KT-562-845

Dark Gold

Christine Feehan

PIATKUS

PIATKUS

First published in the United States in 2000 by
Dorchester Publishing Co., Inc.
First published in Great Britain in 2006 by Piatkus Books
This paperback edition published in 2008 by Piatkus Books
Reprinted 2008 (twice), 2009 (twice), 2010, 2011, 2014

Typeset by Phoenix Photosetting, Chatham, Kent

Printed and bound by CPI Group (UK) Ltd, Croydon, CR0 4YY

Papers used by Piatkus are from well-managed forests
and other responsible sources.

Piatkus
An imprint of
Little, Brown Book Group
Carmelite House
50 Victoria Embankment
London EC4Y 0DZ

An Hachette UK Company
www.hachette.co.uk

www.piatkus.co.uk

For my daughter Domini, who was the inspiration for the character of the heroine with the unselfish way she loves her son, Mason.

For Alicia who took a chance on an untried author and for Leslie, my editor who has unfailing patience with me and all my quirky ways. Thank you both so very much.

Dark Gold

Chapter One

"Joshua, this is a very important business meeting," Alexandria Houton cautioned her younger brother as she parked her beat-up Volkswagen in the large lot behind the restaurant. For a moment she rested her hand on his curly hair, looking down into his bright eyes. A rush of love instantly warmed her, pushing aside her fears and frustrations and her mouth curved into a smile. "You're so grown up, Josh, I don't know why I'm repeating myself. But this is my only chance at a dream position like this. You know we need this job, don't you?"

"Sure, Alex. Don't worry. I'll stay around back and play with my truck." He grinned at her, his beloved sister who had been his only parent since their mother and father died in a car accident before his second birthday.

"I'm sorry the baby-sitter flaked on us. She was—um, sick."

"Drunk, Alex," he corrected solemnly as he gathered up his backpack and toy.

"Where in the world did you hear such a thing?" she demanded, horrified that a six-year-old would know what drunk was. She slid from the car and carefully brushed off her one good suit. The outfit had cost a month's income, but

1

Alexandria regarded it as a necessary investment. She looked far younger than her twenty-three years and desperately needed the edge a sophisticated, expensive suit could give her.

Josh hugged his favorite toy, a worn Tonka dump truck. "I heard you telling her to go home, that she wasn't fit to watch over me because she was drunk."

Alexandria had specifically told him to go to his room. Instead, he had lurked nearby to eavesdrop. He knew it was an invaluable way to pick up information Alexandria considered proper only for adults. Still, Alexandria found herself grinning at his mischievous upturned face. "Big Ears, huh?"

He looked sheepish.

"It's okay, little buddy. We do better on our own, don't we?" She said it with far more confidence than she felt. They lived in a rat-trap, a boardinghouse patronized mainly by prostitutes, alcoholics, and drug users. Alexandria was terrified for Joshua's future. Everything depended on this meeting.

Thomas Ivan, the genius behind the top-selling, wildly imaginative video and computer games featuring vampires and demons, was looking for a new graphic designer. Ivan had graced the cover of nearly every magazine that counted. And he had been intrigued enough with her samples to request a meeting. Alexandria knew she was talented; now if only he wouldn't judge her on her youthful looks. She was competing with many more experienced designers.

Alexandria dragged her slim portfolio from the car and took Joshua's hand. "This might take a while. You have your snacks in your backpack, don't you?"

He nodded, silky curls bobbing across his forehead. Alexandria tightened her grip on his hand. Joshua was everything to her, her only family, her reason for fighting so hard to move to a better neighborhood, a better standard of living. Joshua was a bright, sensitive, compassionate child. Alexandria believed he deserved everything good that life had to offer, and she was determined to get it for him.

She led him across the restaurant's back acreage, graced

2

with a grove of trees. A path led to the cliffs overlooking the ocean. "Don't go out to the cliffs, Joshua. The edges are dangerous. They can crumble right under your feet, or you could slip and fall."

"I know, you already told me." There was a hint of exasperation in his voice. "I know the rules, Alex."

"Henry is here tonight. He'll be looking out for you." Henry was an elderly homeless man from their neighborhood who often slept in the grove behind this restaurant. Alexandria had frequently given him food and loose change and, more important, respect, and in return, Henry kept an eye out to do her favors.

Alexandria waved to the thin, stooped man now hobbling toward them. "Hi, Henry. It's so nice of you to do this for me."

"You were lucky you ran into me at the market earlier. I was going to sleep under the bridge tonight." Henry looked around carefully with his faded blue eyes. "There's been some strange things happening hereabouts."

"Gang activity?" Alexandria asked anxiously. She didn't want Joshua exposed to the dangers or pressures of that kind of life.

Henry shook his head. "Nothing like that. Cops wouldn't allow that in these parts. That's why I sleep here. Fact is, they wouldn't let *me* stay if they knew about it."

"So what strange things have been happening around here?"

Joshua tugged at her skirt. "You're going to be late for your meeting, Alex. Henry and I'll be fine," he insisted, reading her distress. He settled himself under a canopy of trees, sitting cross-legged on a rock beside the faint path leading to the cliffs.

With creaking kneecaps, Henry sat down beside him. "Right. Go along, Alex." He waved a gnarled hand. "We'll just play with this fine truck, won't we, boy?"

Alexandria bit her lip, suddenly indecisive. Was it wrong to leave Joshua with just this worn-out, arthritic old man to look after him?

"Alex!" As if reading her concerns, Joshua glared at her, his manhood clearly affronted.

3

Alexandria sighed. Josh was far too old for his age, exposed to such a sordid life. Unfortunately, he was also right: this meeting was important. After all, it was for his future. "Thanks, Henry. I owe you for this. I need this job." Alexandria bent to kiss Joshua. "I love you, little buddy. Be safe."

"I love you, Alex," he echoed. "Be safe."

The familiar words comforted her as she made her way back through the cypress trees and around the kitchen to the steps leading to the balcony overhanging the cliffs. This restaurant was famous for its view of the crashing waves below. Wind tugged at her hair pulled into a chignon, spraying salt and droplets of sea foam. Alexandria paused at the intricately carved door, took a deep breath, raised her chin, and moved inside with an air of confidence her churning stomach belied.

Soft music, crystal chandeliers, and a jungle of beautiful plants gave the illusion of stepping into another world. The room was divided into private little nooks, its huge, flickering fireplace giving each recess a warm, intimate feel.

Alexandria flashed the maître d' a smile. "I'm meeting Mr. Ivan. Has he arrived yet?"

"Right this way," the man said with an approving look.

Thomas Ivan choked on his Scotch as the beautiful Alexandria Houton approached his table. He often brought his dates to this cozy restaurant, but this young woman was a decided improvement. She was on the short side, slender, but with full curves and fantastic legs. Her large sapphire eyes were fringed with dark lashes, her mouth lush and sexy. Her golden hair was twisted into a severe chignon that emphasized her classic bone structure and high cheekbones. Heads turned to follow her progress. She didn't appear aware of the havoc she was creating, but the maître d' seemed to be escorting royalty. There was definitely something special about this woman.

Thomas coughed to clear his throat and find his voice. He rose to his feet, shook her extended hand, and privately gloated at his good fortune. This gorgeous young creature needed him. A good fifteen years her senior, with money, influence, and and fame, he could make or break her career. And he meant to exploit every pleasurable possibility of that very favorable position.

"It's a pleasure to meet you, Mr. Ivan," she said softly. Her melodious voice played over his skin like the touch of silken fingertips.

"Indeed." Thomas held her hand a moment longer than necessary. The sweet innocence in her eyes made her natural sexiness all the more provocative. He wanted her fiercely and set his mind to having her.

Alexandria kept her hands clasped together in her lap so their trembling would not betray her nervousness. She couldn't believe she was actually sitting with such a brilliant man as Thomas Ivan. Even more, being considered as the artist for his next project. It was the chance of a lifetime. When he remained silent, studying her intently, she searched for something polite and fairly intelligent to say. "This is a beautiful restaurant. Do you come here often?"

Thomas felt his heart leap. She was interested in him as a man! Why else would she make the inquiry? She might look cool and untouched, even faintly haughty, but she was fishing for information about his personal relationships. He lifted one eyebrow and gave her his carefully cultivated smile, the one that always took their breath away. "It's my favorite restaurant."

Alexandria didn't like the suddenly smug look in his eyes, but she smiled anyway. "I brought some sketches with me. Samples of ideas, drawings of the story line you suggested for your next game. I see so clearly in my mind what you're describing. I know you've been using Don Michaels for *NightHawks*. He's very good, but I don't think he captures exactly what you envision. I see so much more detail, so much more power." Under cover of the table, Alexandria twisted her fingers together but tried to remain outwardly composed.

Thomas was startled. She was absolutely right. Michaels was a big name, with a big ego to match, but he'd never fully understood Thomas's vision. However, Alexandria's obvious professionalism irritated him. She looked so cool

5

and untouchable. She wanted to talk business. Women usually threw themselves at him.

Alexandria could see the annoyance gathering on Thomas Ivan's face. She dug her nails into her palms. What was wrong? Doubtless she was coming on too strong. A man with his rakish, debonair reputation probably preferred a more feminine approach. She needed this job; she certainly couldn't start right out making him angry. What harm was there in a light flirtation? Ivan was a wealthy, handsome bachelor, exactly the kind of man she should be attracted to. She sighed inwardly. She never seemed honestly attracted to anyone. For a while she'd put it down to the unsavory men in their neighborhood, to her many responsibilities with Joshua. Now she secretly thought she might be truly frigid. But she could fake it if she had to.

Thomas Ivan's next comment proved her right.

"I don't think we should spoil our dinner with business talk, do you?" he said, flashing a charming smile.

Alexandria blinked away the image of a barracuda and allowed a soft, flirty smile to curve her mouth. It was going to be a long evening. She shook her head when he would have poured her a glass of wine and applied herself to her shrimp salad and the small talk that seemed to make her occasional dates happy. Ivan leaned toward her, frequently touching her hand to make a point.

She managed to escape once to check on Joshua. Under the sinking sun she found Joshua and Henry playing blackjack with a battered deck of cards.

Henry grinned up at her, thankfully took the food she had managed to smuggle out, and waved her off.

"We're doing fine, Alex. Go get that job you want so much," he instructed.

"Are you teaching Josh to gamble?" she demanded with a mock-severe frown. Both culprits laughed mischievously, and it was all Alexandria could do not to hug Joshua close.

"Henry says I could probably support *you* with this game, cuz I always win," Joshua told her proudly. "He says then you wouldn't ever have to pretty up to a no-good hound dog again."

Alexandria bit her lip to hide both her amusement and her overwhelming affection. "Well, until you're a full-fledged card sharp, I'll see to our support. So I'd better get back inside. If you guys get cold, there's a blanket in the trunk." She handed the car keys to Joshua. "Take good care of these. If you lose them, we'll be sleeping out here with Henry."

"Cool!" Joshua replied, his blue eyes dancing.

"Very cool. Cold, in fact," Alexandria warned. "Be careful. I'll be as quick as I can, but this man is not very cooperative. I think he thinks he's might score big tonight." She made a face.

Henry shook a gnarled fist. "He gives you any trouble, you send him my way."

"Thanks, Henry. You two boys behave while I'm working." Alexandria turned and began to make her way back toward the restaurant.

The wind was picking up, blowing the sea toward land, spitting foam through the air. Mist was seeping in, shrouding the trees in melancholy white tails. Alexandria shivered, running her hands up and down her arms. It wasn't really that cold, but the aura of fog and mystery distressed her.

She shook her head to clear away notions of evil lurking behind every tree. For some reason she was especially on edge tonight. She put it down to the enormity of this interview. She had to get this job.

She made her way back through the restaurant, winding through the jungle of potted plants and hanging green vines.

Ivan jumped to his feet to seat her, well aware that he was the envy of the other males in the room. Alexandria Houton just had some special magic that made him think of hot nights and untamed passion.

He ran his fingers over the back of her hand. "You're cold," he said, his voice a little hoarse. She made him feel like a blundering schoolboy, while she remained aloof, slightly haughty, an untouched siren watching him squirm.

"I stepped outside for a moment on my way back from the ladies' room, and the night was so beautiful, I couldn't resist looking at the ocean. It seems to be acting up a bit." Her eyes seemed to hold a thousand secrets, her long lashes locking up every emotion behind them. Thomas swallowed hard and looked away. He had to bring himself under control. He reached deep into his reserve of famous charm and began telling whimsical stories to amuse her, to engage her.

Alexandria tried hard to listen to his conversation, but it was difficult to concentrate on his anecdotes about the making of his brilliant career, his many social obligations, and the wearying string of women constantly pursuing him for his money. She was growing increasingly uneasy, so much so that her hands were beginning to tremble. For a moment she felt a shiver of terror, as if icy fingers had wrapped around her throat. The illusion was so real, she actually raised a hand to her neck to check.

"Surely you'll have one small glass of wine. It's an excellent vintage," Thomas insisted, lifting the bottle and drawing her attention back to him.

"No, thank you, I seldom drink." It was the third time she'd told him, and she resisted asking him if he had a problem with his hearing. She was not about to cloud her mind with alcohol when this interview meant so much. And she never drank when she was driving, and never around Joshua. He saw more than enough boozing in the halls and on the sidewalks outside their rooming house.

Alexandria flashed a smile to take the sting out of her refusal. As the waiter cleared away the plates, she very decisively reached for her portfolio.

Ivan sighed audibly. Usually women were fawning over him at this stage. But Alexandria seemed immune to his charm, out of his reach. Still, she intrigued him, and he had to have her. He knew this job was important to her, and he would use that if he had to. He could tell there was fire in her, locked behind her easy smile and cool sapphire eyes, and he was looking forward to enjoying some hot, steamy sex with her.

But the moment Thomas saw her sketches, he forgot about satisfying his ego and his lust. Alexandria had captured the images in his mind better than his own words had done. Excitement caught at him, and he nearly drooled over her exceptional drawings. She was exactly what he needed for his newest game. It was a hot concept, frightening and difficult, and it would blow away the competition. Her fresh, inventive approach was precisely what he needed.

"They're just quick sketches," Alexandria said softly, "without the animation, but I hope you get the idea." She forgot she didn't like Thomas Ivan very much as she watched the appreciative way he looked at her work.

"You have such a gift for detail. Such imagination. Such technique. And, looking at these, I feel as if you've read my mind. You actually capture the feeling of flight here," he said, pointing. He was impressed that she had caught such a stomach-churning sensation with her illustrations alone. What might she do with his vast array of computers and design programs?

Thomas studied one scene, feeling as if it were really happening. It was as if she had taken a photograph of a vampire caught in a brutal battle. It was so real, it was frightening. Her drawings, capturing his story line and the images in his mind so perfectly, so completely instantly created the bond between them that had been eluding him all evening.

Alexandria was suddenly aware of the brush of Thomas Ivan's fingers against hers, aware of the strength in his arms, the width of his shoulders, the handsome angularity of his features. Her heart jumped hopefully. Was she actually responding to someone physically? It was amazing what having a passion in common could generate. She watched with pride as he openly admired her renderings of the creatures of his imagination.

But suddenly a cold draft streamed through the restaurant, bringing with it the taint of evil. It crawled over Alexandria's skin like worms through a body. Revulsion welled up, and she sat back in her chair, pale and trembling. She looked around carefully. No one else seemed to notice the thickening air, the stench of evil. Laughter and the low murmur of conversation surrounded her. Its normalcy should have reassured her, but the trembling only increased. She could feel sweat beading on her forehead, running down the valley between her breasts. Her heart was thumping.

Thomas Ivan was far too busy going through her sketches

to notice her uneasiness. He continued to murmer his approval, his head down, his eyes feasting on the richness of her drawings.

But something was wrong. Terribly wrong. Alexandria knew it; she always knew. She had known the very moment her parents died. She knew when a violent crime took place within her vicinity. She knew who was dealing drugs, when someone lied; she just knew things. And right now, while others in the restaurant enjoyed themselves, ate and drank and talked, she knew something evil was nearby, something so malevolent, she had never conceived of such a being.

Her eyes made a slow, careful circuit of the spacious room. Patrons were talking, eating, undisturbed. Three women seated at the table closest to her were laughing outrageously, toasting one another. Alexandria's mouth went dry, her heart pounding. She was unable to move or speak, frozen with terror. On the wall behind Thomas Ivan, a dark shadow crept forward, began to loom over the room, a loathsome apparition seemingly seen by no one else as it reached out, claws extended, toward her, toward the three women talking with such animation. Alexandria sat perfectly still, hearing a horrible whispering in her head like the brush of a bat's wings, issuing an insidious command, buzzing insistently, powerful.

Come to me. Be with me. Let me feast on you. Come to me.

The words beat at her until shards of glass seemed to pierce her skull. The claws on the far wall opened, extended, beckoned her.

A chair scraping to her right broke the spell. Alexandria blinked, and the shadow faded away on the echo of maniacal laughter. She was able to move, to turn her head toward the sound of two more chairs scraping back. She saw the three women rise as one unit, toss money onto the table, and walk in sudden eerie silence toward the entrance.

Alexandria wanted to scream at the women to come back. She had no idea why, but she actually opened her mouth to do so. Her throat closed, and she fought for air.

"Alexandria!" Thomas rose swiftly to help her. She was

ashen, tiny beads of perspiration dampening her forehead. "What is it?"

Blindly she tried to shove her drawings into the portfolio, but her hands were shaking, and the sketches spilled across the table and onto the floor. "I'm sorry, Mr. Ivan, I've got to leave." She stood up so abruptly, she nearly sent him sprawling backward. Her mind felt sluggish and thick, as if some oily evil still clung to it, and her stomach rolled.

"You're ill, Alexandria. Let me take you home." Ivan tried to gather up the precious sketches and hold her by the arm at the same time.

Alexandria jerked her arm away, her only thought to get to Joshua immediately. Whatever the evil thing was, whatever creature was stalking the night, those women, Henry, and Joshua were in grave danger. It was outside. Out back. She could feel its presence like a dark stain on her soul.

She turned and ran, uncaring of the curious stares or Thomas Ivan's bewilderment. She tripped on the stairs, caught the hem of her skirt, and heard the rip. Pain and terror sliced through her. Her chest felt as if it had exploded, her heart torn and bleeding. It was so real, she clutched her chest and stared down at her hands, expecting to see blood. No. Someone else's blood. Someone was hurt—or worse.

Alexandria bit her lower lip hard enough to break the skin. That pain was real, and it was only hers. It enabled her to focus, to keep running. Whatever creature was stalking the grounds had made a kill. She could smell the blood now, was experiencing the lingering vibrations, the aftermath of violence. She prayed it wasn't Joshua. Sobbing, she flung herself onto the narrow path winding around the building. She couldn't lose Joshua. Why had she left him alone with only an elderly man to watch out for him?

She became aware of the fog then. Dense. Thick, like soup. It hung in the trees like an eerie white wall. She couldn't see a foot in front of her. It even felt thick, as if she were wading through quicksand. When she tried to pull air into her lungs, she found it nearly impossible. She wanted to scream for Joshua, but some deep intuition kept her silent.

11

Whoever the madman was, he enjoyed the pain and terror of others. That was his rush, his high. She could not indulge his macabre tastes.

Feeling her way carefully through the trees, she literally stumbled over a body. "Oh, God," she whispered aloud, praying it wasn't her brother. Leaning close, she realized the corpse was far too big. Cold and motionless, he lay in a pathetic heap, tossed aside like so much garbage. "Henry." Grief welled up as she clasped his shoulder to turn him over.

Horror rose when she saw his mangled chest. His heart was literally torn out, exposed and still. Alexandria scrambled away, knelt, and was violently sick. There were ragged wounds on Henry's neck, wounds an animal might make.

Taunting laughter filled her mind. Alexandria wiped at her mouth with the back of her hand. This depraved madman was not getting Joshua. Determined, she moved instinctively forward toward the cliffs. Waves crashing loudly against jagged rocks below and the wind rushing through the trees made it impossible to hear anything.

Without sight or hearing, Alexandria moved steadily forward, every instinct drawing her toward the demented killer. She had the impression that he knew she was coming, that he was waiting. She was also certain he believed he was controlling her, deliberately commanding her to come to him.

Despite the strong wind, the fog remained heavy, yet now, through the thickness, she caught glimpses of more horror unfolding. Three women, vaguely familiar from the restaurant, were inching their way toward the cliffs. The women had been at the table to her right; they'd left just before she had. Alexandria could tell they were in some kind of trance, staring rapturously up at the man silhouetted on the cliff's edge.

He was tall and slender but gave an impression of great strength and power. His face was beautiful, like that of an Adonis, his hair shoulder-length and wavy. When he smiled, his teeth were very white.

Like a predator's. The moment the thought entered her head, the illusion of beauty was gone, and Alexandria saw the blood on the creature's hands. On his teeth and chin.

The welcoming smile was a grimace, exposing vicious fangs. His eyes, on the three women, were black holes glowing a feral red in the darkness.

The women were smiling, simpering, reaching out to him. As they moved closer, he raised a hand and pointed to the ground. Obediently the three dropped to their knees and crawled sensuously forward, writhing and moaning, tearing at their clothing. The fog covered the obscene display for a moment, and when it cleared again she could see that one of the women had reached the man and was winding herself around his knees. She ripped away her blouse, exposing her breasts, touching herself suggestively, rubbing herself against the man's body, begging and pleading for him to take her, use her. A second woman reached the cliff's edge and clung to his waist, staring up provocatively.

Alexandria wanted to turn away from the horror of what was about to befall these human puppets, but she caught sight of Joshua walking slowly toward the man. He didn't seem to notice the women. He looked neither right nor left, just walked forward as if in a dream state.

A trance. A hypnotic trance. Alexandria's heart slammed against her chest. Somehow this killer had hypnotized the women and Joshua. They answered his bidding like mind-less sheep. Her brain was trying to analyze how he had accomplished such a feat even as she hurried to intercept Joshua before he could reach the monster. Fortunately, Joshua was moving very slowly, almost as though he was being pulled reluctantly forward.

Although the thick veil of fog hid her, Alexandria felt the impact of those hostile, unearthly eyes as the creature swung his head toward her, his neck undulating like that of a reptile.

As he examined her through the thickness of the fog, bat wings beat at her skull; the shards of glass pierced her over and over. The soft, seductive voice murmured insistently in her head. Alexandria ignored the pain throbbing in her head and focused her attention on reaching Joshua. She would not give this monster the satisfaction of knowing he was hurting her.

Her hand caught at Joshua's shirt. His feet continued forward, but she planted her feet firmly and held him still. Wrapping her arms around the child, she faced the monster, not more than fifteen feet away.

He was on the very edge of the cliff, his human puppets fawning on him, purring and begging for his attention. He appeared not to notice the women, his entire being concentrating on Alexandria. He smiled at her, a baring of fangs.

Alexandria shuddered at the sight of Henry's blood on his lips and teeth. This madman had killed sweet, harmless Henry.

"Come to me." He held out a hand to her.

She could feel his voice right through her body, pulling at her to do his bidding. She blinked rapidly to keep in focus the bloodstains on his hands and long, dagger-like fingernails. As she stared at the talons, the voice lost its beauty and took on a harsh, quarrelsome ugliness.

"I don't think so. Leave us alone. I'm taking Joshua with me. You can't have him." She spoke with determination, her spine stiffening, her blue eyes blazing defiance.

Absently one of his obscene hands caressed the woman rubbing at his waist. "Join me. Look at these women. They want me. They adore me."

"Keep fooling yourself." She tried to take a step backward. Joshua resisted her effort. She tightened her arms to prevent his moving forward but when she dragged him back a step, he began to thrash, forcing her to stop.

The monster on the cliff raised an eyebrow. "You do not believe me?" He turned his attention to the woman at his waist. "Come here, my dear. I wish you to die for me." He waved a hand behind him.

To Alexandria's horror, the woman licked his outstretched hand, and, simpering and fawning, she crawled past him. "No!" Alexandria cried out, but the woman was already falling into the emptiness of space, down to the greedy water and jagged rocks below. Even as Alexandria gasped, he pulled the second woman up by her hair, kissed her full on the mouth and, bending her nearly backward, sank his hideous teeth into her neck.

The vivid sketches Alexandria had drawn depicting Thomas Ivan's horror stories were springing to life before her eyes. The creature feasted on the blood spilling down the woman's throat, then tossed her aside, over the cliff, as if she were nothing but an empty shell he'd found on the beach. Deliberately he ran his thick, obscene tongue over his blood-smeared lips in a grotesque display.

Alexandria found herself murmuring a prayer, a chant, over and over beneath her breath. Whatever this creature was, he was dangerous and insane beyond imagination. She took a firmer grip on Joshua and lifted him from his feet.

He kicked at her and fought, made little growling noises, and snapped his teeth at her. Alexandria managed to move two more feet backward before she was forced to put him down. He remained still as long as she wasn't moving away from his objective.

The monster raised his head again, licked his fingers, and smiled hideously. "Do you see? They will do anything for me. They adore me. Don't you, pet?" He lifted the last woman to her feet. Instantly she wrapped herself around him, rubbing suggestively, touching and caressing him. "You want only to please me, do you not?"

The woman began to kiss him, his neck, his chest, moving lower and lower, her hands fumbling at his trousers. He fondled her neck. "See my power? And you are the one I have been seeking to join with me, to share my power."

"That woman doesn't adore you," Alexandria protested. "You've used hypnosis to make her a puppet. She has no mind of her own. Is that what you call power?" She put as much contempt into her quavering voice as she could.

A low, deadly hiss escaped the monster's mouth, but he continued to smile at her. "Perhaps you are right. This one *is* useless, is she not?" Still smiling, still staring straight into Alexandria's eyes, the man caught the woman's head between his palms and wrenched.

The crack was audible and seemed to vibrate right through Alexandria's body. She was shaking so much, her teeth were chattering. With one hand the monster casually dangled the woman's broken body over the cliff's edge. She hung there like a rag doll, her neck at a peculiar angle, a once beautiful woman now an empty, lifeless shell. The monster discarded her by merely opening his hand and allowing her to fall into the greedy water below.

"Now you have me to yourself," he said softly. "Come to me."

Alexandria shook her head violently. "Not me. I'm not going to come to you. I see you as you are, not what you made those poor women see."

"You will come to me, and of your own free will. You are the one. I have searched the world for one such as you. You must come to me." His tone was soft, but held a whip of warning, a hiss of command.

Alexandria tried to take a step backward, but Joshua erupted into a growling frenzy, kicking and biting. She stopped again and got a firmer grip to prevent his escape. "You're sick. You need help. A doctor or something. I can't do anything for you." She was searching desperately for a way out of this nightmare, praying someone would come. A security guard. Anyone.

"You do not know what I am, do you?"

Alexandria's mind felt almost numb with terror. She had spent considerable time reading and doing research on ancient legends of vampires to work on her sketches for Thomas Ivan. And this monster was the epitome of that mythical creature, feeding on another's blood, using hypnotic trances to command helpless humans to do his evil bidding. She took a deep breath to calm herself, to try to bring herself back to the world of reality. Surely it was the fog and wind, the dark, starless night, and the eerie crash of the waves below that made her think what could not possibly be. This was a twenty-first century sociopath, not some legendary character of old. She must hold on to her wits and not allow the horror of the night to fuel her imagination.

"I believe I know what you think you are," she said evenly, "but the truth is, you're simply a vicious murderer."

He laughed softly, wickedly, the sound scraping like nails on a chalkboard. She actually felt icy fingers along her skin.

"You are a child hiding from the truth." He raised a hand and beckoned to Joshua, his glowing eyes on the boy's face.

Joshua struggled madly, fought and kicked, biting at Alexandria's arms in an effort to get free.

"Leave him alone!" She concentrated on subduing her brother, but he was strong enough in his trance-induced state to wiggle free. Instantly he ran to the monster on the cliff, hugged his knees, and gazed adoringly up at the man.

Chapter Two

Alexandria's heart skipped a beat. She straightened very slowly, her mouth dry with terror as she saw those claw-like hands sink into her brother's shoulders.

"You will come to me now, will you not?" the monster inquired softly.

Alexandria lifted her trembling chin. "This is what you call free will?" Her legs felt so rubbery, she could take only a few steps toward him before she had to stop. "If you use Joshua to control me, that isn't my coming to you of my own free will, is it?" she challenged him.

A long slow hiss escaped him, and then he caught Joshua by one leg and held him over the cliff's edge. "Since you like freedom so very much, I will release my hold on the child's mind so that he can see and hear and know what is happening." The fangs gnashed and clicked as he uttered the words in a precise, icy tone.

His words propelled Alexandria forward once more. She stumbled to within a couple of feet of the monster, reaching for Joshua. "Oh, God, please, don't drop him! Give him to me!" There was pain in her voice, real fear, and it fed the monster's excitement.

He laughed softly as Joshua suddenly came to life,

screaming, his face contorted with fear. He screamed for his sister, his eyes on her face, his only salvation. The monster fended Alexandria off with one hand as he easily held Joshua over the cliff with the other.

She forced herself to stand perfectly still in front of the man. "Just give him to me. You don't need him. He's only a child."

"Oh, I think he is very necessary—to ensure your cooperation." The madman smiled at her and moved Joshua back to the relative safety of the cliff's edge. He waved a hand, and the child ceased to fight or scream, once more under the man's demonic control. "You will join with me, become what I am. Together we will have power such as you cannot imagine."

"But I've never wanted power," Alexandria protested, edging closer to try to snatch the boy from him. "Why do you say I'm the one you've been searching for? You didn't know I existed until tonight. You don't even know my name."

"Alexandria. It is easy to read young Joshua's mind. You persist in thinking me a mere human, but I am so much more than that."

"What are you?" Alexandria held her breath, afraid of his answer, knowing this creature *was* somehow more than human, *was* the powerful beast from legend. He could read minds, control others, draw his prey to him, even from a distance. He had ripped out Henry's heart. He had broken a woman's neck and drained blood from another right in front of her. Whatever he was, he was not human.

"I am the nightmare of foolish humans, the vampire come to feast on the living. You will be my bride, share my power, my life."

He said it perfectly seriously, and Alexandria was torn between needing to cry and hysterical laughter. Thomas Ivan could not have written more bizarre dialogue. This man believed what he was saying, and what was worse, she was beginning to believe it, also.

"It . . . it really isn't my kind of lifestyle." The words came out in a husky whisper, and she could not believe she was pleading for her life, for Joshua's life, with such a silly answer. But how did one address such insanity?

"You think to mock me and get away with it?" His hands closed so hard on Joshua's shoulder, she could see his fingers nearly meeting.

She shook her head, stalling for time. "No, I was serious. I like the sunshine. Vampires hang out at night. I seldom drink wine, let alone blood. But I do know a bar where you can find lots of girls who are into kinky things. They wear black and worship the devil and say they drink each other's blood. But not me. I'm ultra-conservative."

How could she be having such a strange conversation with a killer? Wasn't there a security guard around? Hadn't anyone found Henry's body yet? Where was everyone? How long could she stall, keep this creature talking?

His laughter taunted her, low and insidious. "No one will come to save you, my dear. They cannot. It is a simple matter to keep others away, as easy as it is to draw them to me."

"Why me?"

"There are few like you in existence. Your mind is very strong, which is why you cannot be controlled. You are a true psychic, are you not? That is what my kind requires in a mate."

"I don't know about that. I sometimes know things others don't," she conceded, pushing a nervous hand through her hair. "I knew you were here, if that's what you mean." Someone had to come and rescue them soon. Surely Thomas Ivan was looking for her. "Please, let me take Joshua home, somewhere safe. You don't need him, only me. I'll give you my word, I'll come back tomorrow night. And if you're so powerful, you can always find me if I don't return." She was desperate to get to Joshua. It was terrible to see him so limp and lifeless, his eyes glassy. She wanted to gather him up and hold him close, to keep him safe, to know this creature could never touch him again. If she could save Joshua, nothing else would matter.

"I cannot allow you out of my sight. There are others seeking you. I must stay near to protect you at all times."

Alexandria rubbed her pounding temples with her palms.

The creature was trying to invade her mind, and the constant struggle to keep him out was becoming very painful. "Look, mister—what is your name, anyway?"

"Are we to be polite and civilized then?" He was laughing at her.

"Yes, I think that would be best." Her control was crumbling, and she knew it. She had to find a way to get Joshua away from him. Joshua had to live whether she managed to do so or not. Deliberately she dug her fingernails into her palms and concentrated on the sensation to keep her focus.

"By all means, then, let us be civilized. I am Paul Yohenstria. I come from the Carpathian Mountains. You may have noticed my accent."

She held out her arms for her brother, unable to stop herself. "Give Joshua to me, please, Mr. Yohenstria. He's just a little boy."

"You wish him to remain alive, and I wish you to accompany me, I think we can work out something mutually beneficial. Do you not agree?"

Alexandria allowed her empty arms to fall to her sides. She was exhausted and frightened, and her head hurt terribly. Somehow he was amplifying her discomfort, wearing at her defenses with his mental battering, the voice in her head driving her mad with its relentless pressure. "I'll go with you. Just leave my brother here."

"No, my dear, I will not do that. Come to me now."

She went reluctantly. She had no other choice. Joshua was her life. She loved him more than anything. If he was gone, she had nothing. The moment Yohenstria touched her, she felt sickened. His bloodstained fingers curled around her upper arm, and she could see the blood trapped beneath the long, dagger-like nails. Henry's blood. He allowed Joshua to drop to the ground, but the boy simply remained where he had fallen.

"You don't need to hold me. I just want to check on Josh," Alexandria said. The contact with such an evil being was making her stomach churn, and she feared she would have to vomit again.

"Leave him for the moment." His fingers tightened like a

vise, dragging her close so that his body touched hers. She could smell his fetid breath, the scent of blood and death. His skin was clammy and ice-cold.

Alexandria struggled in his hold, trying to escape, although she knew she was helpless in his grasp. He bent closer to her neck, and his breath, hot and foul, touched her skin.

"Don't. Oh, God, don't," Alexandria whispered, her voice failing her. If he released her, she would fall, her knees buckling, but he held her still as he bent even closer.

"Your God has abandoned you," he whispered. And his teeth closed over her throat, puncturing deeply, a pain so intense that everything swirled blackly. He dragged her into his arms and feasted, gulping at the rich blood. She was small, and he nearly crushed her in his arms as he drank. She could feel the fangs hooked in her body, connecting them in some dark, ugly way. Her body felt weak and sluggish; her heart stuttered and labored as he continued to drain her. Her lashes swept down, and even as she told herself she had to live to fight for Josh, black dots whirled and danced before her eyes, and she slumped helplessly against the vampire's wiry frame.

He lifted his head, blood trickling from the side of his mouth. "And now you must drink to live." His teeth tore open his own wrist, and he pressed it to her lips, watching as his tainted blood dripped into her mouth.

Alexandria had enough life left in her to try to avoid ingesting the hideous liquid. She tried to turn her head, to close her mouth, but the vampire held her easily and forced the poisonous drink beyond her lips, his hand stroking her throat until she swallowed convulsively. But he did not replace most of what he had taken, deliberately keeping her weak, wanting her more amenable to his bidding.

Paul Yohenstria dropped his victim beside her brother and lifted his face triumphantly to the dark, moonless night. He had found her. Her blood was hot and sweet and her body young and supple. She would provide what he needed to bring his emotions back, to make him feel again. He roared his triumph to the heavens, shook his fist to defy God.

He had chosen to lose his soul, and what did it matter after all? He had found this special one, and she could bring him back.

Her weak, instinctive movements away from him brought his attention back to her. Alexandria crawled to Joshua's side and gathered him protectively to her. The vampire snarled jealously. Many would want her, but she was his. He would not share her with anyone. The moment the transformation was complete, and she came to depend on him, came to him of her own free will, he would dispose of the brat. He reached down, caught the boy by his shirtfront, and pulled him away from her.

Alexandria managed to sit up, but everything was spinning, making it almost impossible to get her bearings. But she knew unerringly where Josh was. And she knew she would never allow him to share this fate. If this murderous creature could actually make them like him, death was the better alternative.

Without warning she launched herself forward. Her arms outstretched, she caught Joshua close to her, and her momentum carried them over the edge of the cliff. The wind rushed up at them; salt spray stung and cleansed. The waves reached high to welcome them to their watery graves, smashing like thunder on the jagged rocks just below the surface.

Talons caught at her, wings beat furiously, and hot, fetid breath heralded the arrival of her enemy. Alexandria cried out as the nails bit deeply into her and the creature carried them away from their only salvation. She could not bring herself to drop Joshua. There might be a chance, a moment when their captor was not watching, for her to help Josh escape. She buried her face in his blond curls and closed her eyes, whispering that she was sorry she wasn't strong enough to allow him the mercy of death while she still lived. Tears burned in her throat, and she felt tainted by the evil in the monster, knowing he lived inside her now, forever binding them together.

The place he took them was dark and dank, a cave cut

deeply into the cliffs, surrounded by water. There was no visible way to escape. He tossed their drained bodies contemptuously on the wet sand at the cavern's mouth and paced restlessly back and forth, trying to control his anger at her rebellion.

"You will never do such a thing again or I will make that child suffer hell unlike anything you have ever imagined. Do I make myself clear?" he demanded, towering over her.

Alexandria tried to sit up. Her body felt battered, and she was weak from loss of blood. "What is this place?"

"My lair. The hunter cannot track me, surrounded as I am by water. His senses are confused by the sea." Paul Yohenstria laughed harshly. "He has defeated many of my kind, but he cannot find me."

She looked cautiously around. As far out as she could see, there was only the rough ocean waves. The cliffs loomed above, barren, slick, steep, and impossible to scale. He had them trapped as surely as if he had placed them in jail. And it was cold, icy cold. She was shaking with it. Mist was falling lightly, and she tried to cover Joshua's body with her own to protect him.

But the tide was coming in, and the sand and pebbles they were lying on were already awash in salty water. "We can't stay here. The tide is coming in. We'll drown." It was an effort to speak. She cradled Joshua's head in her lap. He seemed oblivious to what was happening to him, and for that she was grateful.

"The cave winds upward into the mountain. The farther back one goes, the dryer it is." He cocked his head to one side and regarded her with his bloodshot eyes. "You will have a slightly uncomfortable day, my dear. I do not trust you enough yet to allow you near me while I sleep, yet I cannot leave you to run around on your own. I do not think there is a way for you to escape, but you are far more clever than I gave you credit for. You leave me no choice but to chain you inside the cave. It will be wet, but I am certain you will endure."

"Why are you doing this? What do you hope to accomplish? Why don't you just kill me outright?" she demanded.

"I have no intention of allowing you to die. Far from it. You will become like me, powerful and insatiable in all our appetites. We will rule together, be invincible. No one will ever be able to stop us."

"But don't I have to come to you of my own free will?" she protested hastily. There was no way she was going to accept his life. There could be no way unless he used force. There was no reason powerful enough to make her do as he wished. But even as she thought it, she felt Joshua stir in her arms.

The vampire looked down at her. "Oh, you will, my dear. Eventually you will beg for my attention. I guarantee that you will." He reached down and hooked her under one arm, dragging her to her feet.

Even as she swayed in the rush of wind and salt spray, Alexandria held on to Joshua with every bit of strength she possessed.

Paul shook his head. "For a human, you are stronger than you should be. Your mind is very resistant to control *or* persuasion. An interesting problem. But do not try my patience too far, my dear. I can be quite cruel when provoked."

Alexandria felt a hysterical sob welling up, choking her. If this was showing patience, if this was not an example of his cruelty, she didn't want to consider what he was capable of doing. "Someone will miss those three women. They'll find their bodies. They'll find Henry."

"Who is Henry?" he asked suspiciously, jealousy contorting his features.

"You should know. You killed him."

"The silly old man? He got in my way. Besides, I sensed you in the restaurant, defying me, and needed to get your attention. The old man and the boy belonged to you. They served my purpose."

"Is that why you killed him? Because you knew I cared for him?" Alexandria's horror was deepening, even as her insides were burning from the tainted blood. She felt as if someone was taking a blowtorch to her internal organs, and her heart ached for dear, sweet Henry.

"I cannot allow remnants of your old life to divide your loyalties. You belong to me. Only me. I will not share you."

Her heart pounded, and involuntarily she clutched Joshua closer. The vampire was going to kill her brother eventually. He had no intention of keeping the child in their lives. She had to find a way for Joshua to escape. She swayed again and would have fallen, but Yohenstria reached out and caught her arm.

"The light will not reach so far back into the cave that your skin will burn. Come, let us go within before the dawn arrives."

"I can't be in the sun?"

"You will burn easily. But you are not wholly changed as of yet." Ruthlessly, uncaring that she was so weak, he dragged her, still clinging to Josh, inside the bleakness of the cave.

Alexandria fell several times, incoming waves splashing over her clothing. He continued walking, forcing her along, sometimes dragging her behind him. She held Joshua close, trying to impart some of her body heat into his shivering form. He was terribly still, a dead weight in her arms. She tried to think, but her brain was too slow, and she needed desperately to lie down.

A few yards into the cave, the vampire stopped and shoved her against the rock wall, where a thick chain and manacle was bolted. She noticed, as he tightened the cuff around her wrist, that the steel was stained with blood. Evidently he had brought more than one victim to this place to await his pleasure. The metal cut into her soft skin, and she slumped to the ground, uncaring that the water was pouring over her lap and then receding in its endless cycle. She rested her back against the cliff wall and reached to cradle her brother in her arms, all the while shivering, her teeth chattering.

The vampire laughed softly. "I will rest now. I am afraid it will soon become difficult for you to do the same." He turned his back on her and strode away, his taunting laughter echoing behind him.

In her lap, Joshua suddenly stirred, sat up, and rubbed his eyes. The vampire having released him from his trance, he cried out and clutched Alexandria, clinging to her. "He killed Henry. I saw him, Alex. It was a monster!"

"I know, Josh, I know. I'm so sorry you saw such a terrible thing." She rubbed her cheek over his curls. "I'm not going to lie to you. We're in trouble here. I'm not certain I can get us out." Her words were slurring together, her eyelids closing of their own volition. "The water is rising, Josh. I want you, while you can, to very carefully look around and see if there is a ledge you can climb on to be safe."

"I don't want to leave you. I'm afraid."

"I know, little buddy. I am, too. But I need you to be very brave and do this for me. See what you can find."

A wave rushed in, a gush of water that sprayed salt and sea up to her chin, then receded in a carpet of foam. Joshua screamed in fear and threw his arms around her neck. "I can't do it, Alex. I really can't."

"Try going outside the cave and finding a place to wait where the water can't get to you."

He shook his head so adamantly, his blond curls bounced. "No, Alex, I won't leave you. I have to stay with you."

Alexandria didn't have the energy to argue. She had to concentrate just to think. "Okay, Josh, don't worry." She braced herself against the wall and managed to get to her feet. Then the water was only up to her calves. "We can do this together. Let's look around."

It was nearly impossible to see anything in the gloomy interior of the cave, and the sound of the water crashing on the rocks was thunder in her ears. She was shivering uncontrollably, and her teeth were chattering so hard, she feared they might shatter. The salt caked on her skin and hair; the wound on her neck burned. She swallowed with difficulty and tried not to cry. The only niche that could possibly hold Joshua was too far above her head. Had she been taller, she might have been able to boost him up to it, but neither of them could possibly reach it.

The force of the next wave nearly lifted Joshua off his feet. He caught at Alexandria's hips and hung on. She closed her eyes and leaned against the wall. "I'm going to have you stand for as long as you can, Josh, and then I'll pick you up for as long as I can. After that, we'll put you on my shoulders, okay? It won't be so bad." She did her best to sound encouraging.

Joshua looked scared, but he nodded trustingly. "Is that man going to come back and kill us, Alexandria?"

"He'll come back, Josh, because he wants something from me. If I can hold out, that might buy us some time to figure out how to get out of this mess."

He looked up at her solemnly. "When he bit you, Alex, I could hear him laughing in my mind. He said he was going to have you kill me personally. That once you were like him, you would want to kill me because I was in your way. He said you would take all the blood from my body." He hugged her tighter. "I knew it wasn't true."

"Good boy. That's part of his plan. To make us afraid of each other. But we're a team, Josh. Never forget that. No matter what, you know I love you, right? No matter what happens." She laid her head on his and let the waves wash around her legs. She was so tired and weak, she wasn't certain she could make it through the day, let alone face the vampire again. She prayed silently over and over until the words ran together in her mind and it was impossible to think.

Light was streaming in through the cave entrance when Joshua's frantic cries woke her as she slept standing up. Water was lapping at his chest, literally knocking him from his feet. He was digging into her leg, trying to keep from being washed away by the pounding surf.

"I'm awake, Josh. I'm sorry," she whispered. She was exhausted and almost too weak to stand. The light hurt her eyes, and the salt water was chafing her skin. Taking a deep breath, she lifted Joshua into her arms in an attempt to protect him from the rising sea.

There was no way she could possibly hold him for long, but the feel of him next to her brought them both a measure of comfort. Something large bumped her leg, brought in on a wave. She shuddered and held her brother tighter.

"It's so cold." Joshua was shaking, every bit as drenched as she was.

"I know, little buddy. Try to go to sleep."

"It hurts, doesn't it?"

"What?" A wave slammed her backward into the wall, and she almost lost her grip on Joshua.

"Where he bit you. You were moaning while you were sleeping."

"It hurts a little bit, Josh. I'm going to try to lift you to my shoulders. You might have to climb up by yourself, okay?"

"I can do it, Alex."

She was so weak, the waves were bouncing her into the rock wall behind her, but somehow Joshua managed to make it onto her shoulders. His weight nearly sent her to her knees, and her hair, long since down from its chignon, was trapped under his legs, hurting her. But she didn't protest. She just held on for dear life. The water was rising steadily, up to her waist now, a relentless assault. Her wrists burned from the salt water, the wound in her neck was raw, and her insides ached. She could feel things brushing against her legs, nibbling at her skin. It was all too horrifying, but Alexandria was determined to keep her will strong for her brother.

"We can do this, can't we, Josh?" she said.

He leaned his weight against the wall and wrapped an arm through the thick chain to help steady them from the constant buffeting of the sea.

"Yes, we can, Alex. Don't worry. I'll save us." He was very determined about it, very firm.

"I knew you would." She closed her eyes again and tried to rest.

Alexandria slept on and off, a few snatched moments here and there. The salt spraying over her was pitiless, flaying the skin from her body. She was thirsty, and blisters were forming on her swollen lips.

At last the water began to recede, and the endless battering slackened. Joshua had to climb down by himself; Alex was no longer able to lift her arms. As she had suggested earlier, he made his way out of the cave to explore their prison. Alexandria usually had a million safety rules for him to follow, but this time she just watched him with glassy eyes.

He studied the cliff walls to find a place he could climb up, but they were too steep and slick. He was very thirsty, so he looked for a place where fresh water might run down the wall of rock, but he couldn't see anything. The sun felt good on his cold, wet skin, and he lay down on the sand to dry his clothes and warm up.

Alexandria slumped over and struck her head against the rock wall. All at once she jerked awake, staring wildly around her. Joshua! He was gone! She had fallen asleep, and the waves had carried him off! She struggled to her feet, fighting the manacles on her wrists, and screamed for her brother.

Her voice was hoarse, nearly nonexistent, and refused to carry beyond the mouth of the cave. The meager sunlight filtering in burned her eyes, burned her skin, but she pulled and tugged at the chains, calling out again and again for Joshua.

By the time Joshua ran into the cave, and to her side, she was huddled against the wall sobbing. "What is it, Alex? Did that man come back and hurt you again?"

Alexandria lifted her head slowly. Joshua touched her bleeding wrists. "He did come back, and I wasn't here to protect you."

She stared up at him through her tears, unable to believe it was really her brother and not some figment of her imagination. She caught at him, hugged him tightly, and ran her hands over him to assure herself he was unharmed. "No, the man didn't come back. I don't think he can, with the sun up."

"Should I go look? I can sneak." The sunlight was making him feel braver.

"No!" Alexandria tightened a hand around his arm. "Don't you dare go near that man." She wiped her swollen lips on her sleeve. Blisters burst and began to bleed. "Is there any way for you to get out? Can you climb up the cliff?"

"No, there's no foothold anywhere. There isn't even a

good hiding place. I haven't looked farther back in the cave yet. Maybe there's a way through there."

"I don't want you to try it, Josh. I can't help you if he finds you in there." She wasn't certain if Paul Yohenstria really was an honest-to-God vampire, but whatever he was, Joshua could not possibly handle him. She had visions of the six-year-old finding the vampire asleep in a coffin. Did they really sleep in coffins?

"But you're really hurt, Alex. I can tell. And he's going to come back here. That's why he chained you up, so he can come back and hurt you some more." He sounded near tears.

"He's very sick, Josh." She thumbed a tear from his face, then kissed the top of his head. "We might have to pretend a lot around him. He thinks I am the woman he wants to marry. Isn't that silly, when we don't even know each other? But I think he's hurt in the head, you know, something wrong with his brain."

"I think he's a vampire, Alex, like on TV. You said there wasn't really such a thing, but I think you're wrong."

"Maybe. I don't honestly know anymore. But we're a hard team to beat, Josh." Actually, she was so weak, she could no longer stand and didn't even bother to try. If the vampire returned right then, he would have very easy pickings. "I think we're too smart for him. What do you think?"

"I think he's going to eat us," Josh said honestly.

"He said something about a hunter. Did you hear him say that? There's someone hunting him. We can hold out until the hunter finds him." She was so exhausted, her eyes were closing again.

"I'm scared, Alex. Do you think the hunter will get here before the vampire wakes up and kills us?" Joshua's lower lip was quivering along with his voice.

She made a supreme effort to rouse herself. "He'll come, Josh. You wait and see. He'll come at night, when the vampire least expects him. He'll have blond hair, just like you. He's big and strong and powerful, like a jungle cat." She could almost see him in her mind, the hero she was attempting to create for her brother.

"Is he more powerful than the vampire?" Joshua asked hopefully.

"Way more," she said firmly, weaving a fairy tale for the child, wanting to believe it herself. "He's a magical warrior with shining gold eyes. The vampire can't stand looking at him because he sees himself reflected in those burning eyes and is frightened by his own ugly appearance."

There was a small silence, and then Joshua touched her face with his fingertips. "Really, Alex? Will the hunter really come and save us?"

She saw no harm in giving him hope. "We just have to be brave and strong. He'll come for us, Joshua. He will. We'll stick together and outsmart that old vampire." Her words were slurring, and with her blood supply low, her body temperature was dropping, her strength ebbing quickly. Alexandria didn't see how she could possibly survive until nightfall. Her lashes drifted down again, so heavy she had no way to lift them.

Joshua didn't want to tell his sister, but she looked terrible. Horrible, even. Her mouth was swollen and black. White salt covered her skin, giving her a monsterish look. Her hair hung in grayish-white strands all around her face, and he couldn't even tell its natural color anymore. Her clothes were torn and streaked white, and strings of kelp hung off her skirt and her ragged, torn nylons. Her legs had hundreds of beads of blood on them where something had nibbled away her skin. Even her voice sounded funny, and her neck was swollen and raw looking. But Alexandria didn't seem to notice. Josh was very scared. He sat down next to her, took her hand, and waited while the sun slowly fell from the sky.

Alexandria was aware the moment the sun went down. She felt an uneasy stirring of the earth and knew immediately that the vampire had risen. She put an arm around Joshua's shoulders and pulled him close. "He's coming," she whispered softly into his ear. "I want you to go out of the cave and be very quiet and stay out of sight. He'll try to use you against me, try to hurt you in some way. Maybe he'll forget you if you stay out of sight."

"But, Alex," he protested.

"I need you to do this for me, honey. Stay very quiet, no matter what happens." She kissed him quickly. "Go now. I love you, Josh."

"I love you, Alex." He ran from the cave and pressed himself against the cliff wall.

Alexandria watched him go with troubled eyes. The tide was coming back in again, and he was only six years old. Then, though she heard no sound, she suddenly knew the vampire was watching her. She turned her head and met his stare.

"You look a bit worse for wear," he greeted her congenially.

She remained quiet, simply watching him. His grotesque smile stretched across his face. He crossed the distance that separated them and, lifting her wrists, examined them. He brought one to his mouth and, staring into her eyes, licked the blood from the painful wounds.

Alexandria winced visibly, trying to jerk her hand away. He tightened his hold until he threatened to crush bone. "You want me to release you, do you not?"

She forced herself to be still and endure his hideous touch. When the cuffs fell to the ground, she struggled to get to her feet.

"You wish to leave this place?" he asked softly.

"You know I do."

He caught her neck with one clawed hand and jerked her to him. "I am hungry, my dear, and it is time for you to choose whether the child lives another night or dies."

She didn't have the strength to fight him, so she didn't even try. She couldn't stop the cry of pain that escaped her as his fangs sank deeply into her neck. He made a growling noise as he fed, his fist in her tangled hair holding her still while he drank greedily. She knew her life was sliding away from her, down his throat. She was suffering from loss of blood and hypothermia. Nothing seemed to matter.

Yohenstria felt her slump against him and had to catch her in his arms to prevent her from falling. Her heart was laboring, her breathing shallow. He had taken too much again. His teeth tore open his wrist, and he clamped it hard over her mouth, forcing the dark liquid down her throat. Even with her life hanging in the balance, Alexandria fought him. He could not seize her mind and force her under his complete control. Although he was able to compel her to swallow some of his tainted blood, he knew it was only because she was so close to complete collapse. Still, each time he forced her to feed, he brought her closer to his dark world. She would not die; he would not allow it. He would have to force her to accept far more blood to keep her alive.

But even as he determined that, he felt the disturbance in the air. A slow hiss escaped his lips, and he turned his head slowly. "We have been found, my dear. Come, you will see what the hunter is like. There is nothing like him in this world. He is relentless." Paul Yohenstria half carried, half dragged Alexandria from the cave into the night air.

All around them the waves crashed to shore, spitting up white spray, and sea foam doused the cliff walls. The vampire shoved Alexandria to the ground and centered himself in the middle of the open beach, his eyes scanning the sky.

Alexandria crawled across an expanse of sand to reach Joshua. He was huddled in a shadow, rocking back and forth, trying to comfort himself. She dragged herself to his side and positioned herself between him and the vampire. Something terrible was about to happen. She could feel the air thickening around them. The wind swirled, and fog blanketed the cove.

There was a rush of movement somewhere in the dense fog, and the vampire screamed, the sound high and filled with fear and rage. Alexandria's heart nearly stopped. If the vampire was that afraid, whatever was out there was something for her to be terrified of too. She caught Joshua to her, covering his eyes with her hands. They clung together, shaking.

Out of the fog a huge golden bird seemed to materialize. It came in at the beach so fast, it was a blur, talons extended, golden eyes gleaming intensely. The heavy fog swirled, then parted to reveal a shape half human, half bird. Alexandria stifled a scream of her own.

Then the creature became a man, huge, tall, and heavily muscled, with bulging arms and a massive chest. His hair was long and blond, flowing in the wind. His body moved with supple fluidity, like a jungle cat stalking its prey. His face was shadowed, but she could see eyes like molten gold pinning the vampire in their intensity.

"So, Paul, we meet at last." The voice was beautiful, a ripple of notes so pure, the tone seemed to seep into her very soul. He stood tall and relaxed, a perfect reincarnation of a Viking warrior. "I have had much work cleaning up the messes you have made around my city. Your challenge was quite clear. I could do no other than oblige you."

The vampire moved backward, putting more space between them. "I never challenged you. I kept my distance." His voice was so fawning, Alexandria went cold. This hunter was so great a force to be reckoned with that he struck terror into the heart of the vampire.

The hunter tilted his head to one side. "You killed when it was forbidden. You know the law, unclean one."

The vampire launched itself then, a blur of wicked claws and fangs as it leapt to strike the intruder down. The hunter simply stepped aside and casually whipped a claw across the vampire's throat, laying him open. Blood erupted in a red volcano.

Alexandria was horrified to see the golden head contorting, the face lengthening to a muzzle, fangs exploding into a wolf's mouth. The hunter snapped the vampire's femur like a twig, the sound carrying across the beach and resonating through her body. She flinched and hugged Joshua tighter, holding his head down to prevent him from witnessing such a terrifying and gruesome scene.

The vampire wiped at the blood running down his chest and stared with hateful eyes at the golden hunter. "You think you are not like me, Aidan, but you are. You are a killer, and you rejoice in the battle. It is the only time you feel alive. No one can be one such as you and not feel the joy and power in the taking of life. Tell me, Aidan, is it not true that you can see no color in this world? That there is no emotion in you unless you are in battle? You are the ultimate killer. You, Gregori, and your brother Julian. You are the darkest shadows in our world. You are the real killers."

"You have broken our laws, Paul. You chose to trade your soul for the illusion of power instead of greeting the dawn. And you turned a human woman, created a deranged vampiress to feed on the blood of innocent children. You knew the penalty."

The voice was purity itself, a cool, clean stream of beauty. The tone seemed to flow into Alexandria's mind, made her want to do whatever he asked. "You know there is no way to defeat me," the voice continued, and Alexandria believed it. It was so soft and gentle, so true. There was no way anyone could successfully oppose the hunter. He was truly invincible.

"It will not be long before one must come to hunt you," Paul Yohenstria taunted, struggling to stand. His form seemed to shimmer, dissolve, but even as he mutated, the hunter struck again.

The sound was sickening. The fog cloaked the actual assault, and the hunter was such a blur of motion, Alexandria could not possibly follow his movements. But out of the fog rolled an obscene sight—the vampire's head, the hair a tangle of blood and gore, the eyes open and staring. The head rolled toward her, spilling a crimson trail behind it.

Alexandria struggled to her feet, clutching Joshua to her, her hands over his eyes as the grotesque ball stopped mere inches away. The fog swirled and thickened, and, to her horror, the hunter turned his head, and the molten gold of his eyes rested on her face.

Chapter Three

Aidan Savage heaved an inward sigh as his gaze settled on the crazed vampiress clutching the small boy to her breast. The demon in him was strong today, struggling for freedom, the red haze in his mind clamoring for control. And the vampire was correct. Suppressing the killer within was becoming more and more difficult. He did feel the power and joy in battle, and the fighting was addicting because it was the only time he felt anything. He had endured centuries of a cold, barren, black-and-gray existence, enjoying no real color or emotion except the lust for battle.

He allowed his gaze to sweep the beach, then turned his attention back to the hag threatening the child. Suddenly he stilled. After more than six hundred years of seeing no color, he now saw the trail of tainted blood from Paul's head not as a black streak but a bright scarlet ribbon, leading his gaze straight to the vampiress.

Impossible. Color and emotion would return to him now only if he found a lifemate. And there was no one here but the pitiful human Paul had attempted to turn. He looked at her, his heart heavy. He almost felt sorry for the poor woman. Again he was puzzled by this unexpected burst of sympathy, of emotion, after so many centuries, but he continued his inspection of the female. It was impossible to tell her age. She was small, almost childlike, but the suit she wore, as torn, wet, and dirty as it was, clung to full curves. Her legs were a mass of bloody welts, her mouth swollen and black with oozing blisters. Her hair, tangled with kelp, hung in a rank clump down her back to her waist. Her blue eyes held terror but also defiance.

She was going to kill the child. The rare woman could become Carpathian. Contrary to the popular myth, most human women could not be turned by a vampire without dire consequences. They immediately went insane and preyed on innocent children. This woman had suffered horribly. The ragged wounds on her neck gave evidence of the vampire's hard usage of her, and the cuts on her wrists were cruelly deep.

Aidan reached mentally for her mind, wanting to make her death as painless for her as possible. Shocked by her resistance, he took a warning step toward her. She was incredibly strong. Her mind had some kind of natural barrier, resisting his will. Instead of placing the child on the sand in front of her as he had directed, she pushed the boy to

36

one side, picked up a large piece of driftwood, and launched herself at Aidan.

He sprang forward, swiping the staff from her hand. The impact cracked a bone—he could hear it, see the pain in her eyes—but she didn't scream. Evidently she was beyond screaming. He reached for her, intending to end her life before she suffered further. She struggled, still resisting his mental compulsion. He bent his head to her throat.

She was so small and cold, shivering uncontrollably, and his every protective instinct leapt into being, feelings he had never before experienced. He wanted to cradle her close, shelter her in the warmth of his arms. His teeth pierced her soft throat, and instantly everything changed for him for all eternity. His entire world. Colors whirled and danced, nearly overwhelming him with their beauty and vividness. His body reacted with a wild urgency he had not known he was capable of feeling, not even in the old days, when he still had emotions.

Her blood was hot and spicy, a sweet, addicting feast giving nourishment to his depleted body. The hunt and fight had cost him strength, and he had not fed this night. Her body shared its life-giving fluid with his. He was aware on some level when her struggles ceased and she rested passively against him. He lifted her easily into his arms, cradling her against his chest as he fed. Then something hit him hard across his legs. Startled, he closed the wound with a caress of his tongue and turned to stare down at the child. It was a measure of his current bemusement that he had all but forgotten the boy, had not even heard his approach.

Joshua was furious. He struck the hunter across the legs a second time, swinging the piece of driftwood as hard as could. "Stop hurting my sister! You were supposed to come and save us! She said you would come if we held on long enough. You were supposed to help us, but you're just like him!"

Tears streamed down the child's face. Aidan could clearly see that the youth had blond hair and blue eyes. The colors nearly blinded him. He looked down into the ravaged face of the woman in his arms. Her heart was laboring, slow, her lungs fighting for air. She was dying.

"I *am* here to help you," he murmured softly, almost absently, to the boy. He reached inside himself, found a calm, tranquil pool to rest in, and sent himself seeking outside his own body and into the woman's. He could not believe he had found her after all these long centuries. But it must be. Only finding his lifemate could bring about these astonishing changes in him.

She was fading away, not fighting anymore. His will surrounded hers. *You will not leave me. Take my blood, which is freely offered to you. You must drink in order to live.*

Her mind moved away from his. Her spirit was still strong enough to evade his compulsion. Aidan changed tactics. *Your brother needs you. Fight for him. He cannot be without you. He will die.*

With one fingernail he slashed the heavy muscles of his chest and pressed her to him. She resisted at first, but he was relentless, surrounding her, herding her will, battering at the barrier until, in her weakened state, she gave in to his enthrallment and fed.

"What are you doing?" Joshua demanded.

"She has lost much blood. I must transfuse her." Aidan planned to erase the child's memories of this nightmare. A satisfactory explanation would not harm him at this point. The boy was very brave and deserved to hear anything that would ease his terrible fear.

It had taken careful tracking of the vampire to find him. He always left a bloody mess behind yet remained one step ahead of his hunter. The night before, Aidan had arrived too late. He had gone to the restaurant on the cliffs, tracking the disturbances in the air, but Paul Yohenstria had already killed an elderly man, ripping his heart out and leaving behind a corpse too hot to allow the police to discover. Aidan had disposed of the body and made certain the vampire's three female victims would never be found. But he had lost the undead's trail just before dawn. Still, he had been certain he was nearing his lair, and finally he had found and destroyed him.

Now he had no choice but to burn the vampire and take these two lost ones back to his home. For this pitiful, disfigured woman was clearly the mate he had been seeking these eight hundred years. His astonishing responses to her proved it. He had no idea what she was like, or even what she looked like, but she had brought his body and heart back to life. This was the one.

"What is your name?" Aidan asked the child. It seemed kinder than merely reading his mind. Not that he had given great thought to kindness before.

"Joshua Houton. Is Alexandria going to be all right? She looks so white and horrible. I think that bad man really hurt her."

"I am a healer for my people, Joshua Houton. I know how to help your sister. Do not worry. I will ensure that this bad one can never hurt another living soul. Then we will go to my home. You will be safe there."

"Alex is going to be upset. Her suit is ruined, and she needs that suit to get us a great job and lots of money." Joshua sounded forlorn, as if he might cry at any moment. He was looking up at the hunter for solace.

"We will get her another suit," Aidan assured the child. He gently stopped the woman from feeding. He needed strength to transport all of them back to his home, and it also took tremendous energy to heal another. He would have to find time to hunt this night for sustenance.

Aidan placed Alexandria on the sand and pulled Joshua gently to her side. "She is very ill, Joshua. I want you to sit right beside her so she can feel your presence and know you have not been harmed. She will need us to take care of her for a while. You are a big boy. You can handle that, even if she says things that are scary, can you not?"

"Why would she say something scary?" Joshua asked suspiciously.

"When people are very sick, fever can make them delirious. That means they do not know what they say. They can be afraid of people or things for no real reason. We have to stay close to her and make certain she does not harm herself."

Joshua nodded solemnly and sat down in the wet sand beside Alexandria. Her eyes were closed, and she didn't respond even when he bent down and kissed her on her forehead as she sometimes did to him. Sand and salt caked her skin. Joshua stroked back the wet strands of hair gently, singing softly as she often did to him when he was sick. She seemed very, very cold to him.

Watching them together brought a lump to Aidan's throat. They looked the way a family was supposed to look. The way Marie, his housekeeper, had looked at her sons as they grew, the way she looked at him and he could never reciprocate. Sighing, he went about the grim business of disposing of the vampire's remains. Vampires were always dangerous, even after they were dead. He had extracted the heart, but even now it was pulsating, broadcasting to the undead its location, that the vampire might reunite its form. Aidan concentrated on the sky, built a storm in his mind, and created a whip of lightning that sizzled and danced as it struck the ground. Flames rushed along the path of crimson, leaving behind black ashes. The vampire's body shriveled. Blue and orange flames whirled together, and a low shriek seemed to rise above the wind.

The smell was putrid, rank. Joshua held his nose and watched wide-eyed as the vampire simply vanished in the black, noxious smoke. He was shocked when the hunter held his hands in the orange flames. The flames didn't burn him.

Aidan tiredly wiped his palms along his trousers before turning back to the little boy trying so hard to guard his sister on the beach. A faint smile softened the hard line of his mouth. "You are not afraid of me, are you, Joshua?"

Joshua shrugged and looked away. "No." There was a small, almost defiant silence. "Well, maybe a little."

Aidan hunkered down beside the boy and looked directly into the blue eyes. His voice dropped an octave, became a pure tone, silver notes that entered Joshua's mind and took possession. "I am an old family friend you have known all your life. We care a great deal for one another and have shared all kinds of adventures." He sent himself outside his body and into the boy, studying the memories the child had of his young life. It was easy to implant a few memories of himself.

Aidan maintained eye contact with the child. "Your friend

Henry had a heart attack and died. It was very sad. You called me to come and get you because your sister was so ill. You and Alexandria have been planning to move in with me. The two of you have already brought some of your things into my house, and you have met my housekeeper, Marie. You like her very much. Stefan, her husband, is a good friend to you. We have been arranging the move for weeks. Do you remember?" He implanted memories and images of his housekeeper and caretaker so the two would be familiar and comfortable to the child.

The little boy nodded solemnly.

Aidan ruffled Joshua's hair. "You had a bad dream, something about vampires, but you do not really remember it. It is all very hazy. You talked to me about it, and if it ever returns to haunt you, you will come to me, and we will discuss it. You always feel free to talk with me about things that sometimes do not make sense. You want me to be with your sister always. We talk about it together and plot together to make her want to stay with me as my wife, as family. You and I are the best of friends. We always look out for Alexandria. You know she belongs with me, that no one can care for her and protect the two of you as I can. This is very important to you, to both of us."

Joshua smiled his assent. Aidan held the child's mind a few minutes longer, letting the boy recognize his touch and feel soothed by it. The child had suffered a terrible trauma. Aidan made certain that the method by which he took them home would be instantly forgotten, and the child would remember a large black car, one he would like.

The trip back was made on the heels of a storm. Swirling black clouds protected the large golden bird and his burdens from any prying eyes as they swept through the sky. Aidan entered the three-story house through the upstairs balcony so no neighbors would see him carry the boy and his sister in.

"Aidan!" Marie, his housekeeper, rushed to help him as he came down the winding staircase. "Who are these youngsters?" She caught sight of Alexandria's swollen face, the blisters and sores. "Oh, my God. You caught up with the vampire, didn't you? Are you all right? Did he hurt you? Let me call Stefan."

"I am fine, Marie. Do not worry about me." Even as he said it, he knew it wouldn't change the way she was. She and her husband had been seeing to his needs, to his household, for nearly forty years. Before her, her mother and father had served him. For all his life, members of her family had served him willingly, without the aid of mind control. He had bestowed money enough that none of them ever had to work, but they were loyal to him and his absentee twin brother, Julian. They knew what he was—they were the only humans he had entrusted with the knowledge of his kind—yet it didn't matter to them.

"The vampire has harmed her?"

"Yes. I need you to care for the boy. His name is Joshua. I have implanted memories of our friendship so he will not fear being here. Stefan must go to their rooming house and collect their belongings and bring them here. Her car remains in a restaurant parking lot." He told her where. "That must be collected. The boy has the car keys in his pocket. Healing his sister will take some time. The child must not interfere in any way. I will have to go out and feed. She needs much care, and I must keep up my strength."

"Are you certain she is not unclean?" Marie asked with great trepidation. She reached for Joshua's hand.

The little boy smiled up at her in recognition and willingly took her hand. He even stepped close and tugged on her apron conspiratorially. "He is going to make Alexandria well. She is very sick."

Marie shoved aside her own anxiety and nodded at Joshua. "Of course. Aidan is a miracle worker. He will make your sister well in no time." After settling the child down at the kitchen table with cookies and milk, she followed Aidan across the room, raising an eyebrow at the hunter, silently demanding an answer to her question.

"He did not turn her, but I am afraid I inadvertently may have. She was protecting the child, but I misunderstood. I thought she was going to kill him." He took two steps away from the housekeeper, then turned back to face her. "Marie?

I see colors. You are wearing a blue-and-green dress. You look beautiful. And I feel again." He smiled at the woman. "I know I have never told you in all our years together, but I have great affection for you. I was so lost, I was unable to feel it before."

Marie's mouth formed a perfect O, and tears shimmered in her eyes. "Thank God, Aidan. At last it has happened. We hoped and prayed, and at last our prayers have been answered. This is tremendous news. Go now. Care for your woman, and we will see to all that is necessary here. I am certain this young man is very hungry and thirsty."

There was such joy on her face that Aidan felt it reflected in his heart. It was amazing to feel. To be able to feel. Without his mate, a Carpathian male lost all wants, needs, emotions after two hundred years. He lived in an abyss, void, and from that moment on he was at risk of turning vampire. The longer he survived, as the centuries passed, the Carpathian distanced himself more and more from his community and all it stood for. Only two things could save him from his empty, desperate fate. He could choose to meet the dawn and end his life, or a miracle might happen and he would find his lifemate.

A handful of very lucky Carpathian males had found the one they searched for. The Carpathian male was by nature a dark, dangerous predator, and he needed the balance of his other half. Needed to find the woman whose soul perfectly complemented his own. Two halves of the same whole, her light to his darkness. There was only one true lifemate for each male. The chemistry had to be just right. And Aidan had finally found his.

Now he moved through the house with his silent, fluid stride. Alexandria's weight was nothing to him. His lair was located far below the first story, a long underground chamber fully furnished with every luxury. He laid her carefully on the bed and stripped away the remnants of her suit. His breath caught in his throat. Her body was so youthful, her breasts full and firm, her skin beautiful. She had a narrow rib cage and a ridiculously small waist. Her hips were slim, almost like a boy's. Despite the fact that her face and limbs were covered in sores from long exposure to the pounding of salt water, Alexandria Houton might, after all, be a pretty woman.

He took great care to wash the salt from her skin and hair, then disposed of the damp quilt beneath her. She lay on the sheets, her long hair wrapped in a towel, her breathing labored but steady. She was severely dehydrated, and she needed more blood. While she was in an unconscious state, Aidan supplied her with more. Aside from her fragile state of health, he was certain her body still had to go through the rigors of the change. And it was very necessary to dilute the vampire's blood. It was easier to access her mind and make the repairs to her damaged body while she was unconscious.

She stirred uncomfortably, moaning softly. Aidan began the soft, healing chant, centuries old, in the ancient tongue of his people, while he crushed herbs around the room.

Alexandria's long lashes fluttered, lifted. For a moment she thought she was in the middle of a bad dream. She hurt everywhere, her body bruised and battered. She looked around the unfamiliar room.

It was beautiful. Whoever owned this place had an eye for elegance and the money to indulge his tastes. Her fingers twisted in the sheet. She found she was too weak to move. "Joshua?" She called his name softly, her heart beginning to pound in alarm when she realized she was awake and not dreaming.

"He is safe." That voice again. She would recognize it anywhere. It was so beautiful, unearthly, like the voice of an angel speaking to her. Yet she knew the truth. This man was a vampire with supernatural powers. He was able to shape-shift, to kill without hesitation. He fed on the blood of humans. He could read minds and force others to do his bidding.

"Where is he?" She didn't bother to move. What would be the point? He clearly had the upper hand. She could only wait and see what he wanted.

"At this very moment he is eating a nutritious dinner prepared by my housekeeper. He is safe, Alexandria. No one in this house will ever harm that boy. On the contrary, every one of us would give our lives to protect him." His voice was so soft and gentle, she could feel the notes soothing her mind.

She closed her eyes, too tired to keep them open. "Who are you?"

"Aidan Savage. This is my home. I am a healer as well as a hunter."

"What are you planning to do with me?"

"I need to know how much blood the vampire forced you to accept. I imagine Yohenstria was quite stingy, wanting to keep you in a weakened state. You are very dehydrated, your eyes black and sunken, your lips cracked, your cells crying out for nourishment. Still, whatever blood he gave you is tainted, and your body is about to go through the conversion." Very gently he applied a soothing salve to her tortured lips.

His words penetrated her foggy brain. Blinking, Alexandria stared up at him, horrified. "What do you mean, conversion? I am going to be like you? Like him? I am to become one of you? Kill me, then. I don't want to be like you." Her throat was so raw, she couldn't speak above a hoarse whisper.

He shook his head. "You do not understand, and there is little time to teach you. Your mind is very strong, completely different from that of most humans. You are resistant to mind control. I want to help you through this. You will go through it, with or without my help, but it will better for you if you allow me to aid you."

She closed her eyes against his words. "My arm hurts."

"I expect it does. I expect most of your body hurts," he answered, his voice somehow penetrating her skin and reaching into her aching arm to touch the bone. A warm tingle started and begin to spread, easing the throbbing. "Your arm is broken, but I have begun repairs. The bone is in line, and the mending has started without trouble."

"I want Joshua."

"Joshua is just a little boy. He thinks you are ill with a virus. He does not need to be frightened and traumatized further. Do you not agree?"

"How do I know you're telling me the truth?" Alexandria asked tiredly. "Don't all vampires lie and deceive?"

"I am Carpathian. I am not yet vampire. I must know how much blood Yohenstria has given you." He spoke patiently, gently, his voice never changing inflection. "How many times did he exchange his blood with you?"

"You're very dangerous, aren't you?" She bit at her lower lip, then winced when she painfully scraped blisters and sores. "You have this way about you, making everyone want to do everything you say. You made the vampire believe you could defeat him, didn't you?" It hurt her to talk, but it was comforting that she could.

"I use the power of my voice," he acknowledged gravely. "Less wear and tear on the body when hunting vampires, although I have had my share of wounds." He touched her then, the lightest of caresses across her forehead. "Do you not remember your own story to young Joshua? I am the hunter, come to rescue my fair lady and her brother. Joshua recognized me as such. He told me so. Do you not find it a strange coincidence that you described me so accurately?"

Her mind refused to think about that, so she changed the subject. "Joshua saw the vampire kill Henry. He must be so frightened."

"He remembers Henry's death as a heart attack. To him, I am an old friend of the family. He thinks he called me to come and help you because of your illness. He believes you fell ill at the restaurant."

She studied his appearance. He was physically beautiful. His hair was rich and thick, waves of gold reaching past his wide shoulders. His eyes, a peculiar molten gold, intense and frightening, gazed back at her with the unblinking stare of a jungle cat. His lips were impossibly sensual. It was impossible to judge his age. She would have guessed he was somewhere in his thirties. "Why don't you erase *my* memories?"

A small, humorless smile curved his mouth, revealing strong, even, white teeth. "You are not so easy to handle, *piccola*. You are resistant to my direction. But we need to address what is happening to you."

46

Her heart began to pound. "What is happening to me?"

"We need to further dilute the tainted blood in your system."

Alexandria wanted to trust him. The smell of the herbs, the sound of his voice, his seeming honesty all made her want to believe he was trying to help her. And he didn't force her decision, or even attempt to rush her, though she sensed he was concerned that whatever was going to happen would happen before he was adequately prepared to deal with it. She took a deep breath. "How do we do that?"

"I must give you a large amount of my blood."

He said it quietly, matter-of-factly. Alexandria looked away. Those golden eyes of his never blinked. She was afraid if she stared into them too long, she would fall forever into their depths. "You will give me a transfusion?"

"I am sorry, *piccola*, that will not work." There was real regret in his voice. He touched her again, turning her chin so she would face him again. The feather-light stroke sent her heart pounding.

"I can't . . . I can't drink blood."

"I can put you under compulsion if you are willing for me to do so. It will aid you. It is our only chance, Alexandria."

The way he said her name sent butterflies winging through her stomach. But was it possible that drinking more blood was the only way to make her well?

"If it is impossible for you to drink of your own free will, you must consent to my aiding you," he said.

"I'm not sure I can do it." The very thought repulsed her. Her stomach was churning, already rebelling at the idea. "There must be another way to make me well. I don't think I can do it," she repeated.

"His blood is tainted, Alexandria. Even though he is dead, he can cause you much pain and suffering. We have to dilute it before you go through the transformation."

There was that word again—*transformation*. She shivered.

He reached behind him for an immaculately white silk shirt, clearly one of his own, and, his eyes holding hers, he gently put it on her, handling her as if she were a fragile

47

porcelain doll. They both pretended the act was impersonal, but there was something in his touch, some quality in his gaze that could only be described as possessive.

Exhausted, Alexandria tried to think. The vampire had been grotesque, and the thought of any part of him living in her bloodstream was terrifying. "All right. Do it." Her blue eyes met his golden gaze. "Put me under compulsion to get rid of the vampire in me. But nothing else. Don't take away or put anything else into my head. Nothing else. You have to give me your word on that." For whatever that would be worth.

He nodded. She was far too weak to sit up, so Aidan cradled her on his lap. She began to tremble, her heart pounding so hard, he was afraid it would shatter before he could heal her. Deliberately he reached behind her to braid her long hair, to soothe and distract her. Then he silently began a low chant in her mind, murmuring in the ancient tongue, bringing a measure of relief to her. She visibly relaxed.

"I want to command you to sleep through your conversion. It is quite brutal, *piccola*. I will wake you when it is over." His velvet voice made the suggestion, and she felt the notes wrapping around her like safe, warm arms, compelling her to do as he wished.

Instantly she pulled back, her mind slamming shut, turning away from him. She simply was not willing to be that vulnerable, to give up all control, even consciousness, to a stranger. Especially one capable of the things this man could do. What was he, after all? Possibly another vampire, despite the distinction he drew about being "Carpathian, not yet vampire," whatever that meant.

"I will assist you in diluting the vampire's tainted blood, Alexandria, nothing more, if that is your wish." He chose his words carefully. He had been in her mind several times already, and the bond was strengthening with each mental sharing. She was unaware of it as of yet, and for now it was better to keep it that way. He knew she was confused and mistakenly hoping that the conversion about to take place would restore her to human life. For now he would have to mildly deceive her in that regard to spare her the agony of the inevitable transformation, already begun, to Carpathian life.

Alexandria sighed. The feel of his hands in her hair, the soft whisper of his husky voice, the total confidence he exuded was mesmerizing. "Let's get it over with before I lose my nerve."

As soon as the words slipped out of her mouth, he shifted her slight weight, cradling her on his lap, and bent his blond head slowly to her throat. The touch of his mouth was like hot silk on her skin. She felt that wildly erotic touch right down to her toes.

Alexandria stiffened, suddenly afraid of losing far more than her life. His lips were on her throat, right over her pulse. *You have to trust me, piccola. Let yourself feel me in you. I am part of you. Reach for me now, as I reach for you.* The words seemed to be in her mind rather than spoken aloud. He was strength and heat, fire and ice. He was power and protection from the insanity engulfing her.

A white-hot heat pierced her throat, and then she felt an erotic intimacy so beautiful, it brought tears to her eyes. She had never felt so cherished, so beautiful, so perfect as she did at that moment. She felt him in her mind, exploring her secret thoughts and desires. He was soothing and healing her, tasting her, sharing her mind. He examined every memory, the strength of her block against him.

When he was certain he had taken enough of her blood to ensure a proper exchange, his tongue reluctantly stroked over the wound and closed it.

With a fingernail he opened a line over his heart. *Drink, Alexandria. Take what is freely offered.* His mind was ready, reaching to take control of hers, to compel what she did not wish to do. His body clenched as her mouth moved over his skin, found what it was seeking, and his life's blood flowed into her. His heart slammed hard against his chest. He knew she was the one. She was his. His entire being responded to her. The chemistry between them was electric, exact. He had waited so long, seemingly forever, for her. And now he was taking no chances on losing her. He began the chant that would bind them together for all time.

I claim you as my lifemate. I belong to you. I offer my life for you. I give you my protection, my allegiance, my heart, my soul, and my body. I take into my keeping the same that is yours. Your life, happiness, and welfare will be placed above my own. You are my lifemate, bound to me for all eternity and always in my care.

He spoke the ritual words in her mind, both in her language and in his native tongue. The ritual would not be complete until her body was bound to his, but, this done, no one would be able to take her from him, nor could she escape him.

Aidan gave her as much blood as he could. He wanted the vampire's blood thoroughly diluted when the conversion began, during which she would expel whatever might remain. They had little time before the transformation would begin, and he was weak and pale. He desperately needed to hunt before she needed him again, which would be very soon.

Alexandria lay back, her long lashes thick crescents resting on her cheeks. Even in her hypnotic state, he could see the pain twisting her body. It was difficult to keep his promise and not command her to sleep the deep, healing sleep of immortals. But if Alexandria was ever to trust him, he had to keep every promise he made. She had exceptional cause to despise his kind. Her trauma and terror would never be fully erased, even as she came to understand their race.

His call to Marie brought the older woman to the chamber immediately. "You will stay with Alexandria while I hunt this night."

Marie watched him, appalled as he staggered with weakness. She had seen him weary and wounded from battle, but she had never seen him so starved before. He was nearly gray. "You must take my blood before you go out, Aidan," she said. "You are too weak to hunt. If a vampire caught you is such a state, he would destroy you."

He shook his head, touching her arm gently. "You know I would never do such a thing. I do not use those I care for, those I protect."

"Go then, and hurry." Marie watched with anxious eyes

as he bent to brush his mouth across the girl's forehead. He was suddenly so tender, this man she had come to know so well. He had always been aloof, remote, even to those he called family. This rare gesture of tenderness made her want to cry.

Aidan whispered the command to awaken Alexandria from her trance. "I must go now," he told her. "Marie will stay with you until my return. Call to me if you have need of me."

For some strange reason, Alexandria didn't want him to leave her side. She curled her fingers in the sheet to keep from calling out to him. But he moved quickly with his peculiar grace, like a great jungle cat, and soon was gone.

Marie held a glass of water to her lips. "I know you're sore, Alexandria—may I call you that?—but some water might help. I feel I know you, what with young Joshua telling me such tales of his wonderful sister. He loves you very much."

The rim of the glass hurt her mouth, and Alexandria pushed it away. "Just Alex, that's what Josh likes to call me. Is he okay?"

"Stefan—that's my husband—looked him over very carefully. He was hungry and tired, a bit hypothermic and dehydrated, but we attended to that. He's eaten and is in good spirits. He fell asleep by the downstairs fire. Under the circumstances, with him so worried about you, we felt he should sleep close to us and not alone in his room."

"Thank you for looking after him." She tried to sit up. With the infusion of the hunter's blood, she felt stronger. "Where is he now? I'd like to go see him."

Marie shook her head. "You must not even attempt to leave this bed. Aidan would have our heads. You're very weak, Alex. I guess you haven't seen yourself yet either. In your condition, you'd scare Joshua to death."

Alexandria sighed. "But I need to see him, to touch him, just so I know he's all right. Everyone tells me he is, but how do I know for sure?"

Marie stroked back stray strands of gold hair from Alexandria's forehead. "Because Aidan does not lie. He would never harm a child. He is one who, at great risk to himself, hunts the vampires preying on the human race."

"Are there really such things? Maybe I'm just having a terrible nightmare I can't wake up from. Maybe I'm just sick with a high fever." She said it hopefully. "How could there really be such things as vampires in our society without everyone knowing it?"

"Because of those like Aidan who stop them."

"What is Aidan? Isn't he a vampire, too? I saw him turn from a bird to a man to a wolf. He grew fangs and claws. He drank my blood. I know he intended to kill me. I still don't know why he changed his mind." Suddenly she felt her body beginning to burn. Her muscles began to tighten into hard knots. Even the thin sheet covering her felt too heavy and warm against her skin. Her muscles seemed to be contorting, the heat migrating throughout her body.

"Aidan will explain everything to you. But rest assured that he is no vampire. I have known him since I was a young girl. He watched me grow up, have children of my own, and now I have become an old woman. He is a powerful, dangerous man, but not to those of us he calls his own. He will never harm you. He will protect you with his life."

Alexandria was panicking. She did not want to belong to Aidan Savage. Yet she realized he would never let her go. How could he? She knew far too much. "I don't want to be here. Call 911. Get me a doctor."

Marie sighed. "No doctor can help you now, Alex. Only Aidan can. He is a great healer. They say there is only one other greater than he." She smiled. "Aidan will return, and he'll take away your pain."

Her insides twisted so hard and abruptly, Alexandria was nearly thrown from the bed. She cried out, screamed. "You have to call me a doctor, Marie. Please! You're human, like me, aren't you? You have to help me. I want to go home! I just want to go home!"

Marie tried to hold her down on the bed, but the pain was so intense, Alexandria's body convulsed, and she hit the floor hard.

Chapter Four

Aidan inhaled the night as he walked along the San Francisco sidewalk. Creatures winged their way across the sky. The breeze carried the scent of prey. Half a block away, an alley, narrow and dark, opened onto the street. He could feel the presence of three men. He smelled their sweat, heard their crude laughter. They were would-be assailants waiting for a lost soul to brighten up their otherwise dull lives.

His hunger rose sharply with every step he took, the demon rising so that his mind became merely a red haze demanding to feed. He smelled the night. It had taken him some time to get used to the sounds and sights and smells of this foreign city. The sea salt carried on the wind, the thick fog, the patterns of the night life were all so different from the ways of his homeland. But someone had to hunt the vampires. Once the undead had learned they could leave their lands and travel far from the Dark One's justice, they had begun to branch out. Aidan had volunteered to leave his beloved Carpathian Mountains and go to a new land to protect the humans residing there. And San Francisco had become his home base. Over time he had come to enjoy the city and its diverse people, to even think of it as home.

The art centers were wonderful. Theater and opera were plentiful. And there was a ready supply of prey. He moved silently, muscles rippling as he neared the alley. The three thugs were shuffling back and forth, whispering, unaware of his stalking. Their mutterings were loud in his ears, despite the fact that he had deliberately lowered his hearing, wanting to escape the assault on his senses. Sensations, intense emotions, even the vivid colors he hadn't experienced in so many centuries were overwhelming to him. The night seemed so brilliant, it took his breath away. He found it beautiful, the clouds, the stars, the moon, all of it.

Aidan shrugged his powerful shoulders to relax the tension in his body. He was more obviously muscular than most of his kind. The majority of his people were slimmer, more elegantly built. Also unlike the others, he and his twin were blond with golden eyes. His race customarily had dark hair and eyes.

As he approached the alley, he sent forth a call. He didn't need to do so. The moment the men spotted him, they would have attempted to attack him. But this way would be calmer. Although the predator in him would welcome a battle, brief as it would be, he didn't have the time to indulge his nature just now. In any case, having come so close to the edge of madness and transformation to vampire by waiting so many centuries for his mate, and so soon after the killing battle with Paul Yohenstria, he would not allow himself to explode into violence. He had a purpose now, a reason for existing, and he would not allow his predatory nature to overcome his intelligence and will.

One of the trio had just lit a cigarette, its pungent aroma wafting along the street, but abruptly he turned and began to shuffle out of the alley. The other two followed him, one cleaning his greasy fingernails with the point of a pocketknife. Their eyes were slightly glazed, as if they were drugged. Aidan frowned, unhappy that the prey was using narcotics, but blood was blood, and the drugs wouldn't affect him.

"It is cold out on the street," Aidan said softly, slipping an arm around the smoker's shoulders. He led the men back into the darkened alley, away from prying eyes, and bent his head to drink. The other two waited like cattle, pushing close to him for their turn. Their unwashed bodies and rather useless minds sickened him, but he had to feed. Sometimes he wondered why humans like these were allowed to exist. They seemed little different from those of his race who had chosen to forfeit their souls and turn vampire, preying on those less powerful than themselves. Why didn't someone stop these humans? Why had God created them? Why had he given the gift of breath to them, knowing they would fail to live a life of honor and integrity? Carpathian males endured for hundreds—some of them thousands—of years before they sought the dawn and self-destruction or made the decision to turn renegade and lose their souls for all time. Yet some human males could not endure even beyond their teen years.

Aidan dropped the first victim carelessly on the ground, his hand curling around the nape of the next donor. The man came to him easily, under hypnotic trance, eager to please. Aidan fed voraciously, heedless that the three men would be weak and helpless for some time. He needed the nourishment, and he was disgusted with their existence. Men like these searched to exploit those weaker than themselves. They were cruel to their women and avoided their obligations to their most precious treasure in life, their children. Who cared how they got this way? Aidan was a firm believer in choosing one's own destiny, not taking the easy way out. Carpathian males had all the instincts of a predator, sometimes more dangerous than wild animals, yet they would never abuse a woman or a child. They held to a strict code of honor even in their oftentimes kill-or-be-killed world. All of them knew the consequences of their actions, and they accepted the responsibility of their gifts. In Aidan's race men such as these three would soon be exterminated. As powerful as Carpathians were, they could not be allowed to abuse those weaker than themselves.

The second victim swayed and fell nearly on top of the first. Aidan dragged the knife-wielding man close. The man looked up at him. "Are we going to party?" the reprobate asked with a crude laugh.

"One of us is," Aidan agreed softly, and he bent his head to find the pulsing jugular.

The first ripple of unease hit him. He lifted his head for a moment, and his prey's blood spurted out. He bent once more to his task, this time all efficiency and quickness. It was Alexandria. He could feel the first wave of pain hitting her.

He meticulously closed the wound, ensuring that there was no evidence on the man's neck to betray the presence of his kind in the area, and allowed his prey to sink to the ground. To anyone passing by all three men would appear drunk. Doubtless the trail of blood down one man's shirt would be attributed to a bloody nose.

It was starting within Alexandria, as he knew it would. The conversion. And, ultimately, if inadvertently, he was responsible. The guilt didn't sit well with him. He had observed two wounds on Alexandria's neck, which could only mean one thing: the vampire had bitten her twice, made his exchanges. When Aidan had assumed she was a vampiress, already turned, he had nearly killed her. Then, when he had realized his error, he had replaced her lost blood with his own. Four blood exchanges would put the human through the transformation process—to vampire or Carpathian. Either way, there was no turning back. In most humans, attempts at conversion either killed the woman outright or drove her insane. Only a few women, those possessing psychic abilities, had managed to come through the ordeal alive and well. And they would be the ones to help perpetuate the Carpathian race, since their own females were proving barren.

The fourth blood exchange, converting Alexandria, would also keep her chained to him forever. Selfish though it might be to make that decision without her consent, she was, after all, his only salvation. He had held on for so many centuries, awaiting his lifemate, avoiding turning vampire himself. And, consenting or not, she *was* meant to be his lifemate, not Yohenstria's; all the signs, and their perfect chemistry, confirmed that. And at least he had done what he could to give Alexandria as much of his own powerful, ancient blood as he could to dilute the vampire's taint and make her transformation to Carpathian easier.

He felt her scream in his mind, a helpless cry filled with desperate pain. She was confused and afraid, linked with him yet unknowingly sharing her thoughts. She was terrified of him yet afraid he had deserted her, afraid he might even be enjoying her pain as the vampire had. Mostly she was afraid for her brother, Joshua, believing he was alone, unprotected in the house of a vampire so powerful, he had killed another of the undead in a matter of moments.

Aidan launched himself into the night sky, needing to cover the distance between them as quickly as possible. At that moment he didn't care if someone saw a strange night owl, huge beyond belief, winging its way over the city. She needed him. She was begging Marie for a doctor. Marie was in distress, wanting to accommodate her yet knowing Aidan was the only one who could help her. He heard it all clearly, the soft voice begging for help, the housekeeper nearly in tears. He was sharing Alexandria's mind, experiencing everything she was experiencing. Confusion. Pain. Fear amounting to terror.

He flew to her, to be close when she called out for him. And he hoped, for both their sakes, that that would be soon. She needed him, but he had promised to compel her no further than the blood exchange. She had to call for him.

Outside the underground chamber he paced, Alexandria's pitiful cries sending shards of pain through his own heart. A dozen times he reached for the door, wanting, even needing to kick it in. But she had to call to him. She had to express faith in him or she would never believe he was helping, not harming, her. He rested his forehead against the door, then was shocked to see a crimson stain from the contact. He was sweating blood, in agony hearing her pleas and feeling the pain twisting and burning within her body. The physical agony he could manage, but his heart and his mind were in torment.

It seemed an endless nightmare. He knew the moment when she tried to crawl across the floor in a blind attempt to escape her own body. He knew when she vomited blood, the tainted blood of the vampire. He felt her insides burning and rebelling against their mutations. Her internal organs were reshaping, renewing themselves, becoming different. Her cells—every muscle, tissue, every inch of her skin—were on fire with the transformation.

Where are you? You promised to help me. Where are you?
He had waited so long for the invitation, he thought he

was hallucinating when it actually came. He hit the door with the flat of his hand and burst inside. Marie was kneeling, tears streaming down her face, trying in vain to hold the convulsing body.

Aidan nearly dragged Alexandria from Marie's arms, cradling her protectively against his chest. "Go, Marie. I will help her."

Marie's eyes were eloquent with sympathy for Alexandria and anger and accusation for him. She twitched the hem of her skirt smartly and slammed the door hard as she left.

The moment the housekeeper was out of sight, Aidan put her out of his mind. His total attention centered on Alexandria. "Did you think I had deserted you, *piccola*? I did not. But I could not interfere if you did not wish me to do so. Remember? You made me promise."

Alexandria turned her face away, humiliated that Aidan Savage would again see her so vulnerable, so disheveled. She didn't have time to dwell on it though, because the next wave of heat was starting, clawing at her stomach and liver and kidneys, taking a blowtorch to her heart and lungs. Her cry echoed through the room, a wrenching scream of agony. She wished she would stop so she could breathe, but it went on and on. Tears streamed down her face.

Aidan thumbed away her tears, and his hand came away stained with blood. He breathed for her, for both of them.

Aidan's hands were cool and soothing on her skin, his ancient chants centering her mind so that she had an anchor to cling to in an insane world. After a time Alexandria realized he was somehow taking part of the pain from her. He was there in her mind, shielding her from the terrible burning, from complete awareness of what was happening to her. Her mind seemed hazy, as if she was in a dream state. She forced her eyes open. She could see her own agony reflected in his eyes. There was a scarlet smear across his forehead.

When the terrible spasms let her loose from their grip to give her a few moments' reprieve, she reached up and touched his face with wondering fingers. "I can't believe you came back." Her voice was husky, her throat swollen. "It hurts."

"I know, Alexandria. I have taken the brunt of it, but I cannot do more at this time, and the poisoned blood you took in makes it so much worse." He said it with honest regret, guilt, and humbleness, all powerful new emotions.

"How can you do what you're doing?" Her tongue touched her dried lips, felt the terrible sores.

"We are connected now through the sharing of our blood. That is how I heard your call to me. It is how you feel me in your mind." Once more he touched some soothing salve to her lips, one small relief he could provide.

"I'm so tired, I don't think I can do this anymore." If he could really read her mind, he would see she was telling the truth. He was rocking her back and forth, oblivious of her hideous condition, holding her as if she was the most precious, beautiful woman in the world. He was there in her mind, his arms keeping her sheltered next to his heart. It was soothing, comforting; it made her feel less alone. But even with his help, she could not stand another bout of this agony. She knew she couldn't. And it was coming; already she could feel the heat beginning. Her fingers circled his arm; her blue eyes rose to meet his liquid gold gaze. "I really can't."

"Allow me to put you to sleep. Do not be afraid. It will merely be the unconscious state of humans, not the sleep of our kind. Your body must convert before I can put you into our truly healing sleep." His velvet-soft voice was compelling and beautiful.

"I don't want to hear any more." Her body was stiffening. Even with Aidan's enormous strength, a spasm of pain nearly wrenched her from his grasp. A low moan escaped her clenched teeth, her nails bit into his arms, but she clung to him while her body rid itself of the tainted blood and her cells and organs continued to reshape into those of another race. Her mind was chaos and pain, a place of fear and agony.

The spasm lasted a full three minutes, the intensity peaking and then ebbing like the waves of the sea. She was beaded in blood, sweating it. Her breath came in ragged gasps; her heart was nearly exploding. "I can't do this," she gasped.

"Then trust me. I came back for you, did I not? I will not harm or desert you while you sleep. Why do you resist?"

"At least awake I know what's going on."

"You don't know, *piccola*. I share your mind. You cannot comprehend anything other than pain. Let me help you. I cannot take much more of your agony either. I am afraid I will lose control and be forced to break my promise not to further compel you. Do not force me to break trust with you. Give your consent that I may put you to sleep."

She could hear the pleading and honesty in his voice. She also felt that warm, sensuous velvet that wrapped her up and made her want to do whatever he wished. It frightened her that his voice alone held so much power. This man, whatever he might be, was dangerous, lethal. She sensed it, but at that moment, with the heat starting and the mixture of pleading and warning in the golden eyes, she gave up the fight. "Don't hurt me anymore," she whispered against the warmth of his throat.

He read the submission in her voice, in her eyes, and Aidan took no chances that she would change her decision. He instantly sent a sharp command, seizing her mind, pushing past its barricade to take control. He put her to sleep, beyond the pain, in a place where neither the agony of the conversion nor the vampire's blood could reach her.

He held her in his arms for a long time before gently cleaning her and laying her to rest more comfortably on the bed. Putting the chamber in order took longer, but he did it himself, not wanting Marie or her tacit criticism to intrude on this intimate time with Alexandria. He used candles and herbs to fill the room with healing aromas.

He was becoming familiar with Alexandria's mind, with her strengths and weaknesses. It was inevitable that soon he would unlock the barrier she was able to erect against him. His thumb caressed her forehead as she lay asleep and vulnerable in the huge four-poster bed. It was amazing to be in her mind. She was an incredible human. She had struggled against nearly impossible odds, losing her parents so young, single-handedly raising her little brother, loving him with the same fierce, protective instincts of a mother. She worked hard to provide Joshua with a decent life. She was also funny and mischievous and irreverent, filled with a love of jokes and pranks. She was warm-hearted and generous.

She was a bright light to cast out the growing darkness within him. Alexandria was compassion and goodness, everything he was not.

He sat down on the edge of the bed, thankful the herbs were working their magic. The odor of vomit and blood, the taint of evil, was gone from the chamber, leaving only the pungent aroma of the healing plants. He checked each of Alexandria's wounds and sores, in time-honored fashion mixing some of the precious soil of his homeland with his saliva to speed the mending of each laceration. The ragged tears at her neck were the worst. The vampire had made the wounds, and they festered with his poison. Aidan packed them carefully, chanting in the ancient tongue, once more sending himself into Alexandria's body to heal it from the inside out. The conversion was almost complete, he noted with relief.

He stretched out beside her on the bed, aware that he still had a long, uphill battle ahead of him with his new lifemate. She was going to be very resistant to his advances. She would fight the truth of her conversion, hate it when she realized what it meant. And she would blame him. Rightfully so. With the vampire's gruesome torture and his own clumsy handling of her at their first meeting, she had nothing to thank his species for. Still, she had no choice; she was bound to him, her mind to his, her soul his other half. Joining them together completely was now a matter of patience. Aidan sent up a silent prayer that he would have whatever it took to give Alexandria the time she needed. She deserved it, and as her true lifemate, he could do no other, than to provide her with whatever she needed. Only he knew how dangerous every moment of that time would be to both of them, how vulnerable she was without him, and how he would no longer endure if anything happened to her. In addition, she was in danger from her own predatory nature, which would clamor to claim her even without her consent.

Aidan sighed, then scanned his home and the surrounding

area. He checked windows and entrances. Placed strong spells at the door of the underground chamber and even more deadly, potent spells to guard the chamber itself. He was taking no chances with his mate now that he had found her. Aidan pulled her into his arms, waited until he was certain the change had completely taken place, then sent her into the deep, healing sleep of his race. His body wrapped protectively around hers, he closed down his heart and lungs and lay as one dead.

As the sun began to set, a disturbance found its way into the chamber. Then a single heartbeat interrupted the silence, and lungs drew in air. Aidan lay still, scanning the house for the cause of his early awakening. Above him, on the first floor, someone was rudely pounding on the door to his home. He could hear Marie's soft footfalls as she moved to answer. Her heartbeat was audible to him. She was nervous about the caller. The pounding at the front entrance was loud and authoritative. A smile curved his mouth. Behind his housekeeper, he heard Stefan, ever ready to defend his wife, to defend Aidan's home.

Aidan rose, his body supple and strong. His gaze slid to Alexandria. Shock went through him. She was beautiful! There were a few bruises marring her soft skin, but it was otherwise healthy, flawless skin. Her lips were soft and lush, her lashes long and heavy. Younger even than he had imagined, she was unlike any woman he had ever seen. And she belonged to him, and nothing on Earth would change that. His body stirred unexpectedly with a sudden, urgent ache that shocked him. She lay there helpless, a virtual stranger, yet he had been in her mind and knew her more intimately than one could ever know another after years of living together. He bent to brush her forehead with his lips, a salute to her courage, her capacity for loving, and the goodness in her. But proximity to her only deepened the throbbing ache in his body.

Quickly he put distance between himself and temptation. It had been six hundred years since he had felt a biological urge, yet this surpassed anything he had once known. This was no mild desire to appease the needs of his body. This was a raging hunger for one woman, the only woman. He needed her now in every sense of the word, and it didn't help his self-control that she was young and beautiful, rather than the hag he had initially thought her.

The caller on the floor above them was yelling at Marie. Aidan could hear the man clearly. It was someone obviously used to having his way. Wealthy, clearly difficult. He was demanding to see Alexandria Houton. He went so far as to threaten Marie with deportation if she did not produce Alexandria immediately, obviously thinking her accent made her vulnerable to such a threat.

Fangs exploded in Aidan's mouth, and his golden eyes glowed hot and vicious, the beast in him stronger than ever. Was it because he was jealous of any male coming near his lifemate? Because he was feeling anger—another powerful new emotion—that someone was yelling at his house-keeper? Or perhaps a combination of both? He did not know; but he recognized he was dangerous and would have to exercise great self-control. A long, slow hiss escaped his lips as he floated up the stairs and entered the kitchen through the secret passage. He moved with supernatural speed, invisible to the human eye. All Carpathians were capable of such things, and it was second nature to him.

In the entryway of his home, a tall, handsome man raged at his housekeeper. "You produce Alexandria immediately or I'll call the police. I think foul play has been committed, and you're in some way a party to it!" He was looking at Marie with contempt, as if she were an insect he could eas-ily crush beneath his foot.

Abruptly the stranger fell silent, a cold shiver unexpect-edly running down his spine. He had the distinct impression something was stalking him. Wildly, he looked around the immaculate yard. Empty. Still, the impression of danger was so strong, his heart began to pound, and his mouth went dry. Thomas Ivan's heart slammed against his chest when a man appeared virtually out of nowhere. He simply seemed to materialize behind the stubborn housekeeper. The man was tall, elegant, well-dressed. Long blond hair flowed to his broad shoulders, and unusual golden eyes regarded him with the unblinking stare of a cat. He exuded power. Power and strength. Danger clung to him like a second skin.

Thomas registered that the house reeked of money, and that this occupant was no one he could easily intimidate. The man seemed to glide forward, his muscles rippling beneath his silk shirt, his movement so fluid his feet barely seemed to touch the floor. He certainly made no sound as he moved. The hand putting Marie to one side was extraordinarily gentle, yet it conveyed a sense of menace to Thomas.

"Marie is here legally, and it is extremely rude of you to threaten members of my household. Perhaps those who work for you are simply servants, but my people are my family and under my protection." The words were spoken in a soft, pleasant voice the texture of velvet. A polite smile accompanied the words, a brief show of white teeth.

For no reason at all, Thomas felt a shiver of fear run down his spine. The hair on his body actually bristled in alarm. His mouth was so dry, he wasn't certain he could talk. He took a breath and decided to backpedal. A housekeeper he could handle; this man was altogether different. He held up a hand in the age-old symbol of peace. "Look, I'm sorry we got off on the wrong foot. I apologize for coming on so strong. It was definitely the wrong way to handle the situation, but my friend is missing, and I'm very worried. I'm Thomas Ivan."

Aidan recognized the name immediately. The rising star of the computer-games industry, the imagination behind some astonishingly popular recent vampire video games, had come to call. Aidan raised an eyebrow, his face expressionless. "Am I supposed to know you?"

Ivan was disconcerted. This interview had suddenly shifted ground, and he was no longer in control. Even his famous name didn't buy him the usual awe or entree. For some reason this man, as soft-spoken and polite as he was, scared the hell out of Ivan. He was frankly scarier than the vampires of his imagination. There was menace lurking just below his surface, as if the veneer of civilization was very thin, and a wild animal, powerful and predatory, prowled impatiently for release.

Thomas tried again. "I was dining with my friend, Alexandria Houton, two nights ago. She became ill and raced from the restaurant, leaving behind her portfolio, never to return. Her sketches are very important to her; she would never just leave them behind if she were all right. Three other women disappeared that night, along with a homeless man. There was a terrible storm that night, and the police believe the missing people somehow went over the cliff. Alexandria's car was found the next morning in the parking lot but soon thereafter removed by your caretaker." Ivan had given the parking attendant a good sum of money for that information.

"Alexandria is a close personal friend, Mr. Ivan," Aidan told him. "Her younger brother was waiting outside the restaurant for her when she became ill. He called me, and I brought them both here. Miss Houton is still quite ill and cannot receive visitors. I am certain she will be pleased to hear you have returned her briefcase. I will tell her you called." Aidan nodded in dismissal, those molten gold eyes never once blinking.

The smooth, pleasant voice made it clear that Thomas Ivan meant nothing to him. The odd part was, Ivan wanted to do as the man bade him. He actually extended the briefcase toward the man before he realized what he was doing. He quickly lowered his arm. "I'm sorry, I didn't get your name." He said it almost belligerently. He was not going to be pushed around. And he was not going to turn the briefcase over to a perfect stranger. How did he know this was the truth?

The perfect white smile appeared a second time. The smile sent chills crawling over Ivan's skin. It was a predator's smile, as if the beast lurking below the surface had just been unleashed. It held no warmth, and those golden eyes glittered dangerously at him.

"I am Aidan Savage, Mr. Ivan. This is my home. I believe we both attended a party for Senator Johnson a year ago, but we were never introduced. I seem to recall now that you make up games of some kind."

Thomas winced visibly. The voice was musical, its notes

so pure he couldn't help but want to hear it again and again. It seemed to work its way inside him and twist and turn until it was difficult to resist anything this man said. Yet somehow, despite the purity of Aidan Savage's voice, the words stung. Ivan was a huge success with his famous games; they were the hottest thing on the market. Worse, he had heard of the illusive, highly regarded, much sought-after Aidan Savage, and if a man with such a reputation and wealth were to reject Thomas outright, the social circles he ran in, both professional and personal, might also eject him. This was turning into a nightmare. Only his need for Alexandria Houton—also personal and professional—kept him rooted to the spot.

"I really must present this to Alexandria myself. Her work is very important to both of us. She was eager for a job with me, and I certainly am eager to give it to her." Ivan attempted to put himself back on firm footing. "When would be a good time to call again?"

"Perhaps in a day or two. Marie will supply you with my number. Alexandria and her brother Joshua are residing here now, but we have not yet had time to install Alexandria's private phone. Her sudden illness, you see, advanced the move before we were quite ready with her apartments. You will, of course, turn over Alexandria's personal property to me immediately. She is under my protection, Mr. Ivan, and I always take care of my own."

The golden eyes caught Ivan's gaze and held him captive. Thomas found himself meekly handing over the briefcase. Then the eyes released him from their mesmerizing stare. At once Ivan was appalled at what he had done. What had gotten into him? He had never intended to give up the portfolio, not to anyone but Alexandria. His gaze found Savage's hand, the thumb caressing the imitation leather as if it were Alexandria's skin. At once he felt jealous. Just what was Aidan Savage to Alexandria? A man like Savage would eat an innocent like Alexandria alive. Thomas completely forgot, in his surge of chivalry, that that had been his own intention until he had discovered her exceptional artistic talent.

"Thank you for coming by, Mr. Ivan. I regret I cannot ask you to stay longer, but I have several appointments. I will see to it that Alexandria phones you in a couple of days, or that you are otherwise informed of her progress. Good evening, sir."

Ivan soon found himself outside the closed door, unable to place Savage's European accent or to stomach the house-keeper's rather smug smile as she reopened the door briefly to hand him Savage's unlisted phone number. He had made no friends in this house, a big mistake. If Alexandria needed his assistance, and he was more certain than ever that she did, he had no allies in this fortress Savage called home.

Aidan turned to Marie and touched her hair lightly, a brief, affectionate gesture. "Did that imbecile upset you?"

She laughed lightly. "Not nearly as much as he upset you. You didn't know you had a rival for the lady's affections. A famous millionaire, no less."

"He makes up drivel."

"Still, from what I gleaned from his conversation, Alexandria wants to work with him." She was openly teasing him. "And his vampire games have made the news. I've seen him on the covers of magazines. He's quite taken with Alexandria, isn't he?"

"He does not have a chance. And he is much too old for her."

Marie and Stefan both laughed. They were fully aware that Aidan had lived for centuries. Aidan suddenly grinned himself, surprising them both. They had never seen a gen-uine smile light his golden eyes.

"How is the child, this night?" he asked them.

Marie and Stefan sobered. "He is very quiet, that one," Stefan answered. A few inches taller than Marie, wide and muscular, he was a force to be reckoned with. "I think he needs to see his sister before he can be a little boy once again. He has lost too much in his short life."

"He is a sweet child, Aidan. He already has Stefan wrapped around his little finger," Marie pointed out.

"Ha!" Stefan protested emphatically. "It is you who weeps for him and fills him full of food at every turn."

"I will speak to him," Aidan reassured the couple, "and

tell him that his sister will see him later this evening after she rises from the underground chamber."

"After she wakes up," Marie corrected with a frown. She wanted no allusions made to the otherworldly life in front of the innocent boy. "Do you think it wise to promise such a thing? What if she . . ." She hesitated.

Stefan filled in. "Has problems accepting what she has become? Or worse, what if she is not the true one you seek and is now completely deranged?"

"She is the true one. Can you not see her presence, her light, in me already? She has given me life, light, emotion. I see colors once more, and they are radiant. I feel things, everything from anger to a melting warmth. She has returned the world to me. She will wake as one of my people, and yes, I expect considerable resistance from her, but not in front of the child. She loves him very much, and she will try to appear as normal as possible for him. He has been her prime motivation for years, and he will continue to be so. It will be as important for her to see him as for the child to see her. I suspect that if Joshua can accept me into his life, that will be half the battle."

"Aidan!" Joshua ran into the room and flung his arms around Aidan's legs. "I've been looking everywhere for you. Marie told me where your bedroom is on the third floor, but you weren't there."

"I told you to stay out of Mr. Savage's rooms," Marie said with her best scolding tone, but there was no way to conceal the warmth in her expression.

Joshua looked a bit ashamed but answered her with spirit. "I'm sorry, Marie, but I have to find Alexandria. You know where she is, don't you, Aidan?" he asked.

The Carpathian male rested his hands gently on the boy's silky curls. His heart twisted, a funny, melting sensation. There was so much trust and faith in those blue eyes looking up at him. "Yes, Josh. She is still asleep. I want you to give her another hour or so to rest, and then I'll bring her to you. How is that?"

"Is she all better? I've been afraid she wouldn't come

back—you know, like Henry and my mom and dad." The young voice trembled with fear.

"Alexandria is not going to leave you, Josh," Aidan assured him quietly. "She will always be here, and we will look after her together so that nothing will ever take her from either of us. You know I will always protect her, and I am not easily defeated. No one will take her from the two of us. Is that a deal?"

Joshua grinned up at him trustingly. "We're best friends, aren't we, Aidan? You, me, and Alexandria."

"We are more than best friends, Joshua," Aidan replied soberly. "All of us who live in this house are a family."

"Marie says you want me to go to a new school."

Aidan nodded. "I think it would be best. The one you were attending is far from here, and the school we have in mind for you is very good. You will have friends and good teachers there."

"What does Alexandria say? She usually takes me to school. She thinks it's dangerous for me to go by myself."

"Not this school. In any case, Stefan and Marie will go with you if you like. They will escort you there every day until you feel comfortable with the arrangement."

"I want you to go with me if Alex can't take me." Joshua managed a decent pout.

Aidan laughed softly. "You little devil. I can see you are used to getting your way. Alexandria is a soft touch where you are concerned, is she not?"

Joshua shrugged, then laughed, too. "Yeah, she lets me have just about anything I want, and she never gets mad when I don't do what I'm supposed to do. Sometimes she tries to yell at me, but she always ends up hugging me instead."

"I think you need the firm hand of a man in your life, young Joshua," Aidan said, reaching down to lift the boy up to his broad shoulders. "A great big strong man who will not take all your nonsense."

Joshua's arms circled Aidan's neck. "You don't ever yell either."

"No, but I mean what I say when I say it, right?"

69

"Yeah," Josh admitted. "But I still think you should take me to school when I have to go."

"I have to stay here to make certain your sister does everything she is supposed to do to get well. Her illness was very dangerous, and we have to be very careful for a few days. She can be quite stubborn, as you know." Aidan said the last with a conspiratorial wink.

Joshua nodded with a small smile. "I know if you're with her, nothing bad can happen to her. I'll go to school with Marie and Stefan. Of course, if you took me, all the other kids would think I have a big daddy, and they wouldn't try to pick on me." He shrugged. "But Stefan's big. Maybe he'll work."

"I am certain Stefan will scare off any bullies. But this is a nice school, Joshua, with nice children. No one carries weapons, and no one is going to try to hurt you there. If something like that were to happen, you would come to me right away and tell me." The golden eyes stared directly into the blue ones.

Joshua nodded. "I would tell you, Aidan." He blinked and squirmed until Aidan put him down. "Marie said dinner was ready. She's a good cook, better than Alex, but don't tell Alex, 'cuz it'll hurt her feelings. Are you going to eat with us tonight?"

Aidan found himself grinning for no reason at all. He suddenly felt as if he had a family for the first time. People had cared for him for centuries, been loyal to him, and that had helped keep him a part of the world of sanity. Now, though, he had more than mere loyalty, fine as that was. He had emotions choking him, tearing at him, warming him. He loved it, even as he found it somewhat overwhelming. "We will never tell Alexandria that one," he agreed solemnly.

Marie took Joshua's hand. "He just compliments me so he can stay in my good graces. He likes to lick the frosting bowl."

Joshua was shaking his head so hard, his blond curls bounced. His voice was solemn, his eyes earnest. "No, Marie, it's really true. Alexandria is a terrible cook. She burns everything."

Chapter Five

She heard noises first. A drum beating. Wood creaking. Water running. Whispers of conversations, rumbling car engines, and the distant laughter of a child. Alexandria lay perfectly still, not daring to open her eyes. She knew she wasn't alone. She knew it was night. She knew the drum beating was her own heart—and that of another in a synchronized rhythm. She knew the conversation she could hear so clearly was taking place at a distance from her, on the first floor, in the kitchen. She knew the child laughing was Joshua.

She didn't know how she knew these things, and it terrified her. She could smell cookies and spice. She could smell . . . him. Aidan Savage. He was there watching her with his beautiful eyes. Liquid gold. Penetrating. All-seeing. She let herself breathe. Hiding like a frightened child beneath the covers was not going to change anything. She was whatever he had made her. And he had somehow made her . . . not human. But, the voracious hunger now crawling through her body in a way she had never known was a fact she had to deal with.

Her long lashes lifted, and the first thing she saw was his face. It was amazing how beautiful he was, in a purely masculine way. She studied him carefully, thoroughly. He was strong and powerful. It was there, all of it, the violent nature hidden just beneath all that civilized charm. His eyes were like a cat's, golden orbs, unblinking and steady, lashes long. He had a strong chin, an elegant nose. His lips were very defined, inviting, his teeth exceptionally white. His hair was a tawny mane of shimmering gold flowing to his broad shoulders. His muscles were ropey and rippled when he moved. But now he remained utterly still, like a part of the room, almost blending in, watching her intently. He was a magnificent predator. She knew he was, knew there was no other quite like him.

She touched her tongue to her lips to moisten them. "So, what do we do now?"

"I need to teach you our ways."

His voice was quiet and matter-of-fact. Did that mean people turned into vampires every day? Alexandria sat up tentatively. Her body was sore and stiff but not agonized as it had been before. She stretched her muscles gingerly, testing them. "I don't have any desire to learn your ways." She glanced up at him, a flash of blue eyes quickly concealed by long lashes. "You tricked me. You knew I thought I would become . . . human again."

He shook his head, the force of his will so strong, she had to look up at him. At once the molten gold captured her gaze. "No, Alexandria, you know that is not true. You wanted to believe it, so you convinced yourself. I chose not to confront you with the truth, but I never at any time misled you."

A small, humorless smile touched her mouth. "Is that what you think? How noble of you to absolve yourself of any responsibility."

He stirred, a slight ripple of muscles, and her heart leapt in alarm. He subsided, motionless once more, as if reading her fear. "I did not say I do not hold any responsibility in this matter. But I cannot change what is. Nor could I change what occurred last evening. Believe me, Alexandria, I would give anything that you not have had to endure what the vampire put you through. Had I been able to do more to spare you such agony, I would have done so."

His voice, so soft and gentle, rang with honesty. He seemed incapable of lying. But didn't vampires have that ability, that power to mesmerize their victims? Alexandria didn't know what was reality anymore, but she was not going to allow anyone to take over her life without a fight. She had a brain, she was strong, and she was determined. She had long ago learned patience. Fortitude. Survival skills. Right at this moment she didn't have enough information to make any decisions.

"Am I like you now?"

His mouth quirked in the smallest of smiles; then his face was once again a cool, blank mask, his golden eyes soulless, reflecting back her own image. "Not exactly. I was born Carpathian. My people are as old as time itself. I am one of the ancients, a healer of our people, and a hunter of the vampire. I have knowledge and power from centuries of study."

She held up a hand. "I'm not sure I'm ready for all this. Mostly I want to know if I'm still me."

"Who did you think you would become? There is no longer any lingering taint of the vampire's blood in your system, if that is what concerns you."

She took a deep breath. Drew on her knowledge of vampire lore. Hunger was a clawing ache. "What concerns me is . . . whether or not I can walk in the sunshine. Whether or not I can eat like a regular person, go to a fast-food place with Joshua and eat whatever I want."

He answered calmly. "Sunlight will burn your skin. Your eyes will have the worst reaction, swelling and tearing. In daylight you must wear dark glasses, made with special lenses for our people."

She let her breath out slowly. "That answers one question. I'm trying hard not to get hysterical here. Just say it out straight."

"You must have blood to survive."

"You could have broken it to me more gently, in stages or something," she replied wryly, her customary irreverence clearly intact even though her mind was spinning, in total chaos. It was hard to think, to breathe. This couldn't really be happening. It just couldn't. "I hope you don't expect me to sleep in a coffin." She tried to make it a joke, to help her mind accept the possibility of such a thing. More than anything, she wanted to scream.

His eyes were absorbing her, drawing her to him. She could almost feel him reaching for her, an illusion so real that she felt the warmth of his arms, his soothing touch in her mind. "I do not think that will be necessary."

Her tongue found her suddenly dry lips. "I can't breathe."

He physically touched her then, his hand curling around the nape of her neck, forcing her head down. "Yes, you can," he said calmly. "This panic will pass."

She dragged great gulps of air into her burning lungs, fighting the sobs tearing at her throat. She could not cry aloud. She couldn't do anything but try to inhale. His fingers began a slow massage, so gentle, so light, but her body responded, an easing of the terrible tension at the calm command of his hand.

"Why didn't you just kill me?" The words were muffled by the quilt, by her aching throat.

"I have no intention of killing you. You are innocent of any wrongdoing. I am not a cold-blooded killer, Alexandria."

She looked up at him then, her large eyes meeting his. "Please don't lie to me. This is hard enough as it is."

"I *am* a hunter, *piccola*. But I do not kill the innocent. I am a sentinel of justice for our people, appointed by our Prince, the leader of our people, to guard this city."

"I am not your kind. I'm really not." She knew she sounded desperate despite her every intention to remain calm. "There's been some kind of mistake. You have to undo it." Her voice was trembling, her body shaking. "If you would just listen to me, you would understand. I'm really not like you."

His hand closed over hers, eased her clenched fingers, his thumb lightly stroking the frantically beating pulse in her wrist. "Stay calm, Alexandria, you are doing fine. You will heal fast. I know you did not get a look at yourself last night, but you are already remarkably healed. And you will find much to love in your new life. You will be able to see in the darkness as if it was high noon. You will be able to hear things never before heard, see things never seen. It is a beautiful world."

"You don't understand. I already have a life. And I have to take care of Joshua. Joshua can't be without me during the day. He's just a little boy. He needs me to take him to school. I have to work, too."

Aidan said he was no killer, but Alexandria was not blind. He was beautiful but deadly beneath a thin veneer of civilization. She could not, would not, become like him. She had to care for Joshua. Aidan sighed, soft and gentle, a quiet exhalation she felt right down to her toes, and she had the horrible feeling that he knew what she was thinking, that he really was somehow in her head with her, sharing her thoughts and emotions.

"You will be able to care for Joshua. Your things have been moved into the second-floor rooms. You and Joshua will maintain living quarters there. It will be essential for you to keep up the illusion of human life. Only during the afternoon, when you are at your most vulnerable, will you come down to this chamber and sleep. Joshua remembers nothing of the vampire. I could not allow him to be traumatized for life."

"You can't allow him to know the truth," Alexandria guessed shrewdly. "We have our own home. As soon as I'm able, I am going to take him away from here." *Out of this city if need be, away from you, so far away that no harm can ever come to him.*

There was a small silence that seemed to stretch into eternity. For some reason, she could feel her heart pounding in alarm. When Aidan moved, every muscle in her body froze. He was silent, but he terrified her, the way he moved so silently.

"There is a bond between us, Alexandria." His voice was pure, like the sound of a clear stream running over rocks. "It is unbreakable. I will always know where you are, as you will always be able to find me. If I was going to harm Joshua, I would have disposed of him long before now. You will stay here and learn what you must to survive. At least give yourself time to adjust to your new life."

"I want to see him, right now. I want to see Joshua."

For some inexplicable reason, she was finding it impossible to breathe again. Emotions whirled and danced, raged and exploded, until she thought she might go mad. Instead she sat quietly like a polite child awaiting his agreement. He stood staring down at her with his golden eyes, his face an expressionless mask.

Afterward Alexandria had no idea how it happened. One moment she was sitting quietly, the next she had launched herself out of the bed and flung herself at him, unable to contain the rage racing through her. Aidan's sensual features remained cool and calm even as he caught her small, flying figure. She was already desperately fighting to regain self-control, horrified at her behavior. She had never done such a thing before. Aidan restrained her easily, clasping her wrists behind her back so that she was held tightly against his hard frame.

And at once she was aware of the thin shirt covering her bare skin, her curves fitting against his body. She was aware of him as a man, of herself as a woman. That horrified her. Everything about the situation horrified her.

"Shh, *piccola, cara mia*, be calm," he soothed her, one hand pinning her wrists while the other tangled in the heavy fall of hair at her nape. "We will get through this together. Hold on to me. Use me. Use my strength." He released her wrists even as his hand tightened on her neck.

She thumped his chest once, twice, trying not to scream out her frustration. "I'm crazy. My mind is crazy. It won't stop." She rested her head against the heavy muscles of his chest, the only refuge, the only sanctuary left to her. Her brain was racing, a terrible, chaotic jumble of desperate thoughts. Aidan was solid, an anchor of strength, the calm in the eye of the storm.

"Breathe, Alexandria. With me, breathe." The words whispered softly over her skin, seeped in through her pores, penetrated to her heart and lungs.

He seemed to be doing it for her, his breathing regulating hers. Aidan held her almost tenderly, not asking anything of her, simply holding her until the terrible trembling ceased and she was able to stand on her own two legs. Almost reluctantly, he released her, putting space between them, his hand trailing down the length of her thick braid until his arm once more dropped to his side.

"I'm sorry." Alexandria pressed her fingertips to her temples. "I'm not normally a violent person. I don't know what got into me." *It was so unlike her, this craziness. The vampire's blood must be still in her, and Aidan did not want to reveal the truth to her.*

Aidan could read her fear, that the vampire was still in her, directing her actions. What nonsense. He shook his head. "Fear itself can make us act out of character. Do not worry yourself so. Are you ready now to see Joshua, to be calm enough to reassure him? I know you need more time to adjust to all this newness, and I will not insist, but your brother is beginning to worry. Young Joshua thinks of himself as your protector. As much as he trusts me, he needs to see you, to touch you." Deliberately, he directed her thoughts to the child, the only one capable of taking her mind off her terrible transformation.

With a shaking hand, she reached for the jeans Aidan had had brought from her boardinghouse. "Fill me in on what I should know, what Joshua expects. I can't remember everything you told me."

Aidan couldn't drag his gaze away from the slender length of her legs. His body hardened unexpectedly, his blood pounding and hot. He turned away from her to hide his hunger. Hunger for erotic, steamy sex. He had never felt its pull with such intense heat.

"Aidan?" He heard the whisper of the zipper as her voice skimmed over his skin. Fangs exploded in his mouth, and his body clenched with need. He was barely able to suppress a low growl of aggression. His fingers curled into fists, his knuckles white. As Carpathians aged, everything increased in intensity. Including emotions, if they could feel. Pain, happiness and joy, sexual need. He had known that, but he had never experienced it before. It was not easily controlled when it was so new.

He let his breath out slowly, the red haze before his eyes receding, the demon struggling for supremacy leashed and muzzled. He had an eternity to win Alexandria. She was bound to him, soul to soul, mind to mind. He would find the patience to give her time to come to him willingly.

"Aidan?" This time her voice trembled. "Is something wrong?"

"No, of course not. Let me review things for you. Joshua believes me to be an old family friend. He believes that the two of you had been planning for some time to move into the suite of rooms on the second floor and that your illness at the restaurant merely moved the schedule forward."

Her large sapphire eyes glinted at him; then her long lashes swept down. "Just how good of friends are we supposed to be?"

A small smile tugged at his mouth, and for one brief moment he looked almost boyish. Then the illusion was gone, and he was a powerful predator once more. "Oh, I would have to say close. Very close. And, fortunately for me, Joshua likes it that way. He is my staunch ally."

One eyebrow shot up, and the dimple near her mouth deepened. "*You* need an ally?"

Again he glimpsed her mischievous nature, and it prompted another small smile. "Absolutely."

Aidan had a way of tipping his head to one side and looking at her with such hunger that it took Alexandria's breath away. It might have been a trick of the light, except there was no light. She concentrated on his words, trying not to react to his sensual looks or the mesmerizing sound of his voice.

"A rather odious friend of yours tracked you down here and demanded to see you. Aside from upsetting my staff, he did not get very far, he did return some property of yours. You are aware, of course, that both your friend Henry and little Joshua instinctively disapproved of this childish game maker. In fact, Josh has secret plans to make money so you do not have to sell your art to such a man." Aidan reached behind his head to secure the thick mane of hair at the nape of his neck. "He has a smile reminiscent of a shark, do you not agree?"

Alexandria was held spellbound by Aidan's simple act of

securing his hair, finding the way he moved incredibly sexy. She shook her head, angry that such a ridiculous thought should even occur to her. "Are you talking about Thomas Ivan? Because if you are, show some respect. The man is brilliant at what he does. He actually came by here looking for me?"

She grabbed on to that notion. It was human and normal in a world gone mad. Thomas Ivan was someone she could relate to. Someone who had things in common with her. She ignored the fact that Thomas Ivan's smile *was* exactly like a shark's toothy grin. She ignored the fact that this creature in front of her was the most purely masculine man she had ever seen and that *his* smile alone held a fascination for her.

"The man's story lines are idiotic drivel. He does not know the first thing about vampires." There was contempt in Aidan's voice, yet it still held such a purity of tone, she found herself leaning toward him and had to pull herself up sharply.

"No one knows anything about vampires," she corrected firmly, "because they don't exist. They can't. And his work isn't drivel. His games are brilliant."

"I had not heard that about vampires not existing," Aidan responded with a mocking grin. "I wish I had known earlier. It might have saved me a great deal of trouble over the centuries. As for Ivan, I fear I must agree with Joshua. The man is a pompous ass. In any case, he returned your briefcase, and I told him you would get in touch with him when your doctor says it is all right to do so."

"I don't have a doctor."

Aidan's white teeth flashed, and his golden eyes gleamed with wicked amusement. "I am your doctor. I am your healer."

She could not meet that heated gaze. His amusement was as sexy as his sculpted mouth. "I think I'm getting the picture. So, what else has my little brother been told?" She glanced about the room. "Aren't there any shirts of mine around here?" She lifted the tails of his elegant silk evening shirt. "Some that don't reach my knees?"

He cleared his throat. He liked her wrapped in his shirt,

surrounded by him. "Well, actually, as Joshua knows, that is one of your annoying habits. You like to run around in my shirts. You think they are much more comfortable than your own clothes."

Alexandria regarded him with wide blue eyes. "Oh, I do, do I? I take it you grumble about it."

"Often, to Josh. We laugh together about the idiosyncrasies of women. He thinks you look cute in my shirts."

"And what would give a little boy an idea like that?"

He looked unrepentant. "I might have mentioned it a time or two."

His golden eyes slid over her body, making her aware of her bare skin beneath his shirt, of every curve of her body, of the fact that they were completely alone in some secret chamber of his home.

"It is true, after all. You do look cute in my shirt."

"Why do Joshua and I have to stay here?" She was going to keep this conversation on track and away from these frighteningly new sensual sensations.

"Joshua is a beacon to guide our enemies to us, as Marie and Stefan are. As long we have human ties, we are anchored to them, and those who wish to destroy us can easily find us. Where most of our kind can remain hidden at will, our enemies know that we will never be far from our human connections, especially Josh, a small child. You are far safer from our enemies, here in my home."

"What enemies? I don't have enemies." Aidan spoke matter-of-factly, yet Alexandria could feel her heart begin to pound all over again. She sensed he was speaking the truth, and whoever the enemy was, it was no ordinary assailant.

"Paul Yohenstria was not the only vampire in this city. There are others, and they know I am hunting them. They will know of your existence quickly, and they will turn their powers to acquiring you."

Alexandria felt her stomach muscles clench. "Why would they want me? I don't understand any of this. Why is all this happening to me?"

"You are a true psychic, a human woman capable of becoming one of us. And even vampires are Carpathians before they turn. There are few women among our people, and they are greatly treasured."

Her chin rose belligerently. "I have news for you, Mr. Savage. 'Your people' hardly seem to treat women like treasures. No wonder there are so few." She touched the ragged wounds still visible at her throat. "I can't imagine too many women wanting the honor. I can truthfully say *I'm* not happy about it."

"I have asked you to call me Aidan. It is necessary, even when we are alone, that we continue to behave in the human manner and keep up the pretense that we are close friends until it becomes so." His golden eyes glinted for a moment, nearly stopping her heart.

Her fingers twisted in the tails of his shirt, her agitation increasing at the quiet, soothing tone of his voice. "Who else lives here? I know there is a woman. I remember she wouldn't call an ambulance even when I begged her to." Despite her attempts at normalcy, Alexandria could not keep the fear and bitterness from her voice.

Aidan advanced a step, suddenly close enough that she could feel the heat radiating from his body. "My house-keeper, Marie, was extremely distressed over your condition, Alexandria. It was not her fault, and I hoped that you would not place the blame with her. She knew no human doctor could help you. I was the only one who could ease your suffering. Just so you are aware, she was very angry with me over your condition. She has been my housekeeper and a member of my family for many years. She is the one who will look after Joshua for us while we are unable to do so in mid-afternoon. For that reason alone you should find it in your heart to become her friend."

"Do you control her? Drink her blood? Make her do whatever you want, like a puppet?" Alexandria burst out.

"I have never taken blood from Marie, nor have I ever controlled her thoughts. She has chosen to stay with me, as did her family before her, of her own free will. She stayed by your side while you were so ill because she felt compassion. I will repeat myself one last time so that you might understand. She did not call an ambulance because no human physician could have eased your suffering." He felt it unnecessary to inform her that, in addition, the human doctors would have discovered the new abnormalities in her blood, and his species could never allow such a discovery. They were often hunted by more than only the undead. Human "vampire-slayers" sought them out as well.

Again his voice was cool and even, yet her mouth went dry with fear. He could convey menace quietly far better than most people could with roaring anger. She nodded, trying to look agreeable when in truth she was crumbling inside, her mind fragmenting and her body trembling almost beyond her capability to control it.

"Take another breath. You keep forgetting to breathe, Alexandria. Your mind is trying to deal with the trauma of what has happened to you a bit at a time. Every time a new piece of information is processed, your body reacts to it. You are a very intelligent woman; you have to know this will not be an easy transition, but you will get through it."

A small, humorless smile curved her trembling mouth. "I will? You're so certain of that. Is that because you've decreed it?" Her chin lifted, and for a moment her eyes flashed in defiance. "You're so sure of yourself."

He simply watched her in that calm, infuriating manner she was becoming familiar with. Alexandria finally sighed. "Don't worry. I don't blame the woman."

"Marie." He whispered it softly between his white teeth, a whisper of velvet over iron. His golden eyes were growing hot, molten gold that could so easily engulf her.

She swallowed hard. "Marie, then. I'll be nice to her."

He held out a hand. Alexandria stared at it a moment, then, carefully avoiding contact, slipped past him to the door. Aidan moved with her, a silent shadow, yet she was aware of his every rippling muscle, body heat, his very breath. He was so close to her, she felt their hearts were beating the same rhythm.

The tunnel they entered was narrow and wound its way upward toward the first floor. She was forced to stop no more than halfway to their destination, a wave of dizziness overcoming her. She gripped the stone wall and fought for breath. At once Aidan curved an arm around her waist.

Her fingers curled into his shirt. "I can't do this. I'm sorry, but I can't." There was an involuntary plea in her voice, her fear overcoming her sense of self-preservation against Aidan's power. He was enormously strong and as solid as a rock. He was all she had to cling to when her mind rebelled against the trauma it had been subjected to.

He held her like a child, his body giving comfort when, inside him, the beast raged for fulfillment. "For now, think only of the boy. He is lonely for you and afraid. I have done my best to reassure him, but he has lost so much in his young life, and the memories he has of this place and of me and my family are merely implanted, no substitute for the reality of his love for you. The rest of the future can wait, can it not?" His voice was pure sorcerery, impossible to resist. It whispered sensuously in her mind, assuring her that if she simply did as he suggested, all would be well with her world.

His chin brushed the top of her head, lingering for a moment while he drank in her scent, made certain their scents mingled. His golden gaze held possession and hunger; his arms were gentle and tender.

"Come with me now, Alexandria. Come into the warmth of my home of your own free will. Share some time with me and mine. Forget everything for now but this respite from your nightmare. You need the relief, and there is no harm in it."

"In the illusion of normalcy?"

"If you care to put it that way, I suppose it can be said." His fingers, on the nape of her neck, were working a kind of magic.

In her life there had been too much adversity, no warmth other than what Joshua had provided. Aidan was so gentle, and even if that was the biggest illusion of all, Alexandria took comfort in his arms. On some level she was aware of clinging to him, of leaning on his strength, but she refused to dwell on it; for her sanity, she didn't dare. She needed to immerse herself in a small measure of normal life, if only for a short while.

She took a deep breath. "I'm all right now. Really. And I'm going to pretend you're a nice man, not some snarling beast about to eat me if I don't do everything you say."

Against the satin skin of her neck his mouth curved into a smile, his breath warm against her pulse, his teeth scraping gently. The sensation was far more sensual than frightening. "I do not know where you get these ideas, *cara*. Perhaps from Thomas Ivan's games? You should cease playing them. They seem to influence you unduly."

"But he is so good at what he does. You have played his games, haven't you?" she asked, guessing as much and trying to goad him a bit. She remained very still, almost holding her breath, enjoying the feel of his mouth on her neck, yet terrified of this strange reaction in herself.

"I will admit reluctantly to wasting my time investigating his foolish propaganda . . . but you are not to tell anyone. I might lose my status as a *true* vampire-hunter." His arm slipped back around her waist, and his body urged hers upward along the narrow tunnel.

"Aidan! Are you a snob?" she teased, trying to ignore the unfamiliar feelings his hard muscles brushing against her body were creating. He was so close to her, his arms made her feel protected, a sensation she had never experienced before.

"Probably."

His voice whispered over her skin, making her insides tremble.

"You forgot your shoes," he pointed out. "This floor is cold. You should have put on the slippers I left for you." There was a trace of censure in his voice.

Alexandria glanced up at him over her shoulder, a quick flash of blue eyes. "Actually, that's another one of my habits that will no doubt annoy you—I have many, you know. I always like to go barefoot in the house."

Aidan was silent a moment. She couldn't even hear his footfalls. He seemed to glide rather than walk. "So, just how many annoying habits do you have?" he asked.

His voice created a funny melting sensation inside her.

"So many I can't count them. And they're bad, really bad."

There was a teasing note in her voice, a warmth that hadn't been there before. Aidan searched her mind and found that she was trying to do as he said, put aside all that had happened and live only in this moment. Her natural warmth and humor were beginning to surface in spite of all the odds against it. He found himself feeling pride in her. She was constantly amazing him. This woman, so unexpected in his life, was certainly worth the effort and patience it would take to win her completely. No one had ever teased him before. Marie and Stefan had been in his life a long time. He saw their affection for him, but it was always tinged with respect for what and who he was.

"You do not know the meaning of the word *bad*. You have no vices. You don't even smoke, and you very seldom drink alcohol. And before you accuse me of reading your mind, let me explain that Joshua has spilled all your secrets. He wanted me to know of your virtues."

"Oh, did he?" There was a wall facing her, and Alexandria stopped abruptly. It seemed made of solid, immovable stones.

Aidan reached past her and casually placed his fingertips on one of the oddly-shaped stones. A panel swung outward, allowing them access to stairs leading up from the basement to the kitchen.

Alexandria rolled her eyes. "How very melodramatic. Secret passageways and everything. You should write a book, Aidan. Or perhaps a video game."

He leaned close, his warm breath sending a shiver down her spine. "I have no imagination."

Her pulse beat right beneath his mouth. Aidan felt her heat beckoning him, the scent of her, the spice of her blood, so addicting, calling to him. For a moment his eyes glowed with hunger and need, molten gold shooting fiery sparks. His blood leapt in anticipation, and in his mouth his fangs fought for liberty.

"Oh, really? I think one of *your* annoying habits is to lie whenever it suits you. It took great imagination just to design this place. And don't tell me you didn't do it yourself."

It was his prolonged silence that gave him away. Alexandria sensed the sudden danger she was in and froze, holding her breath. Her stillness, the scent of her fear, beat at him. His fingers circled her fragile wrist gently. "I am sorry, *cara*, it has been a long time for me. To experience emotions is slightly overwhelming. You will have to forgive me when I blunder."

His voice once again wrapped her in safe arms, offered a haven. Alexandria bit her lip hard enough to produce a drop of blood, hoping the pain would dispel that illusion of safety he had created. She tried to step away from him.

Aidan refused to relinquish control. His fingers never tightened, but, just the same, his grip was unbreakable. He bent his head to hers, his golden eyes holding her blue ones captive. "Do not place temptation in my way, Alexandria. I have little control around you."

He whispered the words, a velvet seduction, his voice alone stirring a small flame in her midsection. His mouth brushed hers in the lightest of caresses, but he stole her breath as his tongue stole the tiny red droplet of blood from her lower lip.

When he lifted his head the same slow, sensual way he had lowered it, she could only stare up at him helplessly, mesmerized by the unexpected fire in her blood and the need in her body. It shocked her, the strength of her first real sexual awareness. That it should be with this man, that she could feel such heat and hunger for a creature like Aidan Savage, made her tremble.

He could feel the tremor that ran through her slender body, see the sensual awareness in her blue eyes. Her tongue darted out nervously, touching her lower lip right where his tongue had touched. He found his body tightening in demand, urging him to claim what was rightfully his, the demon lifting its head and roaring.

"Aidan?" Her hand went protectively to her throat. "If you're going to hurt me, get it over with. Don't play some sort of game with me. I'm not a very strong person, and I don't think I can handle much more without going crazy."

"I have said I will not harm you, Alexandria, and I will not." He stepped away from her to give his body some small respite.

For the first time, his voice was husky, but the huskiness only deepened the beauty of it, increased its enthralling effect. Alexandria could barely breathe with the effort to keep from being ensnared by him. She found herself wanting to comfort him, to be the one to take that hungry look from his golden eyes. There seemed such a need in him, and she wanted to sate it. "I think I'm more afraid of you than I was of the vampire. At least I knew he was evil. I could feel it in him, and I knew whatever he wanted from me was more horrible than dying could ever be. Tell me what you're planning to do to me."

"If you do not recognize evil in me, Alexandria, then trust your instincts. Have you not always been able to recognize evil?"

"I saw what you did to Paul Yohenstria. Shouldn't I believe my own eyes?"

"What did I do that was so evil? I destroyed a vampire preying on the human race. My only mistake was in believing he had turned you vampiress. I believed you were about to feed on the child." He touched her face, his palm warm and comforting, the feel of him lingering even after he lowered his hand. "I deeply regret that I frightened you, but I cannot regret that I destroyed the vampire. That is what I do; that is the reason I continued my existence for so long alone and far from home. For the protection of both our races, human and Carpathian."

"You say you aren't a vampire, but I saw the things you can do. You are far more powerful than even he was. He was afraid of you."

"Do not most criminals fear justice when it finds them?"

"If you are not a vampire, then what are you?"

"I am Carpathian," he reiterated patiently. "I am of the earth. We have existed from the beginning of time. We are of the soil, the wind, the water, and the sky. Our powers are great, but we have limitations, too. You have not become vampire, a wanton destroyer. You have become like me, like my people. As I told you, only a handful of humans can become as we are. Most die or become deranged and must be destroyed. I tell you this not to alarm you but to help you to understand that I do not mean you harm."

Alexandria was silent, studying his face. Physically he was the most beautiful man she had ever seen. He exuded masculinity and power. Yet always that danger lurked beneath the surface, and it was that she was afraid of. Should she believe him? Could she?

The hard line of his mouth softened, his amber eyes warming to molten gold. "Do not worry about it this moment, *cara*. Get to know me better before you attempt to make such a judgment." His hand brushed the length of her hair, a touch of his fingertips, no more, yet she felt it in the pit of her stomach, in the nape of her neck, on every inch of her skin. "A truce, Alexandria, for this night with your brother, while you heal and grow stronger."

She nodded mutely, afraid to trust her voice. She was both repelled by and drawn to Aidan. She felt safe, and yet she knew she was in danger. But for the moment she would try to put aside her fears, her suspicions, and simply enjoy her time with Joshua.

Aidan smiled. It was the first real smile she had seen on his face. It warmed his eyes and stole her breath. There was something very sexy about it that made Alexandria even more afraid. She had never had to fight her own feelings before.

"The door is in front of you," he said.

She turned her head slightly so that she could keep an eye on him even as she observed the basement door. "Any tricks up your sleeve? A secret password?"

"Turning the knob will do it."

"How very mundane." Alexandria reached for the door-knob at the same time he did. His arm curved around her, bringing their bodies close so that she smelled his clean, masculine scent and felt the heat of him right through their clothes. Hastily she dropped her hand. As he opened the door, she could have sworn she heard soft, taunting laughter in her ear. When she turned to glare at him, his face was all innocence.

Alexandria refrained from kicking his shins and with great dignity walked into the brightly lit kitchen, proud of her self-control.

Aidan leaned close as he trailed behind her. "I can read your mind, *cara*." His voice was teasing, velvety, sliding over her skin like the touch of his fingers, fanning flames she hadn't known existed.

"Don't brag about it, Mr. Savage. What a great name for you, by the way. Savage. It suits you."

"If you do not call me Aidan, I am going to have some explaining to do to Joshua. That boy is very smart, you know."

She laughed softly. "And you said you had no imagination. I can't wait to hear what you come up with."

Chapter Six

The kitchen was huge, larger than the entire suite of rooms Alexandria had rented for Joshua and herself at the boarding-house. It was beautiful, all windows opening out onto a huge garden. Plants hung everywhere, healthy and green, and the tiled floor was spotless. She turned around in a full circle, trying to take in everything at once. "This is so beautiful."

"We have a microwave in case you take a notion to cook something, and the garbage disposal works quite well."

"Very funny. I'll have you know I *can* cook."

"So Joshua assured me—I believe it was when he was devouring Marie's cookies."

"So she bakes, too. I don't know if I'll be able to stand such a paragon of virtue." Alexandria made a face. "I suppose she's the one responsible for cleaning this showplace? What can't she do?"

"She does not have your smile, *cara*," he replied softly.

For one brief moment, time seemed to stand still while she fell into the mesmerizing gold of his eyes, liquid heat pouring over her, into her.

"Alexandria!" Joshua was banging the door open and hurling himself at her, releasing her from Aidan's spell as he did so. "Alex!"

She caught him to her, hugging him so tightly, she nearly smothered him. Then she was looking him over for any signs of wounds or bruises. She paid close attention to his neck, making certain Aidan had not taken his blood. "You look great, Joshua." She hesitated, then said, "Thank you for calling Aidan the other night when I was so sick. It was very smart of you."

He grinned at her, his blue eyes lighting up. "I knew he'd come and he'd know what to do." His mouth suddenly turned down at the corners. "I think that other man made you sick. Poisoned you."

Alexandria tried not to look alarmed. "What other man?"

"Thomas Ivan. When you were having dinner with him, I think he made you eat poison," Joshua said firmly.

Alexandria turned to glare at Aidan's innocent face. "Thomas Ivan wouldn't poison anyone."

"In any case," Aidan said in his gentle, compelling voice, "he'd be more likely to put the poison in something she drank, not something she ate. Much more efficient and like-lier to hide any bitterness."

"You would likely know," Alexandria growled at him. "But stop encouraging Joshua to dislike Thomas Ivan. Evidently I'm soon going to be working for him."

"Henry said Thomas Ivan was known as a rake—whatever than means, other than a garden tool—and that he was probably trying to get something besides your drawings from you," Joshua informed her candidly.

A vision of Henry's lifeless body rose up in Alexandria's memory, and her grief was stark and gripping. Instantly she felt Aidan in her mind, soothing her, his soft, ancient chant providing a calming influence, an anchor allowing her to smile down at Joshua. "Henry sometimes said things that maybe weren't quite the truth," she managed. "He was a little colorful."

"I do not know about that," Aidan volunteered. "Henry seemed a pretty wise old man. I believe Thomas Ivan *is* interested in more than your drawings. He was adamant and aggressive when he demanded to see you. Hardly the demeanor of someone searching only for an employee."

Joshua was nodding his agreement solemnly, looking at Aidan as if he was the smartest man in the world.

Alexandria did kick Aidan's shin; she couldn't stop herself. "Stop being such a pain! I'll never be able to counteract your influence if you keep this up. Joshua, Aidan is only teasing. He doesn't really dislike Mr. Ivan, do you, Aidan?" she prompted, admonishing him with her eyes.

There was a small, telling silence as Aidan thought about it. "I would like to help you out, *cara*, but the truth is, I am of the same opinion as Henry and Joshua. I think Thomas Ivan is up to no good."

Joshua puffed out his chest. "See, Alex, women just don't know when a man is gonna try something."

"Where in the world did you hear that?" Alexandria glared accusingly at Aidan.

"Henry," Joshua said immediately. "He said most men are really no good and are usually after only one thing and that Thomas Ivan was known to be the worst of them all."

"Henry had a lot to say, didn't he?" Alexandria gave a little sigh.

Aidan nudged her, raising his eyebrows expectantly.

She tilted her chin, deliberately ignoring him. "We both loved Henry, Joshua, but he did have some strange opinions about things."

Aidan nudged her again.

"What?" Sounding rather haughty, she put on her most innocent expression.

"Perfect example of how devious women can be, Joshua. Your sister practically accused me of filling your head with all kinds of ideas, and now she wants to pretend she did not

91

make a presumption." Aidan bent down and lifted Joshua, spiriting him from the room.

"Hey!" Alexandria trailed after them into a formal, elegantly appointed dining room, her mouth opening in speechless astonishment.

Aidan had an almost overwhelming urge to kiss that look right off her face. "Do you think she should apologize for jumping to conclusions, Joshua?"

"In your wildest dreams," she denied. "You aren't nearly as innocent as you'd have me believe."

Joshua reached out and touched a bruise on the side of her chin. His eyes went to Aidan's gold ones. "What happened to Alex's face?" There was a hint of suspicion in his voice, and he seemed to retreat into some private torment.

"Aidan?" Instant fear caused Alex's voice to tremble.

Aidan simply caught and held Joshua's gaze with his own. His voice dropped an octave, becoming like pure running water rippling over the child, seeping into his mind. "You remember Alexandria falling because she was so weak with illness, do you not, Joshua? Remember? She ruined her beautiful suit when she fell on the path. You were very upset until I came and carried her to the big black car and brought her here to our home."

Joshua was nodding in agreement, the suspicion and tormented look gone as quickly as they had come. Thankful, Alexandria held out her arms for the boy.

Aidan shook his head. "We will go into the living room and sit down before you hold him, *piccola*. You are still shaky."

His voice felt like a caress, yet she knew it was a command. Velvet in iron. He was clearly in charge. She tried not to let it annoy her and meekly followed him down a wide hallway. She stumbled several times because, instead of watching where she was going, she was staring in awe around her. She had never been in a house as beautiful as this one. The woodwork, the marble floors, the high beamed ceilings, the paintings and sculptures were all magnificent. A Ming vase sat gracefully on an antique mahogany stand near a wide stone fireplace. Aidan had to catch her arm twice to keep her from walking right into a wall.

"It is customary to watch where you are going, *cara mia*," he reminded her gently. "It is not as if you have never seen the house before," he added wickedly to make her smile.

She made a face at him. "Don't you think this is all a bit much? What if Joshua comes tearing through the house and knocks over the Ming vase? Somehow, I'm beginning to think we made a big mistake in accepting your hospitality. Some of these things are priceless." Two could play at his game.

"I believe we already had this conversation," he said smoothly, steering her into the living room. "We agreed that if Joshua broke anything, we would not cry over spilled milk." His golden eyes gleamed at her, daring her to continue.

"Aidan, really, a Ming vase?" Horrified at the thought of destroying such a treasure, Alexandria considered grabbing Joshua and running from the house.

Deliberately Aidan leaned close so that his warm breath stirred the tendrils of hair falling over her ear. "I have had centuries to admire the piece. Losing it might give me the incentive to patronize a modern artist."

"That is sacrilege. Don't even think it."

"Alexandria, this is your home. This is Joshua's home. Nothing in it is as important as the two of you." His golden eyes glittered at her as his gaze ran up and down her body. "Now sit down before you fall down."

She swept a hand through the hair tumbling across her forehead. "Would you just try not to sound like a drill sergeant? It's getting on my nerves."

He looked unrepentant. "One of my annoying habits."

"And you have so many." Alexandria chose a leather recliner to curl up in, and at once she realized just how weak she really was. It felt good to sit even after a short walk. Joshua immediately came to sit in her lap, needing the closeness to her as much as she did to him.

"You look so white, Alex," Joshua pointed out with a child's candid nature. "Are you sure you're all right?"

"I'm getting there, little buddy. It takes time. Do you like your room here?" She again examined him for marks.

"It's great, really big. But I don't like sleeping up there without you. It's kinda *too* big. Marie and Stefan let me sleep downstairs near them." He hugged her bruised, lacerated neck and didn't notice when she winced.

Aidan's golden eyes narrowed to slits. With deceptive indolence he reached out a lazy hand and drew the child to his side. "We have to be careful of Alexandria for a while. Remember what I said? She needs tender care. It's up to you and me to see that she gets it. Even when she rebels, as she's thinking of doing now."

"I'm okay," Alexandria said resentfully. "If you want to sit on me, Joshua, of course you can." *No one*, except her, told Joshua what to do.

Joshua shook his head, his blond curls bobbing in the way that always made her heart melt. "I'm big, Alex, not a baby. I want to take care of you. That's my job."

She raised her eyebrows. "I thought I was the one in charge."

"Aidan says you only think you're in charge but that we have to let you think that because women like to think they're in control, but men have to protect them."

Her blue eyes met golden ones over the blond curls. "He said all that, did he? That's a lot of *thinks,* Joshua. I *am* in charge, not Aidan."

Joshua smiled conspiratorially at Aidan. Aidan mouthed, "I told you so." Both looked at her in complete innocence, their expressions so similar, it unexpectedly turned her heart over.

Joshua moved closer to Alexandria, playing with the braid hanging over her shoulder. She could hear his heart beat, hear the blood pounding and surging through his young body. All at once she was aware of the pulse beating in his neck. Every stroke, every beat. Horrified, she thrust him away from her and jumped to her feet, searching for a way out. She had to run as far and as fast as she could, away from Joshua. She was a monster!

Aidan moved so swiftly, she didn't even see him coming,

yet he was there with her, his arms surrounding her, holding her captive and still. "It is nothing, *cara*, only your heightened senses." His voice was barely discernible, yet she heard him clearly. The tone was soft and gentle and calm. "Do not be alarmed."

"I can't risk being near him. What if you're wrong? What if I still have the vampire's blood in me? I couldn't bear it if I harmed Joshua. I can't be here with him."

She kept her voice low, muffled against his chest, a whisper of sound that tugged at Aidan's heart. He pulled her closer into the shelter of his arms, felt her relax instinctively against him. She didn't trust him, didn't know him, but her body did. "You could never harm the child, Alexandria, never. I know you feel hunger, that you are unusually weak. Your body has been through a tremendous ordeal, your mind has suffered a trauma, but nothing could ever induce you to harm Joshua. I know it absolutely." His voice was soothing black velvet seeping into her mind, a balm.

She allowed him to hold her, to calm her, as she rested her head against his hard frame. She could hear his heart beating the same rhythm as her own. He was so calm, so gentle, his voice never rising, always so certain, so confident. A solid rock to lean on. Of their own volition, her lungs slowed to match his breathing pattern.

Aidan stroked her hair, massaging the nape of her neck as he drank in the scent of her. "Better now?"

She nodded and stepped away from him just as an older couple approached. Alexandria recognized the woman carrying a tray with two long-stemmed cut crystal wineglasses and three English bone china mugs. The man behind her carried a tray with a bottle of red wine and a pitcher of something steaming.

Marie flashed Alexandria a tentative smile. "It's good to see you up and around. Are you feeling better now?"

Aidan's hand on Alexandria's neck tightened perceptibly. His thumb stroked across her pulse, once, twice, a gesture meant to soothe even as it served notice that he was in control.

Alexandria's chin lifted. "I'm fine, Marie, thank you. It was good of you to try to help me while Aidan was gone." She sounded sweet and polite, wishing the entire time that she could detect a hint of corruption in any of these people. She was determined not to like them, not to be drawn into their circle. She didn't want to be lured into a trap by the silken web of this fantasy home, this place of beauty. The older couple seemed warm and giving, looking into each other's eyes with love, looking at Aidan and Joshua—her Joshua—with great affection. She wanted to see none of it.

The trays were placed on the coffee table, and Aidan reached with lazy contentment for the bottle of wine. Marie poured hot cocoa from the steaming silver pitcher into three mugs. "Joshua loves his hot chocolate before bedtime, don't you, honey?"

The boy eagerly accepted the mug and grinned mischievously up at Marie. "Not as much as you and Stefan do."

Alexandria's stomach was rebelling at the sight and smell of the chocolate. Aidan handed her a wineglass and filled it with the ruby-colored liquid. Even as she shook her head, he was pushing it toward her lips, his golden eyes staring directly into hers. "Drink it, *cara.*"

She felt as if she was falling forward into the fathomless depths of his eyes, mesmerized, hypnotized. She could feel him in her mind, a dark shadow pressing his will on her. *You will drink it, Alexandria.*

She blinked, then found the empty wineglass in her hand, her eyes locked with Aidan's. He smiled, that flash of white teeth, lifted his glass to her in a small salute, and drained the contents. In total fascination, she watched his throat work. She could barely pull her gaze away from him. Everything about him was so sensual.

Alexandria tasted the sweetness, the addicting spice that seemed so familiar in her mouth, on her tongue. Aidan was watching her closely, with that unblinking stare of a predator. She turned away from him, close to tears, afraid to spar with him in case she made a fool of herself in front of the older couple. She was confused and tired and scared. She lifted an unsteady hand to push at her hair.

"Aidan says we can get a computer just for me," Joshua blurted out.

Alexandria glanced at Aidan. He was pouring himself a second glass of "wine," and he held up the bottle, offering her more. Everything in her demanded that she comply, so she backed away from him, shaking her head. Why was it so important to her to do as Aidan wanted? It was unlike her to follow anyone's lead so blindly. It frightened her to think he had such power over her.

"You know, Joshua, we haven't really had time to settle in and think about what we're doing," she cautioned, her eyes never leaving Aidan's face. "We don't even know yet if we're going to stay here. This is more of a trial to see if we can all get along. Sometimes roommates just don't work out, no matter how much they like one another."

Joshua looked as if he might cry. "But it's great here, Alex. I know we should be here. It's safe here. And you can get along with me, can't you, Aidan? I'm not too loud or anything."

Aidan's hand rested in the boy's silky curls even as his golden eyes held Alexandria captive. "You know you aren't. I like having you here, and I don't expect us to run into any problems. Your sister is worried that the two of you might be extra trouble for Marie and Stefan, but I know better."

Marie was nodding in agreement. "We love having you, Joshua. You brighten up the house. And boys are supposed to be loud."

"Of course everyone would want you, little buddy," Alexandria hastily assured her brother, making a supreme effort to free herself from Aidan's mesmerizing golden gaze. "Sometimes adults can't live together. I'm used to doing things my way, and Aidan is set in his medieval ways."

"What's *medieval?*" Joshua wanted to know.

"Ask Aidan. He's good with answers," she replied resentfully.

"*Medieval* refers to the days of knights and ladies, Joshua. Alexandria thinks I would have made a great knight. They were men who served their homeland with honor and always rescued and took care of fair maidens." Aidan drained the contents of a third glass of ruby liquid. "A fitting description, and quite a compliment. Thank you, Alexandria."

Stefan coughed behind his hand, and Marie hastily turned to look out the window.

Alexandria found a reluctant smile curving her soft mouth. "That's not all I could call you, but for now, we'll leave it at *medieval.*"

Aidan bowed formally from the waist, his golden eyes warming. She could drown in those eyes. His palm cupped the side of her face almost tenderly, the pad of his thumb sliding over her skin in a brief caress. "Sit down, *cara mia*, before you fall down."

Alexandria sighed and did as he ordered, mostly because her legs were wobbly. She was certain it had nothing to do with being close to such an attractive, masculine man and everything to do with her recent ordeal with the vampire. No mere man could make her weak in the knees.

Aidan settled beside her on the couch, as Stefan had acquired the leather recliner since she had abandoned it. Aidan's thigh brushed hers, sending a tremor rushing through her. His breath warmed her ear. "Fortunately, I am no mere man."

"Stop reading my mind, you . . . you nightmare from a Thomas Ivan game." It was the worst insult she could think of, but he only laughed softly, the sound in her mind, not in her ear. It was blatant seduction and wrapped her in heat.

"It's very late, Josh." She turned her attention to her brother to save herself. It was the only sane thing to do. "Time for bed."

Aidan leaned even closer, his lips brushing her ear. "Little coward."

"Ah, Alex, I don't wanna go to bed. I haven't seen you for days," Joshua wheedled.

"It's past midnight, young man. I'll stay with you and read you stories until you fall asleep," she promised.

Aidan stirred, a sleek movement of muscles, no more, but she felt the heavy weight of his disapproval. "Not tonight, Alexandria. You need rest, too. Marie can put the boy to bed."

Marie was frantically signaling Aidan. She had already sensed Alexandria's ambivalence toward her and knew most of it stemmed from the impression of her usurping Alexandria's position with Joshua. Aidan was only making it worse with his dictatorial manner. As always, Aidan simply ignored what he didn't want to see. He had no intention of allowing Alexandria to do anything he thought might be harmful to her. Aidan was used to having his way in all things.

"I don't think you're going to tell me what I can or can't do with my own brother. I've been putting him to bed for years, and I intend to continue doing so. I'm certain Marie has no objections." She glared a challenge at the older woman.

Marie smiled at her. "Of course not."

Aidan took Alexandria's fist, gently pried open her fingers, and laced his through hers tightly enough that she knew better than to fight his grip. "I am the one to object, *piccola*, not Marie." His voice was gentle enough to melt a heart of stone. "I am responsible for your health. You are weak yet and need to rest. Tomorrow or the next night will be plenty of time for you to take back your job." He turned to look at Joshua. "You will not mind if Marie puts you to bed tonight, will you?"

"I can go to bed all by myself," Joshua bragged. "But I do like Alexandria's stories. She always tells me one after she reads me a book. Her stories are always better than the book."

"Not like her cooking?" Aidan asked.

Joshua wisely did not reply.

"I can cook." Alexandria felt she needed to defend her domestic abilities in front of Marie.

"No one microwaves quite like Alexandria," Aidan teased her.

"As if you would know," she said scornfully. The aroma from the wine bottle was drifting up to her, beckoning, causing hunger pangs so intense, she was almost unable to control her instinct to reach for it.

"Leave her alone, Aidan," Marie admonished. She had never heard him tease before, and it was something she found welcome and astonishing. But they were all on thin ground with the newcomer, and Aidan had to keep Alexandria with him to survive. They all had to tread cautiously, to be careful not to drive her away.

Perversely, Alexandria didn't want Marie to stand up for her. She didn't want to like the older woman. She wasn't going to like any of them. She absolutely would not. And why did she have to be so aware of Aidan's body against hers, the strength in his fingers? She didn't have to be afraid of him any longer. What more could he do to her? She was already the walking dead, wasn't she? She was going to defy him.

He brought her knuckles to his mouth, whispering, "No, you are not. And the silly things you think. 'The walking dead.' Where do you come up with this nonsense?" His mouth brushed her skin, sending darts of fire racing over her nerve endings. "Allow me to guess. Thomas Ivan."

"Maybe he does use that term. I don't remember."

"Is Mr. Ivan the gentleman who came to see Miss Houton?" Marie inquired cautiously.

"Call her Alexandria, Marie. This is not a formal household, and you are no servant. You are my family and friend."

"Please do," Alexandria seconded at the pressure on her fingers.

"I would like us to be friends," Marie said.

That made Alexandria feel small and petty. After all, this woman she was resenting was the one taking care of Joshua when she was unable to do so. Immediately on the heels of that thought came anguish, as a bit more of the truth slid into her brain. Her breath caught in her throat, and she fought for air, strangling, choking.

Aidan pushed her head down toward the floor. "Breathe, *cara*. It is not so difficult. In and out. Keep breathing. Marie, please take the boy into the other room."

"What's wrong with my sister?" Joshua demanded, clearly rebelling.

Alexandria fought the madness swirling in her brain. She would not allow Joshua to be affected by this whole insane nightmare. She sat up and smiled at him, a bit pale, her smile tentative but there all the same. "I'm just a bit weak, like Aidan said. Perhaps he's right, although I hate giving him the satisfaction, he's so bossy lately. You go on with Marie, and I'll just sit here until I feel well enough to get to bed myself."

Joshua's eyes lit up. "Maybe Aidan should carry you. He's very strong. He could do it, you know, like in the movies." He sounded eager.

"I could do that," Aidan agreed, winking at Joshua.

He looked very sexy, enough that he seemed to rob her breath again. "I don't think so." Alexandria sounded firm.

Aidan suddenly stood, inhaling sharply, his attention clearly on something other than those in the room. Alexandria felt it, too. A disturbance in the air, a dark, creeping evil moving slowly but surely toward them. It spread like a dark stain over the sky, the air thickening until it was difficult to breathe. A low murmur began in her mind, the words foreign, beckoning, impossible to understand, but she knew their significance. Something was tugging at her, attempting to draw her outside.

A sound escaped her lips, an inarticulate cry of terror, so muffled it was nearly nonexistent, but Aidan turned his golden eyes to her immediately. Horrified, Alexandria clutched his arm. *He's out there,* she thought in terror. She dragged Joshua to her protectively, inadvertently clutching him too tightly.

Do not alarm the child, cara. The voice in her mind was calm and soothing, so gentle it reached into the chaos of fear and found strength. *He cannot enter this house. He does not know for certain you are here. He is seeking to draw you out.*

Alexandria kept her fingers curled around Aidan's wrist, needing the contact with him. She took a deep breath and smiled down at Joshua. He was looking up at her with curious blue eyes, wondering at her sudden gesture. Marie and Stefan were staring at her, alert.

101

Aidan gently pried Alexandria's arm from around the child. "Marie, you and Stefan should close down the house at once, then put Josh to bed."

There was command in his voice, and the couple reacted instantly. They had been through an attack before and knew the danger, even though they couldn't detect it as Aidan and Alexandria could. They hurried Joshua through his good-nights and began to usher him from the room.

"Keep Joshua with you tonight. I must go out," Aidan instructed them. Then he touched Alexandria's face with gentle fingers. "*Cara*, I have to go out and remove this threat. You will stay here. If anything happens to me, take the boy and go overseas to the Carpathian Mountains. Find a man named Mikhail Dubrinsky. Stefan and Marie will help you. Promise me you will do this." *It is the only way Joshua will be truly safe.* He did not inform her yet that their bond was already strong enough to endanger her if he were to die. Aidan did not even allow the possibility to enter his mind. He could not die. Would not allow it, now that he had reason to live.

There was something so compelling in his voice, in his eyes, in the push at her mind, that Alexandria reluctantly nodded. As divided as she was in her opinion of what Aidan Savage was, of who he was, and what his intentions toward her were, she did not want him to leave the house and face whatever was out there.

"I thought Paul Yohenstria was dead." She whispered the words, the fear in her a living, breathing entity.

He is dead, cara. This is another. The words were in her mind only, and for the first time she recognized the bond between them. He could talk to her at will, enter her mind, and see her thoughts. *As you are able to do with mine. Reach for me, and you will find me at any time. I must go now.*

Alexandria tightened her hold on him, unwilling for him to go out into the thick cloud of evil surrounding the house. "If it is not Yohenstria, then what is out there?" She was trembling, not even attempting to hide it from him.

"You know, Alexandria. You already know there are oth-ers." Aidan bent his head and brushed the top of her silky hair with his mouth, lingering for just a moment to breathe in her scent. "Do not leave the safety of this house." It was a clear order.

Alexandria nodded. She had no intention of going out to face another evil creature. How many of them were there? How had she gotten into this endless nightmare? How far did she trust Aidan Savage?

She watched him stride away from her, complete confidence in every line of his powerful body. He never turned his head, never once looked back at her. He moved with the silent precision of a predator, already stalking his prey. Fear for his safety curled in her stomach. She should be rejoicing. She was free of him for the moment. She could take Joshua and run away, far from this place, far from this city, where none of his kind could ever follow them. Yet the thought of never seeing Aidan again was suddenly as terrifying as being in his possession.

Alexandria followed Aidan to the door. As he went out, she was left staring at the heavy oak door he closed behind him. It was quite beautiful, with intricate stained-glass panels unlike any she had ever seen before. But her mind could not focus on anything. Not the artistry of the glass, not even Joshua. It registered only the bleakness of her existence without Aidan.

She stood there, alone and frightened, trembling with fear for him. She could feel the heavy shadow moving away and knew that Aidan was drawing the danger away from the house, away from Joshua, away from Marie and Stefan—and away from her.

She closed her eyes and concentrated, seeking him, seeking the truth of Aidan's words. She found him in fierce battle, his mind a red haze of joy in the hunt. She felt his pain as claws raked his chest. She clutched her own chest, her heart pounding.

Aidan was so powerful, she had never really expected him to be injured. She tried to study her sensations, to look for the danger to Aidan. Whatever, whoever, was out there was creating illusions, multiplying, using his ability to confound Aidan and keep him off balance. The attacks were swift and brutal, then gone so quickly, Aidan couldn't retaliate. She could sense his confusion and growing consternation.

Alexandria probed farther into the darkness. Something was very wrong. Aidan, assaulted from all sides, could not discern the nature of his attacker the way she could from the sanctuary of the house. The illusion the creature out there was fabricating was too thick, too evil. Then she knew what to do. "Aidan." She whispered his name aloud, everything in her going completely still. She could not allow him to die. She didn't know why she felt that way, but she knew it in her deepest soul.

She reached again for his mind, waited until she could penetrate the red haze, until she could gather her strength and focus. As she did so, Aidan struck hard and fast at his opponent, and she got an impression of a stream of bright red blood and a howl of haunting fear.

Behind you, Aidan. The danger is behind you. There is another. Get out of there! She screamed the warning to him in her mind but was sure it was too late. She felt the impact as he was struck, the blow meant to kill, raking his throat, his stomach, his thigh. But Aidan *had* turned at her frantic call, so that the second attacker could not deliver the mortal blow he expected.

Alexandria could feel the pain slicing through Aidan, but he remained calm and cool under the onslaught. His own speed was incredible, and he used it almost blindly, slashing at his assailant as he turned to face him. His blow was delivered with deadly precision. Even as the vampire fell away from him, flopping to the ground screaming, the first attacker took to the air, clutching his own wounds as he retreated.

"Stefan!" Alexandria called out with surprising authority. "Get the car—now! Bring it around to the front. I can find him."

"Aidan does not want you leaving the house," Stefan said as he approached her, but his hand was already going to the keys in his pocket.

"Well, that's just too bad. His majesty is hurt and unable to make his way home. He can yell at both of us later, but we can't leave him out there to bleed to death. Which, by the way, is what he's doing." Alexandria gave Aidan's man her coolest stare. "I'm going after him with or without you."

Stefan nodded. "Of course I will come with you. But he'll be very angry with us."

Alexandria flashed a smile of camaraderie. "I can take it if you can."

Hear me, cara. I cannot make it home this night. Go to the chamber, and I will attempt to come to you tomorrow night. He was trying to hide his pain from her, to cover the fact that he was dragging himself to shelter, trying to find a piece of ground he could safely open to crawl into.

Just stay put, Aidan. I'm coming for you.

Do not! There is great danger to you. Stay in the house!

Give it up. I've never been very good at minding anyone. In case my little brother neglected to inform you, I've been the boss for years. Stefan is with me, and we're already on our way, so just stay put and wait for us.

She followed Stefan to the driveway, her eyes jumping to the gun in his hand. He was searching the sky, clearly half expecting an attack from that direction.

"I don't feel any of them close by, but the air is thickening around Aidan. We have to hurry. One of them is dead or dying, but the other is returning to finish the job."

"How weak is Aidan?" Stefan did not question her connection to his boss or how she was attaining her knowledge of Aidan's situation as he drove.

"He's trying to hide it from me, but I'm not certain he can sustain another attack. He acts confident, but he feels the approach of the other one." She laughed softly to herself, helping to suppress her own fear. "He's warning me off. In fact, he's actually angry. I've never heard him anything but cool and collected. That's so annoying, don't you think? Always being so in control? If I wasn't terrified, this would be comical. Go left here. I know this is the way."

Stefan slowed the car in hesitation. "Let me go by myself. The other doesn't want me. But if something were to happen to you, we would lose Aidan."

"You'll never find him on your own. We don't have time

105

for this. Come on, Stefan. He's out there alone." She didn't stop to think why it was so important, but she would do anything to save Aidan Savage.

You do not understand, cara. You cannot come here. This one is stronger than Yohenstria, and I am weak. I do not know if I can protect you from him.

You will protect me where you would not protect yourself. He comes now. He is close to you.

You do not even trust me. You still do not know if I am vampire. Why are you placing yourself in danger? He was frustrated with her disobedience; she could feel his impotent rage at not controlling her. But he could not expend the energy it would take and still protect himself and fight the rapidly approaching vampire.

Pay attention to what is happening there. I have a plan. That was the biggest lie she had ever told anyone in her life. And she was becoming more terrified the closer they were to their destination. Why was she doing this stupid, crazy thing? She didn't like Aidan, didn't trust him, and she was terrified of him, of what he might be, of the control he had over her. All she knew for certain was that she couldn't allow him to die.

"We need a plan, Stefan. A really good plan. If you shoot that thing with the gun, will it kill it?"

"No, but if I hit something vital enough, I can slow it down, maybe keep it from going to ground. Then the sun would kill it," Stefan informed her grimly.

"Okay, here's the plan. I'll keep telling you where the creature is, and you keep shooting while I pull Aidan into the car. Then we drive away as fast as we can and hope we leave it behind."

That is the worst plan I have ever heard. In spite of his dire situation, there was a hint of humor in Aidan's voice.

Stefan snorted aloud. "That is absolutely the worst plan I've ever heard. You aren't strong enough to get Aidan into the car. And we can't trade places, because you've probably never fired a gun in your life."

"Well, I don't hear anything brilliant from either one of

106

you," she snapped indignantly. "Isn't it funny how men stick together even when they can't hear one another?"

"What are you talking about?" Stefan was looking nervously up at the sky, in his rearview mirror, out the side windows.

"Never mind. Turn on this road. He's near the ocean—no, the other way, down the hill. He's close by." She could barely breathe, the air was so filled with evil now. "The vampire is somewhere close also. I can feel him."

Go back, cara, go back. There was pleading in Aidan's voice.

He is searching for you, Aidan. I can feel his triumph. He thinks he knows where you are. He's in the form of a bird— no, something else that flies—but he's injured. He's favoring his right side. Alexandria rubbed her temples; the energy it took to communicate mentally was draining. Her head throbbed, her thigh was burning as if she had somehow incurred an injury there.

Go back, Alexandria. He feels your presence. That is why he is triumphant. He has drawn you out of safety. Do as I say! Aidan placed one hand carefully over the deep cut on his temple and pressed the other over the wound on his thigh that was draining away his life-force. He had lost so much blood; the precious fluid pooled on the ground, seeping into the soil.

The smell of the blood would draw the vampire to him. But he could also smell, and the vampire's scent was as strong as the disturbance in the earth's natural harmony. He did not need Alexandria's warnings to know the vampire was close. This one held far more power than Yohenstria, and his ability to create illusions was flawless. Aidan had fought others as strong, but not with such a mortal injury himself. With Alexandria so close, he had no recourse but to fight and win. Even had he gone to ground, the vampire probably would have found him before dawn. He forced his protesting body to move, to climb to his feet. He pushed the pain from his mind. He pushed the thought of Alexandria away. He could do no other than defeat the vampire. He stood very still. Waiting. Just waiting.

107

Chapter Seven

The wind blew up from the bay. Waves rushed toward the shoreline below. The stars glowed overhead. The night itself seemed far too beautiful to hide such a perverted, demented creature as *nosferatu*, the undead. Aidan lifted his face to the wind and inhaled sharply to sort out the information the night chose to share with him.

The vampire was high overhead, winging its way toward him from the ocean side, hoping the spray and sea salt would conceal his scent. Like Aidan, the vampire was wounded, and the blood spoor was easy to follow. Ravenous from blood loss, Aidan's fangs exploded into his mouth at the mere smell. Tainted blood was the last thing he wanted, yet without an infusion of blood, he would die soon. He had made a promise to himself centuries ago that he would never touch a member of the family that served him, no matter what the cost, and he meant to keep that promise. And Alexandria was far too weak; it would be dangerous for her to provide for him. She had no knowledge of the consequences to both of them should he lose her.

He had long ago begun to accept death, greeting the dawn as the only, inevitable choice open to him. But he was not prepared to relinquish his life now, when the possibility of happiness had finally come his way. He would fight. He would at least manage to save Alexandria and Stefan from their own folly. He would take the vampire with him into the dawn if that was his only option.

Standing up had increased the bleeding from the deep wounds on his thigh and temple, and a steady stream ran down his neck and over his shoulder to his arm and chest. A wave of weakness washed over him, and for a moment everything blurred. He blinked to bring things into focus, but it was only after he brushed at his eyes and his hand came away smeared with blood that he could see again. He waited patiently, breathing in and out, because he had no other choice. He had to bring the vampire down to him.

A large bat made a pass at his head, grimacing to reveal tiny pointed teeth. It settled on the ground yards from him, crawling toward him, stalking him.

"Come, come, Ramon, must we play these childish games? Come to me like a man or not at all. I grow weary of your foolishness." Aidan spoke softly, his voice compelling and hypnotic. "All your tricks will not aid you this night. If you choose to continue this battle, we will have done with it here and now. You cannot win. You know it. You feel it. You have come here to die at my hand. So be it. Walk like a man to your death." His golden eyes caught the starlight and glowed with red flames, the flickers of ruby matching the blood on his face.

The bat hesitated, then began to lengthen and grow into a grotesque creature with talons and a razor-sharp beak. The creature moved sideways, approaching Aidan but favoring its right side.

Aidan remained motionless, a statue carved from stone. Only his eyes were alive, flaming with deadly resolve.

His stare stopped the creature, intimidating it until it changed again, reshaping itself into a tall, thin, pale man with cold, pitiless eyes. Ramon regarded Aidan warily. "I do not think you are right this time, Aidan. You are gravely wounded. I will prevail, and I will take the woman for myself."

"It is an impossibility, Ramon. You may bray like a donkey, but no one, not even you, will believe your bravado. Come to me, and accept the justice of our people, as you know you should. You have committed crimes against all humanity."

"I have power! You are weak, a fool. Your life has been dedicated to a false purpose. Where are those you fight to save from one such as me? The humans you protect would drive a stake through your heart if they knew of your existence. Your own people have condemned you to a solitary existence, without even the soil of your homeland to nourish you. They have left you here alone in this place. Join me, Aidan. I can save you. Join with me, and we will take over this city. Do you not believe we deserve to do so? We can have it all. Riches, women. We can rule here."

"I have everything I have always wanted, my old friend. Come to me as you know you should. I will make your end swift and painless." He had to make it swift. Time was running out. His life's blood was on the ground now, his enormous strength draining away.

The vampire was edging closer, attempting to throw Aidan off with the illusion of bats winging right toward the Carpathian's blood-streaked body. Aidan remained still, those red-starred golden eyes never leaving Ramon's gray face.

The vampire launched himself. As he did so, Aidan felt Alexandria merge with him, pouring her strength, her will, her courage, her belief in him, into his mind. It was a priceless gift, and Aidan used it with all the speed of which he was capable. At the last possible moment he simply stepped aside, his arm locking around the vampire's neck, snapping it like a twig. The head flopped to one side, and Ramon began to howl, a high-pitched, agonized cry that went on and on.

Taking a deep breath, Aidan finished it, plunging his hand straight into the thin chest until he reached the pulsating heart. He removed the organ and flung it away from the vampire, stepping back quickly to avoid the spraying blood. Almost immediately his strength gave out, and he found himself sitting on the ground, helpless, open to any attack.

She came out of the darkness. Her scent reached him first. Though the smell of blood was driving him slowly insane, he did not attempt to utilize the vampire's contaminated blood to replenish himself. Then suddenly she was there, fresh and clean and pure in the face of evil. And he had tainted blood on his hands and death surrounding him. He could not look into her eyes and see the condemnation there. He couldn't face it.

"Stefan! Tell me what to do."

Her voice was musical, as soft as an early-morning breeze. To die with her voice in his mind and heart was not so bad. But Aidan did not want her in this place of death. "There is nothing you can do. Walk away, Alexandria. Go to the Carpathian Mountains, as you promised me." His eyes were closing, far too heavy to keep open. "Go to my home-land, and I will feel as if you took a part of me with you."

"Oh, shut up," she snapped impatiently, horrified at the sight of him. She didn't even glance at the fallen vampire. "No one asked you, Aidan. And you're not going to die. I won't allow that, so stop the macho act and cooperate. Come on, Stefan! What do I do for him?" She was already applying pressure to the worst wound, the one in his thigh. She had never seen so much blood spilled. It was a red river soaking into the ground. She concentrated on Aidan, keeping her gaze away from the fallen, disfigured bodies.

"He needs your saliva mixed with soil. Pack the mixture into the wounds," Stefan said quickly, kneeling beside them.

"It's so unsanitary!" she protested, appalled.

"Not for a Carpathian. Do it if you want to save him. Your saliva contains a clotting agent. Quickly, Alexandria."

"Dispose of the bodies, Stefan." Aidan issued the com-mand without opening his eyes. He found himself floating in a dream world.

"Will you shut up?" Alexandria admonished. Spitting was more Joshua's talent than hers, but she did her best, making mud patties while Stefan dragged the vampire bod-ies to the edge of the curving dirt road and, using the gas can from the car trunk, began a fire.

The stench made Alexandria gag. She closed her mind to everything but what she was doing. She did not have time to examine why she was saving Aidan, why it mattered, but her every bone, every cell, her very soul cried out to her to do so.

Aidan appeared unconscious as Alexandria meticulously packed his deep wounds and lacerations. She knew he wasn't, though, that he was aware of her every movement; she could feel him in her mind. Somehow he had slowed his heart and lungs to impede the seepage of blood to give her

111

time to seal the wounds with soil and saliva. But his hunger was a living thing, crawling through his body with slow, torturous intent. It gnawed at him relentlessly; she could feel it through their mind link. He was very much aware of her living, surging blood, hot and beckoning, so close to him. The demon in him crouched just below the surface, threatening to break free.

Stefan returned to her side. "You must talk to him. Tell him he can't leave you alone. You won't be able to live without him."

"No way! He's arrogant enough as it is. That's all I'd need, to simper like some besotted idiot over him. He'd hold it over my head forever. And he's so egotistical, he'd probably even believe it." Even as she said the words, her fingers were tenderly pushing back clotted strands of hair, wiping the blood from Aidan's face.

Stefan frowned at her but refrained from expressing his opinion. "He needs blood. I will give it to him. You must drive us home. This fire will attract attention from the authorities soon, and we need to be away from here."

No. Aidan's voice was strong in its protest, but only in her mind. She realized he was too weak to attempt speech. *It is too dangerous. I would kill him. I cannot take from Stefan.*

She believed him. It was in the purity, the honesty of his voice. It was in the alarm in his heart and soul, his mind a raging protest. "No, Stefan, you drive. Aidan refuses to allow you to donate, so I guess it'll have to be me." She brushed back Aidan's hair again with gentle fingers. *That's what you're trying to tell me, right? I can donate but not Stefan. Don't say no; it isn't as if you haven't helped yourself before. Just do it, and don't argue with me, or I might lose my sweet nature.* And my courage, she added silently to herself.

I am not certain you will be safe.

Big deal. I told you, I don't have a lot to lose. This really isn't my kind of life. Go for it, Aidan. Just don't hurt me, okay?

Never, cara, he assured her.

It took both Stefan and Alexandria to get him into the car.

His face was gray and etched with pain, but he didn't make a sound until they had him settled with his head cradled in her lap. "The spilled blood must be destroyed," he said. Only Alexandria caught the words. He was so weak, he could barely whisper.

"He wants you to clean away the rest of the blood, Stefan." Her heart was beating fast. This was it. She would die this night, giving her life for this man. She didn't know what he was, only that he was the most courageous being she had ever known. She wasn't certain that what she believed about him was true, or that she even liked him, but this was right. She knew it in her deepest soul.

Stefan swore softly. "We are bound to be seen, the longer we stay," he groused, but he hastily went back to the gas can he had left for the investigators and set to work on the pools of blood. It was necessary to remove any trace of Aidan's participation in the battle, and they had little time to do so.

Alexandria laid her head over Aidan's. "You can't wait. Do it now. But promise me you will always look after Joshua. That this insane life will never touch him. Promise me."

Always, cara mia. The voice in her mind was faint, and she knew they didn't have much time.

She felt his hand move first. His fingers stroked the slim column of her neck, sending a shiver down her spine. His fingers parted the buttons of the silk shirt, his shirt, covering her bare skin. The brush of his knuckles against the soft swell of her breasts sent flames licking through her blood. She relaxed into him, arching even closer so that his warm breath touched the pulse over her beating heart. The touch of his teeth scraping gently, erotically over her skin sent liquid heat pooling in her body, producing a heavy, unfamiliar ache.

She made a sound, a soft moan, as white-hot heat exploded through her when his teeth pierced her skin and sank deep. She cradled his head to her, drowsy with contentment, offering herself up to him. It was a sensual experience, her blood flowing into his body, replenishing damaged cells and tissue, warming cold muscles, bringing him life.

She could feel strength building in him even as it slowly

113

flowed from her. It was like a hazy, erotic dream. And then he was in her mind, murmuring softly, seductively, words of love, words she had never heard, ancient, beautiful sounds. The car was moving, a vague swaying adding to the surreal timelessness.

Stefan drove the car up close to the side door and ran to lock the heavy iron gates behind them, nervously checking the skies. When he returned to the car, he was shocked to find that the situation in the back seat had changed so dramatically. Now it was Aidan sitting upright and alert, covered in blood but his color returned, while Alexandria lay motionless, gray-faced, like one dead. She looked small and lost in Aidan's arms, almost like a child.

Stefan looked away. He had spent a good portion of his life with this man, yet the reality of Aidan's existence was almost too much for him to accept. He knew in his heart that Aidan would never harm the woman, yet to see her like that, so still and lifeless, after she had displayed so much courage . . .

"Clean the car, Stefan. I will go to ground for a day or two. It will be up to you to field any questions if the police come around. You must protect the child and Marie from any intruders. Remember, no harm can come to you in this house at night, but vampires can use humans to do their bidding."

Stefan helped Aidan from the car, watching as he reached into the back seat to lift Alexandria's limp body into his arms. "I know what they and their minions can do, Aidan. I will be alert for an attack," he assured him gruffly.

"Place blood inside the chamber for me this night, and then leave and stay away. Keep Marie and the child far from the chamber. It will not be safe for any of you until I replace the volume I have lost." He said it tersely, his strength already waning. Alexandria was a small woman, and he had taken all the nourishment he safely could from her, then had placed her in the deep sleep of his people to keep her alive until he could replace her blood loss.

He allowed Stefan to assist him through the house. Marie came running, crying out when she saw him. He heard the boy's feet on the hardwood floor. Aidan swung around, his golden eyes flaming with warning. "Keep the child away from me," he snapped, beating down his voracious hunger.

Marie stopped in her tracks, one hand pressed to her throat. Aidan was covered in blood and dirt, Alexandria lifeless, cradled in his arms. Blood and soil littered the hardwood floor on a trail from the door. Aidan's eyes were flaming red, his white teeth sharp and gleaming like a predator's.

"Marie!" Stefan's voice propelled her into action. She rushed to intercept Joshua before he could witness the horror of this night. Tears were pouring down her face as she caught the child up and began to run down the hallway toward the stairs.

Joshua touched the tears on her face. "Don't cry, Marie. Did someone hurt your feelings?"

She made an effort to gain control of herself. The house would have to be cleaned before the boy could come downstairs, so somehow she had to get him to sleep. "It's nothing, Joshua. I had a bad dream. Don't you ever have bad dreams?"

"Alexandria says if you say a prayer and think about really good things, you know, things you like, you'll have good dreams." Joshua rubbed his cheek against hers. "It always works when she does it with me. I'll say prayers with you like she does, and you won't have bad dreams ever again."

Marie found herself smiling at the simplicity and innocence in Joshua. She had three children, now grown, and Joshua brought back memories of the sweetness of childhood. She hugged him close. "Thank you, Joshua. Your sister is a very smart woman. You're lucky to have her." She stifled a sob. "And what are you doing out of bed at this time of night anyway? It's nearly four in the morning. Shame on you, young man."

"I thought Alexandria was in her bedroom, but she wasn't. I was looking for her." Joshua's eyes betrayed his fear of losing his sister.

"Aidan had to take her to a special place of healing. She's still sick, Joshua, so we have to have patience until he makes her better."

"Will she be all right?" he asked anxiously.

"Of course. Aidan would never let anything happen to her. He'll watch over her very closely. You know that."

"Can I talk to her on the phone?"

Marie laid him in the bed, pulling the covers up to his chin. "Not for a while. She's sleeping, just like you should be. I'll stay with you until you're sound asleep."

He smiled, a sweet, angelic smile that put warmth back into Marie. "I can teach you the prayer."

She pulled a chair up to the bed and took his hand, listening to his child's voice saying soft, innocent things to God.

Stefan wrapped an arm around Aidan's waist to support him. He could feel Aidan's disturbance at his touch and knew it stemmed from his battle with the ever-present demon within him fighting for control.

Aidan's enormous strength was drained, his hunger voracious, his need for blood so strong it ruled his every sense. It wrapped around his organs and crawled through his mind with burning need. "Hurry, Stefan, get out of here," he said hoarsely, trying to push the older man away from him.

"I will get you to the chamber, Aidan," Stefan said firmly. "You will not harm me. You hold your woman in your arms. She is your salvation. In any case, I have offered my life to you on more than one occasion. If it is your wish to take it at this time to save yourself and your woman, I have no objection."

Aidan gritted his teeth and clamped down hard on his predatory instincts. The will to survive was strong, the need for fresh, hot blood paramount. He tried not to hear Stefan's heart beating strong and steady, the pulse of blood surging through the body of this man he was so close to.

Once in the chamber, Stefan released him and backed away, knowing he was causing Aidan distress. He knew in his heart that Aidan would never harm him. He trusted the Carpathian far more than Aidan trusted himself. "I will bring the blood, Aidan."

Aidan nodded curtly and placed Alexandria's nearly lifeless body on the bed. He sagged down beside her, his hand curling around the thick braid of her hair. She had saved him, assuming she would die in the process. She had willingly, freely, offered her life for his. Their bond was much stronger than he had realized. She would never have survived his death. They were linked for all eternity, true lifemates. He had uttered the ancient words binding their souls together. Two halves of the same whole.

He sighed and lay beside her, inwardly cursing his need for blood. He could not go to ground without taking in more sustenance. He waited, the demon within him roaring and raging, until he sensed the human near, heard the soft pad of footsteps. The heavy door creaked, and Stefan placed several bottles of blood on the floor, then retreated, leaving Aidan and his lifemate alone in the chamber.

Aidan staggered across the floor and wrapped his hand around the neck of a wine bottle. He drained the contents and reached for the next one. Stefan had brought five full bottles, and Aidan consumed them all, and still his body craved more.

But with renewed energy from the blood supply, he moved the bed with a wave of his hand and opened the trap door to the cool, waiting earth below. It took concentration to peel back the layers of soil to make a space for his body and Alexandria's. Gathering her into his arms, he floated into the protection of Mother Earth. Aidan settled his frame around his lifemate and began the intricate ancient spells guarding the entrance to his lair. The trapdoor shut, and the bed above moved back into position. He closed the earth over them, around them, and slowed his heart and lungs as he felt the healing properties in the soil coiling around his wounds. His heart stuttered, his lungs rose and fell, and then all bodily functions ceased.

Stefan closed the door to the basement, knowing it could be days before Aidan made another appearance. He hoped he had brought him enough blood. Aidan would provide for Alexandria when he rose again and hunted his human prey. Until that time it was up to Stefan to guard the house, Marie, and young Joshua.

He found Marie cleaning the floor. She turned to him

immediately, her eyes questioning. He held her tenderly. "He will live, Marie. Don't worry for him."

"And his woman?"

Stefan smiled tiredly. "She was amazing. She wants nothing to do with him or us, yet she saved his life."

"She will be his salvation. But you're right, Stefan, she doesn't want to be here with us." Marie sounded sad, her heart filled with compassion.

"She doesn't yet understand what has happened to her," Stefan said with a sigh. "And the truth is, I wouldn't want to have to face what she is facing. She doesn't understand the difference between Aidan and the vampires. She's been roughly used, and her freedom is gone for all time. Even her ability to be with Joshua is restricted."

"We will have to be patient with her."

Stefan smiled suddenly. "*He* will have to patient with her. And she will stand up to him as no one in his lifetime has ever done. Modern American women are far different than what he is used to."

"You think it's rather funny, don't you, Stefan?" Marie observed.

"Absolutely. Aidan has never understood how you wrapped me around your little finger, but he is soon to find out." He kissed her gently and patted her shoulder. "I will clean the car and driveway, and we'll go to bed." He grinned suggestively.

Marie laughed lovingly and watched him go out into the night.

The sun was high in the sky, burning off the fog coming off the ocean. Marie and Stefan escorted Joshua to his school and lingered for a time outside, making certain no one was watching the boy. The morning paper had speculated that the two men found dead, burned beyond recognition, had most likely fought with one another. It was presumed that one of the men had accidentally drenched himself when he had thrown gasoline on the other. The blackened gas can found near the scene held the fingerprints of one of the victims.

Stefan avoided Marie's questions, not wanting to remember how he had pressed the hand of Ramon around the can. He wasn't certain he had covered every detail and was still nervous that the police would come knocking on their door.

When they returned home, however, it wasn't the police they found, but Thomas Ivan. Dressed in an expensive, tailored Italian suit, he was waiting somewhat impatiently at the front door. He carried an enormous bouquet of white and red roses mixed with ferns and baby's breath. He gave the couple his most charming smile, even managing a slight bow toward Marie.

"I wanted to stop by and see if Alexandria was feeling any better yet. I thought it might be a good time, too, to apologize for my rude behavior the other day. I was worried about Alexandria, and I took it out on you."

"She was happy to have her briefcase returned," Marie returned noncommittally. "She was given your message, and I'm certain she will contact you as soon as she is feeling up to it."

"I thought the flowers might cheer her up," Thomas said easily. He could handle servants anytime. As long as the lord of the manor didn't show up, he might get past the door this time. "Perhaps I could just take a peek in, wish her well. I'll only stay a moment."

The housekeeper didn't budge from her position. Standing directly behind her, looking every inch the Mafia hitman, Stefan remained deadpan. Ivan pushed down his temper. It wouldn't do any good to alienate these people. He needed to win them over to his side.

Marie shook her head. "I'm sorry, Mr. Ivan, that would be impossible. Mr. Savage left specific instructions that Alexandria should not be disturbed—on doctor's orders."

Thomas nodded. "I understand that you have to do what you were told, but you see, I'm really worried about her. I just want to look in on her, see for myself that she's all right. What do you say? We don't have to tell Mr. Savage. I won't stay long, just a quick peek to assure myself that she's okay." He pulled several twenty-dollar bills from his pocket, crinkling them expectantly.

Marie's indrawn breath was indignant. "Mr. Ivan! Are you suggesting I would sell out my employer?"

He swore under his breath. "No, of course not. I just meant to give you something for the extra trouble."

"Alexandria is no trouble, Mr. Ivan." Marie deliberately misunderstood. "She is a part of our household. She's considered family, as is her brother. You do know her brother?" She knew very well he didn't, and her voice said it all.

Thomas Ivan was furious. This battle-ax was openly defying him. Deliberately taunting him. He wished he could have her deported, preferably to someplace cold and wet and uncomfortable. Instead he smiled again, clenching his teeth as he did so. "I was not implying in any way that Alexandria might be a bother to you. Perhaps your understanding of English is not so good. Where are you from originally?" He tried to inject interest into his voice.

"Romania," Marie said, "but I have no problem with the English language. I have been here for many years. We consider San Francisco home now."

"Is Mr. Savage also from Romania?" He was very interested in the answer to that. Maybe he could have the arrogant bastard deported right along with his hired help.

"I cannot discuss my employer with someone not known to me, sir," Marie said politely, her face expressionless.

Thomas knew the old hag was secretly laughing at him. He took a deep breath. Well, she and the caretaker were making an enemy more powerful than they knew. He had friends in high places, and they were foreigners. "I just wondered, because his accent is different from yours." He wanted to say more educated, more cultured, just to insult her, but he refrained. He could bide his time and wait for his revenge. He would bring the entire house down, have the police and immigration people swarming over the place in no time.

"Well, I'm sorry you feel you can't cooperate with me. I'm extremely worried about Alexandria. If you refuse to allow me to see her or to speak with her on the phone, I have no other recourse than to take this matter to the police. As a possible abduction." He thought he saw alarm in the woman's face, but the man behind her didn't flicker an eyelash. Thomas began to wonder if the man carried a gun. Maybe he was the enforcer in the group. The back of his neck began to itch uncomfortably.

"You go ahead and do whatever you think you should, Mr. Ivan. I can't go against my orders," Marie said firmly.

"Then perhaps I could speak to Mr. Savage personally," he suggested tightly.

"I'm sorry, Mr. Ivan, but that isn't possible at this time. Mr. Savage is not at home, and there is no number where he can be reached."

"How very convenient for Mr. Savage," Thomas sniped, his fury at being thwarted beginning to surface. "We'll just see how much he likes talking to the police!" He swung around, hoping the enforcer wouldn't shoot him in the back. His eye started to twitch the way it always did when he was upset.

"Mr. Ivan?" Marie's voice was soft and sweet, almost placating.

He swung around in triumph. At last he'd said something to scare the pair of idiots. "What?" he snapped, making a show of his displeasure with her.

"Did you want to leave the flowers for Alexandria? I'll see to it that she gets them. I'm certain they'll cheer her up, knowing they came from you." Marie was trying not to laugh at the man. He looked so silly, all puffed up with his own importance, so certain he could intimidate them. She was not looking forward to a confrontation with the police, but she could use the flowers.

Ivan shoved the roses at her and stormed off, in no way appeased by her feeble attempt to get into his good graces. These foreigners were going to be sorry they crossed him. They obviously had no clue what kind of power a man like him wielded.

Marie glanced up at Stefan, and they both laughed. "I know what you're thinking, you wicked woman. You want to use those flowers to drive Aidan crazy with jealousy."

"How could you think such a thing, Stefan?" Marie demanded innocently. "I simply could not abide such beautiful flowers going to waste. I'll put them in the refrigerator until Alexandria rises. They'll brighten up her room or, better yet, the living room."

Stefan kissed her lightly on the cheek and made to depart. "Aidan is in for some interesting times."

"Where are you off to? You aren't going to leave me here alone to deal with the authorities. That man is going straight to the police station, and they'll likely listen to him."

"He's sure to make them angry with his obnoxious demands, and Aidan is well known to the local police. He always donates to their causes, and he's been careful to maintain a good relationship with them. I don't think Mr. Ivan is much of a threat, but I want to take a look around and make certain everything is in place for their upcoming official visit," Stefan reassured her.

"We can always have them talk to Joshua if we have to," Marie suggested, vaguely uneasy, as she always was when Aidan was vulnerable.

"It will not come to that," Stefan assured her.

Chapter Eight

The sun sank into the sea with a brilliant explosion of colors. Then the fog unexpectedly rolled in, a white, eerie haze that hung low over rooftops and streets, inching through the dark alleys and parks, until it filled them completely. No wind came to move the veil, and cars had to crawl from block to block.

Midnight. Aidan clawed his way to the surface. Hungry. Ravenous. Eyes red-rimmed and glowing with fierce need. His insides twisted and rolled. Cells and tissues cried out, demanding nourishment.

The loud sound of hearts beating close by, calling, beckoning, nearly drove him mad. His face was pale, almost gray, his skin dry and lined, his mouth parched. Fangs dripped with anticipation, and long, razor-sharp nails tipped his fingers.

For a moment his eyes rested on the lifeless body lying so still beside him in the open earth. Alexandria. His lifemate. His very salvation. The one thing standing between him and the fate his kind dreaded. Because of her he would not turn, would not become vampire, the undead. She had freely given her life for his. She had sealed their fates as nothing else could have, irrevocably bound herself to him for all eternity. She had chosen life for him; therefore, she had chosen it for herself. It didn't matter to him that she wasn't aware, exactly, of what she was doing. It had been done.

She needed blood. Her situation was even more desperate than his. He could not wake her until he could feed her. Her body was depleted, and without nourishment to revive her, she could not remain alive more than a few scant moments.

He smelled blood. Warm and fresh. Beating, surging, ebbing and flowing like the timeless call of the ocean itself. The demon inside roared and raged, desperate for control, yet desperate to save his lifemate. Desperate to feed the gnawing, clawing hunger. A man. A woman. A child. Aidan pulled back from the brink of disaster just in time, controlling himself enough to make the necessary preparations.

Minutes later he sped through the narrow underground tunnel, a blur of speed so fast that even a mouse would not detect his presence. He exhibited no traces of blood or dirt. His clothes were elegant, his hair clean and secured in a thick ponytail at the nape of his neck. He traversed the stone passageway into the basement without mishap. As he placed his hand on the door leading to the kitchen, he detected the presence of the woman entering the room from another door. For a moment his heart accelerated in excitement, and saliva anticipated his repast, but he fought down the responses. With his forehead resting against the door, he concentrated on reaching the woman mentally, on removing her from harm's way.

Marie would find herself inexplicably in the front room, but it would save her from the haunting hunger growing with every step Aidan took. The moment she was at a safe distance from him, he glided through the kitchen and out into the garden.

Instantly the smells saturating the night air assaulted his senses, flooded him, told stories. Only feet away a rabbit crouched, frozen with fear, aware of the deadly predator hunting blood. Its heart thudded wildly. In the houses up the street he knew where each warm body was and what it was doing—sleeping, snacking, making love, fighting. A veil of fog surrounded him, cloaked him, became a part of him.

Three days and two nights he had lain in the ground healing. With a new infusion of blood, he would be stronger than ever. Hunger fought for control, and he snarled and launched himself into the sky, more dangerous than anything Thomas Ivan had ever conceived. He was hunting living, breathing, human prey, and those moving below him were at risk this night that for once he might not stop his feeding in time to spare their lives.

He was a dark shadow winging overhead, invisible to those below. Aidan intended Golden Gate Park, with its rolling landscape and groves of trees, to be his hunting ground. The fog lay heaviest there, waiting for him, covering his advance. He landed lightly, silent feet touching the ground even as the wings were folding.

Only a few yards away lurked a group of men, barely out of their teens, displaying their gang colors, waiting for their rivals, pumping themselves up for a fight. All were armed, a good two-thirds of them were jacked up on drugs, and they were passing around a bottle of cheap wine.

Aidan smelled their sweat, their pores steaming with the adrenaline and fear their loud, belligerent bluster was meant to hide. It was the sound and smell of the blood flowing in their veins and arteries that interested him. He concentrated on them one by one, finding the blood least affected by substance abuse. *Come to me. Come here quickly. You need to be here now.* He sent the call easily, his hunger so strong he beckoned several of them. The rest of the group he merely instructed not to notice the absence of the others.

He seized the first man and sank his teeth deep, unable to

control the compulsion to feed long enough to be gentle. He gulped the hot liquid, his starving cells soaking it up greedily. It rushed through his body like a fireball, pouring strength into his muscles. He was barely able to prevent himself from taking the last drop of blood and gaining the ultimate power. It was the thought of Alexandria that pulled him back from the brink of such sure ruin. She had freely given her life for his. He could not allow himself, his hunger and his predatory nature, to throw that precious gift away by killing and condemning his soul.

Aidan concentrated on his knowledge of her, the curve of her cheek, the length of her eyelashes. She had a smile as rich as honey. Her mouth was lush and hot, like silk warmed by the sun. He dropped his victim and dragged the next one to him.

The liquid of life poured into him, and he closed his eyes and thought of her. She had eyes like blue gems, stars in their centers. She was brave and compassionate. She would never drop her prey at her feet as he was doing. He caught the third man close, his hunger beginning to ease. He took more care this time.

A sound penetrated his feeding frenzy, and he knew the other gang was approaching, trying to make their way through the thick fog, their cars still too distant to alert those waiting in the park. He pushed away the third victim and reached for the fourth.

It really wasn't fair to allow this gang to fight with several of their men out of commission, he considered. Then a slow smile curved his mouth. Already Alexandria was getting to him. To him, people like these men were without honor, without a code, willing to hurt or brutally mow down even those uninvolved in their conflicts, even women and children. Those without honor had no place in Aidan's world. Yet under Alexandria's influence, he was considering intervening to allow this group of killers an equal chance in their ridiculous battle for power. Not that any of them knew what true power really was.

He dropped the fourth man and reached for the fifth. His hunger was appeased, his full strength restored, but this was

125

for Alexandria. His white teeth glistened for a moment, poised over the exposed throat. The gray, bleak, and empty world was now filled with brilliant colors and exciting smells. Once again it held fascination and beauty. He allowed the knowledge to finally sink in. A true lifemate. Salvation at last. He could feel emotion. He would never be alone again. Never to be alone again. Centuries of emptiness gone in a moment. Alexandria.

With a little sigh that he had to follow a few more rules than he might like, he dropped the last man to the wet grass and sent out a call to the incoming gang. Waves of terror hit them as a group. They fell silent, looking from one to the other. Aidan found himself grinning. Maybe he had to be good, but that didn't mean he couldn't enjoy himself along the way.

The lead driver pulled his car over to the side of the road, dragging great gulps of air into his lungs. He was sweating profusely.

You are going to die tonight. All of you. The fog covers a monster. Death. It is calling.

Just to make his point, Aidan leapt into the sky, his body stretching, contorting, until he was a giant winged lizard with sharp, conspicuous teeth. His tail was long and thick with scales, and his eyes were ruby red. He came out of the fog, right at the line of showy cars, and breathed fire across their hoods.

Doors sprang open, and gang members burst out onto the street, shouts of terror echoing through the fog. Aidan laughed softly as he landed just to the right of the lead car, shape-shifting as he did so. His long muzzle shortened, fangs exploded, and his body compacted itself into lupine muscle and sinew. Fur rippled down his back and arms, emerging in a wave over his skin. He loped after the men, red eyes glowing.

"Wolf! Werewolf!" The scream caromed along the street, and a gun went off. It was impossible for anyone to see more than a scant foot in front of him, but to Aidan the air was perfectly clear, and he knew the exact location of his prey. He chased them for some distance, reveling in his ability to run so swiftly. There was joy in his heart. The joy he had felt some seven hundred years earlier. He was having fun.

"It was a dragon!" a harsh voice yelled as they all ran, their footsteps loud in the darkness.

He followed another voice. "This isn't real, man. Maybe we're having some kind of mass hallucination."

"Well, you stay and check it out then," someone called back. "I'm getting the hell out of here."

The wolf loped closer, scenting the human. The man was slowing down, certain none of this could be reality. The wolf leapt, covering a considerable distance in a single spring and catching the human by the seat of his pants. He got a mouthful of denim, and the man gave a high-pitched scream. Without looking back, he bolted to join his friends, his boots loud on the street as he escaped.

Aidan laughed out loud this time, the sound echoing eerily, carried on the thick bed of fog. He couldn't remember the last time he had had so much fun. The gang members were yelling back and forth, cries of fear. To even the odds a bit more, he concentrated on the cars, rolling them over, one by one, so that each car was sitting on its roof, the wheels spinning uselessly in the air. Then he did the same for the rival gang. They needed to rest in the park for a time anyway.

After assuring himself that neither gang had any fight left in them, he took to the air once more, this time racing back to Alexandria. He landed on the stone pathway in the garden outside the kitchen. A fish leapt in the pond, and the sound of splashing was loud in the night air. The wind was beginning to gently shift, slowly pushing its way through the fog. Tails of the white mist swirled lightly and drifted here and there like veils of lace. The effect was beautiful. It was all beautiful.

Aidan inhaled deeply and looked up at the sky. This wasn't his homeland, but it was his home. The vampire had been wrong about that. Aidan had grown to love San Francisco over the years. It was an interesting city with interesting people. True, he missed his own kind and the wildness of the Carpathian mountains and forests. He would give almost anything to touch the soil of his homeland. The ancient land of his people was forever in his heart, but this city had its own call, its diverse cultures melding and making for an incredible world to explore and enjoy.

Aidan used his keys to open the kitchen door. The house was quiet. Stefan and Marie were asleep in their room. Joshua slept fitfully, obviously uncomfortable at being so long separated from his sister, though Marie had allowed him to sleep in the little sitting room off their bedroom on the first floor. Stefan had kept his promise; the house was locked up tight, its iron grills shut over the windows to protect against invasion.

Aidan's safeguards were holding strong. Spells that were ancient and strong, known only to a few of the oldest of his people, were woven into the doors' intricate stained-glass windows. Gregori, the dark one, the most feared of the Carpathian hunters and their greatest healer, had taught him much—the safeguards, healing, even the ways to hunt the undead. Mikhail, their leader and Gregori's only friend, had agreed to send Aidan to the United States as a hunter once it was known the betrayers had begun to branch out and seek other worlds for use as their killing fields. Gregori trained few hunters; he was a loner and avoided others as a rule.

Julian, Aidan's twin brother, had tried to work with Gregori for a time, but he was too much like the dark one. A loner. He needed the highest peaks, the deepest forests. He needed to run with the wolf and soar with the eagles, just as Gregori had chosen to do. Theirs had not been the way of people, of cities, or even of their own kind.

Aidan moved through the spotless kitchen to the basement door. It suddenly occurred to him how good the kitchen always smelled, with its aromas of fresh-baked bread and spices. Marie, and her family before her, had always made his house a home. He had never really appreciated it before. Their loyalty had remained the wonder of his life, but he had never noticed the way they had made his heretofore bleak life bearable.

He breathed in the scent of his family. Warmth spread through his body, his heart. After centuries of a cold, barren existence, he wanted to fall to his knees in gratitude at the unexpected joy of family. He had never noticed the rustic efficiency of the basement before, either. It wasn't simply a musty, underground space but a bright, expansive room boasting Stefan's rich wood carvings and a well-organized array of tools. Work benches and tables were clean and orderly, garden tools gleamed with care, and to their left were countless bags of rich soil stacked carefully. Stefan. He owed the man so much.

Aidan himself had meticulously cut out the tunnel leading down to his hidden chamber after studying the rock forming the cliff and knowing that the secret chamber would be impossible to penetrate or detect so close to the large body of water. The undead might know he was sleeping close by, but they would never pinpoint his exact location.

Aidan had chosen the site of his home with care. As money was seldom an object when one lived for centuries, he had more than enough for several lifetimes. It was simply a matter of finding the right location and building to his specific needs. He wanted a few neighbors so that he blended in with his new society, but he needed space and privacy, grounds he could roam in and the freedom of the countryside in his own backyard. He needed the sea with its crashing waves and scents and mist that he could manipulate when necessary.

His property, overlooking the ocean on a bluff, was as close to perfect as he could find. He owned plenty of land around the house to use as a buffer between himself and the neighbors, yet there were other houses along the road. He had the privacy he needed if one of the betrayers found him and he had to fight without danger of someone coming upon them.

Setting up a new home in a new land had been one of the most difficult things he had ever done. But now, as he approached his sleeping chamber, that difficulty paled in comparison to what his brave Alexandria faced in her new life. She expected to die, even welcomed death, especially if it meant saving another—him. He had felt in her mind that she was not willing to prey on the human race for nourishment. She did not have a predatory nature or predatory instincts. And she feared she was vampire. No amount of explanation would overcome her distrust. Only time could do that, and he somehow had to buy himself enough of it with her to convince her that neither of them was vampire, neither of them a heartless killer. He needed the time to make her realize she belonged to him, with him, that they could never be apart.

He brought her out of the earth cradled in his arms. Stretching out on the bed, he motioned with one hand and closed the earth and trap door. She did not need to face the evidence of their unusual life all at once. She would awaken in a bed in a chamber. She would have enough to deal with without finding herself virtually buried in the earth itself.

He would have to work fast. The moment she was awake, he would have to seize her mind, before she became aware of what was happening and attempted to resist him. He did not want to start their relationship by forcing her to do something abhorrent to her; still, he had no choice but to replace her huge blood loss.

He took a breath, stroked back her hair, then opened his shirt. *Wake*, piccola. *Wake and take what you need to live. Drink what I freely offer. Do as I command.* Beneath his hand her heart stuttered, laboring to awaken as he bade even without sufficient blood to sustain life. His fingernail sliced his chest, and he pressed her mouth to the steady red stream.

He held her mind firmly as her body slowly warmed, as her heart and lungs found a rhythm. With the infusion of his blood, so much more powerful than most, her strength returned quickly. Without warning, she fought him, abruptly becoming aware of what was happening to her. With a small sigh, he allowed her to prevail, deliberately loosening his hold.

She dragged herself away from him, falling onto the floor, trying to spit the blood from her mouth, trying desperately to hate the taste of the sweet, hot fluid building strength in her.

"How could you?" She crawled away from the bed, scrambled to her feet, and pressed herself against the wall, wiping at her mouth over and over. Her eyes were wild with horror.

Aidan was forced to close the wound on his chest. He moved slowly to reduce her fear. Very carefully he sat up. "Be calm, Alexandria. You did not yet take in enough nourishment to restore your strength."

"I can't believe you did this. I'm supposed to be dead. You promised to take care of Joshua. What have you done?" She was gasping for breath, the wall holding her up. Her legs felt like rubber. He had lied to her. *Lied.*

"You chose life for me, Alexandria. And I cannot live without you. Our lives are bound together now. One cannot survive without the other." He spoke gently, making no move to go to her. She looked as if she might bolt at the slightest provocation.

"I chose to save *your* life. We both knew what that meant." She said it desperately, jamming a fist against her mouth to keep from screaming. She could not, would not, live like this.

"I knew what it meant, *cara.* You did not."

"You're a liar. How can I believe anything you say? You made me the same as you, and now you're forcing me to live on blood. I won't, Aidan. I don't care what you do to me, but I won't take someone's blood." She shuddered visibly and slid down the wall to the floor. She drew her knees up to her chest and rocked, trying to comfort herself.

Aidan took a breath, careful not to react too quickly to her words. She was totally withdrawing from him, her mind blocking him out. Or so she thought. He was familiar with her mind now, and he slowly entered, a slight shadow, ever watchful. "I have never lied to you, Alexandria. You decided that if you saved my life, you would be giving up your own." Deliberately his voice was velvet.

"You were afraid for Stefan."

"Why would I choose to allow Stefan to live and take your life? There is no sense in that. I did not trust myself to stop with Stefan. I had lost far too much blood, and my survival instincts were too strong. You were the only one safe."

He said it softly. His musical, hypnotic voice washed over her, seeping into her and tempering the horror of what she had become, easing a bit of the tension between them. "Why? Why would I be safe? Stefan has been your friend for years. You don't know me. Why would I be safe when he is not?"

"You are my lifemate. I could never harm you. For you I could control myself, and you I could replenish. I have told you this on more than one occasion, but you insist on ignoring the information."

"I don't understand any of this!" she blurted out. "I just know I want away from you. You're confusing me to the point that I don't know if you're putting thoughts into my head or if they're my own."

"You are not a prisoner, Alexandria, but the truth is, you need to remain close to me. There is no way you can protect yourself and Joshua without me."

"I'll leave the city. Evidently it's overrun with vampires anyway. Who would want to stay?" she asked, somewhere between bitterness and hysterical laughter.

"Where would you go? How would you live? Who would take care of Joshua in the daytime while you are forced to sleep?"

Alexandria clamped her hands over her ears in an attempt to block out his words. "Shut up, Aidan. I don't want to listen to you again." She lifted her chin, her sapphire eyes meeting his. Very slowly, unsteadily she pushed her way back up the wall.

He rose slowly, his movements mirroring hers. He looked so powerful, so invincible, she couldn't believe she was defying him. Hunger crawled inside her. The small amount of blood he had given her had merely whetted her appetite. Her starving body cried out, was insistent, impossible to ignore. Alexandria pressed a hand to her mouth. She was evil; he was evil. Neither of them should be alive.

That is not true, Alexandria, not true at all. He glided slowly toward her, silent, unpredictable, his voice so velvet soft, so very persuasive.

She rubbed her forehead. "God, you're in my head. Do

you really think I'm going to believe it's normal to talk to one another in our minds? That you always know what I'm thinking?"

"It is normal for Carpathians. You are not a vampire, *cara*. You are a Carpathian. And you are my lifemate."

"Stop it! Don't say it anymore!" Alexandria admonished.

"I will keep saying it until you understand the difference."

"I understand you made me like this. And that I'm not supposed to be alive. And no one is supposed to live for centuries. And no one is supposed to kill others to survive."

"Animals do it all the time, *piccola*. And humans kill animals to eat. But in any case, we do not kill when we feed, as vampires often do. It is forbidden, and the act itself taints the blood, destroys the soul," he said patiently. "There is no need to fear your new life."

"I don't have a life." Watching his every move, she inched toward the door. "You took my life away from me."

He was several feet from the heavy stone entrance, she only inches. But even as she jerked it open, his hand was already stopping her. His body, so much larger, so much stronger, was blocking her way to freedom.

Alexandria went still. "I thought I wasn't a prisoner."

"Why do you resist my aid? If you leave this chamber with your hunger as it is, your distress will increase."

Aidan wasn't touching her, but she could feel his heat. Her body seemed to reach for his. Even her mind sought his touch. Horrified, she pushed at him. "Get away from me. I'm going to sit with Joshua for a while. I need to think, and I don't want you around. If I'm not your prisoner, then get away from me."

"You cannot go near the boy looking as you do. You are covered in dirt and smeared with my blood."

"Where's your shower?"

He hesitated, then decided against mentioning she wouldn't need one if she didn't want one. Let her be as human as she needed to be. It cost him nothing. "You may as well use your private bathroom on the second floor. Your clothes are in your room, and everyone is asleep. You will not be disturbed there." He stepped back and gestured toward the passageway.

Alexandria ran through the tunnel and burst into the basement. She had to leave this place. What was she going to do with Joshua? Aidan was dragging her further and further into his world. A world of madness, of insanity. She had to leave.

She had never been on the second floor, but she was so distraught, she scarcely noticed the ornate banister, the plush carpets, the elegance of each room. Marie had done the best she could to place Alexandria's things around, to make her feel more like this was her home. Alexandria peeled off her filthy clothing and stepped into the large glass-doored shower. It was immaculate, as if no one had ever used it.

She turned on the water as hot as she could stand it and turned up her face to the flow, trying not to give in to hysteria. She was not a vampire, not a killer. She didn't belong in this house. Joshua certainly didn't belong here. She closed her eyes. What was she going to do? Where could they go?

Slowly she threaded her fingers through her thick braid, loosening the weave so she could wash her hair. Long and fast-growing, it fell past her hips as she massaged the shampoo into her scalp. What was she going to do? She had no idea, and none seemed forthcoming.

Hunger was ever present, gnawing at her until her mind seemed consumed with it. She could taste the spice of Aidan's blood on her tongue. Her mouth watered, and her body cried out for more. Tears mingled with the water pouring over her face. She couldn't pretend this wasn't happening. Worst of all, she could barely tolerate being apart from Aidan. She could feel her mind, of its own accord, reaching for him. Her heart was heavy, almost grief-stricken, away from him. She could not stop thinking about him.

"I hate you, what you've done to me," she whispered aloud, hoping he was listening to her mind.

She dressed slowly, choosing her clothes carefully. Her favorite pair of jeans, worn and faded with two rips in them. She loved the feel of them against her skin. They were so normal, so much a part of her everyday life. Her favorite ivory lace cardigan, with the little pearl buttons that always made her feel feminine.

As she unwrapped the towel from her hair, she looked at herself in the mirror for the first time. She was slightly shocked there was even a reflection. She had a hysterical impulse to call Thomas Ivan and tell him he needed to rethink some of his ideas for his silly vampire games. He didn't seem quite so brilliant anymore. Still, she looked fragile, pale, her eyes too large for her face. She touched her neck. There was smooth, satin skin, no scars, no faded wounds. Lifting her hands in wonder, she studied her long fingernails. She had never been able to grow long nails. Her fingers clenched into fists.

She could not stay in this place. She needed to figure out how to get Joshua to safety. On bare feet she padded down the hallway. There was no need to turn on lights; she could see quite clearly in the darkness. Once again her mind was tuning itself to Aidan's, and she forced it away, out of danger. She didn't want him to know what she was thinking or feeling. She didn't want to acknowledge that she was any different from any other human being. Very slowly she walked down the stairs.

She knew exactly where Joshua was. Unerringly she found her way to the room where he was sleeping. She stood in the doorway and simply watched him, her heart aching for both of them. He looked so small and vulnerable. His bright hair was a curly halo on his pillow. She could hear his soft breathing.

Alexandria approached the bed slowly, misty tears blurring her vision. Joshua had lost so much. She had been a poor substitute for their parents. Not that she hadn't tried, but she had never managed to get Joshua out of the worst neighborhood in the city. It seemed a terrible irony that now, at last, he was in a mansion, surrounded by everything money could buy and going to one of the most prestigious schools around, and the man who had made it all possible was a vampire.

She sat on the goose down quilt and smoothed a palm

over its thickness. What was she going to do? The burning question. The only question. Could she take Joshua and run? Would Aidan let her go? She knew, somewhere deep inside herself, that he had allowed her to pull away from him when he was forcing her to feed. He was far more powerful than she could conceive, and he was concealing the full extent of it from her.

She let her breath escape slowly. She had no relatives to take Joshua to. There was no one to help her. Nowhere to run. She leaned close to kiss the top of his head. At once she became aware of the ebb and flow of his blood. She could hear it as it throbbed through veins bubbling with life. She became fascinated by the pulse beating in his neck. She could smell the fresh blood, and her mouth watered with need. She inhaled deeply, her cheek brushing Joshua's neck.

Alexandria felt the incisors then, sharp and ready against her tongue. Horrified, she sprang away from the bed, away from the sleeping child. That she reached the door in a single leap barely registered. With one hand clamped tightly over her mouth, she fled down the hall and through the house, jerked open the front door, and ran into the dark night, where she belonged.

She ran as fast and as far as she could, each step draining the strength from her, sobs tearing at her chest. The fog was now no more than a thin mist, stars scattered across the sky in their timeless pattern. When her adrenaline was spent, Alexandria sank onto the ground beside a wrought-iron fence.

She was so evil. What had she been thinking? That she could just take her brother away and everything would be as it was before? Joshua would never be safe from her. Aidan might have told the truth about Stefan after all. Hunger clawed and bit at her until her very skin crawled with need. Her fingers found the solid weight of an iron bar, and she wildly considered stabbing herself through the heart with it. She pulled at it experimentally, but it was embedded solidly in concrete. Weak from lack of blood, she could never remove it by herself.

Biting her lip hard to stabilize herself, she considered her options. She would never endanger Joshua. There was no way she could ever return to that house. She could only pray that Marie and Stefan would grow to love Joshua half as much as she did and protect him from the insanity of Aidan's life. She had no desire to hurt any human being. And that left her only one option. She would stay here until the sun came up and hope the light would destroy her.

"Not a chance, Alexandria." Aidan's tall, muscular frame appeared out of the mist. "That is not going to happen." His face was a mask of implacable resolve. "You are so willing to die, but you are not willing to learn to live."

She gripped the fence until her knuckles turned white. "Get away from me. I have the right to do whatever I want with my life. It's called free will, although I'm sure the concept's beyond your understanding."

In a lazy display of rippling muscles, he stretched to his full height. A certain elegance clung to him like a second skin. "Now you are trying to provoke me."

"I swear, if you keep using that calm, cool, Alexandria, you-are-hysterical tone on me, I will not be responsible for what I do." She kept her fingers tightly around the bar in case he tried to force her to go with him.

Aidan laughed softly, without humor. It was a masculine, mocking taunt that sent a shiver down her spine. "Do not try me too far, *piccola*. I will not allow you to meet the dawn. There will be no discussion on this matter. You will learn to live as you should."

"Your arrogance astonishes me. I will not, under any circumstances, go back to that house. You don't know what I almost did."

"There is no such thing as secrets between us. You smelled Joshua's blood, and your body reacted normally. You are hungry. More than hungry, you are starved and in need. Naturally you reacted to the proximity of nourishment. But you would never have touched him. You would never harm your brother."

"You can't know that." She didn't know it. How could

he? She rocked back and forth in agitation, lowering her head to her knees to hide her shame. "It wasn't the first time. It's happened twice now."

"I know everything about you. I am in your mind, your thoughts. I can feel your emotions. The hunger you experienced was natural. You cannot neglect the demands of your body. But Alexandria, you could not harm a child. Any child, let alone Joshua. It is not in your nature."

"I wish I could believe you."

She sounded so forlorn, it nearly broke his heart. He hated this, the terrible burden of confusion and misinformation she carried. She had mixed the myths and legends of vampires, her horrifying encounter with the real thing, and his powers all together.

His fingers were gentle beneath her chin. He tilted her head up so that her eyes were held captive by his. "I cannot lie to you, *cara*, for you can touch my thoughts at will. Merge your mind fully with mine, and know I speak the truth. There is no danger to Joshua. I am part wild animal, a hunter, a very efficient killing machine, I believe were your thoughts. And that is true of me at times. But that is not the case with you. A male Carpathian is responsible for the protection, the health, and the happiness of his lifemate. I am the darkness to your light. You have compassion and goodness in you. You are Carpathian now, but as with all Carpathian women, your true nature is one of gentleness. There is no danger to Joshua."

She wanted to believe him. There was something in the purity of his voice, in the directness of his steady gaze, that nearly convinced her. More than anything in her life, she wanted to believe him now. "I can't take the chance," she said sadly.

"And I refuse to lose you." He bent down, pried her fingers from the fence, and lifted her easily into his arms. "Why will you not allow me to help you? I know this is all a shock, but listen to your heart, your mind. Why did you choose to save me if you thought me evil?"

"I don't know. I don't know anything anymore, except that I want Joshua safe."

"And I want you safe."

"I can't bear to be close to him and have such strong feelings of hunger like I had. It was awful, thinking of blood, looking at his pulse." She pressed a hand to her stomach. "It made me sick. And it scared me, made me so afraid for him."

His mouth touched her hair in the lightest of caresses. "Allow me to help you, Alexandria. I am your lifemate. It is my right as well as my responsibility."

"I don't know what that means."

He could feel the resistance draining out of her. She looked up at him hopelessly. There was no trust in the depths of her eyes, only a terrible sorrow. She couldn't fight his strength or his implacable resolve.

"Allow me to show you," he said softly, his voice low and intense, a black velvet seduction.

Chapter Nine

Aidan's arms tightened a fraction as he held Alexandria to him. There was an expression on his face, a look in his eyes she was afraid to name. Possession. Tenderness. A mixture of both. She didn't want to know. It made her feel cherished, treasured. It made her feel sexy and beautiful. The way his gaze moved over her face, touching her lips like a physical kiss, sent her heart racing.

A slow smile curved his sensual mouth. "I see you are barefoot. I was going to suggest a walk under the stars, but your annoying habit seems to have surfaced again."

She swallowed hard, making an effort to gain some semblance of control. She did not want to go back to the house. She needed to distance herself from Joshua and sort out what had happened. "Since I ran here, I don't think walking is going hurt me. Put me down, Aidan. I won't take off."

His laughter ruffled her hair. "As if you could get away from me." Very gently, slowly, savoring the feel of her next to him, Aidan lowered her to her feet.

She glanced up at him. There was something new in their relationship that had not been present before. She was very much aware of him as a man. Tall, strong, handsome, sensual. Her mind pulled away from the thought, and she hastily ducked her head again.

She missed Aidan's sudden smile.

"It is a beautiful night, *cara mia*. Look around you," he instructed softly.

Because she was so aware of him moving easily beside her, she did what he said, wanting to avoid thinking about him and the strange power he seemed to hold over her. The stars were a brilliant blanket above them. She took a deep breath, inhaling the salt breeze coming off the ocean.

Behind them was the thick grove of trees growing along the hillside, in front of them, the bluff overlooking the ocean. The street wound its way up the hill; the houses dotted here and there along its path were large, yet blended in well with their surroundings. The city lights rivaled the stars, an iridescent pattern that went on for miles. The view was breathtaking.

Aidan moved closer to her, just a shifting of muscles really, but she felt the warmth of his body. Liquid heat unexpectedly pooled deep in her lower abdomen. Her heart beat faster. *Fascination*. He fascinated her. Captivated her. Casually she inched away to put a little space between them. He glided rather than walked, his golden eyes taking in the landscape surrounding them, a slow sweep of his penetrating gaze that missed nothing, including her retreat.

"If you fed properly, Alexandria, there would be no need for you to ever feel as you did around your brother." He broached the subject impassively, his tone carefully neutral.

She felt as if he had punched her in the stomach. "Do we have to talk about it?" *To feed.* What did that mean, exactly? Not *eat,* but *feed.* Her brain shied away from the word and all its connotations.

His hand slipped over her silky hair, following the wild

mass down her back to her rounded bottom. The gesture was unbearably tender. Warmth seeped under her skin, and her mouth went dry. His hand accidentally brushed hers. Their fingers tangled, then his closed around hers so that they were linked. "It is best, *cara*. Your fears are so groundless."

She took a deep breath, trying to force herself to concentrate on the distasteful subject, but Aidan's nearness was turning her world upside down. She could feel electricity arcing and crackling between them. The tip of her tongue darted out to moisten her lips. She was acutely aware of his golden gaze following the simple movement, turning it into something erotic.

"What do you suggest? Should I make Thomas Ivan my food supply?" She proposed it flippantly because her throat was raw with fear. "I guess I could always seduce him— that's what female vampires do in the movies."

Aidan knew she said it out of fear; he was in her mind. But the image of her body tangled with the software mogul's was instant and vivid. The warning growl escaped him before he could stop it. White teeth gleamed—a threat. He pushed his free hand through his long, tawny hair. At that moment he was dangerous, and that shocked him. He had never been a real threat to any human unless he chose sides in a war. Humans were something to feed on, to protect, and he seldom got involved in their squabbles. Like all Carpathians, when their land ran with blood and their countries were torn apart, they had utilized their skills to fight. But this was different. This was personal. And Thomas Ivan would never be completely safe again.

Alexandria sensed the change in Aidan immediately. He was fighting something lethal in himself, a private battle with a demon she had no concept of. Her fingers tightened around his. "What is it, Aidan?" she asked softly, concerned.

"Do not even make a joke of such a thing. I doubt Ivan would survive if you seduced him." He said it starkly, without softening the blow. His voice was velvet soft but dripped menace, far worse than a shout. He brought her knuckles to the warmth of his mouth, lingering over her satin skin. "Ivan does not need to tempt fate by touching you."

She pulled her hand away, disturbed by the heat in her body, the ache that was becoming an urgent demand. Absently she wiped her palm on her denim-clad thigh to try to erase the sensation of his lips on her skin. "You know, Aidan, half the time I can't understand a thing you say. Why would Thomas be tempting fate? Are you saying I would kill him?" She tried not to hold her breath, waiting for the answer.

His body was against hers again as they matched steps like tango dancers. "Not at all, *cara mia. I* would kill him. I doubt very much if I could stop myself. I would not even want to stop myself."

Her sapphire eyes grew wide as she stared up at his face. "You really mean it, don't you? Why would you do that?"

He hesitated a moment, the silence lengthening while he carefully chose his answer. "I'm responsible for your protection. That man is after more than your beautiful drawings, Alexandria, and, innocent that you are, you cannot see it."

Her chin tilted. "For all you know, Mr. Savage, I might have had a dozen lovers. If I choose to seduce Thomas Ivan, you won't need to worry about me. I can take care of myself."

Her silky hair was suddenly bunched in his hand, and she came to an abrupt halt. He stepped so close, her slender body was bent backward. His golden eyes molten, alive with passion, with possession, stared directly into hers. "You are my lifemate. You have never been touched by another man. I have been in your mind and have access to your memories. Do not try to tell me there have been a dozen men in your life."

She remained passive, still. His body was aggressive against hers, yet there was no pain, no sense that she was in danger. There was only his terrible intensity, as if his inner demons were riding him hard. Her blue eyes flashed right back at him. "On top of everything else, you have to be a male chauvinist. Like I'm supposed to believe there have never been women in your life. And another thing—get out of my head. You don't have a right to my private life. Whatever this lifemate thing is, I don't want any part of it." She

142

tried to sound defiant, but it was difficult when his perfect mouth was only inches from hers. It was embarrassing, the things his mouth made her think.

She couldn't take her eyes from his. She saw their gold became heated, the purpose clear in their depths. His hard mouth softened, and very slowly, with infinite patience, he touched his lips to hers, a brief, feather-light stroke that sent a shaft of desire curling painfully through her body.

"Just so you remember, seducing men is out," he murmured almost absently against her mouth.

She could taste the words. Taste his breath. His mouth was hot and enticing. His body stirred, and she could feel him pressing against her, hard with need. His hand framed the curve of her cheek, his thumb sliding in a caress across her pulse. The wind blew the silken mass of her hair across his hand and arm, binding him to her almost by design.

She could smell his scent calling to her, wild and abandoned, like an animal calling to its mate. Her entire being responded, against all intellect, all reason, against all sanity. Alexandria had never felt such sexual attraction toward any man, and the intensity of her response to him was beyond her comprehension. This was strong and compelling, hot and steamy, a driving need as elemental as time. She wanted him right there in the night, wild in her arms, needing her.

She jerked away from him. "Stop it, Aidan. Just stop." She held up a hand to pacify him. "I'm not ready for this." He was so intense, so much the domineering male, he would sweep her away until she couldn't exist without him. Until she didn't exist without him. "You're not going to take over my life," she whispered to him.

He stroked the pad of his thumb across her lower lip. "I barely touched you, *cara mia*, and you run from me like a rabbit."

"Anyone in her right mind would run from you, Aidan. You're talking crazy. It shouldn't matter to you how many lovers I've had—or have. That's my private business. I didn't ask you about your love life, did I?" Suddenly she thought about his arms around another woman, and the idea made her sick. "You're such a hypocrite. In all the centuries

143

you claimed to have been alive, there's probably been more women than I care to know about. Hundreds." She thought about it. "Thousands. You're a dog, Savage. A hound dog."

He couldn't help laughing. Reaching out, he took possession of her hand again and began to walk slowly back toward his home. Her hand was small and fragile in his, her skin soft and inviting. The wind, determined to have its way, playfully touched her hair, blowing it across his arm, weaving them together with a hundred silken strands.

Alexandria walked along beside him, trying not to feel cherished and protected as he moved alongside her. It was the way he moved—confident, supple, powerful—that made her feel so vulnerable to his possession, yet his fingers were gentle around hers. With every step she took, she became more annoyed that he had access to her personal life.

"I think you're getting the wrong idea, Aidan, about me. I may not have actual lovers, but that's only because I haven't loved anyone yet. I've been attracted, though. There's nothing wrong with me."

His mouth twitched. Manfully he refrained from smiling, but it was necessary to walk several steps before he could reply in his usual neutral voice. "I never, at any time, thought there was something wrong with you. If *you* are worried about it, though, I will be happy to demonstrate otherwise."

She tugged at her hand. He was too close, too vivid and alive. The chemistry between them was explosive. He couldn't touch her, let alone kiss her. It just wasn't safe. "I'll bet you would. But it isn't going to happen. I have a rule about vampires—I don't get involved with them."

His eyebrows shot up. "Good rule. I am pleased you are beginning to show some sense. And you were not attracted to human men."

"Thomas Ivan is very attractive."

His amber eyes glittered at her. "You thought he was a shark. And that cheap cologne he used made your head ache."

"He kind of grows on you," she protested. "We have a lot

in common." Her blue eyes held defiance. "His cologne is not cheap. And he's very handsome."

All at once his large frame was blocking her path, and she ran right into him, her face pressed into the niche of his sternum. One of his hands circled the slender column of her throat. "Not to you, he is not." His thumb drew a line over her lower lip.

At once her body was throbbing with need. Just like that. He blocked out the cool night air, the very stars, everything but his solid muscles, his heat and strength. Her breasts felt uncomfortably taut; her blood rushed through her body.

She could hear his heart pounding. In his veins, blood was singing, calling to her. Hunger gripped her, acute, biting. She tried to pull away, a small moan escaping her. She had been enjoying herself, actually managing to forget for a time that she needed to feed on another being to exist. But the realization drowned out everything else, so that the beauty surrounding her was at once barren and ugly. Fear for him surged through her. Planting both palms on his chest, she attempted to shove him away. It was like trying to move a wall of concrete.

Aidan simply smiled at her. "Stop fearing what is natural to you. Do you really think you could harm me?" His arms closed tightly around her, and she felt her feet leave the ground. His mouth brushed her ear. "But I do thank you for the concern."

Clutching his waist, Alexandria peeked beneath his arm to see the ground dropping away. They floated upward, a lazy, casual motion that struck terror into her heart. "Now might be a good time to tell you I'm afraid of heights," she ventured, her heart thudding loudly in her ears.

"No, you are not, little liar. You are simply afraid of things you do not understand. Have you not always dreamed of flying? High above the earth? Look at our world, *piccola*. Look at the wondrous things you are capable of doing." There was tender amusement in his voice. "You can soar free at your will."

"Dreaming about it and doing it are two different things. And I'm not doing it; you're the one in control."

His laughter was low and wicked. "Would you like me to let go of you? It is not as if you are not capable of floating on your own."

Her fingers twisted convulsively in his shirt. "Don't even joke about it, Aidan." But he never once loosened his hold on her, and she felt safe and protected. Taking a deep breath, Alexandria looked around her.

Wisps of fog drifted past her. She wanted to reach out and touch one, just to see if she could, but she wasn't quite comfortable enough to relax her death grip on Aidan. The stars glittered overhead, and below her the waves raced across the ocean and crashed on large rocks, spraying white foam in all directions. The droplets looked like sparkling diamonds scattered across the deep blue of the sea. The wind was tugging at the treetops, so that they bowed and swayed, branches waving up at her.

Alexandria felt a burst of joy. She felt free. The heavy, oppressive weight crushing down on her was lifted for the moment, and she was laughing, really laughing. The sound of it pierced Aidan's heart, wrapped it up, and squeezed hard. His arms tightened even more. He wanted to hear her laugh like this all the time. The scent of her, the feel of her, was pushing at his control, calling to the wildness in him.

She felt the change in him. The way his body stirred against hers, the way it hardened in urgent demand, the possession in his arms as he held her to him. They were on the balcony of his house now, the one that wrapped around the third story, his private quarters. His feet touched down, but hers didn't, and he carried her easily to a plush lounge chair just outside the intricate stained-glass sliding doors.

"Aidan!" It was a breathless protest. Panic welled up. She could not be alone like this with him. He was too much of a temptation, and she was too vulnerable, her emotions ragged and raw.

His mouth skimmed over her eyelids, her cheeks. "Did I not tell you that you should trust me?" He settled her on his lap, his hips cradling her bottom. She was pressed against him intimately, and it didn't seem to matter to him that she could feel his violent need of her. Secrets between them did not exist. She could have easily reached into his mind and found the same information.

Alexandria shivered, suddenly afraid. There was something different about him, some elemental change she had noticed since he had awakened her this last time. He looked at her differently, as if she was his alone, as if his right to her was complete, unchallenged. There was tenderness but also a deep resolve, a relentless purpose. She touched his face with trembling fingers.

The night shone on his masculine beauty, the thick mass of tawny hair spilling to his broad shoulders. She could see his lush eyelashes, the elegant nose, the strong jaw and perfect lips.

"Merge your mind with mine." It was a soft command.

She stiffened and shook her head. Her life had already been taken over, changed forever. Instinctively she knew he was dragging her closer to him, drawing her further into his world. She had to control something. "I won't, Aidan. I don't want this."

"I only intend to feed you, *cara*, nothing more, although I will admit the temptation is almost more than I can bear. Merge your mind with mine." This time his voice dropped an octave, became mesmerizing, hypnotic, a low, lazy, seductive lure.

She struggled against the hard strength in his arms. Her mind echoed the words *feed you*. Her stomach somersaulted. Her heart pounded. Instead of revulsion, there was hot anticipation, the sexual tension between them rising even higher. She stifled a low sob. This wasn't her. None of it. She didn't want a man so badly that her entire mind and body ached and burned with need. She would never consider biting into someone, yet at the thought of her mouth against his chest, his neck, her body clenched and throbbed in reaction. Liquid heat pooled deep inside, a steamy sensuality she had never known.

"Merge your mind with mine," he whispered again, the words like a seduction against her skin. His tongue caressed her pulse, and her body tightened in anticipation.

In desperation she did as he wished. His mind was a haze of hunger—physical hunger, urgent, demanding. Erotic pictures danced in his head. His tongue stroked again, lower this time, as his fingers slowly threaded through the pearl buttons on her sweater. She was bathed in heat, need, hunger. Her skin was ultrasensitive. She heard herself moan, felt the cool air blow tantalizingly across her breasts.

He touched her, his hand sliding up her narrow rib cage to close possessively over the satin skin below her breasts. His teeth nipped her neck, her throat. He murmured something inarticulate. *I want you, Alexandria. You belong to me. You are mine.* His teeth skimmed down to one breast, lingered, scraped erotically. His velvet tongue stroked the hard peak, once, twice. *I am your lifemate. You will take from me what you need. Feed,* cara mia. *Take from me what only I can give you.* She felt his mouth close over her softness, the heated pull erotic and strange.

Her eyes closed. She was in a dream world. Her body felt heavy, was unfamiliar with yearnings she had never experienced and her entire being raged for a release she needed as desperately as she hungered. His hand opened his shirt, and they were skin to skin. For a moment he held her there, savoring the feel of her creamy flesh against his hard muscles. Aidan's hand came up, and he brought her head to his chest, simply holding her there in an unbreakable grip.

His mind reflected back her need to feed, amplified it until the red haze in him was in her. Her cheek nuzzled his taut muscles, felt the roped sinews beneath the skin, breathed in the surge of his life's blood. She felt his body harden even more, hot and full with need. A slow, feminine smile of satisfaction curved her mouth. Her tongue tasted his skin, the flavor of him, masculine and spicy. Addicting. Her lips brushed his pulse.

Aidan's muscles contracted, clenched. His teeth came together, and he closed his eyes against the demands of his body. She was like hot silk and white lightning. Fire skimming over his chest. It spread across his flat belly, lower still, to torment him with a painful, unfulfilled promise of release. Her tongue teased, dancing over his skin until he thought he might go mad.

Alexandria possessed a natural sensuality, heightened by the Carpathian blood now flowing strongly in her veins. Aidan was her lifemate, and despite the fact that she refused to acknowledge what was happening, her body craved his, needed and hungered for him. Her natural inhibitions were being pushed aside, her humanity swept away on a tide of rising passion. Her blood, raging with fire, cried out to his. Her body moved against his, seeking a closer bond, skin to skin without the confines of their clothing. Her mind was meshed with his, woven together beyond all solitary thought. What he wanted, she wanted. What she needed, he needed.

Her tongue caressed his pulse, swirled lightly over his muscles, stroked a brown, flat nipple. He threw back his head and groaned aloud. A fine sheen of sweat coated his skin, and his body swelled in urgent demand, his jeans far too tight, his body straining to break free. Her teeth scraped lightly, insistently. A trembling started somewhere in his legs and took over his body. His very blood pulsated with waves of urgency, a molten volcano ready to explode. He wanted her more than he had ever wanted anything in all the long centuries of his existence. His arms tightened possessively. He bent his head to brush his mouth over her silky hair, her closed eyelids, her temples.

And then he was gasping for breath, a strangled sound somewhere between a moan and a hoarse cry escaping. His muscles and sinews clenched as white-hot pain coursed through his body, as unbelievable pleasure flooded his every cell. Her teeth had pierced deep, and his blood flowed into her, her mouth moving in a sensuous feeding frenzy. Erotic. Hot.

Her hand slid over his chest, stroked his flat belly, followed the trail of golden hair until her fingertips were brushing the waistband of his trousers. Aidan shifted his weight, tried to ease the tightly-stretched cloth covering his throbbing body. He needed relief, was desperate for it.

His incisors were sharp against his tongue, his mouth filled with hot need. He nuzzled the nape of her neck as she fed. The act was more erotic than all the times, faded now, in his memory of sexual encounters over the earlier centuries, before his emotions, urges, and feelings had disappeared. His teeth clamped down of their own accord on her shoulder, pinning her in place in the age-old Carpathian display of dominance, an instinct he hadn't known he possessed until this moment. His body clenched, drenched itself in sweat, pulsed with need, and burned with fire.

Her hand moved over the constriction of cloth. Her mind, so deeply merged with his, was lost in fiery need. She could see the images in his head of the two of them tangled together in ecstasy. She knew exactly what he so urgently wanted, what his body demanded. His need was hers. Her hand freed him from the confines of his tight trousers. She felt him shudder as her fingers wrapped around the thick length of him, as she stroked and caressed the hard shaft.

His teeth came together, his body arching. There was thunder in his ears and a haze of red desire before his eyes. Jackhammers were beating at his skull. His hands pushed at her sweater, rough and insistent, wild and dominant. His teeth bit down when she would have moved.

Some small sense of self-preservation surfaced, and Alexandria became aware of what she was doing. It had been like some erotic dream, but now she was conscious of the cool night, the heat of his body, the demands of his hands, her own uninhibited behavior, her mouth feeding so sensually at his chest.

"Oh, God!" She let go of him as if burned and tried to move away. His hand held her head to him, and she felt the trickle of blood making its way down in his chest.

"Close the wound with your tongue. Your saliva carries a healing agent. There is no mark unless we wish it." His voice was like a caress, soft and husky yet gravelly with need. His hand forced her compliance.

She did as she was told because she was terrified to defy him. He was in such a state of arousal, with one wrong move he would sweep her resistance aside. And he could. She knew it. He knew it. They were locked together with one mind. She held her breath as he struggled for control. His body was as hard as a rock, taut with leashed aggression, and so hot they both were burning up in the flames. A low growl rumbled in his throat. He was more beast than man, and she realized she had no concept of what kind of being she was dealing with.

"I'm sorry, I'm sorry." She chanted it like a litany, humiliated that she could have been so bold, so wanton. "Please tell me that you hypnotized me and made me do those things. You did, didn't you?"

She was pleading with him. It was in her voice, in her eyes, in her mind. But they were locked together, and lifemates could not have untruth between them. As much as he wanted to spare her the truth, he could not. Aidan shook his head, but the dawning comprehension was already in her mind. Alexandria moaned and covered her face with both hands. "I'm not like this. I don't respond to men this way, I don't drink blood, and I am not a tease. What have you done to me? It's even worse than I thought. I'm some kind of vampire nymphomaniac." She attempted to pull herself out of his arms, but Aidan tightened his hold on her.

"Be calm, *cara*. Breathe your way through this. There is a rational explanation." Everything in him wanted to throw her to the floor of the balcony, claim what was rightfully his, and once and for all put himself out of a living hell. But he could not do that to her. Her outrageous thought, *vampire nymphomaniac*, nearly made him smile. It certainly turned his heart over, even while his self-control was in savage, relentless meltdown.

Alexandria was very aware of the restraint he was showing, of how hard he was fighting his natural instincts, his belief in his right to have her. She swallowed hard and stayed very still, not wanting to enflame him further. She was trembling, fighting her own needs and desires, feelings she had never experienced. Why for him? Why did it have to be for him that she burned and needed? *She drank his blood willingly. She drank it and wanted more, wanted to give herself to him, wanted him to touch her, to possess her, wanted to touch him.* She groaned again, humiliated. She could never face him again as long as she lived. And, for God's sake, he had some pretty vivid and explicit pictures in his head, too. His intentions toward her were anything but avuncular. Aidan Savage wanted with her a desire, a hunger so beyond anything human, she could barely conceive of it.

"You are shaking, *piccola*," he pointed out softly, his breathing a little more ragged than he would have liked. He wanted to keep her right where she was. If he allowed her to run now, he would lose valuable ground. His hand moved over her silky hair in a soothing gesture. "We are both all right. Nothing happened."

"What do you mean, nothing happened?" she demanded. "I drank your blood." The very thought of it now made her sick, and her stomach lurched convulsively. She had wanted to do it, needed to, and her hunger was sated for the time being, but her body was alive with need.

"I told you there were ways. You have no need to worry you will harm Joshua. I will see to all your requirements. It is my right." His voice softened to velvet. "It is my privilege." His hand found her throat, settled there possessively, her pulse beating frantically into his palm. The edges of her sweater were still parted, revealing the enticing swell of her full breasts. Alexandria didn't seem to be aware of it, still so shocked at her wanton behavior and her feeding on Aidan's blood that she couldn't think of anything else. The sight of her was not helping to cool his hot blood. He had a sudden desire to crush her to him, to bury his teeth in her, and drag her fully, kicking and screaming, into his life.

Alexandria carefully avoided looking down into his lap. His masculine body was exposed to the night, hard and thick, with no apologies. Unlike her, Aidan didn't appear in the least embarrassed. In fact, it was obvious he felt he had a right to her. She stared up at the stars pushing their way through the scattered wisps of clouds. The night was beautiful and calming. The feel of his hand wrapped around her throat should have frightened her, but instead she felt cherished.

Alexandria moistened her lips. None of her emotions, so

intense, were characteristic of her. "Are you certain you didn't direct my actions?"

"You are my lifemate, Alexandria. Your mind and body recognize me as such. The bond between us will only grow, as will the need. Such is the way of our people. It is probably a protection for our longevity. Rather than paling over time, our sexual need for each other gets stronger. There will come a time when we must give in, or the consequences will be dire." He tried to choose his words carefully, yet still be honest.

She picked the image out of his mind, blushing furiously. "Violence? We would come together in violence? I don't have experience—we've already established that—and I'm not even certain I like you. Why is this happening between us?"

His breath came out in a long sigh. At least she was talking instead of running. He had to hand it to her, she had courage. "You have never felt physical attraction for another man because you were made for me. Your body needs mine. You are my lifemate."

"I hate that word," she snapped resentfully. "You've taken my life away from me. I don't even know who I am anymore." Her blue eyes met his. "I am not going to just hand myself over to you without a fight."

His thumb brushed her jaw, sending waves of fire beating at her. "I have already taken over your life, as you have taken over mine. It is done."

"I don't think so," she objected, her chin lifting defiantly. All at once she became aware of her sweater gaping open. With a little gasp of dismay, she dragged the edges together. "Do you mind?" she said indignantly, pointedly glancing at his all-too-masculine display.

He gave a lazy shrug. "It is not exactly as if I can comfortably put everything back together again."

She blushed furiously. "Well, don't talk about it, for heaven's sake!"

He found himself smiling in spite of the raging demands of his body. With unhurried movements he positioned himself within the confines of the tight cloth and buttoned the fly. "Does that make you feel safer?" he teased tenderly.

His voice sent a shiver of pure pleasure down her spine. No one deserved to have a voice like his. And his mouth. She stared up at it, caught by the chiseled perfection of it. No one should have that tempting a mouth. Her heart was slamming painfully against her chest. His mouth was mesmerizing, like his voice. Close. So close. She could almost feel the heat, the hot beckoning of his mouth.

His lips brushed hers, and her heart stopped. His tongue traced her full lower lip, teasing an opening to sweep inside the silken interior. Her heart began to pound. There was only feeling, a curious shifting of the earth, a slow spinning that kept her senses off balance. He explored every inch of her mouth with complete authority, building the heat between them once again. It was Aidan who slowly, reluctantly, lifted his head. His strange eyes were hot, molten gold, roaming her face possessively. His thumb caressed her chin while his palm spanned her throat.

"You did that this time," he whispered, a dark sorcerer, ensnaring her further in his spell. "I deny all responsibility."

His voice whispered over her skin. She stared up at him helplessly. How did he do it so easily? Wrap her up in sexual feelings when she was so certain she had none?

"I did not do this," he reiterated. "You are looking at me as if I am some spider and you are the little moth caught in my web." He shifted again in an attempt to give his body some relief.

She felt every masculine muscle imprinted on her soft form. She wanted to stay there forever, never be away from him. Horrified, Alexandria wrenched herself up. She got nowhere. Her body hadn't moved an inch from his. The gold eyes never wavered from her face.

"Let me up. I mean it, Aidan. You're seducing me. You're doing something with your voice. I know you are. Like you do with Joshua."

"If only I could, *piccola*. It would be nice to control you. It would present all sorts of interesting possibilities."

She could see the wicked thoughts in his mind, the tangled bodies, bare skin, his mouth moving over every inch of her. "Stop!" she cried-desperately, feeling her body going into meltdown at the erotic pictures in his head.

He looked innocent and nuzzled the top of her head with his chin. "I am merely enjoying the night, Alexandria. Is it not beautiful?"

She glanced up at the fading stars. Light was beginning to streak the darkness, turning the skies silver-gray. Her breath caught in her throat. Where had the night gone? How long had she lain here with Aidan? She didn't want to go down to the chamber and sleep. "I want to see the sun."

His hand stroked her hair. "You can see the sun, but you cannot be in it. And you can never forget dark glasses, or the time."

She swallowed fear. "The time?"

"You will become lethargic at first, then the weakness will hit and you will be completely vulnerable. You must be in shelter by noon."

His voice was calm, matter-of-fact, as if he was not crushing her, taking her life from her. All at once she hated his voice.

"What about Joshua?" she demanded. "What about his life, school, birthday, parties, sports? He might play baseball or football. Where will I be during his games, his practice sessions?"

"Marie and Stefan—"

"I don't want another woman raising my brother. I love him. I want to be there when he does these things. Can't you understand that? I don't want it to be Marie sitting in the stands when he hits a ball for the first time. And what about parent-teacher conferences? Does Marie do those, too?" Her voice was bitter, and once again the awful blockage was tearing at her throat, threatening to strangle her.

"Breathe, Alexandria," he commanded softly, his hands massaging her shoulders. "You keep forgetting to breathe. This is all so new. Things will work themselves out. Give yourself some time."

"Maybe if I saw a doctor. A researcher specializing in blood disorders. There must be a way to go back," she said desperately. The truth was the worst thing to face. It wasn't just the abhorrent practice of drinking blood. Evidently she could overcome that aversion; Aidan had just given her proof. It was her growing obsession with Aidan that terrified her. *He* terrified her. His dominating her life terrified her. She wanted all of that to just go away and leave her normal again.

He stirred slightly, the jungle cat stretching. She could feel his muscles rippling with power. His hand moved to her neck, and there was stark possession in his gaze. "You will not do such a foolish thing. There are those who hunt our people, and the methods they use to destroy us are not pretty. You would die a hard and ugly death. I cannot allow such a thing."

"I hate that condescending I'm-so-calm-and-you're-so-out-of-control voice you use. Don't you ever get mad?" she blazed at him, little sparks flying from her sapphire eyes. "I'm just going to ignore you. How do I know any of this is real? I've never acted this way before. This could all be a dream."

His eyebrows lifted, and a small, mocking, suggestive smile touched his mouth. "A dream?" he echoed.

"A nightmare," she corrected with a frown. "A very bad, very vivid nightmare."

"Would you like me to see if I can wake you up?" he offered helpfully.

"Don't sound so arrogant and macho. It makes my skin crawl," she snapped, because her heart was pounding all over again with fear. Did he have to be so sexy, so tempting? She didn't know the first thing about men, but surely they weren't all like this. Lethal. A threat to freedom.

A lazy smile softened his perfect mouth, instantly drawing her attention. "Was I sounding arrogant?" His thumb was stroking back and forth over her pulse.

She could feel each separate, caressing stroke go right through her body to collect in the pit of her stomach, to brush there like the wings of butterflies. She turned her head to escape his penetrating golden gaze, to escape that perfect mouth, and she saw the thin ribbon of scarlet that formed a path down his chest, tangled in the fine gold hair, and trickled lower still to his flat belly. Before she could think, instinctively, sensually, she lowered her head, her tongue tracking the ruby streak.

His every muscle clenched hotly, contracted and bunched. His teeth came together, and his throat worked convulsively. She possessed such a natural sensuality, and her body was so familiar with his. Her every instinct cried out for him. Alexandria was so innocent, so unaware of how close to peril she really was. Centuries of discipline were rapidly disintegrating, leaving only the dark, starving beast, needing—no, demanding—to claim its mate. Aidan couldn't help himself. His fingers tangled in the silken hair at the nape of her neck and held her to him while the earth spun and wanted to fragment, while his body pulsed and throbbed somewhere between pain and pleasure.

Without warning, Alexandria leapt up, shoving him as hard as she could so that, in his rather precarious state of arousal, he landed on the balcony floor with a thud. He blinked up at her through hooded eyes, trying to hold back the laughter that threatened to consume him. "What?"

"Stop being so . . . so . . ." Words failed her. *Sexy. Attractive. Enticing.* Hands on her hips, she glared at him. "Just stop!"

Chapter Ten

The kitchen was already warm from the blaze Stefan had built in the stone fireplace. The aroma of coffee and cinnamon laced the air. Alexandria walked beside Aidan into the room, their bodies brushing occasionally. He glanced down at the top of her bent head. She was wary now, afraid of him and the implications of her physical response to him. Yet now, without her knowledge, her body instinctively sought the shelter and comfort of his. She was beneath his shoulder, his arm sliding easily around her waist, across her back. She didn't even seem to notice.

The feel of her skin against his was driving him mad, but he walked with his usual easy grace and revealed none of his emotions on his face. He smiled at Marie as she turned from the counter, where she was beating an egg mixture in a bowl. She had so much warmth and affection in her for so many, not least for him. She humbled him with her ability to take so many into her heart.

"Aidan! Alexandria! I had no idea you were in the garden." She was smiling at them, but her sharp eyes were taking in his carefully blank expression and the shadows in Alexandria's eyes. "Joshua slept a little fitfully—I think he's really missing you, dear. He's such a sweet little boy. And his beautiful curls!"

Alexandria smiled. "He detests those curls."

Marie nodded. "What little boy wouldn't?" Alexandria wasn't nearly as pale as she had been all the other times Marie had seen her, and she certainly didn't look dead, as she had when Aidan carried her into the house. She had been well fed by Aidan, Marie was certain. She took a deep breath. "I wanted to thank you for what you did for Aidan the other night. It took courage. Stefan said Aidan would have died had you not gone to his aid. Aidan is like a son to me, or a brother. He is our friend and our family. Thank you for bringing him back to us."

Aidan stirred restlessly beside Alexandria, but she ignored him. "You're welcome, Marie, although I'm certain he would have found a way without me. Aidan is nothing if not resourceful. I'm indebted to *you* for all you've done for Joshua."

Aidan bent his head to brush a kiss onto Marie's temple. "I have told you for years that you worry too much about me. But you are correct. Alexandria saved my life."

Alexandria made a face at him. "And it was such a brilliant decision on my part, too," she whispered for his ears only.

His hand came up to caress the nape of her neck. "I thought so."

Stefan came in with an armload of wood. "Aidan! You're up." He beamed at them both. "And Alexandria, you certainly look better than the last time I saw you. But I give you credit—you know how to get things done."

Self-consciously she brushed a tendril of hair from her face. "I can be rather bossy, Stefan. I didn't mean to be. It's just that I've lived for so long on my own, caring for Joshua, that I'm used to doing everything myself and figuring things out. Besides, Aidan is so stubborn, and he seems to have everyone around here buffaloed."

She was taunting him, the little devil! Aidan knew it, and something inside him responded to the teasing. He felt, for the first time in centuries, for the first time since he was young, that he was not alone. He was in his home—not a house, but a real home—with his family surrounding him. Joshua slept peacefully in his bed, Marie and Stefan were laughing and joking in the kitchen, and beside him was the woman who was his life, his very breath, the blood in his veins. She had given him a heart, so he was now capable of knowing love and laughter and appreciating the miracles he had been favored with.

"That handsome man came back," Marie suddenly said, her eyes bright and innocent. She remained very busy at the counter.

Stefan choked on his coffee, and Aidan had to pound on his back. He looked suspiciously from one to the other. "What handsome man?" But he was beginning to have a sinking feeling in the pit of his stomach.

Marie touched Alexandria's arm lightly. "Your Mr. Ivan. He was quite upset and worried about you. He even called the police when we wouldn't allow him in. They were by yesterday morning. Nice, polite officers. I believe you've met them, Aidan, a time or two." Marie was beaming.

"Thomas Ivan came by again?" Alexandria asked, shocked.

"Oh, yes, dear," Marie said guilelessly. "He was quite worried about you."

"He called the police?" Alexandria couldn't take it all in.

"Two detectives. They insist you and Aidan contact them

159

as soon as you return. We told them Aidan had taken you to a private hospital, that you were very ill. Aidan has donated money many times to their causes and even helped a few out individually when they needed it. All on the up and up, of course. Loans with very little interest but certainly within the law. I had the impression Mr. Ivan had angered them with his accusations against Aidan."

"I can imagine he did," Aidan said dryly, glaring at Marie.

Marie didn't seem to notice the signal. "I thought it sweet that he was so worried about your safety. One could hardly blame him for his concern." She smiled. "He wanted them to search the house, but of course, the officers refused. He left his number and wants you to call him, and he left something else. Let me just get it for you." She sounded like an excited schoolgirl.

Aidan leaned one hip lazily against the counter, but there was nothing lazy about his golden eyes. He followed his housekeeper's every movement, unblinking, his stare like that of a great predator eyeing its prey. Stefan moved closer to his wife uneasily, but Marie didn't seem to notice, bustling over to the refrigerator.

"I have to talk to the police?" Alexandria asked, completely unaware of Aidan's menacing stance. "I can't talk to the police. Aidan." She reached for his arm, her hand shaking. "I could never do it. What if they ask me questions about Henry, or something about those women? Thomas Ivan will have told them I was there that night. I can't talk to the police. What has Thomas done?"

With a great sense of satisfaction, Aidan curved an arm protectively around her shoulders. He swept her close to him, offering comfort. Marie pulled open the enormous refrigerator and turned, a huge bouquet of roses in her hands, the vase cut crystal. He felt Alexandria's swift intake of breath.

"For you," Marie said blithely, ignoring the black scowl on Aidan's face. "Your Mr. Ivan brought these for you."

Alexandria moved away from Aidan to cross the room. "They're so beautiful. Roses," she said breathlessly. "I've never received flowers before, Marie. Never." She touched one dewy petal. "Aren't they wonderful?"

Marie was nodding and smiling in agreement. "I thought we might put them in the living room, but if you want them in your private bedroom, that would fine, too."

Aidan's hands itched to strangle the woman. He had known Marie from the moment of her birth—sixty-two years ago—and they had never exchanged a cross word. And he suddenly wanted to strangle her. He should have ripped Ivan's throat out. Flowers. Why hadn't he thought of flowers? Why hadn't Marie mentioned it to him first? Why had she accepted them? Whose side was she on, anyway? Flowers! He had the urge to rip those petals off one by one.

"Look," Marie cooed, "he even had the thorns removed so you wouldn't hurt yourself. What a thoughtful man."

"What time did you tell the police we would see them?" Aidan interrupted, afraid that if he didn't he would erupt into violence. He detested the way Alexandria kept caressing the petals of one of the white roses.

Stefan cleared his throat and glared at his wife. "They asked that you contact them at your earliest convenience. It seems that Ivan is particularly insistent, especially since two bodies, burned beyond recognition, were found a few miles from here. I told the police I was returning from the store when I saw the blaze and called it in from the car phone."

Alexandria's face went white, and she looked up at Aidan as if for direction. "Are they going to question me about that, too?"

Aidan reached out a hand, gently fingering her silky hair. "Of course not, *cara*. Do not be so alarmed. They believe I had already taken you to the hospital. If necessary, we will be able to prove such a thing. The police want only to answer Ivan's ridiculous concerns by seeing you alive and well. I assured him you were safe when he was here last, but he would not take my word. He has thoroughly insulted me."

In spite of her fears, Alexandria laughed. "You were lying to him, you idiot. I wasn't safe. A vampire had bitten me, remember?"

He raised an eyebrow at her. "*Idiot?* In all the centuries of my existence, no one has ever called me an idiot."

"Well, that's because everyone's afraid of you. Thomas had good reason to think you were lying. Don't act like one of those ridiculous men in whatever century who fought duels of honor."

"I have fought more than one duel in my time."

"Idiot," she said disrespectfully, but she was laughing. Alexandria buried her face in the flowers, inhaling the sweet fragrance. Then she raised her head and caught Aidan looking at her with that possessive, masculine intensity that caused her heart to turn over. "Do I really have to talk to the police? Can't you just do it?"

There was some satisfaction in her blaming Ivan, Aidan thought, but it didn't help to have her cuddling those accursed flowers.

Stefan shook his head. "Actually, Aidan, the police are very interested in those bodies. It seems the way they burned was quite remarkable, as if the flames were burning from the inside out. There was nothing left but ashes. They couldn't ID the bodies through dental work either. I think they'll insist on speaking to both of you."

Alexandria slumped against the counter, leaning heavily on Aidan. "I'm not very good at lying, Aidan. Everyone always knows when I'm lying."

She sounded so dejected, as if it was a terrible sin that she couldn't lie, that he smiled. "Do not worry, *cara*. I will handle the police. All you have to do is sit in a chair and look fragile and delicate," Aidan assured her.

She frowned at him as if she thought he was making fun of her. "I can't look fragile. Or delicate. I'm sturdy, Aidan."

He laughed then. He couldn't help it. The sound was deep velvet, a pure note that made Alexandria smile even as she nudged him. "Don't laugh, you ape. I swear, Aidan, you're so completely arrogant, it's scary. Has he always been this way?" She was smiling at Marie—her first genuine smile at the other woman, a sharing of feminine minds.

"Always," Marie said solemnly, her heart lightening. She had not realized just how afraid she had been that the household would change, that she and Stefan would no longer be welcome. She knew Aidan would never throw them out, but if the tension between Alexandria and herself was not resolved, sooner or later she and Stefan would have to find their own place. And Aidan's home had been her home her entire life. When she married Stefan, he had moved in and accepted the life she led, had accepted and grown to love Aidan Savage, too.

"I think the living room is the perfect place to put the flowers," Alexandria agreed. "When Thomas comes over, he'll be able to see them."

Aidan found himself gritting his teeth. Alexandria was already flitting from the kitchen. He caught Marie by the shoulder before she could follow, leaned down, and put his mouth to her ear. "Couldn't you have thrown the damn things out?" The words came out somewhere between a hiss and a growl. "And just for the record, you traitor, Ivan is not her man. I am."

Marie looked shocked. "Not yet, you're not. I believe you still have to court her. And of course I would never throw roses out, Aidan. When a man goes to the trouble of giving a woman flowers, she should at least have the pleasure of seeing them."

"I thought you didn't like this bum."

"He can't be all bad. You should have seen his concern for her. I tell you, Aidan, he's really taken with her." Marie was deliberately, innocently enthusiastic. "I don't think you'll have to worry about her when she's with him." She attempted to sound reassuring.

Behind them, Stefan was choking again. Aidan swore eloquently in three languages and followed Alexandria out of the room, shaking his head over the workings of the female mind.

Stefan put an arm around Marie. "Wicked, wicked woman."

She laughed softly. "This is fun, Stefan. And it's good for him."

"Be careful, woman. He is not like other men. He might kill to keep her. His nature is that of a wild predator," Stefan warned gravely. "We've never seen him like this."

Marie sniffed. "He will behave himself. He wouldn't dare do otherwise. That girl wants to run. She has sense, that one, and plenty of courage."

"Spirit," Stefan agreed. "She will lead him a dance. But she doesn't realize the danger she will always be in. Or the danger Joshua will be in."

"She needs time, Stefan," Marie said softly. "She will have us to help her, and Aidan will guide her."

Aidan paced after Alexandria, pushing down the swirling demon raging against that soft, faraway look that had crept into her eyes. Intellectually he understood the lure Thomas Ivan represented to Alexandria. She wanted to be human. She wanted to feel human. She wanted to work and live in the human world. She believed Ivan could give her that. Even more, she would not have to deal with the unfamiliar, frighteningly intense sexual feelings Aidan evoked in her.

He reached out and caught the length of her hair in his hand, bringing her to an abrupt halt. "Do not worry about the police, Alexandria. They will not ask you anything about the vampires. They have no idea they were vampires, and they believe you were in a hospital. If they ask, just tell them you do not remember anything."

She was quiet a moment as she arranged the roses. He could sense her unease. "Aidan? Can I leave here? Would you let me go?"

Involuntarily his hand tightened in her hair. He let his breath out slowly. "What brought this on, *piccola*?"

"I just want to know. You said I wasn't a prisoner here. Can I come and go as I please?" Her teeth were tugging at her full lower lip.

"Are you planning on dating this joker?"

"I want to know if I can leave this house."

He wrapped an arm around her slender waist and pulled her against his hard frame. "Do you think you could survive without me?" His mouth was close enough to her neck that she could feel the warmth of his breath. Despite her every intention not to respond, her body caught fire.

Her sapphire eyes searched his face. He gave nothing away; she had no idea what he was thinking, and she wasn't going to merge her mind with his to find out. He was drawing her deeper and deeper into his world, a world of the night. A world of sexuality and violence. Alexandria wanted her old life back. She wanted familiar things around her, things she had some control over.

His perfect mouth touched her throat. A brush of flame. His golden gaze met her eyes. "Do not ask questions you do not really want the answer to. I will not lie to you, even to make it easier."

She closed her eyes as warmth flooded her body. He made her feel cherished. Made her feel beautiful. Made her feel unfulfilled and empty without him. Her fingers tightened around the stem of one of the roses. She jerked her hand away with a little cry, cradling one finger.

"Let me see," he said softly. His voice was tender, his touch gentle as he pulled her hand to him for his inspection. A pinprick of blood welled up from her index finger. "Sir Galahad left a thorn," he murmured as he bent his head and took her finger into the healing heat of his mouth.

She couldn't move, couldn't speak. Her body blazed with need. She stood as still as she could, watching him the way a cornered mouse does a cat. He had already taken over her life. It was there in her mind, in her body, her terrible need of him. She wanted to cry. Even if she managed to escape, to somehow get Joshua out and run away from him, she would carry him with her everywhere she went.

Abruptly she jerked her hand away from him before the flames leapt any higher. "His name is Thomas Ivan, not Sir Galahad, and I doubt very much if he personally took the thorns from the roses."

Aidan nodded solemnly. "You are right, *piccola*. He would not think of such a thing himself, nor would he perform the task. He would think it beneath him and a waste of his time." He reached around her and removed the thorn, then examined each stem carefully to assure himself she would not get hurt again.

"Why do you have to make him sound so petty?" she demanded, exasperated. She was determined to be attracted to Ivan. Women all over the world had multiple lovers. If other women could be attracted to more than one man in a lifetime, so could she. It didn't have to be just Aidan Savage. He was worldly, sensuous, impossibly attractive with those haunting eyes and that perfect mouth. Any woman might fall for him, but all it was was physical attraction. She could get over it like a bad case of the flu. A virulent case of the flu.

Aidan turned away from her to stare out the window. He didn't know whether to laugh or be angry at her wild thoughts. She was so determined to find someone, anyone, other than him.

"Aidan?" Stefan walked in. "I informed the police that you and Alexandria had returned and that she would be up to speaking with them this morning. I made certain they understood she would be unable to go to the station or even to stay up long. They're sending a couple of detectives over now."

"Detectives?" Aidan raised an eyebrow. "For so trivial a matter?"

Stefan cleared his throat and shifted his weight uneasily. "I believe Mr. Ivan has some political pull. He went above the department's head and even, according to the detective I spoke with yesterday, went so far as to check to see that all of us were in the country legally. I believe he wished to have us deported."

Alexandria gasped, her chin lifting. "He did *what?*"

"I'm sorry, Alexandria, I should not have repeated that within your hearing. Mr. Ivan was terribly upset at not being able to get in touch with you," Stefan said.

Aidan could have strangled the man for attempting to get Ivan off the hook. Alexandria had been annoyed. Without her even being aware of it, she was already thinking of the members of his household as part of her family.

"That is no excuse for Thomas to throw his weight around and try to get you and Marie deported. He didn't even care about completely disrupting your lives. And what about Joshua? He would have had to go into a foster home." Her anger at Thomas Ivan was rising. She detested people who thought they could have their way because they had money. Though she would never admit it to Aidan, never concede

166

that tiny bit of power, she was less and less inclined to work with the man or be involved with him in any meaningful way. Surely she would find other creative outlets.

"Actually," Stefan confessed, avoiding Aidan's sharp gaze, "I believe it was Aidan he was more interested in deporting. He had an investigator run a background check on him, hoping, I think, to come up with some hint of criminal activities. *Unsavory* is the descriptive I believe he used."

Alexandria bit back a sudden laugh. "Perhaps Thomas has more intuition than we gave him credit for. *Unsavory* is an apt word, don't you think, Stefan? I wouldn't mind having Aidan deported myself."

"I think it would be prudent to retire to the kitchen and eat my breakfast, Alexandria," Stefan said diplomatically.

"Your only choice," Aidan growled.

Stefan grinned at him unrepentantly and paused in the doorway. "You might want to give Mr. Ivan a call, Alexandria. The detectives said it might stop him from harassing them every ten minutes."

"He's been calling them every ten minutes?" A slow smile curved her mouth. "He must really be worried. Isn't that sweet, Aidan? He's worried about me. He must really want me to work for him. What a break. With the money he pays me, Joshua and I can. . . ." She trailed off, looked quickly up at Aidan.

His hand curled around the nape of her neck, his fingers moving in a soothing massage. "I am proud of you, Alexandria. Your work must be extraordinary to have Ivan after you to this extent. You deserve to feel good about yourself." He didn't believe for one moment that Ivan's interest in her was purely business, but he knew she was truly talented. Aidan was a shadow in her mind, seeing her vivid pictures spring to life in her imagination.

She smiled up at him. "I used to dream about working for Thomas Ivan. His company is always on the leading edge of graphic designs, and his games are like full-length movies. When the rumor hit the street that he might be looking for another graphic designer, I started sketching night and day. I didn't believe I'd really get a chance to show him my work, let alone that he would want to hire me."

"From what I saw of your drawings, you are very talented," he acknowledged softly. "But perhaps you might want to correct some of his false impressions of vampires."

Her eyes flashed at him, but a dimple deepened in her cheek. "Make them more ruthless and merciless, you mean?" she asked mischievously. She touched the petals of the nearest rose and bent once more to inhale their fragrance. "I can't believe he sent me flowers."

A rude noise escaped from somewhere deep in Aidan's throat. "I just saved your life. What are roses compared to that?" He was glaring at the long-stemmed flowers, his golden gaze intense and menacing.

Alexandria glanced up at him, saw the dark, determined set of his mouth, and burst out laughing. She spun around and went up on her toes to cover his eyes with her palm. "Don't you dare. If my roses wither, I'll know exactly who's responsible. I mean it, Aidan. You leave my flowers alone. You can probably destroy the entire bouquet with one ferocious glance."

Her body was soft against his, her laughter warm against his throat. His arm circled her small waist, locking her to him. "I was only going to make them droop a little. Nothing too dramatic."

His velvet voice turned her heart over. Little butterfly wings were brushing at her stomach. She could feel his muscles, hard and masculine, imprinted on her form. Why did her body have to melt every time she came into contact with him? Even when he was being bad, a petulant, jealous child, he made her laugh. Why did all this have to be happening with him?

"I'm going to take my hand off your eyes, but you aren't even to look at my roses. If I catch you . . ." She trailed off, meaning to intimidate him. Slowly her palm slid from his eyes, her fingers accidentally touching his mouth. At once her heart slammed hard against his. Or was it his heart slamming against hers? She didn't know, but the electricity was crackling, and he was too close.

"Don't you dare, Aidan." She made it an order. His eyes had gone hot, liquid gold, blazing possessively down into hers, melting her insides.

"Dare what?" he whispered, his sorcerer's voice slipping under her skin like a flame. His gaze was so intense, she felt the same flames licking along her nerve endings.

His mouth was now mere inches away. Her tongue touched her lower lip. Enticed him. Tempted him. She closed her eyes as his mouth came down on hers. Fire swept through her, consumed her. His arms crushed her to him, but it didn't matter. Nothing mattered but his perfect mouth and the earth moving beneath her feet.

She belonged to him, with him. There could never be another. Only Aidan. Only the two of them together. She was his. The words beat in her head, imprinting themselves forever on her heart. On her soul. Alexandria reluctantly pulled her mouth from his, burying her face on his chest. "You aren't playing fair, Aidan," she said, the words muffled in his shirt.

The warmth of his breath touched her neck. "This is no game, *cara*. It never has been." His mouth closed over her pulse, sending it racing. "This is for all time."

"I have no idea what to do with you. I don't even know if you mean the things you say." The confusion in her mind was very real. He was swamping her, giving no relief, no time to figure things out for herself.

That wasn't what Aidan wanted. Alexandria needed to trust him, to see him as a friend as well as a lover. The urgent demands of his body and nature gave them very little time, but he was determined to make the most of it. She could laugh at him, make him laugh at himself. It was a start to friendship. Slowly, reluctantly, his arms released her, and he stepped away, providing a measure of relief for both of them.

"Thomas Ivan needs to be taken out and shot," he said deliberately to make her smile. "He's a spoiled brat who made too much money too fast."

She relaxed visibly. "I wonder if he thinks the same thing about you."

"With his vivid imagination, he probably envisions a stake through my heart," he muttered. "That man has a sick mind, to make up all that nonsense. Did you happen to pick up his last game, the one with the vampires and their army of women slaves?"

"Well, it's obvious you have," she pointed out, pouncing on that. "Secretly you probably love his games. I'll bet you own every one." Her eyes widened, and a slow, wicked smile spread across her lips. "You do, don't you, Savage? You have all his games. You're a secret fan."

He nearly choked. "A fan? That man could not find the truth if it was staring him right in the face. As it was the other evening."

She raised an eyebrow. "His games are fiction, Savage. No truth intended. Only imagination. That's why they're entertainment, not truth. Admit it, you like his games."

"It is never going to happen, Alexandria, so do not hold your breath. And another thing—when you talk to that pompous ass on the phone, do not go all syrupy." He folded his arms across his chest and looked down at her from his superior height.

"Syrupy?" she echoed indignantly, outraged at the accusation. "I never sound syrupy." Her large eyes flashed a warning at him, daring him to pursue his point.

He dared to. "Oh, yes, you do." He clasped his hands together and made a face, his voice rising an octave as he simpered. "Oh, Marie, the flowers are so beautiful. Thomas Ivan gave them to me." He rolled his eyes as he mimicked her.

"I did not say that! And I never act that way. For some reason, you just can't bring yourself to admit you like Ivan's games. It must be some macho kind of nonsense, although a lot of men play them and enjoy them."

"They are pure trash," he insisted. "And there is not a grain of truth or sense in any of them. He romanticizes vampires. It would be interesting to see what he thought if he was introduced to one." It was a veiled threat, nothing less. Aidan fairly purred with satisfaction at the mere thought of it.

Alexandria was horrified. "You wouldn't dare! Aidan, I

mean it, don't you even think about doing something so evil."

"Was it not you who said there was no such thing as a vampire?" he inquired innocently, his white teeth very much in evidence.

His mouth again. She found herself staring up at it, fascinated. His smile had softened its lines into pure sensuality. She blinked to bring perspective back into her life. He should be outlawed.

His smile widened, dispelling any hint of cruelty, and he leaned close to her. "Remember, I can read your mind, *piccola*."

Her blue eyes flashed at him, and one small fist thumped the middle of his chest. Hard. "Well, stop it. And don't flatter yourself. I wasn't exactly giving you compliments."

"No?" His hand touched her face tenderly. "Keep fighting, Alexandria. It will not do you any good, but if it makes you feel better, go ahead."

"Arrogant, primieval ape," she sniffed, turning away before he could read her need of him in her eyes. She deliberately went to the telephone. "I believe you have Thomas's number?"

He reached around her, his arm brushing her shoulders, his scent enveloping her. Any of his kind would recognize his brand, would know she belonged to him just from his scent on her. The human, however, would never notice. Irritated by the thought, Aidan found the business card beneath the phone and handed it to her.

"Call him," he dared softly.

Her chin went up. She was human. She would be human. Even if she wasn't, this . . . this creature, whatever he was, would not rule her life. Defiantly she stabbed at the buttons on the phone.

To Alexandria's amazement, Thomas himself answered. It seemed so out of character. "Thomas? This is Alexandria Houton," she said hesitantly, not certain, now that she had him, what to say. "I hope it isn't too early to call."

"Alexandria! Thank God! I was beginning to think that

man had you locked up in a dungeon somewhere. Are you all right? Do you want me to come and get you?"

Thomas sat up, pushing at the hair falling across his forehead. The sheets had wound around him so tightly for a moment, he had to fight just to move.

"No, no, I'm fine. Well, still a bit shaky, and I have to rest a lot, but I'm doing much better. Thank you for the roses. They're beautiful." She was acutely aware of Aidan standing close to her, listening to every word, listening to the tone of her voice. She had an impulse to try for syrupy. The man had no right monitoring her personal conversations.

"I'm coming over, Alexandria. I have to see you." Thomas said it almost belligerently, determined not to be denied.

"I believe I have an interview with a couple of detectives this morning," she said in a gentle reprimand.

Beside her Aidan stirred restlessly. Her voice was far too soft for his liking. Far too sexy. She was a Carpathian now, with all the sensuality and the mesmerizing effect on humans of one born to his kind.

Aidan's subtle, possessive movement brought his body even closer, and she could smell his scent. It invaded her very being, sending liquid warmth pooling unexpectedly in her midsection. Alexandria hunched her shoulders and stepped away, backing up against the antique cherry-wood piece the phone rested on.

"I was so worried, Alexandria. And that strange man. How well do you know him?" Thomas had lowered his voice to a conspirator's whisper.

Alexandria was acutely aware that it did not matter how quietly Thomas spoke. Her own hearing was so sharp now that she could hear at great distances if she chose. It only stood to reason that Aidan's hearing would be even more intense and his ability to control it far better than hers. She felt color wash into her face.

"You don't know Aidan at all, Thomas. You barely know me. We only met for one dinner, and that was interrupted. Please don't say things against someone who has been a great friend to me." For some unknown reason, Thomas's slights against Aidan annoyed her, but it was the last thing she wanted Aidan to know.

"You're very young, Alexandria. You've probably never met a man of his caliber before. Believe me, he's way out of your league. He's likely very dangerous."

Her fingers tightened around the receiver until her knuckles whitened. *What did Ivan know? And, therefore, how much danger might Aidan be in?* Her teeth bit down hard on her lower lip. She really couldn't bear it if someone suspected the truth and . . . and drove a stake through his heart or something. She might not want to feel that way, she might even be betraying mankind, but she couldn't help herself. The idea of losing him was terrifying.

Aidan reached around her and gently covered her hand with his. In her mind danced the image of a shark with Thomas Ivan's white, practiced smile. Deliberately Aidan teased her with the image until she was forced to laugh.

"This is no laughing matter, Alexandria," Thomas said huffily. "I'm coming over to discuss this. You can't stay in that house with that man."

"I wanted to work for you, Thomas," she replied softly, "not have you dictate my personal life." She closed her eyes. She had wanted the job so much. She also wanted to be human, to live and breathe and function in a world she understood.

"I'm coming over," he said decisively.

Alexandria was left with a loud click and a dial tone. She glared up at Aidan. "Do I look like someone to push around?" she demanded as she banged down the phone. "Is *please order me around* tattooed on my forehead?"

"Let me see," Aidan said, leaning close. His mouth was inches from hers. "Hmm. Not at all. It says, *extremely kissable*."

She pushed at the wall of his chest but found him immovable. "Don't try your winning little ways with me, Savage. I've been told you're a dangerous man and that I'm way out of my league, whatever that means."

"How could I be dangerous?" His body was trapping hers with its heat, with its aggression. She ached for him so easily. "Am I dangerous?" His voice whispered over her lips like silk against her skin.

"If you don't get out of my way right this minute, I'm going to . . ." She pictured bringing up her knee hard and watching him writhe in pain on the floor. The image in her mind was as vivid as his shark's image had been.

Aidan leapt away from her, laughing as he did so. "You have a nasty little temper, Alexandria."

"Another annoying habit," she said smugly.

Chapter Eleven

There was something unnerving about the house. Thomas couldn't put his finger on it, couldn't find the exact word to describe it, but he wished he could. It wasn't just the owner. The house itself seemed alive, a silent sentinel watching him. If he could put this feeling onto computer screen, capture the images to depict the way the house lived and breathed, stared malevolently at him, he would be one of the wealthiest men in the world. There was something very wrong with the entire setup at Aidan Savage's, and he meant to get to the bottom of it.

The setting was dramatically beautiful, the house itself was architecturally perfect, yet he sensed some deeper, underlying monstrous being lurking there. He found himself thankful the usual early-morning fog wasn't present as he climbed the steps to the huge, ornate front door. Even the police car parked in the circular drive was oddly comforting. He knew the detectives didn't like him, but their presence gave him the sense of security he needed to face Aidan Savage.

Frankly, the man scared the hell out of him. It was his eyes. Savage had the disquieting, eerie, unblinking stare of a predator. There was power and intelligence there in that molten gold gaze, yet at times Thomas was certain the eyes had flashed with red sparks and glowed with a weird intensity. A few years back, for one of his games, Ivan had researched jungle cats—tigers, leopards, and the like—and he remembered how well cats could see in the night, a perfect adaptation for predators. Their large round eyes had huge pupils that closed down to slits in the light of day but widened dramatically in the darkness. And he vividly recalled their deadly stare preceding an attack.

Thomas shuddered and tried to shake off his feeling of dread as he stood before the door. His imagination was clearly working overtime. Savage was dangerous not because he was a night predator but because he was staking out Alexandria Houton as his territory, and Thomas Ivan intended to do the same. That was all. They were rivals for the same woman. Nothing sinister, nothing more. He had always had trouble keeping his imagination under control.

He stared at the intricate stained-glass panels in the door. They were beautiful, patterned with strange symbols and shapes. The more he studied the glass, the more he felt as if he were falling into it. Caught in it, like a fly in amber. That nameless dread began to build again, and for a moment he could barely catch his breath. To enter this house was to be trapped forever in an eternity of hell. The pattern began to move and change before his horrified stare. It wanted to draw him into its spiral, carry him into hell. His heart was pounding so loudly, his ears hurt.

Thomas nearly screamed when the door swung open, breaking the spell. Aidan Savage stared down at him from his superior height. The man was dressed casually in a faded jeans and a vee-necked shirt, but he looked at once strangely elegant yet wild and untamed, out of time and place, like some all-powerful tribal chieftain from times gone by. The shoulder-length hair, as golden as his eyes, added to the impression.

"Mr. Ivan." The voice was so perfectly pitched, it seeped into Thomas's heart and soul, coiling itself inside him like a living, breathing thing. "I am so pleased you could take the time to stop in and reassure Alexandria. I am certain your visit will ease her mind. She has been quite anxious that you might not hold the job for her."

Savage's solid weight blocked the entrance to the interior. His voice was pleasant, soothing, but the words stung slightly. It made Thomas a mere employer, nothing special to Alexandria Houton and certainly no threat to Savage's designs on her.

Thomas reached for his own voice. A smoldering anger began to burn in him, giving him the impetus he needed to deal with this man. He was Thomas Ivan. He owned his own company, was wealthy, famous, a force to be reckoned with. He was no coward to snivel on a doorstep. "I'm glad we could meet again under more auspicious circumstances." Smugly superior, he offered his hand.

The moment Savage gripped his fingers, Thomas winced at the man's enormous strength. Savage wasn't even trying, didn't even seem to notice his own casual power. Cursing silently, Thomas shook hands. And then Savage smiled. A gleam of white teeth. Strong. Sharp. No humor, no welcome. A predator's smile that never once warmed those strange, unblinking eyes.

"Do enter my home, Mr. Ivan," Aidan invited, stepping back to give him room.

And all at once entering that house was the last thing Thomas wanted to do. He actually stepped backward, a cold shiver of fear racing down his spine. Savage's mouth curved into a cruel yet almost sensual smile.

"What is it?" The voice, so calm, so smooth, like velvet, was taunting all the same.

The two detectives had been there for well over an hour, and in that time the demon in Aidan had been growing stronger and stronger. He had all but sprouted fangs as one of them did everything but beg for a date with Alexandria. Did she really need yet another suitor? He was going to have to post a sign on the lawn stating that all males courting Alexandria Houton did so at their own peril.

Alexandria walked the two detectives to the door, and at once Thomas Ivan forgot his fear. He couldn't take his eyes off her. She was hauntingly beautiful, more so than he remembered. Even the police officers were staring at her, mesmerized. Thomas choked back the jealous rage welling up out of nowhere, surprised by the intensity of his emotions. Under Savage's steady stare, he forced himself back under control.

Alexandria's face lit up when she saw him, and Thomas sent a triumphant grin Savage's way. He entered the house quickly, pushed past the detectives, and clasped both of Alexandria's hands in his.

Something deep within Aidan coiled dangerously at the sight of her hands in Thomas Ivan's. His breath stopped. His heart ceased to beat. The demon within stirred and roared for release, fangs exploded into his mouth, and the red haze of the beast flamed in his eyes. As Thomas leaned in close, intending to kiss her cheek, Aidan fought for control so that he could casually wave a hand, directing a flurry of dust spores to whirl and dance beneath Ivan's nose. As Ivan inhaled, he began to sneeze violently, the spasms wracking his entire body.

Alexandria stepped away from him and raised an inquiring eyebrow at Aidan. When he looked far too innocent for her liking, she glared at him. It was hard enough for her to deal with the two bewitched policemen. They seemed oddly mesmerized by her voice, her eyes, her every movement. They had been so solicitous of her, so careful of what they said, so worried about her health, that she was beginning to suspect that, along with the exchange of blood, Aidan had somehow shared his sex appeal with her. And she definitely didn't want it.

Aidan showed the detectives out the door, exercising great restraint not to throw them out bodily. He had not anticipated their human reaction to Alexandria's haunting beauty. He certainly had not anticipated his own reaction to their wanting her. He could smell their arousal, read their thoughts, and he wanted them out of his sight before he did something unforgivable.

Something stirred in his mind like the brush of butterfly wings. *Aidan?* Startled, he glanced at Alexandria. She was frowning at him. *Stop being so mean to Thomas.*

Joy surged through him. She had voluntarily merged her mind with his and was communicating in the way of a life-mate. He smiled, completely unrepentant. *Stop holding his hands.*

You're being childish. I am not holding his hands.

And stop letting him kiss you.

He didn't get to kiss me. Aidan, stop. I mean it.

He raised a hand, and the dust dispersed. Embarrassed, Thomas turned away from Alexandria, wondering what had happened. He never had sneezing fits. Never. Why would he suddenly have one now? Was it somehow this house and those damned unblinking amber eyes?

Alexandria was smiling at him with her lush mouth and inviting dimples. "Please come and sit down, Thomas. I'm sorry you were inconvenienced by my illness." Her voice whispered over his skin, and he felt a shaft of desire pierce him. She was dressed simply in torn, faded jeans and a pearl-buttoned cardigan. She was barefoot. Yet she looked incredibly sexy. Thomas had always preferred sophisticated, high-fashion women, yet he couldn't tear his gaze from Alexandria's unpolished beauty.

The housekeeper entered carrying a tray with warm croissants and cream puffs and a silver coffeepot. Unexpectedly, she smiled a welcome to Thomas. "Mr. Ivan, your flowers have certainly brightened up our home."

He settled on the couch complacently. He was winning over the housekeeper. Feeling particularly charming, he bestowed a slight nod and a brief smile in her general direction.

Aidan caught Alexandria by one slender arm and guided her firmly to a high-backed chair facing Thomas. After seating her, he remained behind the chair, his hands resting lightly on her shoulders. "Alexandria must rest soon, Mr. Ivan. She is still quite weak. The interview with the detectives was longer than we expected, and quite hard on her stamina." It was a reprimand, a reminder that it was Thomas Ivan who had forced Alexandria, as fragile as she was, into talking with the police.

"Yes, of course. I'll be brief. I merely wanted to see that she was all right and to discuss our working arrangements." Thomas accepted the cup of coffee Marie handed him, then gazed up at the man standing so protectively behind Alexandria's chair. "Once I lay out my expectations for this project, it's really Alexandria's genius that has to take over. The story line is unique and very frightening, we have top actors willing to read the roles for us, and we intend to create a product unrivaled in today's market. Everything is in place, but I need the perfect artwork."

"That's so exciting, Thomas," Alexandria said, acutely aware of Aidan's hands on her shoulders. His thumb was stroking slowly, sensually over her clavicle.

You are using that syrupy voice, Aidan pointed out wickedly, his voice brushing her mind like the stroke of his thumb. The teasing note in it set her heart to melting. "You mean you need Alexandria's artwork."

Mind your own business. I'm deliberately flirting a little. You have heard of the concept, haven't you? In fact, I think you wrote the book on it.

We will have none of that nonsense, his voice whispered in her mind, his laughter soft and inviting.

Alexandria glanced up at his face. It was a mask, his golden eyes still on Thomas. Yet she had the sensation of such intense intimacy, it was almost as if they had made love. Her feelings for Aidan were strong and growing more so with every conversational exchange, with every blood exchange, with every merging of their minds. At the realization, fear welled up in her, sharp and ugly.

Breathe, piccola. *You always forget to breathe.* Aidan sounded amused, mockingly male.

Alexandria chose to ignore the taunt, instead sending Thomas a high-powered smile that jerked his head up and set his body tightening with urges and demands.

Thomas was intensely aware of Savage standing like some Greek god behind Alexandria's chair, with that damned unblinking stare and his hands on her shoulders as if he owned her. That deadly stare, never once moving from

Ivan's face, was completely unnerving. Thomas had the feeling Aidan could read his lustful thoughts, his every intention. He took a sip of coffee to calm himself.

"Perhaps we could go out for breakfast, Alexandria," he suggested silkily, deliberately challenging Aidan's hold on her, "and discuss the details."

That stare never wavered. "Alexandria is unable to leave at this time. The doctors were very specific as to her resting hours, were they not, Alexandria? Perhaps that should be taken into consideration when you are deciding if Alexandria can do the work you need." Aidan sounded the same—quiet, mild, almost expressionless, as if none of this meant a thing to him and Thomas was no threat of any consequence.

Yet Alexandria stiffened at his words and would have interrupted had Savage's hands not tightened, holding her still.

Thomas noticed with satisfaction the rise in tension between them. The chemistry, the intensity between the two, was unmistakable, and he detested it, knowing that it threatened his relationship with her. But Alexandria wasn't happy with it, and that was good. Ivan smiled his easy, charming smile and leaned forward.

"Alexandria has the job no matter what the restrictions on her hours. I have the contract with me and am prepared to meet any price." Take that, Savage, he thought. Don't think you can push me aside so easily.

Shark attack! Look out, cara, *he is swimming toward you.* Aidan deliberately lightened the mood between Alexandria and himself.

Alexandria glanced back at Aidan and saw his calm mask. The golden eyes never wavered from Thomas's face, but in her mind she could hear the echo of his soft laughter. In spite of her annoyance, she wanted to laugh with him.

"I'm pleased to hear you say that, Thomas," she answered in her most syrupy voice, deliberately trying to annoy Aidan to pay him back. "The doctors are being extremely careful, and as I have the responsibility of my younger brother, I need to be cautious with my health."

"Follow their instructions to the letter," Thomas replied, leaning even closer. "I wouldn't want a repeat of this episode. It scared me to death." He made it personal, his hand reaching out to rest on her knee.

For some reason, his touch repelled her. The coffee cup balanced in his other hand suddenly shifted, and the hot liquid spilled over his hand and wrist. With a cry he clattered the cup onto the tray, in the process managing to drag his arm across the cream puffs. The sleeve of his immaculate suit came away covered in goo.

"Oh, Thomas." Alexandria tried to jump to her feet to help him, but Aidan's hands kept her in place. *I know you did that, you Neanderthal! Don't for one minute try your innocent act, because it won't work. You're deliberately embarrassing the man.* She accused Aidan of it hotly, working hard to avoid any humor welling to the surface.

He can keep his damned hands to himself. Aidan was calmly unrepentant in the face of her wrath.

You keep touching me whenever the mood strikes you. That's rather like the pot calling the kettle black. Stop provoking him. I want this job.

The idiot is so besotted with you, he would stand on his head if you demanded it. The job is not going anywhere.

No one says besotted anymore. She couldn't think of a scathing enough retort. Aidan acted so completely without remorse. To add to her seething anger, she could hear that unmistakable note of amusement in his black velvet voice.

"I'm sorry, Alexandria." Thomas was mortified. It was those damn amber eyes watching his every move, waiting, just waiting. It was eerie and disturbing, that predator's stare. He felt like a rabbit, prey for a wolf. Then he again cursed his own imagination. He gave Alexandria his most winning smile, trying to ignore the man standing behind her chair. Savage gave an impression of indolence, but Thomas wasn't deceived. Whoever this man was, he was a force to be reckoned with. He had staked a claim on Alexandria and was clearly warning Thomas off.

"Don't worry about it, Thomas. The tray was too close. In any case, the damage is to your suit, not me."

Alexandria's voice was so soothing and peaceful, seeming to surround him, relaxing him.

"Alexandria is tired, Mr. Ivan. I must insist she rest now." Aidan's golden stare was unwavering. "I trust you are now satisfied I am not holding her prisoner in my dungeon." He paused. "And in the future, Mr. Ivan, if you wish to know something about me or my staff, I assure you, a private investigator is a waste of your money. I will be happy to answer any questions you have." His smile was amicable, but his powerful white teeth gave Thomas the illusion of being stalked by a wolf. There was absolutely no warmth in those golden, unnerving eyes.

Thomas rose to his feet, hating the fear swirling deep within his gut and the humiliation of being summarily dismissed by the man under the guise of concern for Alexandria's health. But he could be patient. She would be working with him. They would be alone, and there wasn't a thing Aidan Savage could do about it.

"I regret any inconvenience my concern for Alexandria caused you. I was very worried about her well-being."

Ignoring Aidan's hands on her shoulders, Alexandria rose with him. "We understand. Although, I assure you, Aidan is a good man and would never harm Joshua or me. You had absolutely nothing to worry about."

Thomas looked over her head to directly challenge Aidan. "Oh, I'm sure you're right about that." He understood the bastard, but Alexandria was far too innocent to realize just what kind of a man Savage really was. There had to be skeletons in his closet, a body or two in his past. Thomas intended to find every one of them. Deliberately he smiled at the man, a cool, intentional threat. "Mr. Savage and I understand one another quite well, Alex. I will call you later."

She was following him to the door. As he paused on the front porch, he turned and raised a hand to touch her cheek, certain her skin would be as soft as it looked. For a moment his heart seemed to stop, and his breath caught in his throat. No woman had ever affected him as she did. But even as he reached out to cup her face, he heard an angry buzzing, and a huge black bee dive-bombed him from out of nowhere.

With an oath, Thomas jumped back, swatting ineffectually at the persistent insect. As his left foot came down he turned his ankle and nearly fell.

Alexandria's hand covered her mouth in horror. *Aidan, stop it right now!*

I cannot imagine what you are accusing me of, Aidan returned innocently from the living room. His voice was unconcerned, virtuous, and placid.

Thomas fled down the driveway to the safety of his car. Damn the man, damn the house, and damn every awkward thing that had happened! Savage was not going to drive him away forever! From the sanctuary of his vehicle, he waved to Alexandria, happy to see that she looked somewhat distressed for him. He almost wished he had allowed the bee to sting him; she might have insisted on nursing him back to health.

Alexandria shut the door with more force than was necessary. "You are the most infuriating man in the world," she accused him.

Aidan raised an eyebrow. "One of my more annoying yet endearing qualities." His slow, sexy smile was teasing.

Alexandria nearly lost her train of thought, distracted by the melting warmth that smile caused. Abruptly she caught herself, straightening her shoulders and summoning as much anger as she could manage under the circumstances. "Nothing about you is endearing. That was so . . . so—" She broke off, searching for the right word, but her vocabulary failed her. Nobody should have his smile.

"Brilliant?" he prompted, helping her out.

"Insensitive comes to mind. *Childish.* Are you going to behave this way every time he comes here?"

Her hands were on her slender hips, her sapphire eyes flashing sparks. He wanted to kiss her. His golden eyes warmed, and his gaze dropped to her mouth. Instantly her body responded to that dark, sensual look. She backed away from him hastily, her hands up for protection. "Don't you dare, you escapee from an insane asylum."

"Do not dare what?" His voice was soft, mesmerizing, seductive.

She could feel the touch of it like fingers stroking her skin. She ached with it, went liquid with it. "Just stay across the room from me. I mean it, Aidan. You're lethal. You ought to be locked up."

"But I have not done anything." He smiled and moved slowly toward her. "Yet."

"Marie!" In a panic, Alexandria called out as loudly as she could.

Aidan laughed as the housekeeper hurried in. *Little coward, run while you can.* Although they were half a room apart and Marie was squarely between them, Alexandria felt the brush of his fingers on her skin, her face, her throat. They trailed lower, feather-light, to touch the aching swell of her breast before the sensation was gone.

"What is it, Alexandria?" Marie asked, her hands on her hips, glaring at Aidan.

He held up a placating hand, laughing. "I am innocent. I was a perfect gentleman to her visitor."

"He spilled Thomas's coffee, made him sneeze, smeared whipped cream over him, and chased him with a bee," Alexandria accused. While Marie struggled to keep a straight face, Alexandria delivered the final outrage. "And he was going to wither my flowers."

"Aidan!" Marie reprimanded sharply, but there was laughter in her eyes.

Aidan was really laughing now, his head thrown back, his golden eyes glowing, his face transformed, almost boyish with mischief. Neither woman could resist the pure joy, the fun he was experiencing for the first time in centuries. It made Marie want to cry with happiness, and it was an aphrodisiac to Alexandria, knowing she wielded so much power over such a creature.

"She is not telling the truth. Ivan spilled his own coffee and dipped his arm in the cream puffs. I was nowhere near him. And the bee probably just happened by. How can I be responsible for an insect's attraction to that man?" He looked wide-eyed and blameless. "As to the flowers, I was only glowering at them because she was acting so silly over the damned things."

"Silly?" Alexandria echoed. "I'll show you silly, you *savage* beast." She started toward him purposefully, but Marie held up a hand.

"Now, now, children. Joshua is up, and we wouldn't want him to find the two of you fighting."

"We wouldn't want him to find out his hero has feet of clay," Alexandria corrected, glaring at Aidan.

He moved toward her then, a deliberate stalking, gliding around Marie in his silent, fluid way, making Alexandria's heart pound frantically in anticipation. His perfect mouth was curved in a taunting smile. Hastily she stepped backward, tripped, and would have fallen if he hadn't reached out a hand and caught her.

"Running away, little coward?" he whispered softly, teasingly, dragging her close into the shelter of his arms.

Marie discreetly left the room, deserting the younger woman to her fate, hiding a grin behind her hand as she went.

"Aidan." There was an ache in Alexandria's voice. She didn't mean for it to be there. It was just that he was so close, the heat of his body enveloping her. His mouth was inches from hers, their hearts matching the same desperate rhythm.

His thumb brushed her lower lip in a light caress, sending a flame shooting through her soul. His golden eyes held hers as he lowered his head, his mouth finding hers with unhurried hunger, slowly savoring every inch of the silken interior, exploring, coaxing. His hands slid to her hips, his fingers tightening, pulling her against him, pinning her softness against his hard, demanding body.

There was a trace of resistance in her, as if she were still fighting for survival, her sense of self-preservation warning her she was in danger. But the bond between them was growing with their proximity, with each blood exchange, with the explosive chemistry between them. Already her mind sought his; her soul reached for him. Even her heart was softening, becoming willing. Her body cried out to his. Only her head, so stubborn, prevented him from claiming his rights as her lifemate.

His mouth moved over hers, deepening the kiss, sweeping aside her objections on a wave of fire, dragging her deeper and deeper into a world of sensuality, of the night, of all that went with the demands of their blood.

"Holy macaroni!" Joshua's voice was awed and disgusted at the same time. "Do you like that gross stuff, Aidan?"

Alexandria jerked herself out of Aidan's arms and rubbed at her mouth, trying desperately to regain her breath.

Aidan ruffled the boy's blond curls. "Yes, Joshua, I like that stuff, but only with your sister. She is special, you understand. Someone like Alexandria only comes along once in a few hundred centuries."

Joshua was regarding his sister with a speculative grin. There was a devilish light in his eyes. "She seemed to like it, too."

"Well, I didn't," Alexandria denied adamantly. "Aidan Savage is a jerk, Joshua. A big jerk."

The grin spread. "She did like it," Joshua stated. "You must kiss pretty good, Aidan. She never lets anyone kiss her 'cept me." He turned his face up for Alexandria's kiss, his little arms circling her neck as she bent to do so. "Nobody else better kiss you either, 'cept Aidan and me."

"That is the way it should be," Aidan said complacently. "We will have to be especially vigilant now that Mr. Ivan has hired her to do his drawings. He has that look about him. I would be willing to bet he wants to kiss Alexandria."

"Don't worry, Aidan. I won't let him," Joshua said staunchly. "If she does go to work for that guy, I'll follow them everywhere and make him stay away from her."

"That would be just the thing, Josh." The approval in Aidan's voice had the little boy beaming proudly.

"I can't believe," Alexandria interrupted, "that you are having this conversation with a six-year-old." She hugged her little brother tightly to her and returned the warmth she had been missing. He had been too long away from her. But not so long that he couldn't still argue with her.

"I'm almost seven."

"It's still inappropriate."

Joshua smirked at Aidan. "Don't worry. She always says

that when she doesn't know what else to say and wants me to shut up."

Aidan reached down and one-handedly lifted the boy up to his shoulder. "That is because she liked my kisses and is a bit flustered. We will have to forgive her this time."

"Oh, I see how it's going to be." Alexandria glared at the two of them, but her dimple appeared despite her best effort at ferocity. "You guys are planning to gang up on me."

They looked at each other, exchanging a smile. "Yes," they said at the same time.

Alexandria felt her heart turn over. Joshua had never had anyone but her to watch over him. He had never trusted anyone else, never looked up to anyone else. She couldn't help but be happy that Aidan was taking such an interest in him. Aidan was stealing her heart with his gentleness. Joshua was her world. She could see Aidan's genuine affection for the boy, could see that they were developing a real rapport. And she felt tears welling up in her eyes at the sight of the two of them together.

"Come on, big fellow, we need to get you some breakfast. Mr. Ivan left wearing his food on his clothes, the man's so clumsy. You should have seen him," Aidan informed the boy.

Joshua giggled. "He spilled his food?"

Aidan glided easily toward the kitchen, as if Joshua's added weight was incidental. "He was a complete fool. Even Alexandria had a difficult time trying not to laugh, not that she would admit it. She pretends she likes him," he whispered, knowing perfectly well she could hear his every word.

Alexandria trailed along after them, uncertain whether Aidan needed another kick in the shins or whether she should just act dignified and ignore him. It was a difficult choice.

I can read your mind. His voice in her mind was like a physical caress.

Her eyes flashed fire at him. She *would* kick him, the first chance she got. He knew exactly how he affected her, the cad. *Thousand-year-old playboy. Hound dog. Swine.* He deserved to be kicked. Hard.

187

"I never spill my food, Aidan," Joshua confided solemnly. "At least not anymore. When I was baby I did."

"Sisters do not have the same effect on their brothers as they do on grown men. Believe me, Alexandria could make me spill my food."

Joshua shook his blond curls. "No way, Aidan."

"It is true, Joshua. I do not want to admit it, but she definitely could. Scary, is it not, the effect women have on men?"

"Why? She's just a girl." He rubbed his nose and grinned at his sister. "And she's always telling us what to do."

"Right now, I'm going to tell you to eat your breakfast and get ready for school." Alexandria aimed to sound tough, though she was trying not to laugh. Joshua was far too precocious for his own good. "I'll walk you."

Aidan turned slowly and regarded her with his steady golden gaze. Alexandria ignored him, all too aware that he objected to her going out. But she was determined to be assertive. She was not going to change her entire life because of him. The more she allowed Aidan to convince her of things she could and couldn't do, the more she was drawn into his world.

"I'm going," she reiterated firmly.

"You think," he said softly, lowering Joshua to his feet. He ruffled the boy's silky curls. "Someone has to take care of you. Joshua and I are determined to look after you whether you like it or not."

Joshua grinned up at her, innocent, boyish, unaware of any undercurrents. "Because you're sick, Alex. You know, like you always take care of me when I'm sick." He slid into a high-backed oak chair. "Once I was really, really sick, and she never left me, even to go to sleep. I remember that, Alex."

"You had pneumonia," she affirmed softly, reaching down to touch his shoulder affectionately.

There was such tenderness in her expression, Aidan turned away to prevent himself from pulling her into his arms. She was struggling to stay human, and he really couldn't blame her for it. Her entire world had been turned upside down. For someone who viewed him as a fictional creature, the legendary, horrifying vampire, she was doing quite well.

"Marie cooked pancakes this morning," Joshua said. "I told her I wanted them because they're your favorite. She made funny faces out of them."

The blow was almost physical, a punch in the gut. Alexandria's paled, and she suddenly found herself examining the immaculate kitchen floor. Everything reminded her of the terrible price she paid for remaining alive. There had to be a way to change back. If a vampire or a . . . a Carpathian could bring her across, then modern medicine must have an antidote. She would secretly do research, find a way to take care of Joshua by herself, without the help of Marie or Stefan, and certainly without Aidan. He was becoming far too indispensable for her liking.

She sensed his golden eyes on her, knew he was watching her closely, could feel the exact moment when his mind reached out to hers. She deliberately resisted, wanting to exert her independence.

His laughter was soft and taunting. "Are you going to wear shoes when we take Joshua to school, or do you plan to escort him barefoot?" he asked softly, unconcerned with her defiance.

"I don't think you need to come, Aidan. I'm quite capable of taking Josh to school all by myself. You have to remember, I've been doing it for some time now."

He reached out and tugged a lock of her hair. "True, *piccola*, but that is not the point. I had to research the school very quickly, and while Stefan checked it out for me, I really have not had a chance to evaluate it for myself. This will be a good opportunity to do so."

"You're guarding me." She made it an accusation.

He shrugged lazily. He saw no reason to deny it. "That, too."

She flashed him a resentful look. All at once tears were burning behind her eyes, and that only made her more angry. "I don't need a guard."

"I know better."

She caught him by the arm. "Joshua, hurry and finish your breakfast, then brush your teeth. Aidan and I are going to talk. Come into the living room when you're ready to leave."

"Okay, Alex," Joshua replied.

Though her small fingers wrapped barely halfway around his powerful wrist, she dragged Aidan out of the kitchen. "You can't keep me prisoner, Aidan. And I know you aren't guarding me to keep me safe. What's out there that would hurt me? You said yourself vampires can't be out past the dawn. I can go with Joshua alone."

"You have no idea what you are facing. The light, even the early-morning light, will hurt your eyes, and the sun will burn your skin. You will have to wear especially dark glasses and get used to the sun gradually. As your lifemate, I am responsible for your health and safety, and I must protect you at all times, even from yourself. If you wish to accompany Joshua to his school, than I will go also."

"You're making certain I return. Your coming with us has nothing to do with Joshua's school or my safety. You think I'm going to take Josh and run for the nearest airport. If I had any brains at all, I would. You can just stay here, Aidan, and let me take care of my brother. I've been doing it for years." Her blue eyes were flashing at him, fiery with determination and defiance.

Aidan allowed a slow, masculine smile of amusement to soften his mouth. "And a very good job you have done, Alexandria. Joshua is a fine boy. He has stolen the hearts of all of us who reside here. But I would be remiss in not escorting the boy at least once to his new school. Apparently he has had problems in the past with a bully or two, and he made it clear that a show of force could be very helpful in establishing better relationships. I will have Stefan bring the limo around."

"You aren't listening to me, Aidan." But he had successfully defused her anger. She wanted Joshua to be happy. She had been only too aware of his troubles at the old school. If he wanted the big car and a few big adults around to back him up and make a strong first impression, then who was she to deny him?

"I don't think I like you very much, Aidan. You always seem to get your way," she capitulated reluctantly.

He ruffled her hair as if she were Joshua. "Get used to it, *piccola*. Everyone obeys me."

"I'm not afraid of you the way they are."

"Perhaps not in the same way, Alexandria, but you are most definitely afraid. Otherwise you would not try to run away from me, from us, the way you do." The teasing note in his voice was doing things to her insides she didn't want to acknowledge. She had to escape. It was the only way. The only way.

Marie stuck her head in the doorway. "The phone, Alexandria. Your young man again." She winked. "He is eager, this one."

"He is not Alexandria's young man, Marie," Aidan said, annoyed. "He's old enough to be her father."

Marie only laughed as she sailed back toward the kitchen, ignoring his bad mood.

"Hello?" With deliberate malice, Alexandria sounded as sweet as she could as she took Thomas Ivan's call. "Oh, Thomas!" Her eyes were on Aidan as she gushed the other man's name. "The theater? Tonight? It's short notice, and I don't know if I'm quite ready for a night out."

Aidan could easily hear the suave, persuasive voice on the other end of the line. "We would just sit quietly, Alex, and I'd bring you straight home. An early night."

She closed her eyes. A night away from all the tension. A night in the real world. Her world. It was appealing. And by accepting she would also learn whether she was a prisoner or not. "That sounds wonderful, Thomas. But straight home afterward—I don't want the doctor yelling at me." She looked at Aidan when she said it.

Aidan raised an eyebrow, but his features otherwise remained expressionless granite. For some reason, that made her heart beat faster than if he had looked annoyed. Aidan Savage was planning something. She didn't know what, but she was certain of it.

She hung up the phone. "I'm going to the theater," she said defiantly.

Aidan nodded. "So I heard. Do you think it wise?"

She shrugged. "I'm well enough. My health appears to be back to normal."

"I am not concerned with your health at this moment, Alexandria," he said softly, "only his."

Chapter Twelve

"Aidan, may I have a puppy?" Joshua, sandwiched between Aidan and Alexandria in the car, carefully avoided looking up at his sister.

Alexandria stiffened resentfully, her chin up. Aidan's hand slid along the back of the seat and rested lightly on the nape of her neck. His fingers curled around the slim column and began a slow massage. "Joshua, it is fun to tease Alexandria that I am the big boss and can overrule her, but we both know the truth. Alexandria is your sister and your guardian. Why would you ask me such a question?"

"Ah, Aidan." Joshua stared down at his hands. "She always says no. Don't you, Alex? She says it's too hard to find an apartment that will allow a puppy. But now we live with you. A puppy could live there, don't you think?" He looked up hopefully. "Your house is really big, and I'd take care of it, except when I'm at school."

"Well, Joshua, I do not know," Aidan answered seriously, giving the matter consideration. "Puppies can be a significant amount of trouble. Marie and Stefan have many duties, keeping the household running. To be fair, they would have to be consulted also. This is not a decision to be made lightly. In any case, before you take the issue further, I think discussing it with your sister should be your primary starting point."

Joshua shrugged and grinned engagingly up at Alexandria. "She already said we could have one if we ever found a place that would let us."

Alexandria tried to focus, but her eyes were burning even behind the extremely dark glasses Aidan had insisted she wear. The car windows, too, were darkly tinted to help block out the sun, but it still felt as if a thousand needles were stabbing at her when the light touched her face. It was terrifying. And it meant that once again Aidan had been telling her the truth.

"We haven't been in Aidan's home long enough to know if we're even going to stay, Joshua." She ignored the fingers tightening around her neck. "And it isn't fair to saddle Marie with such a job so early. Let's wait and see what happens. I'll be starting work soon, and we're all just settling in. I'm not saying no. I'm just saying we should wait a little bit longer, okay?"

"But, Alex . . ." There was a whining note in Joshua's voice.

"I think Alexandria is being very fair, Joshua." Aidan's tone brooked no argument, and Joshua subsided immediately.

She was oddly grateful to Aidan. Ordinarily Joshua would have tried to wear her down. And right now she was so tired it seemed difficult to think or function properly. Her eyes were streaming, and the muted sunlight was searing her arms and face. She wanted to cry, to scream against the fate that had done this to her. All along she had hoped Aidan wasn't really telling her the truth. That he merely had some devious reason for trying to convince her to believe him.

We will be home soon, cara. The words moved through her mind, wrapping her in velvet and warmth like the comfort of his arms.

"I can't accept this." She said it aloud, oblivious to the fact that Joshua sat between them, all ears. "I just can't, Aidan." It was a measure of her state of mind that she had said anything that might upset Joshua. She was always so careful around him.

Aidan's hand slid lower down her back, tangling in her

silky hair, linking them together. "Do not worry so. All will be well," he said, easily smoothing over the moment.

The car pulled to a stop, and Stefan opened the door on Aidan's side. Instantly unfiltered sunlight poured in, a streak of heat and light, and Alexandria knew immediately that Stefan had been instructed to open Aidan's door rather than her own. Aidan, as always, was protecting her from her own folly. Even with his large frame blocking out most of the light, throwing a protective shadow over her, she clenched her teeth against the burning sensation. With her eyes closed behind the dark glasses, she kissed the top of Joshua's head. "Have a good day, Josh. See you tonight." She was astonished that she could sound so normal.

"Will you be there when I get home?" he asked anxiously. He still hated letting her out of his sight, still feared he would lose her. Lately, the feeling had crept into his dreams—nightmares, really—that Alexandria was gone far from him forever. He wrapped his arms around her tightly and buried his face on her shoulder.

"What is it, Josh?" At once, her own fears and physical pain were swept aside so that she could comfort him.

"Nothing bad is going to happen to you, is it?" His anxiety was in his voice, in the tautness of his small body.

Alexandria wanted to answer him, to reassure him, but the words caught in her throat and refused to come out. Only a tiny sound escaped, of something between terror and pain.

"I will be with Alexandria while you are at school, Joshua," Aidan said softly, the smooth, easy pitch of his voice so pure, it was impossible not to believe him. "I will never allow anything or anyone to harm her. You have my word on that. And even if she is resting when you get home, she will be up in the evening to be with you."

In his sister's arms, Joshua visibly relaxed, and Aidan patted the boy's head, a rush of affection unexpectedly washing over him. Joshua was wrapping himself around his heart.

But behind the dark glasses, Aidan's eyes were restless, searching, an uneasiness growing in him. He was able to tolerate the light of morning, but the price of being Carpathian, a creature of the darkness, would eventually steal up on him and claim his great strength.

"I'll be home at two-thirty," Joshua announced like a little adult, and he kissed Alexandria one last time.

"Your lunch," Stefan reminded him, handing the boy the backpack Marie had purchased for him a few days earlier.

"Thanks, Stefan," Joshua called as he ran after a boy who had already become his friend. "Jeff! Hey! Wait up."

Alexandria tried to watch him run, but the light nearly blinded her, like needles piercing her pupils, making them water continually. She had no option but to close her eyes tightly. She drew her knees up and huddled miserably against the back seat. Aidan shifted, a mere rustling on the rich leather, but she could feel the warmth and comfort of his solid frame beside her. Still, she didn't want his comfort. She didn't want anything to do with him. He had promised Joshua that he would look after her, that she would always be there for the boy, but she couldn't face living the life of a creature existing off the blood of others. No sun. No day. No real sharing of Joshua's life. She groaned softly and covered her face with her hands.

Stefan shut the door, blocking out the terrible light, and Aidan's arm circled her slender shoulders. "It will not be like this for all time, *cara*."

"It's not even nine o'clock in the morning. The sun is barely up yet." Sobs were trying to push past the lump in her throat.

"Your skin must become accustomed to daylight slowly." She felt the brush of his mouth on the top of her head.

Stefan started the car.

"Wait," Aidan commanded, and Stefan obeyed instantly, turning in his seat in inquiry. Aidan remained silent, scanning the surrounding area, a slight frown touching his mouth. "Perhaps we could use the services of Vinnie del Marco and Rusty. Please get them here immediately, and instruct them to remain with Joshua until he is safe within the walls of our home. Arrange for one of their associates to remain with Marie as she goes about her business, and please ensure that she postpones as many errands as possible." His voice was even and calm, without alarm, yet it frightened Alexandria.

"What is it?" she demanded. Stefan was asking no questions. Obviously he was well aware of the significance of Aidan's orders. "Tell me. Joshua's my brother. Is he in some kind of danger?"

Aidan's arm tightened around her as the car pulled away from the school, preventing her from leaping from the moving vehicle in an attempt to get back to Joshua. Alexandria struggled, but he was enormously strong. "It will be taken care of."

"You said vampires can't take the dawn! Who else would hurt him? He's just a little boy, Aidan. Bring him back to the house!" Her voice was veering out of control, bordering on hysteria.

"Joshua needs to live a normal life. Nothing will harm him. Vinnie and Rusty, very reliable bodyguards, will protect him. Joshua is not like us, Alexandria. He remains in the world of humans. We must return to the house and the sleeping chamber until the sun begins to sink."

She hated his voice. So gentle, so compelling, mesmerizing her into doing anything he wanted. So reasonable, while she was out of control. He appeared not to notice her struggles, her hysteria. He made her feel her protests were childish, her behavior unreasonable. She took a deep breath and fought to regain control. "Let go, Aidan. I'm all right now."

"I think I will hold you just a bit longer, *piccola*. I am in your mind, and I know that you seek to deceive both of us with your false composure. Relax, now, just breathe with me, and you will see that I have taken care of everything. Joshua will be safe with the arrangements I have made."

"I don't think you quite understand," she enunciated distinctly. "I am Joshua's sister. I am the one to decide what is safe for him or not. I want him with me."

"He cannot be with you, Alexandria. It is impossible," Aidan said patiently. His thumb found the frantic pulse at her throat and gently stroked it. "Joshua will remain in school."

"It isn't your affair. I want him home."

"Do you think arguing with me is going to change what is? You are what you are, *cara mia*. There is nothing that can be done." When she tried to move away from him, his arm prevented her escape.

"This arrangement is not going to work, Aidan. I refuse to allow you to dictate what I can or can't do with Joshua. It isn't your business." Furious, she strained harder to get away from him, but she was beginning to feel so very tired.

Aidan cradled her head against his chest, his hand wrapped around her throat, her life's pulse beating into his palm. "There is no way for you to live apart from me, Alexandria, and in your heart you know it is true. Perhaps that is why you struggle so desperately. You are not yet ready to surrender your freedom into my keeping."

"I hate you." He didn't understand at all. From a very early age, she had been forced to take control of situations. She was used to it now. Liked it. She was good at it. Having someone else dictate her actions, tell her what she could or couldn't do, was terrifying. And she feared that Joshua was slowly but surely being taken from her.

She made herself go limp, and she did what Aidan said. Breathed in. Breathed out. She felt the familiar push at her mind and tried to resist it. But even that was not something she could control any longer. He was too familiar with her blocks, her defenses. She blanked her mind, picturing a chalkboard and erasing everything that came across it.

Cara, *trust me a little longer. I know what is best for Joshua. He will have to learn to face some things on his own, just as Marie and Stefan and their children have had to do. Bodyguards will ensure that he is safe.*

She did not respond. Where had her life gone? How had things gotten so crazy? So out of control? Perhaps Aidan had simply hypnotized her, and all the things that were happening were merely tricks her mind was playing on her. Or the truth could be even worse. If he was a vampire, if vampires existed, and the legends and tales were true, he could make her his slave. Make her do anything. She had to find out if Aidan spoke the truth or if she was under some spell.

She feared now that she had stayed because every time his

golden eyes rested on her with possession and need, she had melted inside, had wanted him, wanted someone to feel that intensity for her. Sex. Had she allowed him to try to separate Joshua from her for sex? God, she hated herself. Hated what she had become. She needed to find a doctor. A psychiatrist. None of this could possibly be real. She belonged in a padded cell. She needed help. Desperately.

The car pulled into the garage, but it was still not dark enough for her vulnerable eyes. Stefan opened her door, holding out a hand to help her. She took it meekly, determined to hide her intended defiance. She could feel Aidan's golden gaze, his all-seeing eyes probing her face beneath her dark glasses, but he didn't say anything.

She hurried into the house, and the relief from the sunlight was instantaneous. The heat searing her skin was gone, and the needles stabbing at her eyes disappeared. She realized that the heavy drapes were pulled, darkening the interior. Biting down on her lower lip, she made her way through the house, uncertain where to go, which way to turn. She finally reached the huge front entryway, yet she could not go out. Exhausted and in despair, she collapsed by the door and wrapped her arms defensively around her upraised knees. She was terrified for her own sanity.

In the kitchen Aidan hesitated, wanting to follow her yet oddly uncertain, suddenly afraid for her.

Marie and Stefan exchanged a look of anxiety. Aidan never showed signs of indecision, of uncertainty. Alexandria had shaken his self-possession. And they, better than anyone, knew just how dangerous he could be without his vigilant self-discipline, his taut self-control. "Aidan, perhaps if I talked to her," Marie ventured.

"She is so frightened of me, she cannot even trust her own mind, her senses. She knows in her heart that we are one, that I would never harm her, but still she refuses, in her mind, to acknowledge it. She thinks perhaps she is deranged."

"Most people could never accept what you are demanding of her, Aidan," Marie counseled softly. "She is young and innocent, not a worldly woman. Her life has been very narrow. Joshua is her reason for living. She fears him slipping away from her. She needs to feel in control of something."

His golden eyes slashed at her. "What are you saying?"

"You are very dominating. You command people. You make all the decisions. Alexandria is still struggling just to accept what has happened to her. You, better than any of us, know this, yet you still demand she do exactly as you wish at all times."

He shoved a hand through his tawny mane. "I have given her more leeway than I have ever given anyone. You do not understand the demands of a lifemate. I can barely manage to think straight. I need relief, Marie, as crass as that sounds. The beast in me grows stronger each day. I do not know how long I can successfully wrestle him down."

"You are that beast, Aidan," Marie said severely. "Alex is a child. A terrified child. And she has good reason to be. Give her the time she needs to adjust."

"What of the others seeking her? And there are others. At least two more. You read the papers. A serial killer on the loose, they say. But it is the vampires. I feel their presence. They seek her. They can feel her, that she is one of us and unattached as yet."

"That is not so. You are her lifemate. Your blood is in her as hers is in you. There is no way one of them could lure her from you. In all our years together, I have learned that much. It is your Carpathian nature blinding you, Aidan, your urge to keep your lifemate always under your wing, to claim and protect her. Despite outward appearances, that part of you is still wild and uncivilized. But Alexandria is just as essentially human. She was not born Carpathian. She has no idea what is expected of her, what is even happening to her. She doesn't understand yet."

Aidan sighed, rubbing his temples. "She suffers needlessly. If she would but merge her mind fully with mine . . ."

"She wouldn't yet trust what she learned anyway," Marie insisted.

Aidan sighed and turned to Stefan. "We have to retire to the chamber soon. But you know I felt the presence of something unclean watching Joshua's school. I believe the others will strike against us soon. Please be alert to any danger to any of you."

Stefan nodded. "I have made the necessary calls, and the security system is in place. Do not worry about us. We have been through this before."

"Too many times," Aidan replied sorrowfully. "Why you stayed and chose to live this life so far from our homeland, so dangerous for you and your sons, I do not know."

"You know," Marie said softly.

Aidan bent and brushed her cheek lightly with an affectionate kiss. "I guess I do," he admitted. "Please see if Alexandria is ready to go to the chamber. I do not wish her to think I am 'dominating' her."

Marie nodded, and Stefan followed his wife through the house, uneasy with the way things seemed to be going. Aidan was dangerous, powerful, more beast than man when push came to shove. And he would allow no one or nothing to take Alexandria Houton from him. Stefan could easily read that in Aidan's protective, possessive posture when he was close to her. And Aidan's thin veneer of civility was wearing thinner by the day.

Marie and Stefan's search for Alexandria came to an abrupt stop when they saw her huddled beside the front door. She looked small and lost, a forlorn little girl tormented beyond endurance. Her knees were drawn up to her chin, her face down, hair spilling around her, hiding her expression. She was shaking, pale, the terrible daytime lethargy of the Carpathian people slowly creeping over her, taking control. Clearly it was frightening for her to feel her body turning to lead, as if all control was lost forever.

"Alexandria," Marie said anxiously, approaching the huddled figure, "are you all right?"

Her concern seemed genuine, but Alexandria was under no illusions. Marie's first and only loyalty was to Aidan Savage. Anything she said would be reported to him immediately. Alexandria did not lift her head. Inside her was a growing dread that she was utterly helpless, caught in a snare, a maze so tangled, she would never get out. Aidan was far too powerful to fight, and for some reason, he wanted her with him.

"Alexandria?" Marie gently touched her bowed head. "Tell me, should I get Aidan?"

Alexandria squeezed her eyes shut. Aidan. It always seemed to come back to Aidan. "No, I . . . I'm just finding everything . . . overwhelming. I . . . I need time to adjust." Her voice was so tight, she felt so close to a breakdown, she was afraid to speak. She struggled to stop the inner trembling threatening to shake her apart. Was she crazy? Did she belong in a mental institution?

She had to find a way to get Joshua away from these people. She should have asked Thomas Ivan for help. But the truth was, he could never hope to win against Aidan. Aidan would never let her go. She didn't know why, she didn't understand how, but she had an absolute conviction that he would follow her to the ends of the earth. She bit down on a knuckle to keep from screaming. How could *she* hope to fight Aidan? Could she even survive without his help? If she checked herself into a hospital, admitted to hallucinations, what would happen to Joshua?

Without warning she could feel the need to touch Aidan creeping up on her, entering her mind. No matter how hard she tried to wipe the idea away, it persisted. She wanted to know he was there, somewhere close. Insanity! Her own mind had turned against her! The more she fought herself, the worse it became. She needed him. Needed his reassuring touch.

Marie gave a soft exclamation as droplets of blood dotted Alexandria's forehead. She turned toward Stefan, afraid for the girl. They needed Aidan immediately. Clearly the struggle taking place in Alexandria's mind was causing her agony. Tears welling up in her own eyes, Marie knelt beside Alexandria and put a comforting arm around her shoulders. She felt so small, so fragile, her body trembling so hard, Marie was afraid she might shake apart, break into a million pieces.

"Please let me help you, Alexandria," the housekeeper begged softly.

"What can you do?" Alexandria asked hopelessly. "What can anyone do? He'll never let me go." She looked up at the older woman plaintively. "Will he?"

Marie's silence was her answer. She felt the girl's shudder of fear. "Aidan is a good man and means only to protect you. Trust him."

"Do you?"

"With my life. With the lives of my children," Marie said solemnly, truthfully.

"But then, he doesn't want the same thing from you that he does from me, does he?" Alexandria asked bitterly. "He would do anything to keep me here, even deceive me about what is real and what isn't."

Without warning she leapt to her feet, nearly knocking Marie over. Then she was struggling to open the front door. Stefan yelled a warning. Marie shouted for Aidan. And Alexandria jerked open the heavy door and ran out into the relentless, murderous sun.

At once a thousand needles pierced her eyes, and her skin blistered, smoke swirling around her as she burned. She didn't know if she screamed because of the pain or because Aidan had told the truth. This agonizing reaction was not the result of a hypnotic suggestion.

Stefan tore off his shirt, flung it over her head, and lifted her collapsing body into his arms, rushing her back into the safety of the house. Marie was sobbing, reaching anxiously for her, but Aidan got there first, dragging her out of Stefan's arms, cradling her against his chest. For a moment there was absolute silence as he laid his head on top of hers, his eyes closed, his heart pounding, his soul scarred.

"Never again." He hissed the words aloud. *Never again,* cara, *will I allow this kind of defiance.* He repeated the warning in her mind, meaning it, swearing it. He was frightened for her. Furious with her. Furious with himself. The emotions swirled and flared within him until the conflagration was nearly out of control.

She could feel his rage beating at her, in her. His arms were like steel bars as he held her.

"I am in your debt, Stefan," he said simply, his voice, as

always, calm and peaceful, at terrible odds with the rage like a living entity inside him.

He swung around and was gone, his supernatural speed blurring their movement to human eyes. Alexandria heard the bang of the basement door as they moved into the narrow stone hall leading to the sleeping chamber, but Aidan himself made no sound. None. Not even the sound of breathing.

Alexandria remained quite still. Her pain was tremendous, her blisters large and ugly. Aidan was careful not to jar her burns, careful not to hurt her. She was beyond caring. She knew something terrible was about to happen. Aidan, always so cool and calm, was a seething cauldron of black emotion.

The walls of the tunnel rushed by, a blur of granite, then Aidan was placing her on the bed and turning away from her. She sat up carefully. "You're very angry with me," she said softly.

He didn't reply, instead busying himself crushing herbs in a bowl made of agate. She could smell their fragrance rising. Then he lit candles, and a smoky aroma mixed with the scents of the herbs.

Alexandria swallowed hard and lifted her chin in defiance. "I'm not afraid of you, Aidan. What can you do? Kill me? I believe I'm already dead. Or at least living some kind of life I don't want. Will you take Joshua away? Threaten him? Harm him? I've been in your mind, and I don't think you are like that," she said bravely.

He turned his head slowly, his golden eyes resting on her face. A chill went down her spine. Those eyes were soulless, ice-cold.

"You do not know the first thing about me, Alexandria. Nor have you taken the trouble to learn. Do not presume to fight me. You are a mere fledging, I one of the ancients of our people. You have no conception of the power I wield. I can make the earth move beneath your feet and the lightning crack above your head. I can call the fog and become invisible." There was no boasting in his tone, just fact. Just black velvet. "I can do things you cannot imagine."

Alexandria felt the permanent link he had forged between them, and she could feel his rage, black and terrible, seething below the surface. "What I did today, I did to myself," she whispered.

He moved toward her, looming large, towering over her, an invincible figure, powerful beyond imagining. "You betrayed me. You betrayed Joshua. I told you what would happen if you went out into the sun. You pretended to yourself that you would see if I was telling the truth. But you already knew it was the truth. You took a chance on destroying yourself, leaving Joshua to strangers, to an uncertain future without protection."

"You would protect him."

"Without *you, my* existence is no more. We are linked, in life and death. If you choose death, you are choosing death for both of us."

Her hands were trembling as she swept back her hair. "That can't be."

"You do not wish it to be," he corrected her, and he took possession of her right arm. "But it is so. I do not lie to you, Alexandria. I have allowed you a certain amount of resistance, but only because this is all new to you."

The gel he began smearing over her arm was cool and soothing. "You're saying I don't have a choice. That I've never had a choice," she ventured.

"Your body and mine made the choice for us. Your soul is the other half of mine. My heart is your heart. Our minds reach for the reassurance and intimacy of the other. We are not complete when we are alone. We are two halves of the same whole. That is the truth, Alexandria, whether you like it or not."

She swallowed hard, wanting to press her fingertips to her pounding forehead. "It isn't true. It can't be." She denied it out loud because she didn't want it to be true, because she would not believe in him and his nightmare world.

"Why do you think I can touch your burns as I do without causing you agony? I am blocking the pain for you. This treatment would be torture for you without me."

"It isn't true," she repeated in a small whisper.

"I am angry enough with your stupidity to prove my words, *cara*. Do not argue with me. My body cries out for yours. Not with a mere human need, but with the need of the Carpathian male for its mate. I burn for you, night and day. My only relief is when I sleep the sleep of my people, unaware. Do not tempt me to prove my words, because there will be no going back."

She hunched her shoulders, averted her face from him. Aidan could feel hot, seething rage swirling in him, mixing with the urgent demands of his body and the Carpathian male's need to control. He bent closer to her, reckless now, not choosing his words or actions carefully as he so often tried to do. "You are unable to allow a human male to touch you. You feel revulsion, not pleasure, and you know it. I have been in your mind; I have seen your thoughts. You hunger only for me."

The images he reflected back to her were her own. Hot, erotic things she had no real knowledge of. Things she found humiliating to have even thought of. Her kneeling at his feet, touching him, her mouth moving over him; his body atop hers, commanding hers, taking hers, hot and furiously. He knew, and he was taunting her with her own private fantasies of the two of them together.

"You really are a brutal animal with no thought for anyone but yourself," she whispered, pressing her hands to her burning face. "And I care nothing for you. I feel nothing for you."

His hand caught and spanned her throat, his thumb forcing her chin up so that she met his blazing golden eyes. "I *could* make you my slave, Alexandria, teach you to please me in far more ways than you envisioned." Deliberately his thumb feathered across her trembling mouth.

Alexandria could feel tears burning in her eyes even as her body burst into flame, into need. Aidan was right. She had no thoughts, no resistance, when he touched her; she was only a body drowning in desire, going up on flames. There was nothing left of her, of who she was or what she stood for. Never had a man been able to control her before. Whatever Aidan Savage had made her, she was no longer Alexandria Houton.

Aidan's mind sought hers, and instantly the anger in him melted away. She was sliding toward shock. Too much had happened too quickly in the last few days for her human mind to assimilate. He cursed his own body, raging for release, causing him to say and do things he would never ordinarily consider. He wanted her with every cell in his body, and just now he *had* pushed aside her needs for his own. No self-respecting Carpathian male would ever do such a thing. In that moment he realized just how close to turning vampire he really had been. He felt contempt for himself, for his own selfishness and weakness, when she was having such a difficult transition. "*Cara*, I am sorry. Please do not be afraid of me, of us." The words were spoken in his most beguiling voice, but they seemed to fall on deaf ears.

Her mind shut down, protected her, spared her from any further ordeal. She turned her face away and slumped onto the bed, curled up in the fetal position. Aidan stood over her, angry with himself, unsure what to do to repair the damage he had caused with his stupidity. He had been so afraid he had lost her in that moment, etched for all time onto his soul, when she had flung open the door and gone willingly into the killing sun.

He could withstand the light, the burning, because he had conditioned himself to do so over time. Now, after centuries of study, he had nearly unlimited powers. One of them was healing. So he closed his eyes and sent himself out of his own body and into hers, finding the terrible burns so deeply seared into her skin, repairing them from the inside out. He was careful and precise, and when he was finished, he moved through her to once more enter her mind.

There he found confusion and terror. A deep fear of not being fully human and a desire to prove that she was. He could find no intent to kill herself. She had simply wanted to prove him a liar, deceiving her into believing she could not reenter her own world. She had wanted it to be so.

He stretched out beside her, gathering her weary body into the protection of his arms. She had reason to be afraid of him. He was demanding things of her she had no conception of, making her feel things she wasn't ready for. The intensity of her sexual feelings alone was disturbing to her, so much so that she wanted to run from him.

He rested his chin on her head and stroked her silky hair. It disturbed him that she had some crazy idea of going to a human doctor to be cured. Anything but stay with him. On some level he was hurt, but mostly he was amused that she would think she could defeat him, outsmart him. She was so determined. He admired her for that.

"You just need time, *piccola*. I am sorry for the clumsy way I have handled this situation. My only excuse is my fear for your safety." He knew she could hear him, but she didn't respond. He hadn't really expected her to do so, but he tightened his hold a bit. *Sleep now, Alexandria, the healing sleep of our people. Sleep deep.* He took no chances, gave her no choice. He wanted her under, away from her own mind, away from the terrible drain of her thoughts and fears.

Chapter Thirteen

Aidan woke with his body raging at him. Not with the compulsion for nourishment, the need for blood that was always with him, but with stark, urgent arousal unlike any he had ever experienced. He groaned aloud. Beside him, Alexandria lay in slumber. She was pale, her hair spilling over both of them, binding them together. He wanted her. He had to have her. If he stayed beside her for one more moment, he would be unable to stop himself from claiming her.

He leapt away from her as if burned, his skin hot, painful, searing. He swore softly. How could he feed her in this condition without the act turning into something erotic and wild? Inside, the beast, always wild and untamed, roared for her. Hungered. Needed. It had no logic, only that heavy, relentless ache growing more merciless every day.

He ran an unsteady hand through his unruly hair. The situation was explosive now. There was no way to supply her with her life's blood without claiming her body. Yet after what had occurred earlier, he knew she needed more time. The beast within was raging, and he could no longer control it. Marie had believed he could. She had faith in him. But she did not know the demands of the Carpathian male, the heat rising between mates. She did not know how close he had come to turning.

He groaned aloud again and turned away from the figure lying so still on his bed. In his lair. He flinched as the word entered his mind. The beast was becoming more dominant. And the only way to control it was to merge with his lifemate, let her gentleness, her light, guide him away from the darkness spreading a stain across his soul.

He cleaned up before he woke her, dressing with care in a soft silk shirt and black trousers, hoping an old-world elegance would enhance his appeal. He secured his long hair at the nape of his neck. The shirt he left open at the throat, more because he was having trouble breathing than to be sexy.

As he sent his mind to wake her and watched her take her first breath, his body hardened with such an intensity, he found himself swearing again. He could feel sweat trickling down his chest and lower, between his legs. She stretched, her body moving sensually under the quilt. He thought he might burst. Her tongue moistened dry lips, left them glistening and inviting. He closed his eyes against the sight, but he could smell her, hear the rustle of the sheets.

Alexandria sat up slowly, disoriented. She had vivid images of an erotic dream, hands on her breasts, a mouth pressed to hers, fingers moving in her, then a hard, aggressive body blanketing hers, pinning her down. Her body ached with need, craved his touch. She squirmed, felt the creamy invitation calling, beckoning, tempting him. She opened her eyes—and met Aidan's hot golden stare across the room.

Danger. It was there in his carved features, in the intensity of his eyes. She remained perfectly still, not taking her gaze from the predatory creature watching her. She was afraid even to breathe. If she moved, if she sighed, he would be on her. She sensed it, knew the erotic dream was his, knew his control was fragile and that he was battling his every instinct.

"Get out of here, *cara mia*," he whispered hoarsely. The velvet roughness of his voice felt like a tongue lapping at her sensitized skin. "Get out while you can." Red flames seemed to light the gold of his eyes, and beads of sweat dotted his forehead. His muscles bulged with the effort to remain stationary.

She wanted to go to him, to soothe him—or to enflame him further, the consequences be damned. Her body was on fire, a living, breathing flame nearly out of control. It was only her shyness that prevented her from tempting him further. Her shyness and her fear. She rolled off the bed and fled, running as if seven demons were behind her. Running from herself even more than from Aidan.

Behind her Aidan stood as still as a statue. If he moved he was afraid he might shatter with pain, with need. He could not hold out much longer. God help them both if she did not come to him soon.

Alexandria slowed down once she was in the safety of the tunnel. She could feel Aidan still in her mind, still reaching for her, calling to her. She could taste his kiss, feel him touching her. She closed her eyes and leaned against the rock wall for support. Her legs felt like rubber, refusing to take another step. She wanted him. Not with a sweet, gentle longing, but with a savage, wild need that demanded hot, clawing sex.

She shook her head, trying to rid herself of the thoughts she had, the images taunting her. She made her way up the stairs, grateful that Joshua didn't see her. Her shower did nothing to alleviate her hunger, did nothing to wash away the feel of Aidan or the rich, spicy taste of him. The hot water running down her skin, between the swell of her breasts, down her stomach, to her tight blond curls, only served to heighten her sensitivity. She had to fight the urge to call Aidan to her. She ached for him, needed him, her body all liquid heat and throbbing with desire. She had to call him to her to stop this aching. She needed to feel his mouth on her skin, his hands on her body. She needed him in her, an urgent, wild mating that would go on forever.

And then she remembered his words. *He could make her his slave.* He could make her do things she had never even pictured. Well, she was picturing them now. Where did the images come from? "Damn you, Aidan. Damn you for doing this to me." She turned up her face to the spray and shut herself off from him. She heard the echo of his despairing cry, the roar of the wounded animal, the growl of the hunter who had missed his prey.

Without him in her mind to feed her own hunger, the terrible urgency lessened. It did not go away entirely, but real hunger crept in. She was pale and needed nourishment. She needed him. With an unladylike oath, she dressed in jeans and a ribbed top and headed for the sitting room next to her bedroom. It was to become her studio. She found that Marie or Stefan, obviously on Aidan's orders, had already purchased supplies for her. They were top quality, things she had never been able to afford before. Ordinarily she would never accept such a lavish gift, but the artist in her thrilled to the beauty of the tools.

She heard Joshua before he came looking for her. Home from school, he was laughing with Stefan in the solarium, then chatting with Marie in the kitchen over cookies. Alexandria found herself happy and sad at the same time. Joshua needed the company, and the older couple displayed genuine affection for him, but she was sad that her relationship with her brother was changing, that he would no longer rely solely on her.

By the time he came rushing up the stairs, bellowing boisterously for her, she had regained her composure. Joshua flung himself into her arms, and she lifted him, spinning him around in circles until he shrieked happily with dizziness.

"Look at all this stuff!" she cried joyfully, showing off her treasures.

Joshua puffed out his chest. "I helped pick them out. Aidan and I went shopping. I showed him all the things you always picked up and put back. I could tell you wanted them, though. We had fun shopping for you. He said it was to be a big surprise."

She clutched a box of charcoal pencils to her, all at once finding it hard to breathe. "He did, did he? When did you do this?"

Joshua grinned at her. "A few days ago. While you were so sick. He picked out some new clothes, too. Look in your bedroom closet. You should have seen the saleswoman. She was looking at him like—"

"I can imagine," Alexandria broke in dryly. She followed a skipping Joshua back into her bedroom.

"He thought of everything. He said when a woman as beautiful and as good as you got so sick, a man should do whatever he could to make things better for you." Joshua threw open the double closet doors she had never touched, using only the bureau for her jeans and tops.

In her entire life Alexandria had never owned enough clothes to fill a closet of this size, yet it was jammed with dresses, coats, skirts, slacks, and blouses. She bit her lower lip and touched a long black evening gown. It was by a top designer. She dropped her hand to her side. "Why did he do this?" she whispered aloud to Joshua, repeating in her head, *Why did you do this?*

It is only money, cara. *I have nothing else to use to pay for my sins.* He sounded alone and lost, ragged.

She unexpectedly felt tears in her eyes. Everything in her wanted to run to him, comfort him, but his words from that morning continued to echo in her head, and she closed her mind firmly to his tricks. Become his slave. It would never happen.

"Ah, sis, don't cry like a baby," Joshua admonished. "Aidan did it 'cuz he wanted to. You should see all the neat toys he bought me. You know, I asked Marie and Stefan about the puppy—how much work they thought it would be."

"Persistent little devil, aren't you?" She closed the closet doors firmly on the new clothes, determined never to wear them.

"Aidan says persistence pays," Joshua quoted happily.

Alexandria took a deep breath. "He should know." On second thought, she *was* going to wear those dresses. Every last one of them. Wear them when she worked with Thomas Ivan. When she went out with Thomas Ivan. When she fell completely and madly in love with Thomas Ivan.

For a moment she felt Aidan stirring in her mind, the kind of move a large jungle cat might make while stalking its prey—a mere ripple, and then it was gone, as if it had never been. Had she imagined it?

"Quit thinking about him!" she snapped at herself, angry that her mind would not stay away from him.

Joshua looked up at her, wide-eyed. "About who? The puppy? Why? Did you already find one? Is it a boy dog?"

"There's definitely a boy hound dog somewhere around here," she replied grimly. Then, relenting, she ruffled Joshua's curls. "I'm kidding, Josh. And, no, I haven't found a puppy yet. I haven't even made up my mind yet. I want us to be sure we're happy here before we make such a permanent decision."

"I'm happy here," Joshua said instantly, decisively.

She hugged him. "I'm glad you're happy, little buddy, but I'm not certain I am. It's much more difficult for adults to adjust to living together than it is for kids."

"But Marie and Stefan are so great, Alex, and Aidan is the best. He helps me with my homework. We talk all the time. He's cool. And he said—"

"I don't want to hear what he said just now, okay? I have work to do, honey, remember? We have to have money to eat."

"But Aidan has lots of money, and he said you wouldn't have to work if you didn't want to."

She let her breath out slowly, holding on to her temper. She was sick of hearing what Aidan had to say. She was sick of his being in her mind, taking over her every waking moment. "I like to work, Josh. Now find something to do quietly or scoot."

He made a face but settled down quickly with her old set of colored pens and a sketch pad. They settled into the familiar routine easily. Occasionally she asked his opinion on an idea, and sometimes he showed her his drawings. Alexandria felt they were very good for a six-year-old. She corrected a line here and there when he asked her to, but mostly she encouraged him to do it his way. For a short time, she felt as if she and her world were normal again.

But Aidan was always present. She could feel her mind tuning to his, reaching out to find him. Her ears listened for the sound of his beautiful voice. She found herself staring blankly at the paper before her, and twice she actually drew his likeness. Both times she tore it up quickly before Joshua could spot her obsession and tease her about it.

She tried not to be aware of Joshua's heartbeat, of the ebb and flow of the blood running in his veins. She pretended she didn't notice the way Marie's pulse fascinated her when the housekeeper called Joshua to dinner. She ignored the remembered taste in her mouth, the feel of Aidan beneath her lips, the way her body writhed against his, craved his. She groaned and tried to turn away from yet another picture she had drawn of him. His mouth was set in that sensual, inviting line that seemed to mock her, lure her. Pure temptation.

She touched a fingertip to that mouth she had drawn so perfectly. "I won't let you do this to me," she whispered softly. She wanted him so badly. She needed him to comfort her, to make this world of madness and insanity make sense. She needed him to take away the gnawing, frightening hunger that kept her from fully enjoying Joshua's company. Most of all she needed him to merge his body with hers, to feel his mouth and his hands taking away the terrible burning, the emptiness. She needed his heart beating the same rhythm as hers, his mind invading hers, the ultimate intimacy, locking them together, sharing every wild fantasy as his body took possession of hers.

She went through all the normal motions that evening, helping Joshua with his homework, pretending to enjoy a show on television. They argued about the value of a wide-screen TV. Stefan took Joshua's side, saying it was a necessity for old eyes. Marie sided with Alexandria that it was the ultimate in conspicuous consumption. But the blood rushing through all their veins was like a symphony, drowning out

213

the sounds of the program and making Alexandria afraid for them. She tried to enjoy getting Joshua ready for bed, reading to him, having a short pillow fight, tucking him in. She had always loved their time together at night. Joshua was always so clean and sweet. But the loud beating of his heart interfered with her enjoyment now, and she felt trapped in the middle of a nightmare.

Alexandria dressed with care for her date with Thomas Ivan that night. But as the dress slid over her skin, she felt the brush of hot velvet. Her hands shook as she put up her hair. She had not seen Aidan once since she had fled him earlier. She felt him, always there, close, but he had taken care to stay out of her sight. Instead of being grateful, though, she was depressed. Maybe it didn't matter that she was going out with another man. Maybe he didn't care. And why should it? She didn't want him to care. She wanted to find a human man, one she was attracted to. One she wanted to make love with. Not something obsessive and wild, but something gentle and loving. A human, normal man.

She inspected her nails. Formerly frustratingly stubby, they were now long and beautiful, well manicured, almost as if she'd had them professionally done. Even her hair seemed thicker, more luxurious, her eyelashes long and thick. Her skin, however, was pale, nearly translucent.

She sighed at her image in the mirror. She looked the same but different. More . . . She didn't exactly know what. Just more. The dress clung like a second skin, emphasizing her full breasts and tiny waist. It could have been designed just for her. She ran a hand down the soft material covering her thigh. Her heart slammed against her throat when she looked up to find Aidan's golden eyes watching her in the mirror. He stood behind her, his tall, powerfully built frame, his blond good looks complementing her own. She could taste him in her mouth. They made an erotic picture in the mirror, Aidan tall and heavily muscled, with his brilliant, hungry eyes, Alexandria slender and petite and pale.

"You look beautiful, Alexandria," he said softly.

His voice was compelling, whispering over her skin with

the same heat as the velvet dress. She couldn't read his expression, only feel the molten gold of his gaze.

"I—I won't be out late," she stammered like a wayward teenager. And then she would have given anything to take the words back. Aidan didn't smile, didn't change expression.

She felt a shiver go down her spine. All at once her defiance seemed stupid, like baiting a tiger. That unblinking stare. Was he going to let her go? Only moments earlier she had been somewhat depressed that he would. Now she wanted nothing more than to run for her life, far away from him.

He shook his head slowly. "*Dio*, Alexandria. You persist in thinking me a monster. Take great care, *piccola*, that you do not create one." He left the room as silently as he had entered.

She trembled at the threat. She touched her mouth. He had been staring at it. Her lips tingled so, she swore she could feel the brush of his mouth against hers. She closed her eyes, savoring the feel of him, then cursed that he could so easily control her. She was human. *Human!* And she was determined to stay that way.

Alexandria lifted her chin. She would not be swayed by his sex appeal, and she would not be intimidated by his threats. She slipped on her shoes and glided regally down the stairs.

Thomas had arrived precisely on time and was waiting for her in the living room, grateful that Aidan Savage had chosen not to inflict his presence on him. His breath caught in his throat as Alexandria entered. She seemed to be more beautiful each time he saw her. She amazed him, haunted him, wrapped him up until he could think of nothing but her. His work was suffering, as a result. He was daydreaming about her when he was supposed to be completing the story line for his latest video game. He even dreamed of her at night, hot, erotic dreams he had every intention of making come true.

"Thomas, this was such a good idea." She greeted him in a voice that seemed to penetrate right to his heart and stir a response somewhat lower in his body as well.

Then he felt the weight of those damned golden eyes on him. Relentless. Merciless. They saw his reaction and damned him for it. Aidan Savage lounged with deceptive laziness in the doorway, one hip resting against the wall, his arms across his chest. He didn't say anything. He didn't have to. His mere presence struck terror into Thomas's soul.

Thomas took Alexandria's cape and enveloped her in it, breathing in her perfume. "You look extraordinary, Alexandria. No one would ever know you'd been ill."

Aidan did stir then, a mere rippling of muscles suggestive of a lethal predator. "Nevertheless, she has been extremely ill, Ivan. I trust you will see to it that she is well cared for and returned home early."

Thomas smiled suavely, oozing charm. Damn the man, he wasn't a teenager escorting his first date to the prom. He deliberately took Alexandria's hand in his, knowing it would annoy her blond guard dog. "Not to worry, Savage. I intend to take very good care of her." He urged her to the door, anxious to be away from Savage and his living, breathing, monstrous house.

Alexandria went with him willingly, seemingly as eager as he was. Out in the night air she stopped and took a deep breath. "He can be a bit overwhelming, can't he?" she said, smiling. Smiling to rival the stars. Freedom. Blessed freedom. It didn't matter at that moment that Ivan's smile still reminded her of a shark's toothy grin, or that she could hear his heart beating every bit as loudly as Joshua's, or, even worse, that she could smell his arousal. She was away from Aidan Savage and his influence, and that was all she cared about.

"Overwhelming? Is that what you call it? He's completely overbearing. The man acts as if he owns you," Thomas burst out.

She laughed softly. "You get used to him. He can't help it. He's accustomed to giving orders. You probably know what that feels like," she added mischievously.

He found himself laughing with her, relaxing as they made their way to the car he had waiting. He had deliber-

216

ately hired a limo and driver to leave himself free for whatever might happen in the back seat later.

"I made a good start on the sketches, Thomas," she volunteered, "but you didn't specify what character traits were particularly important to you. I think you should decide ahead of time how you want individuals portrayed instead of leaving it all to me."

"I'd prefer your input," Thomas said, opening the door for her himself. He wanted to do it, and that surprised him. Most of the time the small courtesies he performed were only for effect. But Alexandria Houton was haunting. "Doesn't that house bother you?"

She arched an eyebrow. "Bother me? The house? It's beautiful. Everything about it is beautiful. Why do you ask?"

"I sometimes feel as if it's watching me, biding its time, hating me."

"Thomas, you've played too many of your own video games. What a vivid imagination." Her laughter slid over him, touching him in places usually reserved for intimacy.

His hand inched across the seat toward hers. He wanted her more than he had ever wanted any woman. But then he glanced out the window and saw the reflection of eyes. Glowing, red, feral eyes filled with hate and the promise of retaliation, the promise of death. Unblinking cat's eyes. The eyes of a demon. Of death. He shivered, and a moan escaped.

"What is it?" Her voice was soothing, like the soft sound of running water. "Tell me, Thomas."

"Did you see something weird?" He was choking on fear. "Out the window, do you see anything?"

She leaned around him to look at the reflective glass. "What am I supposed to see?"

The eyes were gone as if they had never been. Was it Savage? His own imagination? He cleared his throat and managed a smile. "Nothing. I guess I just can't believe my good fortune."

In the close confines of a car, it was difficult for Alex to ignore her growing hunger. It seemed to gnaw at her insides, spread like a cancer. Her mind seemed to amplify the sound of blood rushing in Ivan's veins. Beckoning, calling. But her stomach heaved at the thought of touching him, and she fought to keep a smile plastered to her face. He seemed to find every excuse to touch her, brush her leg, her arm, her hand, her hair. She hated it. Loathed it. He made her skin crawl. She hated herself for not being able to return his amorous glances, his touches.

She smiled at him, said and did all the appropriate things, but inside her stomach was rebelling. Somewhere deep inside her soul, a dread began to take shape, to spread. Thomas Ivan was an eligible bachelor, wealthy, charming, famous. Human. He shared her love of fantasy; he admired her artwork. They had much in common, yet even his lightest touch repulsed her. Inside she began to weep.

Cara mia, *do you need me?* Aidan's voice crossed time and distance to find her, to wrap her in warm, protective arms.

She bit her lip. The temptation to call for him was nearly overwhelming, but she resisted. She would be human. And she would find a fellow human to love. Maybe not Thomas Ivan, but someone. *I'm having the time of my life.*

Just so long as Ivan is not.

She felt his withdrawal from her mind, and it felt as if he had taken away her soul and left her dead inside. She lifted her chin and flashed Ivan a particularly brilliant smile. She placed her hand in his as he assisted her from the car. Determined to enjoy the evening, she took his arm as they entered the theater.

Men seemed to be pressing against her, breathing loudly. Heartbeats thundered in her ears. The orchestra's overture blended with the surging of blood running hotly in veins. Alexandria concentrated on the play, aware it was exceptionally good, yet she was more aware of Ivan's arm across the back of her seat, of his smell. When he whispered in her ear, his mouth against her skin, she was sickened by it.

Twice she almost excused herself to go to the ladies' room just for a respite from him.

But she was determined to see this through. She was going to be human even if it killed her. There was a burst of applause just as she heard the words in her mind: *It might kill someone.*

Shut up! she answered him, exasperated, that in the midst of her despair, he made her want to laugh. But Aidan was gone once more. Just his touch warmed her, and the silliness of his warning. He was taunting her on purpose because he knew she was repulsed by the man sitting so close to her.

Beside her, Thomas was clapping. The lights came up, and people seemed to swarm around them. He was in his element, with a beautiful woman on his arm and many aquaintances surrounding them. Powerful men he barely remembered meeting were suddenly stopping to exchange comments on the show. Connections he had been seeking to aid his climb even further up the social ladder were introducing themselves, issuing much sought-after invitations to him and his date.

Alexandria Houton was clearly an asset to him and would be to his career. Proudly he put her on display, strutting because she was on his arm. And he saw that he was not the only one mesmerized by her voice, captivated by her smile. Even the women, he realized with satisfaction, she seemed to charm, bestowing her smile regally, enchantingly.

Thomas circled her shoulders with his arm and drew her closer to him, a display of ownership as they walked out into the night, still followed by his many fans. Alexandria's stomach lurched at the proximity. Then Thomas glanced to his right and froze. Standing not six feet away in the shadows was a wolf. Huge. Blond. With gleaming fangs and red, glowing eyes. Those eyes were staring right at him, the beast's muscular body poised as if to pounce.

Thomas's heart actually stopped, then began to pound. He gripped Alexandria's arm and began to shove her back toward the theater.

"Thomas, what are you doing?" she demanded.

"Don't you see it?" He pointed in his excitement. It was Savage somehow, he was certain of it. "It's him, I know it is. He's here." Heads were turning at his raised voice.

"Thomas." Her voice was soft and soothing. "Tell me what's wrong. You're very pale. What did you see?"

He forced himself to look more closely. The shadows were deep and dark—and empty of wildlife. He could see a large planter where the wolf had been. Wiping the sweat from his forehead, he allowed himself to breathe.

"You're shaking, Thomas. Come on, let's get to the car." Concerned, Alexandria took a careful look around, scanned the area, and found only humans. *You'd better not be tormenting him again*, she warned Aidan, but she could not tell if he heard.

"I swear I'm seeing things, Alex. The planter over there looked like . . ." He trailed off, not wanting to admit his imagination was out of control. What was wrong with him, anyway, that his obsession with Alexandria Houton and Aidan Savage, coupled with his macabre imagination, was producing all-too-real hallucinations?

"It moved?" She was looking at the offending redwood box suspiciously.

"No," he admitted. "It just looked . . . strange."

"Well, I had a great time tonight. The play was wonderful," Alexandria said softly.

Little liar. The words taunted her, male amusement mocking her.

Her chin lifted, and deliberately she placed her hand in the crook of Thomas's arm as they headed for the limo pulling up to the curb for them. "Did you like it?" she asked sweetly, her voice oozing syrup. She could almost feel Aidan wince, and he retreated immediately.

Once in the car, Thomas slid close to Alexandria. His thigh rested against hers, and he could feel the soft swell of her breast against his arm. His hand found her chin. "I know you don't know me very well, Alex, but I'm deeply attracted to you, and I'm hoping the feeling's mutual."

His mouth was mere inches from hers, and under his mouthwash and breath mints Alexandria could smell everything he had eaten for dinner—the pasta with garlic, the salad with tarragon-vinegar dressing, the red wine and coffee and mint. She nearly gagged and tried to put some distance between them. "We'll be working together, Thomas. This isn't a good idea. At least not so soon."

"But I have to kiss you. I have to, Alex." He was leaning into her, breathing heavily.

She made a sound, shrinking back, but in his ardor he took it for consent. As he lowered his head, his eyes caught the glint of red. He cried out and fell away from her toward his door, staring at the rear window, through which two glowing eyes watched him with clear malice. To his horror the window bulged inward, then shattered, spraying glass fragments all over him. The huge wolf thrust his muzzle right into the car, fangs exposed and dripping, diving right for his head. Those red eyes glowed eerily without blinking, boring right into him. He could feel the hot breath on him as those white fangs thrust closer still. Thomas screamed and ducked, covering his face with both hands.

"Thomas?" Alexandria touched his shoulder lightly. "Have you been doing drugs this evening?" She already knew the answer; she could smell it in his bloodstream. "Perhaps we should take you to a hospital. Or a private doctor."

Slowly, in fear, Thomas lowered his hands. The rear window was intact. There were no shards of glass. Alexandria was sitting calmly in the seat, her blue eyes anxious.

"This has never happened before. I'm hallucinating. It was just a little coke in the men's room. Maybe it was some bad stuff, I don't know." He sounded scared.

"What did you see?" Again she scanned the area, trying to find evidence of Aidan or any other danger, but they seemed to be alone. Maybe it really was the drugs. "Should I tell the driver to take you to a hospital?"

"No, no. I'll be all right." He was sweating profusely.

She could smell his fear.

221

"There's nothing out there, Thomas, really. I sometimes sense things before they happen, and I don't have any strange feelings," she offered, trying to be reassuring.

"I'm sorry," he apologized hoarsely. "Have I ruined the evening?" His eyes kept shifting from side to side, and he seemed to have developed a nervous tic on the left side of his jaw. He looked far older than he had at the beginning of the evening.

"No, of course not. I had a wonderful time. Thank you for thinking of the theater. I really needed to get out," she assured him. "But Thomas, I don't believe in taking drugs. I have my little brother, Joshua, to think about. I realize it isn't my business what you choose to do on your own time, but I'm not comfortable with cocaine or any other drug."

"It's not like I'm some junkie. I just use it occasionally for recreational purposes."

"Not around me." That alone was a good enough reason not to be with him. She thought much less of him now, knowing that he would use narcotics to enhance the evening, as if he was incapable of enjoying it on his own.

"Fine," he said sulkily, "I won't."

The car was already pulling into Aidan's circular drive. The wrought-iron gates had been left open in anticipation of her return. For a moment she sat still, staring at the heavy gates. They represented a loss of freedom. She wasn't ready to go back to the house and admit defeat. So Thomas Ivan and she didn't have the least bit of chemistry between them. That didn't mean she wouldn't find another man.

She slid quickly out of the car, eluding Thomas's clinging hand. "Thank you again, Thomas. I'll see you soon. Be sure to get back to me on your ideas for the designs." And before he could get out to accompany her to the door, she was running lightly up the marble steps to the wide front porch. She waved once and slipped inside.

Thomas swore and sat back in the seat. Before he could close the door, he saw the heavily muscled wolf stalking him across the lawn. "Go! Go!" he shouted to the driver, slamming the door hard.

The driver fishtailed out of the driveway and away from the house, and Thomas breathed a sigh of relief. All he wanted to do was get home and get very drunk.

Alexandria moved through the house without turning on a light, found the phone, and made a call. She could see perfectly in the darkness and ran easily up the stairs. Aidan thought he had won—he had monitored her all evening—but it wasn't over yet. She was not ready to concede defeat.

In her bedroom, she removed the black velvet dress and reached for her faded, comfortable, worn blue jeans and a simple pale blue shirt. The change took only minutes, and she tugged on tennis shoes and headed back downstairs. The cab she called had not yet arrived, so she sat outside on the marble steps and waited.

"And where are you off to now?" Aidan asked silkily, appearing out of nowhere to loom over her, making her feel small and fragile.

"I'm going dancing." Her eyes dared him to deny her.

His body tightened. "Dream date didn't go well?"

There was the briefest glimpse of amusement in her eyes, but her mouth frowned severely. "As if you didn't know. Try not to look so innocent. It doesn't suit you."

He was unrepentant, grinning at her, turning her heart over. Just the sight of him brought her body surging to life. "Go away, Aidan. I don't want to look at you."

"Am I tempting you?"

"Didn't anyone ever teach you how to be a gentleman? Go away. You're annoying me." She stuck her nose in the air.

Her profile in the moonlight took his breath away. With the blanket of darkness enfolding them, they seemed to be the only two people in the world. He drank her in, her scent, that special fragrance that was hers alone. A small, confident smile curved his sensual mouth, casting a sexy shadow across his masculine features. "At least I have your attention."

"I'm going out dancing," she asserted.

"You are declaring your independence," he countered. "It

will not do you any good. You belong here, with me. You belong *to* me. None of those men out there will make you feel as I do."

She stuck her chin out. "I don't want them to. You're so intense, Aidan. Wild and intense. You make me crazy. I just want to feel . . ." She broke off, unsure how she wanted to feel.

"Normal. Human." He supplied the words for her.

"There's nothing wrong with that. *You* scare the hell out of me." There. She had admitted it to him. Said it out loud. She glanced away into the night, unable to look at him and not burn for him.

"Your feelings for me scare the hell out of you," he corrected gently.

"I don't trust you." Why was the cab so late? She clenched her fists, not wanting to be alone with him like this. She remembered the feel of his mouth on hers, the taste of him.

"You would trust me if you gave yourself fully to me. Allowed your mind to merge with mine completely. I could hide nothing from you if you wanted to examine it. My memories, my desires." His voice whispered over her skin, tempted, beckoned.

She glared at him. "As if I haven't had your desires dancing in my head all night. Thank you very much, Mr. Savage. I don't intend to become anybody's slave."

He groaned, covering his face with his hands. Then his perfect mouth curved into an enticing smile. "Are you going to hold that against me forever? After all, if anyone is a slave here, it is me. I would do anything for you, and I think you know it."

She bit her lip hard to keep from flinging herself into his arms. "The taxi is here. I'll be back later." He was so sexy, and she desperately wanted him.

He touched her as she slipped past him, the lightest of caresses, running a finger down her arm, but she felt it in her deepest core, felt it in her soul. She carried the sensation of his touch with her into the cab.

Chapter Fourteen

The newest hot singles bar was a wild blend of sophistication and sleaze. It made a stab at class by posting bouncers at the entrance to determine who would enter and who would be denied, but it was clear that they took bribes and that any pretty girl was ushered right in. The line was long, but Alexandria ignored it, walking with complete confidence to the door. She had noticed her new effect on people, noticed that her voice enthralled them almost as much as Aidan's did her.

She smiled at the man standing squarely in her path. His head jerked up, and he sucked in his breath audibly. He didn't even hesitate, personally escorting her inside. The music assaulted her ears and vibrated through her body. She felt the crush immediately, the press of bodies against her. Mostly she heard their hearts beating, the rush of blood through their veins nearly overwhelming her.

A tall man in dark leather quickly claimed her, catching her wrist, grinning at his find. He had a scruffy beard and smelled of cologne, whiskey, and sweat. His left arm boasted a tattoo of a black widow spider in the center of her web, complete with red hourglass on her belly and a hint of fangs protruding from her mouth. The man leered at her and dragged her close to him. "I been looking for you all night."

She wanted to feel something besides her rebelling stomach, but he obviously wasn't her type. She smiled up into his eyes. "It's not going to happen," she said softly, persuasively.

The smile faded from his face, and she could see the latent violence in him. This was a man who didn't like to be thwarted. His fingers tightened like a vise.

"Let go of me." She said it calmly, but she wasn't calm

inside. She had somehow counted on enjoying the best of both worlds tonight, thinking whatever creature she had become would protect her from this kind of thing.

The man's laugh was frankly nasty. "Let's go outside, babe." As he made the suggestion into an order by grabbing her wrist, he felt something on his arm. He glanced down and, to his horror, saw his black widow tattoo crawling up his forearm toward his biceps. He could see the fangs clicking angrily, feel its hairy legs on his skin. He froze, then yelled loudly, dropping Alexandria's wrist, slapping and brushing wildly at his arm.

Alexandria saw nothing but took the opportunity to glide away, disappearing into the crowd.

The man stared down at his arm, gasping heavily, his chest heaving. But the only thing he saw was his tattoo. Nothing moved. He raked a hand through his hair, leaving it wild and disheveled. "I've had too much booze, man," he said to no one in particular.

Alexandria slipped through the throng, her head pounding with the beat of the music. Her blood was hot, but her skin ice-cold. Her stomach seemed to rebel at the bodies she brushed against. A stocky man with chestnut hair and a ready smile touched her shoulder. "Dance with me?"

He was lonely, she could feel it, as well as his deep sadness and near desperation to hold another human being. Without thinking she smiled an assent and allowed him to lead her onto the dance floor. The moment his arms surrounded her and he pulled her body against his, she knew it had been a mistake. She wasn't human. She wasn't what he needed. And his illusion was no more desperate than hers. His desperation was no sadder than her own. Neither of them spoke. She knew his thoughts, his terrible sorrow for the loss of his wife some six months earlier. But she wasn't Julia, his wife. She wasn't even the customary, warm body to help him make it through the night. And he wasn't Aidan, and he never could be.

That last thought struck terror into her soul. Why had she thought that? She could find a man. A human man. It wouldn't be this one, but there must be someone.

The man stirred. "Come home with me?"

"It isn't me you want," she said gently, moving to put a few inches between them.

He tightened his hold, pulling her body into his. "It isn't me you want either, but we can help each other," he pleaded, wanting someone to push away the ghosts for a few precious hours.

The smell of his blood called to her. Alexandria's stomach lurched, and she felt bile rise into her throat. She shook her head adamantly. "I'm sorry, I can't do this." When she went to step away, the music changed to a frantic, driving rhythm that seemed to goad the man to clutch at her. As his arm tightened across her back, static electricity seemed to arc from the floor into his arm, jolting him. He swore and released her immediately. Surprised, Alexandria stepped away. "What happened?"

"You shocked me!" he accused.

"I did?" She inched away from him. Had she inadvertently done so without knowing it? Or had it been an accident? She had no idea, but she was grateful for the timely intervention. She ducked into the whirling, gyrating crowd and made her way across the room, the music beating in her head, through her body.

Alexandria found the bar. Several men in suits parted to allow her access. Their greetings were speculative, hopeful. They seemed nice enough. Some were good-looking. Some even seemed legitimately friendly. But she felt nothing. It was as if she was totally empty inside. Dead.

Suddenly wondering what she was doing, what she was trying to prove to herself, she spun around, leaned her back against the bar, and stared down at her shoes. There was no way around it. She had never been a promiscuous person. It just wasn't in her. She wasn't attracted to a man for his looks, and even those who mildly intrigued her, whom she had things in common with, didn't stir her physically.

"You look sad," one of the suits observed. "Do you want to grab a booth and talk? Just talk." He held up his hands, palms out. "I mean it. No come-on, just talk. My name's Brian."

227

"Alexandria," she said, but she shook her head. He was too nice to lead on. He said he wanted to talk, but she could read his deeper interest easily. "Thanks, but I think I'll go home."

Home. Where was home? She didn't have one. The sorrow was almost too much for her to bear. She looked up, and her gaze was caught on the darkest corner of the room. Golden eyes gleamed back at her. Her heart jumped. She couldn't look away, captivated by the intensity in that unblinking stare.

Aidan moved slowly out of the shadows. Glided. Rippled. Stalked like a great jungle cat. He took her breath away. Tall. Sexy. Powerful. Eyes only for her. Locked on her. Beneath his silk shirt his muscles rippled suggestively. He looked elegant, exuded power, was without equal.

She found herself trembling in anticipation of his touch. Just like that, the mere sight of him had brought her back to life. Like the Red Sea, the crowd parted to allow him through. No one touched him, brushed against him, or jostled him. Even the suits pressing close to her moved aside to allow him entrance into their private domain. Then he was standing in front of her, holding out a hand, his eyes trapping her gaze.

Whether it was compulsion or obsession, Alexandria didn't know. She didn't even care. She couldn't have stopped herself for any reason. She was fighting a useless battle. She needed him, and there he was. She placed her hand in his, and when he closed his fingers around hers and drew her to him, it felt as if she was giving herself away.

"Dance with me, *cara mia*. I need to feel you against me." His words, his voice, were far too seductive to resist.

Alexandria slipped easily into his arms. She fit perfectly. He was strong and warm, and the electricity was instantly crackling between them. Her head found a niche in his shoulder. Her body found his rhythm easily; she was born for it, his other half. It was black-velvet seduction, pure magic.

This was home. In his arms. She closed her eyes, savoring the feel of his body against hers. The music was dreamy, unbelievable in such a place. Not once on the crowded floor did another touch them. He moved them in perfect syncopation, the heat rising between them with every step. Flames seemed to lick along her skin, move to his, and come back again.

Aidan bent his head to taste her. His lips, soft, hot, brushed her neck, lingering for a heartbeat on her pulse. He felt it jump beneath the moist heat of his mouth, felt it begin to race frantically. "Come home with me, *piccola*," he whispered urgently, his teeth scraping her skin gently, persuasively, gliding back and forth across her pulse. Her blood sang to him, cried out for him. "Do not torment me any longer."

Her body swayed with his, liquid and pliant. She had never needed anything so much in her life. She made no sound. She couldn't. But he knew her answer even in her silence. He could read it in her enormous eyes.

They moved toward the door, Alexandria barely aware of her surroundings, yet again Aidan protected her from the crush, his body always between hers and the crowd. Outside, the night seemed to greet them, to welcome them, the stars brighter than usual, the air carrying fragrant scents from the ocean.

Aidan slipped an arm around her waist, locking her beneath the protection of his shoulder. She tilted her head to look up at him. "I should have known you would follow me to protect me. What did you do to that poor man in the leather outfit?"

He laughed softly. "He likes black widow spiders. He also likes hurting women. And I do not like other men touching you."

"I noticed."

He stopped her on the street corner, crushed her to him, and lifted her chin. His golden gaze seemed riveted on her lower lip, and she felt her breath catch in her throat. He made a sound somewhere between a moan and a growl and lowered his head. His mouth fastened on hers, and the earth moved beneath her feet. Her body melted into his until there was only Aidan and Alexandria, a part of the night itself.

The surge of hunger, of need, was so strong, so over-whelming, Alexandria clung to him to keep from falling. He wrapped his arms around her, and they were moving through time and space. The wind blew through her hair so that it streamed out behind them in a siren's song, rippling in the clear night like strands of silk.

His mouth moved over hers, consuming, dominating, hungry beyond human boundaries. His tongue explored every inch of the velvet interior of her mouth, demanding her response. Alexandria heard herself moan, the sound low, pleading.

Then the third-floor balcony was beneath his feet. He simply waved a hand, and the glass door slid open. It stayed that way, the breeze from the sea a welcome counterpoint to the heat of their bodies. He followed her down to the quilt-covered four-poster bed, blanketing her body with his own, unable to take the chance she might panic and flee. He could not wait any longer. He could not let her go this time. His hands caressed her soft skin, traced the inviting swell of her breasts, pushed the fabric of her shirt roughly out of his way to expose her body to his golden scrutiny. The cool air felt sensuous on her hot skin, her breasts aching and full under his heated gaze. His hand cupped a breast, held the soft weight in his palm possessively.

"Do you feel the darkness in me, Alexandria?" he whispered, his voice husky and aching. "It is growing, spreading. Feel it in me." His mouth found her eyes, her temple, the corner of her mouth, her throat. Each kiss was feather-light but left a burning brand, his imprint for all time on her soul. "Give yourself to me. For now. For eternity. Feel the darkness in me, and take it away."

It was the voice of seduction, a need so consuming, so great, she could not possibly refuse. She did feel the dark need in him, his battle to be gentle with her, to allow her some kind of choice. She felt his desire, stark and hungry, to rip the clothes from her and gorge himself in the mysteries of her body. Her own body responded to the urgency of his need with creamy heat.

She moved beneath him, arched upward to offer him her

breast. Her eyes closed tightly, and she moaned aloud as he took her into the heat of his mouth. Her arms circled his head, held him to her as every pull of his mouth produced a rush of answering liquid heat from her body.

His body was so hard and heavy, trapped in the confines of his clothes. He pushed them aside, tore at her jeans, wanting every inch of her soft, bare skin against him. Aidan lifted himself slightly, just enough so that he could see her body. She lay naked, her skin flushed with wanting him. His hand spanned her stomach, his palm covering the triangle of tight blond curls, his fingers finding moist heat. Lightning arced through him, through her, and raced through their blood.

He cradled her head in the palm of his free hand, dragging her to his chest. *Feed, cara mia. Feed long and deep. You are my other half, the half that stands in the light. Be part of me for all eternity.* His finger probed the entrance to her tight velvet sheath, finding heat and readiness and need just for him. He could feel tears burning behind his eyes.

He felt her breath over his heart. "I can never go back, can I?" she asked softly in a lost voice.

His fingers moved deeper, a deliberate enticement. He felt hot velvet muscles clench around him. His body was raging for release. "Do you really want to go back, *cara*, and leave me alone in an eternity of darkness? If you had the choice, would you really leave me?" There was a catch in his husky voice. His hand pushed against her, his fingers probing, exploring, deliberately feeding the fire spreading through her body.

His will was merging his mind with hers fully, completely. She could feel it then, the gathering darkness waiting to claim him, a beast crouched and poised, a cold killer without mercy. There was a red haze, desire beating at him, fire racing through his blood. She could feel his agony, his fear that she would not want him enough to choose him, knowing that he would take her anyway, knowing that he could never stop himself. But he wanted her to want him, to need him that much.

Her tongue stroked over his muscles, a soft caress. Her teeth nipped his skin gently, teasingly. "How could I ever leave you, Aidan? Do you really think I could? I thought you knew everything. Even I knew better. Almost from the very start, I knew better." And she had. She had hidden the secret away from both of them.

His hand explored her thighs, secret shadows and hollows, wringing breathless, mewling cries from her throat. Her hands found the roped muscles in his broad back, her shy touch enflaming him further.

He was doing things to her with his hands, by his touch alone, memorizing every beloved inch of her, bringing her into a firestorm of hunger impossible to sate. She kissed his chest, nuzzled the blond hair there, lapped at his nipple. His body hardened until he thought he might go mad.

He forced her knees apart, giving him better access to her feminine heat. He pushed against her aggressively, needing her desperately. Alexandria felt him, hard and thick, insisting on entrance. He felt too large, too much of an invasion. When she would have hesitated, pulled back, he cupped her bottom in his palm and held her pinned against him. *Trust me, Alexandria.* He breathed the words in her mind. *I would never hurt you. Your body has need of mine. Feel it, what it demands of you. We are one body, one heart, one soul, and one mind.*

She found the beautiful pitch of his voice impossible to resist. Her mouth moved of its own accord over his chest, seeking and finding the deep pulse. Her tongue stroked, caressed. His hands tightened on her hips nearly to the point of pain. Her teeth sank deep, and his body surged forward to bury itself in hers. A streak of lightning lit the sky. It sizzled and danced, streaked through the open door, a white and blue whip searing them both, welding them together. She cried out with pain and pleasure. His shout, hoarse and triumphant, mingled with hers.

He moved, nearly unable to bear the tightness of her velvet sheath clenching him, so hot and addicting that he wanted to lose himself forever in her. The fiery friction consumed him, became him, until he was riding a crest so high with pleasure that he lost all concept of time and space. Colors danced behind his eyes, vivid and bright. Their scents, musky and fragrant, mingled, a perfume created from their lovemaking. Her mouth on him, erotic and frantic, matched the wild frenzy of his body. He lost himself in pure feeling, burying himself deeper and harder, wanting to crawl inside her so deep that their very hearts and lungs would be entwined, impossible to separate.

Alexandria clutched at his back, afraid she was being swept away for all time. Her tongue closed the wound on his chest, savoring the wild, masculine taste of him. His hands were hard on her hips, holding her still for his invasion. It was more than she could bear, the untamed look of him with his hair spilling down, his face taut with pleasure. She moved her hands down his back to his buttocks, memorizing every inch of him.

A moan escaped Aidan's throat, deep and husky, the sound dragged from his very soul. He lifted his head, his strange eyes molten gold, hot and fierce with hunger. He kissed her eyes, the corners of her mouth, her chin. She felt his breath on her throat, the stroke of his tongue a caress. Her body clenched in reaction, heightening his pleasure even more, until he thought he might die with it.

His teeth scraped the valley between her breasts, so that she ached and arched into him, pushing against his mouth. "You are mine for all time, Alexandria. You know that now." He made it a statement, a command she dared not disobey.

Alexandria smiled against his shoulder at his demanding ways. She had no idea what Carpathian women were like, but her male was about to discover a whole new breed. And then she was crying out with pleasure, her throat working convulsively as his teeth pierced her breast, as his arms tightened possessively and his body took hers with a ferocious hunger beyond her wildest imagination. Wave after wave of pleasure swept through her, whirling her out of herself and into him. He was everywhere she turned, everywhere she touched, inside her body, inside her mind, her very blood his, until they seemed one being exploding upward into the sky.

They lay together, clinging to one another, their hearts

pounding out a rhythm of intensity unlike either of them had thought possible. Aidan's tongue stroked her breast, sending a shiver racing through her blood, through his. He framed her face with his hands, brushed his mouth gently, tenderly, across her forehead, and feathered kisses down her face to her chin. For the first time in his long, seemingly endless existence, he felt truly alive, truly at peace.

"You have given me a priceless gift, Alexandria, and I will never forget it. You had no reason to trust me, yet you did," he whispered softly, humbly. "Thank you."

She was staring up at him with wondering eyes, unable to come fully back to earth. He was in her, her body wrapped around his. It seemed impossible that those golden eyes could shine with such intensity, burn with such need, only for her. A slow smile curved her mouth and lit her sapphire eyes to match the glow in his. They simply stared at each other, into each other's soul.

She could feel him, thick, hard, beginning to move, an incredible friction of slick heat, so gentle and tender, she felt as if she were melting into him. Aidan moved slowly, savoring each long stroke, his eyes devouring her face. Her initiation had been a wild frenzy. Now he wanted to take his time, build their pleasure slowly.

His fingers tangled in her hair. His mouth tasted her satin skin, finding the pulse beating in her vulnerable throat. "You are so beautiful, Alexandria, so very beautiful."

"You make me feel beautiful," she conceded.

"I still cannot believe I found you." He suddenly lifted his head and stared down at her. His hips continued the slow, languorous movement. "You are going to get rid of that horror-writing video-game mogul."

She kissed his shoulder, then rubbed her face against the golden hair on his chest. "No, I'm not. He's my boss."

"I am your boss."

"You wish you were my boss," Alexandria teased gently. "I work for him."

"I have enough money for both of us to live comfortably," he protested. Then a trace of laughter entered his voice. "Do you know how sick that man has to be to think up that stuff?"

"What about you? You play his games. Worse, you *live* weirder stuff than he thinks up." Her chin lifted. "Besides, I want the job. I love to draw. This is the chance of a lifetime, Aidan, something I've always wanted to do."

He did laugh then, lowering his head to kiss her belligerent chin, to plant a row of kisses in the valley between her breasts. "Your lifetime has been extended considerably, *cara mia*. You can find someone else's fantasies to illustrate, preferably those of a nice elderly woman with no sons and no male secretaries."

She laughed with him, secretly suspecting she would end up doing as he wished and jettisoning Thomas Ivan from both their lives. But for now, Aidan's body was doing incredible things to hers, and she did not care to think about any other man. His slow, rhythmic rocking was taking her breath away and fanning the embers of the smoldering fire somewhere in the pit of her stomach. Her body was moving with his, following his guidance without inhibition. She loved the feel of his hands cupping her breasts, the brush of his chin, his mouth, across her nipples. He was stealing her heart with his tenderness.

"I have already stolen your heart," he teased softly, reminding her he was sharing her thoughts.

"I'm not certain I'm ready for you to know every single thing I think."

"Or feel." His voice dropped an octave, to black-velvet seduction. "Or fantasize."

Her hands found his hips. "You're the one with all the fantasies. I'm just borrowing yours to try them out."

His body surged forward, burying itself more deeply within her. "How am I doing?" He began to move with deeper, stronger strokes, picking up the pace until the smoldering embers were leaping flames. "We have not even started, *piccola*. I have the whole night to worship you as you deserve."

At the unexpected flash of fire sweeping through her body, she bit her lip, and two small pinpricks of red welled up. Aidan's glittering golden eyes focused there, untamed emotion in their depths. Just that look sent her spiraling over the edge, her body erupting in mind-shattering explosions. Her breathless cry was lost as his mouth found hers, capturing the sound forever. His tongue swept across her lip, a curling caress that impossibly heightened her pleasure.

Aidan's every muscle tensed. He was motionless for a heartbeat, and then he threw back his head and surged forward, burying himself in her, her body's shattering reaction to his overriding his control. It went on forever, the release, the spinning world, yet lasted not nearly long enough. He wanted to be there for all time, with Alexandria locked safely in his arms.

They lay together without moving, without speaking, savoring the moment and each other. Aidan was the first to move, reluctantly shifting his weight. He gathered her close, as if she might suddenly realize what she had surrendered into his keeping and try to run away from him, from what she was.

She stroked his arm as it wrapped possessively around her. "Aidan, I can know your thoughts just as you know mine. And I am still me. I don't intend to be locked away in a closet somewhere."

He propped himself up on one elbow. Wind blew through the room, bringing with it a mist from the sea. He lifted a hand, and the sliding glass door closed instantly. He dragged up a comforter to cover her even as he moved closer to warm her with his body heat. "I did not have the closet in mind, *cara*. I thought my bed would be far more appropriate." There was a trace of male humor in his velvet voice.

She pushed the hair from her face and looked him in the eye. "I am going to work, Aidan. You've created a life here for yourself and Stefan and Marie. But Joshua deserves a normal existence, too. I don't want his life to change so much that he loses everything familiar to him. I don't want to lose that either. This is all so frightening. You're frightening. I will not lose whatever part of me is left."

"I want you safe, Alexandria. The women of our race are our most precious treasures. Without you we cannot continue our existence. I need to know you are safe every moment of the day."

Alexandria sat up and dragged the comforter over her breasts, suddenly aware of her nakedness. Aidan carelessly threw a leg over her thigh, pinning her in place. "There is not an inch of you I do not know, *cara*. This is no time to become shy."

She could feel a blush creeping up her entire body until her face glowed pink in the night. The way he had positioned his leg, she could feel his maleness pressed against her, his heat and strength, his growing, hardening need. She knew his words were teasing, but she had never been in a situation like this one, and she wasn't certain how to act or what to feel.

"You're using . . . this to control me."

He grinned at her unrepentantly, rubbing against her suggestively. "*This?* What is *this?* Are you saying I would use our sexual relationship to get my way?"

She began laughing again; she couldn't help it. "You would use anything, Mr. Innocence, to get your way, and you know it."

He cupped one breast, his thumb feathering over the sensitized nipple. "Is it working?" His voice brushed over her skin like velvet.

"You can't possibly want me again, Aidan," she protested, pushing herself away from him and the temptation of his body.

His hands caught her waist and drew her against his already hard shaft. He traced the contour of her hips and stroked her bottom. "You are beautiful, Alexandria," he breathed as he rolled her onto her belly beneath him.

"Aidan." His name came out in a breathless protest. His hands were strong—ruthless, even—pinning her in place, his breath on her back, his teeth closing over her shoulder when she tried to squirm free. The position made her feel intensely vulnerable.

Aidan pressed against her, his need to take control as strong as his need to give her pleasure. "You want me, *cara mia*. I feel it."

"It's too soon."

"Not for your body." Even as he said the words, his hand

237

pushed against her to test her readiness, coming away bathed in liquid heat. "Oh, God, Alexandria, how can I ever resist you?" He needed her all over again. Needed to feel, to be alive, to know she would always be a part of him, his life, that when he opened his eyes and took his first breath each evening, she would be there to give him ever-deepening emotions, and to look at him with something other than fear in her eyes.

Alexandria might have resisted his dominance, but she could not resist his burning need. The intensity of his feelings swept through her mind, and her body caught fire with his. She pushed back against him, consenting, enflaming him further. She was laughing softly, teasing, but her breath caught in her throat when he thrust forward in intimate invasion. Her body tightened around his, holding him, clutching him, rippling with life and heat.

One powerful arm tightened possessively around her waist, his body all at once protective over hers.

"Are we crazy, we two?" he murmured.

"You're the crazy one," she gasped, moving with him, beginning to spin out of control again that fast. "I have work to do, yet you keep me here, locked to you, a prisoner of your passion," she said, panting. He was building the fire fast, with sure, hard strokes, surging into her, his hands holding her beneath him. "I can't believe I'm letting you get away with it." And she couldn't. It seemed impossible that she would be kneeling on a bed stained with her own innocence and loving this man's possession of her, wanting more, wanting him again and again.

When they finally collapsed, holding each other, a fine sheen of perspiration coating their bodies, they were drained, spent, satiated. "I heard you chanting in my head, the first time we . . ." She trailed off. "The words were in your native language, weren't they?"

"I ensured our bond again," he admitted. "The thought of losing you through my own stupidity was too much. I recited the ritual words as I took your innocence, to bind us together for eternity."

"I don't understand."

"Those words make an unbreakable tie for our males. Once said, the bond is eternal."

She rolled over and blinked up at him. "What are you talking about?"

"When a Carpathian male finds his mate and knows for certain she is the one, he can bind her to him with the ritual words even if he has not yet claimed her body. It is like the human marriage ceremony but much deeper. Our souls and hearts are one half of the same whole, incomplete when apart. The ritual words bind them back together as they were meant to be."

Her gaze narrowed in speculation. "I thought the two were bound by chemistry, by blood."

"They are destined, true, and the bond is begun." He pushed his long hair from his face and retreated to one side of the bed, as if uneasy with the conversation.

"So the woman can still escape if the man doesn't actually say the ritual words?"

He shrugged his broad shoulders, his golden gaze all at once unreadable. "Why would he be so stupid as to not speak them when he knows her destiny lies with him? He would be a fool."

"Perhaps it would be nice if he asked the woman what she thought. Human men at least *ask* the woman if she chooses to spend her life with him. Perhaps Carpathian women would also like to have a choice."

He shrugged again. "It is the choice of destiny, fate, whatever you wish to call it. The law of the universe. The law of God. We were made this way. The words cannot be revoked. No Carpathian male is going to allow his woman to run around unprotected and unclaimed."

"You people are living in the Dark Ages! You can't just take over someone's life without their consent. It isn't right," she argued, appalled.

"A Carpathian male cannot survive without his lifemate."

"Well, just how many years do you want to live anyway?" she demanded hotly.

His golden eyes flashed briefly with amusement, and his palm slid up her calf to her thigh. "I would go for another century or two as long as all our nights were like this one."

His voice did something funny to her heart, starting that curious melting sensation she so often experienced around him. She wanted to be angry with him, but the truth was, if she could have more nights like this one, she wanted a century or two with him herself.

"I am reading your thoughts," he teased, his voice a deliberate caress.

"It's time you stopped. Don't you have something else to keep you occupied for a while? And don't think you're off the hook with this thing. You just can't go around making decisions that affect my life without consulting me." She regarded him suspiciously. "What else can you do without my knowledge?"

He leaned across the bed and kissed her full on the mouth, lingering to savor the taste of her. "You name it, *cara*, and I can do it."

She jerked away from him and slapped at the hand that was moving into her tight nest of curls. "Don't be bragging, Aidan. This is not a good thing."

"I think it is an excellent thing. I will need everything in my bag of tricks to keep you in line. I look forward to each minute of it, Alexandria."

"You're forgetting my annoying little habits, and I think they've just begun to multiply."

He groaned. "You are really going to try to reform me?"

"Someone has to do it." Her hand found his. "I'm used to a certain amount of freedom, Aidan. I need it. I could never be happy if you took it away from me."

He cupped her chin in one hand, his gold eyes sweeping intently over her upturned face. "I am aware of the compromises both of us will have to make, Alexandria. I do not expect that they will all be on your side. I ask only that you allow me room to make a few mistakes."

She nodded. He could so easily steal her heart. With a look. A few words. That voice of his, pure black magic. "How can I be so crazy about you and so afraid at the same time?"

"You are in love with me." He said it quietly.

She blinked, shocked, as if she had never considered it.

"That's a little strong, Aidan. You swept me up in all this so quickly, against my will."

"You love me," he asserted calmly.

She made a small retreat, a few inches across the bed. "I don't know you well enough to love you."

"No? You have been in my mind. You have shared my thoughts, my memories. You know everything about me, good as well as bad. And you gave yourself to me. You would not have done so if you were not in love with me."

She swallowed hard. She did not want to face this right now; it was too overwhelming. She tried to be flippant. "It's just the power of sex."

His eyebrows shot up.

"You dance so beautifully?" she ventured hopefully.

"I have been in your mind, too, *cara mia*. There is no hiding the truth from me." He sounded smugly satisfied.

Alexandria assumed her most haughty expression, dragged the comforter around her shoulders, and kept silent.

"Is it really so difficult to admit to loving me?" His voice was a caress, wrapping her up in safe, loving arms.

"Why is it so important to have this discussion right now? I'm with you, and I'm obviously not going anywhere."

"Because it is important to you. You have this idea that you can't feel love for anyone other than your brother."

"I never have been able to before."

"And you think you feel something for me because I put some kind of magic spell on you. What we have together is not from any spell. Perhaps I did bind you to me in the ways of our people, but I could not have done so were you not already mine. You are my true lifemate. You would have given your life to save me, even when you did not trust me."

Her chin lifted. "I thought I was going to die anyway, and I didn't want to live like a vampire. Remember, I thought you were a vampire and that you had made me one."

"Why would you save a vampire, one so evil?" he countered softly.

She clapped both hands over her ears. "You're mixing me up, Aidan."

He gently clasped her wrists and lowered her hands, leaning to kiss her neck. "You knew, deep down, where it counted, that I was the one. That is why your body responded to mine. Not some ancient spell, not even gratitude for saving you and Joshua. Your body and soul recognized me before your mind and heart had a chance to do so. Your mind was traumatized by all that had happened. And it did not help much when I reacted so fearfully for your safety. How could you know what was in your heart?"

"What I feel for you is so . . ." She could not find the words to describe the emotions whirling so strongly within her.

"Intense. Deep. Different from what you expected. And because it is so different, you do not recognize it for what it is. You are no longer human with human limitations. All your senses have expanded, so your emotions, too—pleasure, pain, hunger—will all be overwhelming until you get used to them. At first your new hearing was almost unbearable, was it not?"

She nodded. It had been briefly, but she had already forgotten.

"In a short time you learned to tone down your extraordinary hearing or use it only when needed. In time you will be able to use all your abilities easily, just as I do. The intensity between us will grow, as will our bond. But it is not magic, Alexandria. It is love." Aidan's voice was so tender, so gentle, and so certain, she felt her heart somersault.

Chapter Fifteen

The ocean waves rose high and raced toward the shore, spilling foam and salt spray before crashing against the rocks of the cliff and cascading back into the roiling sea. Alexandria trickled sand through her fingers as she watched the spectacular display nature was putting on. The late hour and wild winds ensured that she had the beach to herself.

She sat on a sand dune, resting her chin on her knees and watched the waves. She had always loved the ocean, but after her experience with the vampire, she'd thought she'd never be able to face it again.

Aidan had changed all that. He had brought beauty and joy to her world again. She could sit here, alone in the dark, surrounded by the wailing wind, the crashing sea, even the ominous clouds gathering overhead, and realize the magnificence of it all. Aidan was working on one of his many businesses, and she had slipped out of the house to be on her own. While part of her loved the closeness Aidan demanded, the way he was constantly slipping in and out of her mind, she was used to her freedom, used to doing things on her own. And she had needed to just sit quietly and allow all that had happened to her begin to sink in.

Aidan was unhappy with her. She could feel the weight of his disapproval. He was with her, in a quiet corner of her mind, but at least he hadn't tried to force her compliance.

I should have.

Alexandria smiled at his complaint. *It's a good thing you didn't. You need to learn I don't mind you the way Joshua does.*

Another one of your annoying habits?

She laughed out loud, the joyful sound carried down the beach by the wind. *If it isn't, I'm going to be sure to cultivate it.*

You are going to do exactly what I say. His voice had dropped an octave, until it was a black-velvet caress, a blatant seduction.

She instantly felt the answering heat in her body. *Get back to work, sex fiend, and leave me alone for a while.*

Just for a short while. That is all the time I can manage to be without your body beneath mine.

You're wicked, Aidan. Very, very wicked. She was laughing, her head back, her heart light and filled with joy after such a long, dark journey.

Miles away, the sky lit up briefly, a white flash illuminating the dark clouds, and then she heard the distant rumble of thunder. A storm was riding the waves in, feeding the sea's playful mood. She leaned back and felt a drop of water splash her cheek, rain or sea spray, she couldn't tell. She didn't care. Her life was coming back together; she was finding her strength again. And now that she was accepting what she had become, she would find a way to deal with life again.

In the darkness a shadow shifted overhead. She blinked, sat up, and tilted her head to scan the skies. She detected no movement. Perhaps it had been merely one black cloud gliding in front of the others. Still, she felt uneasy. She was alone on the dunes, close enough to the water that she could detect the finned predators beneath the surface. And that realization suddenly unnerved her, that beneath the beautiful waves glided prehistoric creatures, forever seeking prey.

A slow smile curved her mouth. She was beginning to let anything spook her. Who would be out on a night like this? The ocean roared, slammed into the rocks, and sent plumes of froth into the sky. Her uneasiness increased with the wildness of the storm.

Perhaps it would be better for you to listen to your lifemate and be alone in the house or on the balcony rather than out in a storm.

His taunt was irritating, and she scooped up another handful of sand in defiance. Still, despite her determination, Alexandria felt a heavy, oppressive weight on her chest, and she anxiously scanned the sky, trying to remain calm enough to feel her surroundings, to detect another's presence. Suddenly, without any real reason, she was certain she wasn't alone, and whatever was stalking her was evil.

Get out of there, Aidan commanded at once. His voice was cool and determined, and in response to the increasing strength of her instincts, she sensed he had taken to the air.

She stood, her eyes searching the immediate area. The wind tugged at her hair, whipping it across her face. She dragged the long strands away and saw a man teetering high on the cliff. The wind was vicious, and she could see he was in trouble, the edge of the embankment crumbling beneath his weight. Alexandria shouted and began to run, instinctively reaching out as if she could somehow prevent his fall.

How could she not have seen him earlier? Felt his presence? Why had she been so selfishly certain that she was the one in danger? How long had the man been up there and in danger?

What is it, cara? Aidan's voice was calm and soothing, and he was closer now, which was reassuring.

She grabbed on to him like a lifeline. *A man on the cliffs—he's falling.* If only she hadn't wasted time feeling sorry for herself, for what she had become. She could have saved him. She should have been learning from Aidan, everything he could teach her. She could have moved with his blinding speed and caught the man before he hit the jagged rocks below.

I am coming. Stay away from him! It was a demand, but one she couldn't obey. Though she had little hope of saving the stranger, she had to try. She ran barefoot over the wet sand, her gaze riveted on the cliff. For one moment she thought the world darkened. Then a burst of lightning danced and sizzled, and a fireball exploded through the night, heading right toward the man.

Alexandria screamed as he tumbled forward, his fall seeming to happen in slow motion, a torturous descent of forty feet or more. The wind whipped her shout back into her face like a slap. She was still a distance away and far too late, but she ran anyway. Without warning, at a full run, she hit something invisible. The impact knocked her to the ground.

Heart beating fast, she sat up, shoving the wild, wind-whipped tangle of her hair from her face. She didn't see an obstacle, the impact hadn't hurt, yet when she reached out, her hand met something solid.

How could you, Aidan? She was bewildered that he would restrain her this way, stop her from going to the stranger's aid. She slowly got to her feet, shaken.

The fog rolled in swiftly from the sea, carried on the wild winds. Out of it, on the other side of the invisible barrier, a man began to materialize. At first he was shimmering, translucent, but then he solidified further, becoming a dark, shadowy being. He was tall, like Aidan, with the same roped muscles. His hair was as black as the night, long and held with a leather thong at the nape of his neck. His face was beautiful, his mouth both sensual and cruel, his jaw strong. But it was his eyes that captured her attention. They were pale, almost light itself, a quicksilver brilliance impossible to ignore.

Alexandria was suddenly very afraid. Aidan exuded power, but this man *was* power. No one, nothing, could ever defeat such a creature. She was certain he was not human. One hand crept protectively to her throat.

The stranger casually waved a hand, and the barrier was gone in an instant. She had never seen the obstruction, yet now she knew it was gone, that nothing stood between them but air. She was terrified, for herself and for Aidan.

"You are Aidan's woman. His lifemate. Where is he that he would allow you to wander unprotected?"

His voice was the most hypnotic, compelling sound she had ever heard. So pure. So enticing. No one could resist that soft, musical voice. If he told her to throw herself into the roiling ocean, she would do so. She curled her fingers tightly into fists.

"Who are you?" she asked. Silently she warned, *Aidan, be careful. There is another here. He knows I am with you, your lifemate.* She tried not to allow the trembling that was seizing her body to creep into her voice.

Look at him, piccola. *Do not be afraid. I am close. I will see what you see. Keep your mind open.* As always, Aidan sounded calm and in control.

The stranger's beguiling mouth curved, but there was no warmth in the slashing silver of his eyes. "You speak to him. Good. I am certain he can see me now. But he is a fool to allow his feelings for you to blind him to his duties."

Her chin lifted. "Who are you?" she repeated.

"I am Gregori. The dark one. Perhaps he has told you of me."

He is the most knowledgeable, the most powerful of all our kind, Aidan confirmed. He was very near. *He is the greatest healer our kind has ever known and my teacher. He is also a master of destruction and bodyguard to our Prince.*

246

He terrifies me.

He terrifies everyone. Only Mikhail, the Prince of our people, knows him well.

"I trust Aidan has good things to say about me." He was facing her, those brilliant eyes seeing right into her soul, but Alexandria had the feeling his attention was elsewhere. His voice was so pure, so perfect, she wanted him to go on speaking.

A rush of wind stirred up a whirling eddy of sand that spun and swirled until it enveloped Alexandria, driving her backward. When she finally regained her balance and uncovered her eyes, Aidan was directly in front of her.

"Very impressive, Aidan," the stranger said with a trace of satisfaction.

"I have not seen one of my own people for many years," Aidan said softly. "I am pleased it is you, Gregori."

"Do you now use your woman as bait?" The tone was mild, but the reprimand was clear.

Alexandria stirred, furious that this man would try to make Aidan feel guilty about her independence. Aidan's fingers unerringly found her wrist behind him, closing around it like a vise. *Do not*, he warned. She subsided immediately, sensing danger thick in the air.

"This one, this betrayer to our people." Gregori nodded toward the man lying so still on the rocks where he had fallen. "He sought to take her from you."

"He could not have done so," Aidan said softly.

Gregori nodded. "I believe that to be true. Still, she takes a risk that should not be permitted." A network of iridescent white veins lit up the sky, sharp, brilliant, a powerful display. The arcing lightning cast a peculiar shadow across the dark, handsome face and flashing silver eyes, making Gregori look both cruel and hungry.

The fingers around Alexandria's wrist tightened even more. *Do not move, do not speak, no matter what*, Aidan cautioned softly in her mind. "Thank you for your assistance, Gregori," he said aloud, his voice gentle and true. "This is my lifemate, Alexandria. She is new to our people and knows nothing of our ways. We would both consider it a great honor if you would accompany us back to our house and tell us the news of our homeland."

Are you out of your mind? Alexandria protested silently, horrified. It would be like bringing home a wild jungle cat. A tiger. Something very lethal.

Gregori inclined his head at the introduction, but the refusal to join them was clear in his silver eyes. "It would be unwise of me to join you indoors. I would be a caged tiger, untrustworthy, unpredictable." His pale eyes flickered over Alexandria, and she had the distinct impression he was laughing at her. Then he turned his attention once more to Aidan. "I need to ask of you a favor."

Aidan knew of what Gregori would speak, and he shook his head. "Do not, Gregori. You are my friend. Do not ask of me what I cannot do." Alexandria felt Aidan's sorrow, his distress. His mind was a turmoil of emotions, fear among them.

The silver eyes flashed and burned. "You will do what you must, Aidan, just as I have done for over a thousand years. I have come here to wait for my lifemate. She will arrive in a few months to do a show, magic show. San Francisco is on her schedule. I intend to establish a house high in the mountains, far from your place. I need the wild, the heights, and I must be alone. I am close to the end, Aidan. The hunt, the kill, is all I have left."

He waved a hand, and the ocean waves leapt in response. "I am not certain if I can wait until she comes. I am too close. The demon has nearly consumed me." There was no change in the sweet purity of his voice.

"Go to her. Send for her. Call her to you." Aidan rubbed his forehead in agitation, and his obvious upset alarmed Alexandria more than anything else. Nothing ever seemed to get to Aidan. "Where is she? Who is she?"

"She is Mikhail and Raven's daughter. But Raven did not prepare her for what was to come on the day of the claiming. She was but eighteen years. When I went to her, she was so filled with fear, I found I could not be the monster I needed to be to claim her against her will. I did not press her. I vowed to myself to allow her five years of freedom. After all, joining with me will be rather like joining with a tiger. Not the most comfortable of destinies."

"You can no longer wait." Alexandria had never heard Aidan so agitated. She stroked her thumb in a small caress across his wrist to remind him he would not have to face the future alone.

"I made a vow, and I will keep it. Once she is joined to me for all eternity, her life will not be an easy one, so she runs from it, and from me." Gregori's voice was so beautiful, so clear. There was no trace of bitterness, no regret.

"Does she know what you suffer for her?"

The silver eyes flashed at the implication of his lifemate's selfishness. "She knows nothing. This was my decision, my gift to her. The favor I ask is that you do not hunt me alone, if such becomes necessary. You will need Julian. He is of the darkness."

"Julian is like me," Aidan instantly protested.

"No, Aidan," Gregori corrected in his mesmerizing voice. "Julian is like me. That is why he seeks out the high reaches, why he is always alone. He is like me. He will help you defeat me should there be need."

"Go to her, Gregori," Aidan pleaded.

Gregori shook his head. "I cannot. Promise me you will do as I have requested. You will not attempt to hunt me without Julian."

"I would never be so foolish as to hunt the most wily wolf without the aid of another. Stay strong, Gregori." There was real sorrow in Aidan's voice.

"I will hold out as long as I am able," Gregori replied, "but in the waiting, there is much danger. I will be unable to destroy myself should it become too late. I will be too far gone. You understand, Aidan. The burden of this decision could fall on your shoulders, and for that, I ask your forgiveness. I always thought it would be Mikhail, but she is here, in the United States. And she will be here, in San Francisco, when my vow has been honored."

Aidan nodded, but Alexandria could feel the tears burning in his mind, in his heart. She made an effort to comfort him, to send him warmth, but she remained as still as he had asked her, not completely understanding what Gregori was saying but knowing it was grave.

"I will attend to this one, destroy all evidence of his existence." Gregori gestured toward the body at the bottom of the cliff. "But, Aidan, he was not alone. There was another. I thought it best to stay and protect your lifemate rather than hunt him down. So close to turning myself, I did not want to chance two kills in one evening." The soft, musical voice could have been discussing the weather.

"Gregori, I thank you for the warning and the help. You need not worry over the betrayer. That is my job, though I admit I have been attending to other things than hunting recently."

"As you should have," Gregori acknowledged with a gentle smile. "A lifemate comes first in all things."

"Why is it you fear yours will not have an easy life?" Aidan asked.

"I have hunted too long to ever stop. I am used to my own way in all things. I have waited too long, fought too hard, and suffered too much to allow her the freedom she will desire. Her life will never be her own, only what I make of it."

Aidan smiled then, and Alexandria could feel him relaxing. "If you do as you believe, put her before your own comfort, you will have no choice but to allow her freedom."

"I am not like Mikhail or Jacques or, it seems, you. I intend that her protection come above all else." Gregori's voice held an edge.

Aidan grinned at him, laughter spilling from his golden eyes. "I can only hope I have the chance to see you, Gregori, under the spell of your woman. You must promise that you will bring her to meet us one day."

"Not if I end up like you or Mikhail. I will not have my dangerous reputation destroyed in such a way." A hint of humor seemed to creep in and then was quickly gone, as if the wind had carried it away.

"I will see to the vampire," Aidan said. "You should avoid confronting death."

"I killed him from a distance. You will find it . . . unsettling," Gregori warned.

"You are even more powerful than I remember."

"I have acquired much knowledge over the years," Gregori conceded. His pale eyes rested thoughtfully on Aidan's face. "You will find your brother much changed, also. He is a fast learner, that one, and unafraid of reaching too far into the shadows. I tried to tell him the cost, but he would not listen."

Aidan shook his head. "Julian always said rules were made to be broken. He has always gone his own way. But he did respect you. You were the only real influence in his life, maybe the only one he ever listened to."

Gregori shook his head. "He could not listen any longer. The wind called, the mountains, the far-off places. I could not hope to stop him. He was dark inside, and nothing would ever satisfy him."

"You call it darkness. But it was that quality in you that made you open the world for us. It made you seek out the healing techniques that you have passed on to me, to others. It allowed you to perform the miracles that you have performed for our people. It has done the same for Julian," Aidan replied softly.

The silver eyes paled to steel. Cold. Bleak. Empty. "It led both of us to things that should never have been learned. In the acquisition of knowledge comes power, Aidan. But without rules, without emotions, without a concept of right or wrong, it is far too easy to abuse that power."

"All Carpathians are aware of that, Gregori," Aidan argued. "You, more than most, know the concept of right and wrong. And so does Julian. Why have you endured, resisted wrong, when others turned? You fought for justice, for our people. You had a code, and you have always lived up to it, as you are doing now. You say you have no feeling, but what of the compassion you felt for your lifemate when she was so frightened? You cannot turn. Every moment is an eternity for you, I know, but you have an end in sight."

Gregori's cold eyes seemed to impale Aidan, but the younger Carpathian did not flinch. He held Gregori's gaze until Alexandria could have sworn she saw a flicker of fire, a flame, springing from one to the other. Gregori's hard mouth softened slightly. "You have learned well, Aidan. You are a healer of both body and mind."

Aidan inclined his head in acknowledgment of the compliment. The wind howled, the waves crashed, and Gregori launched himself into the dark, roiling clouds. A black shape spread across the sky, an ominous shadow staining the heavens, and then it moved north and faded away as if it had never been, taking the storm with it.

Aidan sank into the sand, his head bowed, his shoulders shaking, as if he was trying to control some great emotion that had overcome him. Alexandria circled his head with her arms. She could feel sobs tearing at his throat and chest, yet he made no sound. Only a single, blood-red tear marked his great sorrow.

"I am sorry, *cara*, but he is a great man, one our people cannot afford to lose. I could feel his bleakness, the inner demon waiting to devour him. To have to honor my promise to him, to have to hunt him . . ." He shook his head. "It is such a disservice to one who has dedicated his life to our people, to our Prince."

Alexandria's breath caught in her throat. She had thought Aidan invincible. Capable, even, of hunting vampires and triumphing over their evil power. But Gregori was a different proposition. Even with two hunters such as Aidan, it didn't seem possible that he could be defeated. "Can't you contact this woman, the one who could save him?"

Aidan shook his head regretfully. "He would continue to honor his vow, and her presence would only make things worse."

She touched his hair with gentle, loving fingers. "As I made it worse for you." She rubbed her chin thoughtfully against his hair. "I can understand that girl's being afraid. You scared me. You still do. But Gregori, he's terrifying. I would never want to be tied to such a being. And she's only a child."

"Why would you still be afraid of me?" Aidan lifted his

head and touched her face reverently with his fingertips, with a tenderness that turned her heart over.

"Your power. Your intensity. Maybe when you teach me a few things, I won't be so nervous of it, but now it seems you have too much power for any one person to wield."

"Your mind holds the same powers as mine. You simply have to think of what you want, Alexandria. If you wish flight, you simply hold the picture in your mind, and your body is light, and you float."

His arm circled her waist, and they rose slowly into the air. "Merge with me. See it for yourself. There is no need to ever fear me." He set them gently back to earth.

"Tell me about the 'claiming' he was talking about. What did he mean? And who is Mikhail?"

"Mikhail is the oldest of our people, our Prince. He has led us for centuries. Gregori is only a quarter of a century younger, so in our terms, they are nearly the same age. Our people have been persecuted over the years, driven into hiding, and many were massacred. Our women have become so few, the men cannot find lifemates to bring light to their darkness, and more and more turn vampire. Though no one has yet discovered why, the few children born to us are male, and most do not survive the first year of life. Those women who give birth and lose the child grow despondent and refuse to try after a time. So the men without lifemates are lost, without hope. They either greet the dawn and perish or succumb to the demon within. Become vampire, true predators."

"How terrible." She meant it, sorrow filling her mind and heart.

"Mikhail and Gregori have been trying to find a way to avoid the inevitable, the extinction of our race. They discovered that a small group of human women possessing psychic abilities were capable of bonding chemically with our males."

"Like me."

He nodded. "You did not find human men physically attractive. For some unknown reason, you were not born into our race but were made for me specifically. Your body and mine have a need to be one. Your heart and soul are the other half of mine. Mikhail and Gregori believe that those psychic women of human descent are capable of producing female children, and that those children will also be capable, or at least more likely to produce female children. So you see why you are so treasured."

"What is the claiming?"

Aidan let his breath out slowly. "Alexandria . . ." There was hesitation in his voice.

She stepped away from him, her chin rising. "I guess there's a lot you haven't told me. Am I expected to have a child? A girl? What are the odds that my child will live?"

He reached out, framing her face in his large hands. "I do not want you for a breeder for my race, *piccola*. I want you for myself. I do not know the odds that *our* child will survive. Like you, I can only pray. We will have to cross that bridge when we come to it."

"So we have a girl, she survives her first year and grows up. What happens then?" Her sapphire eyes were steady on his golden ones.

"All female children are claimed on their eighteenth birthdays. The males come from all over to meet the girl. If the chemistry is right, she is claimed by the male."

"That is barbaric. Like a meat market. She has no chance at living any kind of life for herself." Alexandria was shocked.

"Carpathian women are raised to know they hold the fate of their lifemate in their hands. It is their birthright, as is bearing the children."

"No wonder the poor girl ran away. Can you imagine facing a life with that man at such an early age? How old is he? To her he must seem ancient. He's a man, for heaven's sake, not a boy. He's tough and probably cruel, and evidently he knows more about every subject under the sun than anyone alive."

"How old do you think I am, Alexandria?" Aidan asked softly. "I have lived over eight hundred years now. You are irrevocably bound to me. Is it such a terrible fate?"

For a moment there was silence. Then she was smiling at him. "Ask me again in a hundred years. I'll tell you then."

His eyes burned a liquid gold, molten, sexy. "Go home, *cara mia*. I will finish my work here and join you."

"I brought the car," she said. "When my Volkswagen wouldn't start, I took the little sporty-looking thing that no one ever uses. Stefan said it would be all right."

"I knew, and you did not hear a complaint. There is nowhere you go and nothing you do that is not known to me. We are one, *piccola*." He ruffled her hair as if she was a child because his body was starting to make demands, and a vampire's remains were but a few yards away. "Drive home, and I will meet you there."

As he walked her to the car, she fit beneath his shoulder, so that his body was sheltering her. Alexandria was ashamed of herself for liking the feeling it gave her. She was determined to hold on to her independence with both hands, especially in light of what he had told her might be the fate of her daughter. She had to be strong enough to stand up to Aidan, if she wanted a daughter who was able to choose her own way. She had the feeling Carpathian males had never caught on to the twentieth-century women's liberation movement.

Aidan watched the taillights of the little car disappear around the curve leading up to the main road. He shoved a hand through his thick mane of hair and turned to face the mess on the rocks. Several weeks earlier, five vampires had arrived in the area. They had moved across the United States on a killing spree, believing no hunters would follow them so far from their homeland. Still, it was known among their people that Aidan Savage resided in San Francisco. Why had they chosen to come here, to take such a risk? Was it because Gregori's woman was coming? But that was months away. What then? What had drawn the vampires to one of the few places in the United States where a true hunter resided?

He walked across the sand, his strides long and fast. Had they sensed Alexandria's presence when he had not? Was something else drawing them to San Francisco? He knew several renegades had chosen to go to New Orleans because the city had such a reputation for debauchery, for being the murder capital of the United States. Los Angeles, too, drew them because its frequent violence would hide their handiwork. He hunted there, though, when he recognized their doings.

When he reached the vampire's body he found it blackened and singed, the hair smoldering. It gave off the unmistakable stench of evil. If this one had stalked Alexandria, no doubt their home was being watched. He looked up at the night sky and sent his challenge. Clouds raced forward, dark and ominous, heralding retribution. *Come for me. You sought out my city, my home, my family. I am waiting for you.* The wind carried his words over the city, and somewhere, far off, like a distant clap of thunder, a bellow of anger answered him, the frenzied barking of dogs adding to the din.

His white teeth gleamed like a predator's as Aidan sent his silent laughter winging its way to his adversary. The challenge made, he bent over what remained of this vampire. Though he had spent much time with Gregori, he had never seen anything like this before. The vampire's chest was blown away, but his tainted blood had not seeped out because the wound was cauterized by the blast. The heart had turned to black, useless ashes. He shook his head. Gregori was nature at its most lethal.

Aidan stepped back from the abomination with a sense of sadness and inevitability. He had known this fallen creature, had grown up with him. This man was nearly two hundred years younger than he, yet he had turned. Why? Why did some of them hold out and some give in so quickly? Was it strength of character in those who endured? A loss of belief in any future for those who turned? Mikhail and Gregori struggled endlessly to bring their race hope, yet this man was proof they weren't succeeding. Too many of them were turning. The numbers increased with every passing century. It was no wonder Gregori was tired of hunting, of fighting the demon that was always within him. How did one hunt former friends, century after century, without becoming as hopeless as those he pursued?

256

Dark Gold

Aidan had to go home. He needed Alexandria's arms around him. He needed her warmth and compassion. He needed her body burning around his, telling him he was alive and had not become death. But he had become death to many of his kind, those who had turned, those he had hunted, and he knew it.

Aidan, come home to me. You are not deadly. You are gentle and kind. Look at you with Joshua. With Marie and Stefan. Gregori has made you melancholy.

So many of my people are lost, he mourned.

All the more reason to fight, to keep going. There is hope. We found each other, didn't we? Others will, too. She sent him an image of herself, of her sweater floating to the floor of the third-floor bath, the master suite steamy from the frothy Jacuzzi.

He began laughing softly, his spirits rising as quickly as they had plummeted. Alexandria was waiting for him, sexy and sweet. Light to his darkness, a beacon to guide him home.

That's not all I am. Her voice was provocative. A wisp of lace floating to the floor filled his mind. Her breasts were bare, full, enticing. She was smiling, a siren's invitation. *You're keeping me waiting.*

Show me. Holding the picture of her in his mind, he moved away from the scarred corpse and began to rebuild the storm's intensity.

Her hand went to the fly of her jeans. With infinite slowness she slipped each button from its hole. His breath caught in his throat as she hooked her thumbs in the waistband and inched the denim over her hips.

Come home and see. There was need in her voice, a little catch that sent his blood surging hotly. He lifted his face to the heavens, sent clouds whirling and darkening at his command. Like the roar in his blood, the waves leapt and slammed into shore, dousing the cliff with spray and foam. Thunder rumbled ominously, and veins of lightning flashed inside the clouds.

Come to me, Aidan. She was temptation. She was light while he created the darkness.

Lightning flashed to the ground, lit the sand with a shower of sparks, red tongues of flame licking at his very feet. He could feel her moving in his mind, her mouth on his skin, the sensation taking away the pain of death, the death of an old friend. Losing so many of his people nearly drove him mad.

Aidan raised a hand higher and began to gather the sparks into a fireball. He lifted his face to the wild winds. He could not fathom ever doing this to Gregori. Even if he could defeat Gregori, he could not do this. Yet how many times had Gregori been forced to hunt a friend? A relative? A childhood playmate? How many such stains could one's soul bear before there was no redemption?

I am with you, Aidan. Alexandria's voice was a breath of fresh, clean air, untouched by the evil in front of him. *Your soul is not black. I can see it, feel it, touch it with my own. What you do, you do out of necessity, not out of desire. Your friend fights to save himself. If his soul was black, he would not have stayed to protect me. He would have gone after the second vampire for the joy of the hunt, the kill. He stayed, Aidan. And he has gone to be alone where violence cannot touch him, where he has a chance to wait out his vow. That vow alone should tell both of you something. He is no selfish vampire, not even close to becoming one. He thinks of her. Finish your task, ugly as it is, and come back to me. Think of me.*

I will often have to come to you with blood on my hands.

There was a small silence. Then he felt the brush of her hand and was astonished that she had reached out to him when she had never been trained. Her fingertips lingered on his jaw and trailed down his neck, conveying tenderness. *I have been in the hands of a vampire, Aidan. You forget, I know the ugliness of evil. It is not in you, as you seem to think. You hunt because you must, not from a need to kill. Perhaps at one time those who became vampires were good men, but the men you once knew are long gone from this earth. Perhaps Gregori and you give them peace.*

Aidan allowed her words to rinse the sorrow from his mind, the terrible fear and dread that her very presence in his life had allowed him to feel. He shook his head over the irony of that. He had felt no emotion for so many centuries, and now, because Alexandria had come into his life, he knew the terrible burden, the sorrow of the hunter.

He sent the ball of fire racing toward the dead vampire, his attention now focused on his task. The ball entered the ruined chest, and before his eyes the betrayer blackened, withered, became the ash of the earth once again. His gaze on the ashes, he built the wind with one hand. The gust came not from the sea but from the land, scattering the ashes into the waves that would carry them out to a fitting resting place. Aidan whispered an ancient chant to cleanse himself as well as his fallen friend. Squaring his shoulders, he stood tall and straight, then turned to face the direction of his home.

He could hear the sound of water, Alexandria's murmur of pleasure as she stepped into the sunken tub. He could smell her scent, beckoning him. Smiling, he took to the air, feeling it move over his body, cleansing him.

Chapter Sixteen

Alexandria sat in the huge marble tub, her hair swept up into a topknot, bubbles brushing her skin like a thousand tiny fingers. Aidan paused in the doorway, his face drawn, his eyes holding shadows and a sad, haunted expression she wanted to erase for all time.

When she had felt his deep, disturbing sorrow, she had deliberately sent him erotic images, wanting to help him, wanting to comfort him. From a distance, knowing she didn't have to face him, it had been easy to allow her imagination free rein. She had been shy at the thought of his return, when she would have to face whatever repercussions her vivid, wanton images had created.

Now though, seeing his beautiful eyes shadowed, haunted,

holding such sorrow in their depths, washed every vestige of shyness away. She would do anything to remove that grief.

There was such a weariness in Aidan, he felt he might never move again. He could only stand in the doorway and stare at Alexandria, unable to believe his good fortune, unable to believe she was really with him, really forever in his life. Why him? Why was he the one staring into enormous sapphire eyes overflowing with joy at seeing him? Why not Gregori, who had given so much to their people, who had suffered so much and lost so much of himself in the process? Why not Julian, his soulmate, his twin, so dark and twisted with loneliness? Why was it that the gods had chosen to favor him?

"Because we were meant for one another," she said softly, reading his thoughts. "Gregori has his lifemate, Aidan, and he has chosen to give her time to grow up. He'll hold out; he has hope to keep him strong. As for your brother, I know him from your thoughts and memories. He has your strength, and he will endure forever if necessary."

Aidan raked an unsteady hand through his windblown hair. He leaned his weight against the doorjamb and simply watched her with his unblinking golden gaze. She was so beautiful, so brave. Had he really done anything in his lifetime to deserve her, the happiness she brought him, the joy?

Alexandria shook her head, a slow smile curving her mouth, deepening the dimple that so intrigued him. "Of course you don't deserve me. I'm so good and brave and perfect." Her smile was teasing, frankly sexy, and as she shifted slightly beneath the fizzing bubbles her full breasts broke the surface, inviting his suddenly heated gaze.

"And so beautiful. Do not forget beautiful," he said softly and straightened abruptly, his muscles rippling.

She felt her heart jump in anticipation. "Maybe. You certainly make me feel beautiful." She tilted her chin, her sapphire eyes sexy, speculative. The look made his blood race.

His hand went to the buttons of his shirt, and he slowly slipped each one free, his eyes holding hers. She didn't look away or look scared. Instead, she smiled that slow, sexy smile of blatant invitation.

"You have something in your mind, *piccola*," he murmured softly, his body tightening in anticipation.

She shrugged, a lazy movement that sent ripples along the bubbling surface of the water. "I decided now would be a good time to try out something from one of those fantasies of yours."

The shirt floated to the floor unnoticed. She had eyes only for him, an urgent singing in her blood, a fire sweeping through her.

"Do I have fantasies?" he asked softly. His body tightened, hardened, wanted, and needed. He could barely speak, barely move.

Her laughter slid over his skin caressingly. "I'd say some pretty interesting ones. But don't get *too* excited. We're going to start with something easy."

His eyebrows rose as he reached down to remove his shoes and socks. His every movement was unhurried and lazy, but his eyes were molten with heat as his gaze devoured her. Alexandria's breath caught in her throat. He was bending over, that was all, a casual, everyday movement, but his face was so sensual, his body so fluid yet controlled. She bit her lip, her lashes falling to hide her sudden surge of desire.

"I want you to want me, Alexandria," he chided softly. "I need to know you want me. Do not hide from me."

In spite of herself, her mouth was already curving in response, her dimples deepening. "It's just that you're so beautiful, Aidan."

"Women are beautiful, not men."

"You are beautiful," she corrected him. "Look at yourself through my eyes." It was a teasing challenge.

He found it hard to resist. And there *was* something sexy about seeing himself the way she saw him. The wanting, the needing. The hunger. His hands went to his slacks, pushing them from his hips with a deliberate slowness that sent anticipation curling through her.

"See?" She shifted to her knees in the tub, the bubbles fizzing around her narrow rib cage, her breasts bare and gleaming with beaded water. Her eyes were on his lean hips and hard, jutting masculinity as he stepped into the sunken tub, the bubbles swirling around his legs like tiny tongues lapping at his skin.

Alexandria let out her breath slowly. His thighs were strong, muscled columns covered with fine golden hair. Her hands slid up his calves, urging him closer. She felt the tremor that ran through him, and she smiled seductively.

Her fingertips moved slowly over the sculptured muscles, and her breath was warm and tempting along his heavy erection.

Aidan closed his eyes in ecstasy as her tongue moved in a slow, languid caress over his velvet tip. His stomach muscles tightened as her mouth, tight and hot and moist, closed around him. A groan was torn from somewhere deep inside him. He caught her hair in his fists, dragging her even closer to him, and his body nearly exploded with pleasure as her hands sought his buttocks and urged him more deeply into her. With her mouth tight around him and her soft breasts pressed against his thighs, the bubbles tugging at his calves, and her silken hair in his fists, every thought was pushed from his mind until it was filled only with her, with pure sensation.

Her fingers massaged his buttocks, pressing hard into the heavy muscles, urging him on. He moved, a slow, long stroke, gritting his teeth against the pleasure that nearly consumed him. Her mouth moved over him, again and again. His hands bunched in her hair so hard he was afraid he might hurt her, but he couldn't control the involuntary response. His mind sought hers, and he found excitement, need, a total sharing of his pleasure. She was aware of what she was doing to him and reveled in it, in her power over him. Every sane thought disappeared, every care, every worry. There was only his body, her mouth, and the feel of her satin skin and the bubbles bursting around them. Fireworks. Earthquakes. White lightning. He found himself helplessly thrusting against her, his head thrown back, his joy and rapture not only physical but a part of his very soul.

Aidan's hunger rose until the demands of his race overcame him, insisting he put her pleasure before his own. With a soft, possessive growl he pushed her back into the water, his gaze running over her bare skin like lava. She had time for only one inarticulate cry before his mouth was on her throat, her breasts, his hands all over her body. She felt so small, so delicate under his palms, her skin warm and slick with water. He explored her everywhere. Then his fingers found her creamy with need for him. He pushed inside, watching her eyes, and her body responded with a fresh wave of liquid desire. He pushed deeper, his mouth on her now, his teeth scraping her breasts, her stomach. He could feel her muscles clench around him, velvet and hot. He kissed her hips, the little indentation that always drove him crazy, then raised them out of the water.

Slow down, slow down, his mind repeated, but his body had other ideas. He was on fire, his very skin burning. His mouth replaced his fingers, wanting to bring her to the same fever pitch he was experiencing. She moaned, the sound making him wild. She tasted like hot honey, spicy and addicting. He attacked, on fire with need and love and violent, insatiable lust.

Beneath the onslaught of his mouth, she writhed, cried out. Water splashed over the sides of the tub. Her body clenched, released, wave after wave of sensation spiraling through her. She clutched at him for anchorage as she spun out of control, a terrible, wonderful ride that went on forever.

Aidan finally lifted his head, his eyes hungry, his mouth sensual. He pulled her body to his, wrapping her slender legs around his waist. "You drive me wild, Alexandria. You make me completely insane with wanting you." His voice was husky, and he was pressed against her, hard and thick, pushing so aggressively that her body was slowly opening, allowing him entrance. The feeling was exquisite, a slow burn, hot velvet clutching him, tightening around him, the friction almost unbearable. His hands pinned her small waist, holding her firmly while he buried himself slowly, deeply in her hot, moist sheath. "Look at me, Alexandria. Know that I am your lifemate and that you are always in my care," he commanded softly, his golden gaze holding her blue one, forcing the ultimate intimacy, wanting all of her, every inch of her, wanting them to merge completely, body to body, mind to mind, soul to soul.

He began to move then, a slow thrusting of his hips, burying himself deeply with each surge. She bit her lip, the tiny pinpricks of blood triggering the fangs in his mouth. His hands urged her closer yet, so that she arched her body, her head back, her throat vulnerable and exposed, her breasts equally inviting. His tongue took the water from the rosy, hard tips and moved upward, tracing swelling curves until his mouth rested over the pulse in her neck.

He felt her body clench in anticipation, and his teeth scraped gently back and forth until she moaned and caught at his head with both hands. Satisfaction gleamed in his golden eyes. His tongue stroked her pulse as his body moved in hers. He thrust his hips harder and harder.

"Aidan!" Her soft cry was a plea.

"Not yet, *cara*, not yet." With his great strength he stood, taking her with him, the water sluicing down into the tub. Her legs circled his body, her hands around his neck, and he thrust harder still, over and over, wanting every inch of him inside her.

Her nails dug into his shoulders, an exquisite pain. He leaned her against the wall for better leverage, his hips savage, relentless, frenzied. His teeth scraped, nipped. Then she cried out at the piercing pain, so sweet and sensual, as his fangs buried themselves deeply, claiming her blood as voraciously as his body was claiming hers.

She had driven him wild, and his predatory nature took over, the untamed male of his species, dominant possessive, claiming his mate. His mouth worked at her throat, taking her very essence as her body took his, dragging at him, tightening around him, clenching and demanding until he had to cry out with the intensity of the pleasure. Ruby droplets trickled down the swell of her breast, and his tongue followed the trail.

Alexandria was spiraling into the night itself. The ferocity of Aidan's lovemaking should have terrified her, but she matched his intensity, beat for beat, her fists wrapped in his blond hair, her body wrapped around his tightly, her cries muffled against his shoulder.

His shout, husky with passion, rose to the heavens, carried on the wind. And as he held her, breathing hard, leaning both of them against the wall, from far off in the night came a reply. Of anger. Rage. A howl of the suddenly ferocious wind. The sound clawed at them, filled with hate.

Frightened, Alexandria looked toward the window. "Did you hear that?"

Slowly, reluctantly, he lowered her to her feet, his arm still circling her waist. "Yes, I heard," he admitted grimly.

Outside, the clouds began to darken ominously, malignantly. Hail the size of fists beat at the roof and windows. Instinctively Aidan turned her, standing protectively in front of her lest the ice break through and harm her.

"Is it Gregori?" she whispered, remembering the awesome power clinging to the man, seeping from his very pores.

Aidan shook his head. "If Gregori wanted us dead, Alexandria, we would be long gone from this world. No, this is the last one of the group of undead who entered the city together, for what purpose I do not know. With the incredible hearing of our race, I guess he did not like the joy we shared."

"He sounded dangerous," she said. "Like a wounded bear."

Aidan tilted her chin up, his golden eyes moving over her face possessively, tenderly. "He is dangerous, *piccola*. That is why I must hunt his kind and see to it that they do not cause the world misery."

Looking down at her upturned face, her lips swollen and her cheeks flushed from his lovemaking, he couldn't resist lowering his head to hers, claiming her mouth with a gentle kiss. "Thank you, *cara*, for ridding me of my own particular demons."

She sank back into the tub, its jets now silent, and looked up at him with her enormous eyes. "Could he . . . kill you?"

"I suppose, if I became careless." He sat down opposite her, the water rising with his weight. "But I will not be careless, *piccola*, not even for a moment. Tomorrow night I must hunt him. He is waiting for me."

"How do you know?"

He shrugged casually. They might have been discussing the weather. "He would never have sent a challenge if he had not devised a trap. I have acquired a certain . . . reputation among the undead."

She drew up her knees and rested her chin on them. "I wish he would just go away, find another city to terrorize."

He shook his head, his golden eyes loving. "No, you do not. Besides, I would never allow him to kill wantonly anywhere nearby. My work often involves travel, you know."

"He's the serial killer who's been in the papers recently, isn't he?" she guessed shrewdly.

"One of them. The others are dead now."

She twisted her fingers together in agitation.

Aidan laced a hand through hers reassuringly. "Do not worry, Alexandria. I will protect you from him."

"It isn't that. I know you will. It's just that now that I know you, now that I've met Gregori and I know what causes someone to turn vampire, isn't there any way to . . . to cure them?"

He shook his head sadly. "I know you feel sorrow for them and for those of us who must destroy them, but in most cases it is a conscious choice on their part. And once a kill has been made during the taking of blood, there is no way back."

She met his eyes squarely. "Gregori has done so."

His golden gaze was suddenly cold and speculative. "That is impossible."

"I know he has. He regrets it bitterly, and it eats away at him, but he has killed someone evil using that method. I know, Aidan, really. I sometimes see things in people that others can't."

"Is he turned?" His voice was quiet, lacking inflection, and he was very still as he awaited her answer.

She shook her head. "He thinks he's evil, but he has tremendous compassion in him. But he is dangerous, Aidan. Very dangerous."

"Vampires are adept at hiding the truth. They are consummate liars. You are certain Gregori has not turned?"

She nodded. "I was afraid of him. He's afraid of himself. As he said, he's like a tiger, unpredictable and dangerous. But he's not evil."

Outside, clouds were blackening the gray dawn sky. Aidan smiled smugly and waved a hand, and instantly the clouds began to disperse. "The remaining vampire thinks to intimidate me with a display of power, and I allow it to lull him into a false sense of security. But the dawn is upon us, and he must seek the shelter of the earth."

Alexandria relaxed a little. She didn't like to think the vampire could be just outside their window, listening to their conversation.

Aidan shook his head. "If he were that close, *piccola*, I would know."

She laughed. "I still forget you can read my thoughts. Sometimes it's very disconcerting."

"Sometimes it can be very interesting." His strange, brilliant eyes gleamed at her, sending a blush spreading over her entire body.

"Your mind is interesting, too," she agreed, a smile curving her mouth. "It has all sorts of interesting ideas."

"We are just getting started," he said softly. He leaned toward her, cupping one breast in his hand, his thumb feathering over the hard peak. "I love touching you, being able to touch you whenever I wish." His fingertip brushed her throat, the mark he had deliberately left on her.

She felt his touch through her entire body. "You should be outlawed, Aidan. You know, all my recent sketches for Thomas Ivan's characters took on your look. I couldn't help myself. Do you think Thomas will notice?"

His eyes glittered at her. "Thomas Ivan is an idiot."

"His concepts are both innovative and popular, and he happens to be my boss," she said firmly. "You're just jealous."

"One of my more annoying habits, no doubt. I do not intend to share you, Alexandria." Abruptly he released her. "I do not want another man touching you."

"Working together does not mean sleeping together," she pointed out patiently, secretly knowing that she would readily break off even the work relationship with Ivan if it truly caused Aidan deep distress.

"And you believe he will accept that?"

"He'll have no choice. I'll tell him you and I are engaged. He'll have to accept it."

"I will make arrangements to marry you tomorrow morning. I have a few friends who can speed up the process, and we will take care of the license and have done with it."

She sat back, her sapphire eyes suddenly spitting fire. "Have done with it? *Have done with it?*" She repeated his words, unable to believe he had actually said them. Right now she wouldn't marry him if he were the last man on earth. "I wasn't asking for any favors or a commitment from you, Aidan. Nor do you have to protect my honor."

He was watching her carefully, all at once still. "We have the ultimate commitment between us, Alexandria. We are lifemates for all eternity. We will remain together until together we choose to meet the sun. But your very imaginative, idiotic-boss would not respect that bond, would not even understand it. He will, however, understand the human ceremony of marriage."

"I don't understand this lifemate business, either. Yet, like Thomas, I do understand the sacrament of marriage. Not that you asked me. Not that you respect the institution I was raised to believe in. I find your attitude extremely insulting, Aidan." She was working at hiding her hurt from him, but her expressive face, the glittering sheen to her eyes, would have given her away even if he had not been able to read her thoughts.

He shook his head sadly. "We share everything, Alexandria, including our thoughts. I have unintentionally hurt you, and I certainly did not mean to do so."

She stood up, water pouring from her skin. "We may share our thoughts, but we don't seem to understand one another." Grabbing a towel, she wrapped it around her like a sarong, her eyes studiously avoiding his.

"I think perhaps we do. You would have liked me to ask you to marry me in the human way." He reached out, a lazy rippling of muscles, and shackled her ankle with his fingers, a steely vise preventing her escape.

The oddly intimate act sent flames racing through her bloodstream. Alexandria resented his ability to turn her body to liquid fire with just a touch, just a look. She could feel the electricity arcing between them, see the hunger in his gaze.

She shook her head. "Don't, Aidan. This is important. You can't just hurt me anytime you like and then make love to me until I can't think straight."

At once his expression changed. He stood up so abruptly, she stepped back, intimidated by his sheer size. "Do not do that, *cara mia*." His voice was a caress, a plea. "Do not ever fear me. I would never willingly hurt you. We are already one. I thought you understood that. You are irrevocably tied to me for all time. It is a much deeper and stronger tie than a marriage ceremony. I must admit, I should have considered that you would have thought the marriage ceremony important, but I was assuming, as you are now Carpathian, you would realize that we are already 'married,' bound together for all time. It was done the moment the ancient words were spoken. The ritual was completed when we shared our blood, our hearts, our body and soul. But the words alone were irrevocably binding. It is the 'marriage ceremony' of our people."

His arms swept around her stiff, resisting frame. "Forgive the presumption, *cara*, and know that I want to marry you in the human ceremony because it is important to you."

His mesmerizing voice washed over her like water, cleansing away her resentment as if it had never been.

Alexandria rested against him, pressing close for comfort. "This life is so scary, Aidan, I want as many things as possible to be normal, or almost the same as they were. Just simple familiar things. I can handle it better that way."

"You know, *piccola*," he teased, brushing her cheek with gentle fingers, "Carpathian men never ask their mates. They simply claim them. But shall I ask you formally?"

She rubbed her face against his chest. "It would mean a lot to me if you would," she admitted.

"So I guess I had better do it right," he said softly, taking her hand and going down on one knee. "Alexandria, my only love, will you marry me tomorrow morning?"

"Yes, Aidan," she replied demurely. Then she spoiled the effect by laughing. "But we have to have blood tests. You can't just get married in a minute."

He rose.

"You forget the power of mind persuasion. We will be married tomorrow morning. Now get dressed, *cara*. You are tempting me all over again." His hands wandered down her slender body to caress her bottom.

Her smile was slightly wry. "You're going to give me all kinds of trouble with your chauvinistic ways, aren't you?"

He laughed in answer. "I was just thinking you were going to give *me* all kinds of trouble with your independent thinking."

She tilted her chin. "You have heard the word *compromise* before, haven't you? You do comprehend its meaning?"

He looked thoughtful, taking his time before replying. "As I understand it, *compromise* means you do what I say as soon as I command it. Is that about right?"

Alexandria pushed at the solid wall of his chest. "You wish, Mr. Savage. It's never going to happen."

He pinned her arms to her sides and nuzzled the top of her head. "We will see, my love. We will see."

Laughing, Alexandria pulled away from him and began to dress. The dawn was brightening the sky, and with it came the terrible lethargy she was becoming familiar with. She wanted to see Joshua, to have normal mornings with her brother. Dress him, feed him, spend time with him before he went off to school.

Aidan allowed her to escape him, letting her keep her illusions of normalcy as long as possible. He liked to see the happiness in her, and he had a bad feeling about the vampire's blatant challenge. The creature was up to something. He was the last one remaining from the group that had come to the city, terrorizing the population and leading the police on a wild goose chase. The vampire was not stupid; he would have studied Aidan and his strengths and weaknesses before issuing such a challenge. What was the undead up to?

He glided through the house silently, inspecting each entrance, window, and pathway leading to the house. Every safeguard was in place. The house was impenetrable, even with him sleeping beneath the earth in his secret chamber. No, the vampire could not strike at the house. Where, then?

He followed the sound of hoeing and found Stefan in the huge garden. Whenever he was upset or tired, Stefan gravitated to tending his plants.

When Aidan joined him, he leaned on the hoe and regarded his master steadily. "So, you feel it, too. I had trouble sleeping last night." He spoke in their native language, another sure sign of his state of mind.

"The vampire howled last night. A distinct call for vengeance. I thwarted their plans, whatever they were, and now the one remaining undead intends to destroy me. How he will attempt it, I do not know."

"It will be through one of us," Stefan said sadly. "We are your Achilles' heel, Aidan. We always have been. He can bring you down using Marie, the boy, or me. You know he will."

Aidan frowned. "Or Alexandria. I fear her reaction to what must come."

"She is very strong, Aidan, very courageous. She will be fine. You must have faith in your chosen lifemate."

Aidan nodded. "I know what is in her heart and mind, but I want her happiness above all else." He gave a humorless smile. "I remember a time many years ago, I went to the aid

271

of Mikhail. He had found his lifemate, a human woman. She was very strong-willed, and I remember thinking that he should better control her, make her do his bidding at all times so that she would remain safe. We cannot afford to lose even one of our women—you know that. She was so strange to me, so unlike the women of our race. She showed no fear even of me, a Carpathian male she did not know. I vowed if I found my lifemate, I would not do as Mikhail and bow to her wishes. Yet now, I cannot stand to see sorrow in Alexandria's eyes. I feel sick when she is hurt or upset with me."

A grin spread across Stefan's face. "You're in love, my old friend, and that is the downfall of all good men."

"Even Gregori, the dark one, allowed his lifemate her freedom because of her fear of him. How does one strike a balance between keeping a woman happy and protecting her?" Aidan mused aloud.

Stefan shrugged. "You're in the modern world now, Aidan. Women rule their own lives. They make their own decisions and generally drive us all crazy. Welcome to the twenty-first century."

Aidan shook his head. "She thinks she is going to work with that madman, Thomas Ivan. Yet I know what he wants to do with her."

"If she wants to work, Aidan, have you any choice but to allow it?"

The golden eyes flashed. "I have a choice, Stefan. Still, perhaps the line of least resistance is to have a little mind-to-mind chat with Mr. Ivan. I am certain I can make him see things my way."

Stefan laughed. "I wish I had that particular talent, Aidan. It would come in handy with some of my business dealings."

"Do not allow Joshua to go to his school this day. The vampire will, in all likelihood, try to strike at us through him."

"I agree," Stefan said. "The boy is the most vulnerable."

"Use Vinnie and Rusty again. Keep them around for the next few days," Aidan advised. He glanced up at the sky through his dark glasses. "The trouble will come today."

Stefan nodded in agreement. "I will keep a close watch. There will be no fire this time to destroy all we have built." He looked down at the ground, still ashamed of a past catastrophe even though it was not his fault.

Aidan clapped him on the shoulder. "Without you, Stefan, no one would have survived that day, perhaps not even me." He had been safely buried beneath the soil, but the loss of his "family" would have been devastating. Because of that time, so many years earlier, when a vampire had used a human to try to trap them in an inferno, and he had lain helpless beneath the soil, he had redoubled his studies and his safeguards, strengthening his power and abilities. Never again would he be caught unable to aid those he cared about.

Joshua's laughter reached him, and the soft, carefree sound did something to his heart. The child touched him in ways no other had. He was so like Alexandria, so filled with the joy of living, and he had the same beautiful blue eyes.

"No one will harm the boy, not if I live," Stefan said firmly.

Aidan turned away. He did not want Stefan, who knew him so well, to realize how those words filled him with dread. For all his powers, Aidan was vulnerable in the sunlight, and a vampire could use human puppets, minions, to capitalize on the weakness the day brought. Even with his ability to project during the daylight hours, a feat few of his kind had accomplished, Aidan would still be leaving Stefan without his physical aid, and Stefan was no longer a young man. Aidan did not want to lose his friend any more than he wanted to lose Joshua.

Joshua burst from the kitchen laughing, his blond curls bouncing. "Help me, Aidan, she's after me!" he hollered as he charged toward them.

Stefan stepped squarely in front of his prize tulips, while Aidan glided in to wall off the roses. He caught Joshua's flying figure with one hand and swept him up to his shoulders. "Who is after you, young Joshua?" he asked, pretending not to know.

"Don't you protect that little scalawag!" Alexandria came running after her brother, her hair bouncing in a pony tail,

273

her sapphire eyes dancing with mischief. "You won't believe what the little monster has been hiding under his bed!"

Joshua ducked behind Aidan's neck. "Run, Aidan! She's gonna tickle-torture me, I just know it." Aidan obliged, trotting the boy into the shelter of the garage, knowing Alexandria would follow.

"Ha!" Alexandria said, unaware that she had placed herself in danger from the early morning sun. "You wish I'd tickle-torture you. I'm going to do a lot worse than that," she threatened. "Put him down, Aidan, and let me box his ears."

Joshua clutched at Aidan's thick mane of hair. "No! I'm telling you, Aidan, we gotta stick together on this."

"I do not know." Aidan pretended to think about it, winking at Stefan as he twisted and turned to protect Joshua from Alexandria's jumping attempts to reach the boy. "She looks pretty mad to me. I do not want her coming after *me* like that." He shifted slightly, as if he might really turn the child over to his sister.

Alexandria pretended to spring at him, laughing wickedly. At the last second, Aidan turned to keep his body between her and Joshua. Joshua grabbed him even tighter, squealing in feigned alarm.

"I'm gonna tell her!" Joshua cried. "If you don't save me, Aidan, you're gonna go down, too!" His eyes were alight with mischief.

Alexandria stopped in her tracks and glared at Aidan. "You are a party to this mutiny?"

He attempted innocence. "I have no idea what the child is trying to accuse me of to save his own life." His golden eyes were laughing, belying his words. "Remember, Alexandria, that a man will say anything to save his own skin."

"Ha!" Joshua snorted. "You tell her, Stefan. It was all Aidan's idea, and you helped, right?"

Alexandria faced the older man accusingly. "You, too? You were in on this blatant disregard for my orders?" She put her hands on her hips. "And it *was* an order."

The three males hung their heads in unison, looking for all the world like naughty little boys. "I am sorry, *cara*."

Aidan took the blame squarely on his broad shoulders. "I could not resist the little creature."

"Little? You call that *little*? It's a moose!"

Stefan pushed out his chest. "No, Alexandria, it wasn't Aidan. I saw the little thing, and young Joshua's face was so bright, I just had to get it."

"Little? Are we talking about the same animal here? That dog is not little. It is huge. Did either of you two pushovers take a look at the paws on that thing? They're bigger than my head!"

Joshua burst out laughing. "No way, Alex. He's really cute. You are gonna let me keep him, aren't you? You just have to. Stefan says he'll be a good guard dog someday. He says he'll look after me and be a friend if I treat him right."

"And in the meantime, he's going to eat like a horse every day." Alexandria swept a hand through her hair, her smile fading. "I don't know, Josh. I barely make enough money to feed the two of us, let alone whatever that thing is."

Aidan lifted the boy to the ground and circled Alexandria's waist with one arm. "Have you forgotten, *cara*? You promised to marry me. I think I can cover the cost of the dog food."

"You mean it, Aidan?" Joshua shouted, jumping up and down. "You mean it, Aidan? You're really gonna marry Alex? And I can keep my dog?"

"You'd sell me out for a dog?" Alexandria demanded, catching Joshua around the neck in mock aggression.

"Not *just* a dog, Alex, but this neat house and Stefan and Marie, too. Plus, you won't have to work for that bozo."

"Bozo?" Alexandria turned slowly and regarded Aidan with glittering blue eyes. "Now, how would an innocent little boy come up with a descriptive word like that?"

Aidan smiled at her, a sweet, innocent smile that should have made her feel like laughing but instead sent heat curling through her body. She tilted her chin. "You're lethal," she accused him.

He framed her face with his large hands and lowered his head slowly, purposefully. "I would hope so," he murmured right before his mouth claimed hers, sweeping her into their own private world.

But Alexandria was soon reminded they were not alone.

"Holy moly," Joshua said in a loud whisper. "Can you believe that, Stefan?"

"Never saw such a display," Stefan admitted.

Chapter Seventeen

The sun was unusually large in the sky, gleaming a strange red. There was little wind, few clouds, and the ocean itself was tranquil, the surface like glass. Beneath the earth, a heart began to beat. Soil shifted, churned, then spewed like a geyser from the secret chamber beneath Aidan's house.

He lay still, his great body drained of strength. Beside him, as silent and still as death, lay Alexandria. Aidan's eyes snapped open, fury burning in their depths at the disturbance to his sleep. Outside his home, somewhere close, something evil lurked in the bright sunlight on the peaceful afternoon.

He took a deep breath and closed his eyes, his arms folded across his chest. He sent himself seeking outside his body and into the air itself. It took intense concentration and focus to be bodiless, completely without form. He moved upward through the chamber and passed through the heavy trapdoor. Passing through solids was disorienting, a strange wrenching of atoms and molecules, and Aidan mentally shook himself. He had experimented with this process and often found the complete separation of body and mind difficult. In the other forms he took, his body was different but still with him. With only his mind and soul, his senses were altered. Sounds were strangely distorted, as he had no ears, and he couldn't actually touch anything, passing straight through it if he tried, causing a slightly sickening sensation. As he had no stomach, the nausea was even stranger.

Yet it was imperative to stay completely focused; it was essential not to allow himself to be disturbed by the unwanted sensations. He traveled along the rock tunnel deep within the earth. It always seemed so narrow, his shoulders nearly brushing the sides, but without his body, the space was enormous, another sensory distortion.

He passed through the door leading to the basement. Already the dark, oppressive evil that had awakened him deep within the earth was filling the air with its stench.

Aidan proceeded through the basement door into the kitchen of his home, warped vibrations and tones seeming to bounce through his being before he could identify them as Joshua's laughter, Marie's musical voice, Stefan's deeper baritone. The knowledge that the three were still safe gave him a measure of comfort. Whatever was in the air, whatever was stalking those he loved, had not penetrated the safeguards of his home.

The sun blazed through the huge windows, and Aidan instinctively veered away from the rays. He had no eyes, no skin to burn, but he felt the wrenching agony all the same. When every survival instinct screamed at him to go back to the safe, cool earth, far from the burning sun, the stench of evil impelled him forward.

Over the centuries, he had often lived in proximity to humans, more so than most of his kind, yet it never failed to astonish him that they had so few warning systems, or if they did, that they completely ignored them. The air was thick with the stench, the disturbance so great it had penetrated his chamber below the rich earth, intruding on his deep sleep. Yet Marie was singing in the living room as she dusted his jade collection, and Stefan was humming as he tinkered with an engine in the huge garage, one of his many hobbies. Aidan wanted to call to him, to warn him, but in his energy-consuming formlessness, he didn't dare try. He moved through the garage and back into the house, homing in on Joshua in the kitchen.

The child was the obvious target of the madness aimed at both Alexandria and Aidan. Aidan sped toward him, the bright sunlight sapping his energy. His mind rebelled, flinching from the brilliant rays, but he forced himself through the light to reach the boy.

Joshua was playing with the puppy, his eyes dancing, his blond curls bouncing, the picture of boyish joy. He had no idea he was in deadly peril.

Even as Aidan observed, the dog ran to the door, whining softly, and Joshua glanced about, looking for Stefan or Marie, who had told him in no uncertain terms not to go outside. Snapping a leash on the puppy, he opened the door and rushed into the garden.

The heat of the sun pierced Aidan's very soul. He felt as if he were on a skewer, roasting, burning. He followed the boy anyway, putting aside the pain.

"Come on, Baron," Joshua insisted. "Hurry it up." The little boy looked around again to make sure he was alone. "Baron's a dopey name, but Stefan really wanted you to be called that. He says it will make you noble, whatever that is. I'll ask Alexandria. She knows everything. I wanted to call you Alex. That would have made her laugh."

"Joshua!" Vinnie del Marco appeared, his large frame intimidating, his arms folded, his face stern. "Weren't you given orders? Soldiers get court-martialed for less than this."

The air was thick with the stench now. Aidan could see that Vinnie felt safe in the garden as he teased the boy, the high wall around them, the security system in full force. He had no perception of the danger lurking so close. Vinnie bent to scratch behind the puppy's ears.

A rush of wind, sound, and movement displaced Aidan, knocking him sideways as a blurred mass leapt the fence. A furred, powerfully muscled beast hit Vinnie squarely in the chest, its huge gaping jaws going for his throat.

"Run, kid! Get in the house!" Vinnie yelled just before the animal tore open flesh and sinew. Blood sprayed into the air, showering Joshua and the puppy as they stood frozen to the spot.

The boy said one word, whispered it softly like a prayer amid the ugliness. "Alexandria."

A second animal hurtled over the wall and rushed at Vinnie, and its dripping fangs closed over his leg. With a vicious twist of its massive head, it audibly snapped bone, and Vinnie's screams filled the air. Rusty charged around the corner, gun in hand, but Joshua was in his line of fire. A third animal sprang from the wall onto his back, teeth clamping tightly around his shoulder.

Aidan could hear Stefan running, but he knew the vampire had laid his trap all too well. The beasts were sacrificial pawns. Stefan would shoot them to save the two men from the crazed animals, but by then the human puppet moving over the wall had scooped up the terrified child and tugged him back over the wall. The air reverberated with gunfire, then with Stefan shouting to his wife.

"Call an ambulance, Marie, and get out here now! I need some help!" Stefan knelt beside Vinnie and tried to clamp the worst of the wounds pumping out the man's life onto the ground.

"Joshua! Where is Joshua?" Marie cried when she joined him.

"He's gone," Stefan reported grimly. "He was taken."

Marie's sobs faded behind him as Aidan followed the human and child. Joshua was thrown into the trunk of a car, and the puppet walked with the characteristic jerky motions of a vampire-induced trance to the driver's seat. Aidan streamed in through the open window and hovered, but the puppet could not detect his presence. The vampire could not direct this assault while he lay beneath earth in the daylight hours, but he had implanted his orders into his minions' minds before he had sought the safety of his lair.

The car swerved along the winding road, the driver drooling and staring vacantly ahead with the gaze of the possessed.

Aidan moved away from the abomination and into the trunk. Joshua lay in a stupor, the left side of his face swelling, his eye already turning black. Tears rolled down to his chin, but his sobs were silent.

Aidan concentrated, calling on all of his strength to communicate silently with the boy. *Joshua, I am here with you. I will have you sleep. You will stay asleep until I come for you. When I say to you, "Alexandria needs to see your blue eyes," you will know it is safe to awaken. Only then will you do so*. The mind meld was draining, and he had so little energy during this terrible time of the day. He also needed to cast spells, the most intricate, dangerous ones Gregori had taught him. If the vampire was somehow able to rise before Aidan could return to the boy, it would take a time to unravel the spells, and Joshua would be safe from harm and further trauma in his sleep.

Aidan wove his spells as the car moved northward, toward the mountains. Toward Gregori's new home, came the unbidden thought.

It couldn't be Gregori. Aidan wouldn't believe it. The vampire simply had no idea Gregori was anywhere in the vicinity. It wasn't Gregori. Gregori was so powerful, he would not need the deceitful tricks, the beasts, the mindless puppet doing his bidding, or even the child. Gregori would need no help. This was not Gregori. Aidan held on to that certainty while he wove the spells. Ancient, binding, dangerous to any who tried to harm the boy.

When he was finished, he rested, exhausted. He had done all he could. Once he knew the child's exact destination, he would have to make his way home. He dreaded the journey in the bright sun; there was no pain quite like it, nothing more sickening to one of his kind.

The puppet stopped the car at the entrance to an old, run-down hunting lodge with rotting timbers and overgrown with vines and bushes. Aidan knew at once that the vampire was close, most likely beneath the decaying planks of the floor. Rats scurried visibly, the sentinels for the undead. The walking marionette, the minion of the undead, already drained of his mind and free will, opened the trunk and reached in to pull the child out by his shirtfront.

The protective spell instantly sent fire racing up the puppet's arm to his shoulders and enveloped his head. The thing, no longer really alive, programmed to do one thing only, continued to try to clutch the boy even as his flesh burned.

Aidan was thankful Joshua was asleep. The putrefying stench was incredible, even to one without a nose. The blackened carcass fell to the ground, bits of charred flesh dropping away. The puppet issued a low, keening vibration, his death slow and difficult, the macabre caricature still trying over and over to drag the boy to the vampire. Aidan hated the torment resulting from the vampire's twisted schemes. But then, the undead liked his minions to suffer as much as possible.

When the thing was finally still, the last breath dragged from its lungs, Aidan inspected the remains to ensure it was truly dead and to leave no smoldering ember that might accidentally ignite any vegetation. Satisfied that he had done as much as he was able, Aidan had to leave, to travel through that terrible sunlight, back to his home.

His strength completely drained, the journey took the better part of the afternoon, and he feared that when he did reach home he might not have energy enough to rise with the setting sun and return to the vampire's lair. He was growing ever weaker, his being becoming even more insubstantial, a feather blown about in the elements. Only the thought of Alexandria sustained him. And a welcome dense, blanketing white fog eased his passage home.

Once there, with his last ounce of energy, he made his way unerringly to his resting place beside Alexandria. The wrench of reuniting with his body contorted his very bones, his muscles contracting and locking in hard, swollen masses. Vulnerable and without strength, his great power drained completely, he lay as one dead, the cool earth closing over him. A soft hiss escaped, the last breath from his lungs.

Upstairs, above Aidan and Alexandria, Stefan could only try to comfort his wife as they huddled together awaiting the setting sun, awaiting the moment Aidan would arise. The sun seemed as if it wanted to stay up for all time, but unexpectedly a slow, thick fog began to roll in just before six o'clock. Stefan felt some of the terrible tension leave his body, though the guilt remained as he waited.

Deep below the earth, Aidan arose, voraciously hungry to replenish starving cells and sinews depleted from his earlier task. Yet his first thought was of Gregori. There could be only one answer. The Carpathian had intervened. He was great enough, powerful enough to feel the disturbances in the land even from beneath the earth itself. He had sent the fog to aid Aidan when he knew Aidan was far too drained to build it himself. And the fog remained, here before the sun set, giving him a head start on what he must do.

Aidan had studied for centuries, believing, as Gregori did, that knowledge was power, yet he could not do all the things Gregori was able to do. He would not have detected a bodiless being while sleeping in the ground, and Aidan was certain Gregori had not only done so but had also sent the fog to aid him. Aidan found himself smiling. The vampire was not Gregori.

Glancing down at Alexandria's face, he brushed his fingers tenderly through her hair before floating them upward to the underground chamber. Alexandria always went to sleep on a bed and awoke on one, but as long as a vampire preyed in their city, Aidan always brought her beneath the healing soil, where she was impossible to detect.

Wake, piccola. *Wake and look at your lifemate.* He whispered the words softly, dreading her coming pain, a lump forming in his throat.

When she took her first breath, a soft sigh, it went straight to his heart. Her blue eyes opened, her gaze locked on his. At once her warmth surrounded him, seeping into the cold pores of his body. She smiled, a loving, sweet smile that was an arrow piercing his soul.

"What is it?" she asked. Very gently, tenderly, she lifted a hand and traced his mouth with a fingertip. "What have you been doing to yourself? You're gray, Aidan. You need to feed." Her voice was a soft invitation.

"Alexandria." He said her name, nothing else.

She surprised him as she always did, her eyes darkening to a deep blue, her voice a mere thread of sound, her body very still. "Is he alive?" There was no hint of condemnation, no anger that he had not kept the child safe.

He closed his eyes, unable to meet her gaze. He simply nodded.

Alexandria took a deep breath and caressed his jaw with her palm. "Look at me, Aidan."

"I cannot, Alexandria. I will face you when I have returned Joshua safely to our home, to your arms."

"I said look at me." Her fingertips were on his chin, raising it.

He could do no other than her bidding. She was tearing him up inside with her acceptance, her understanding, her gentleness. His golden eyes blazed at her. Then he felt her, merging, instantly with him, so swiftly and completely that he had no chance to hide any of it—the beasts attacking those guarding her brother, Stefan and Marie's anguish, Joshua's terror, his own efforts and pain in the sun, the charring of the human puppet. It was all laid out in front of her in stark, ugly detail. When she heard the soft whisper of her name on Joshua's lips, she made a single sound.

Her pain went so deep, Aidan felt the demon rise and rush through his body, taking control. A slow, murderous hiss escaped from deep within his throat. His golden eyes glowed with deadly intent. "How dare he try this?" His voice was as lethal as his expression. "How dare he use the boy as a challenge to bring me out into the open?"

"Shh, Aidan." She put a finger over his mouth. "You have no need to blame yourself. Come to me. Take what you need to do this thing, to get Joshua back." She was slowly pushing aside the silk shirt she wore, her slender arm circling his neck, bringing his head down to her breast.

"I will hunt. You have need yourself." He clenched his teeth against the hunger beating at him.

She moved her breasts against his skin, her scent enveloping him, a creamy invitation, a temptation impossible to resist. "You're gray, Aidan, weak. It is my right and responsibility to aid you, isn't it? I am your lifemate." Her fingertips were massaging his neck, her mouth moving over his hair, his temple. "Give me this gift, Aidan. Let me help you."

He swore eloquently, but the demon in him demanded blood, demanded strength, and his body was aroused and painfully full. Cursing his own weakness, he bent his golden head to her skin. So soft, so perfect. Her blood beckoned him with its heat, with the promise of addicting spice. His body clenched as his tongue swept over her pulse.

She was heat and light and the promise of paradise. His hands moved over her hips, her tiny waist, her narrow rib cage. Her breasts filled his palms with their softness. "*Cara mia*," he whispered against her creamy skin, "I love you."

His tongue touched, caressed, sending a tremor through her. Her arms tightened around him. *Please, Aidan, do it now,* she whispered in his mind, her lips in his hair. *I need to make you strong again. I need to take away your pain.* And she did. Alexandria knew his every moment in the terrible sun, what he had suffered for her, for Joshua. She had never needed to do anything more in her life than supply him with nourishment, to show her overwhelming love and support for him.

She cried out, her head thrown back, her body arching into his as his teeth pierced her breast. Tears came to her eyes as she cradled him to her. He was unbearably gentle, holding her with love and tenderness, as if she were the most precious treasure in the world. She could feel her strength waning even as his grew. She could feel it in his mind first, then in the beating of his heart, in the ripple of power in his muscles and sinews. It was an incredible feeling to provide Aidan with such strength and purpose. Her entire body clenched and protested when his tongue lapped across the wound in a rough caress, closing the link between them.

He dragged her into the circle of his arms. "That is enough, *cara.*" His hands stroked her hair. "I must go now. I am counting on you to soothe Stefan and Marie. Stefan always blames himself when he cannot stop whatever a vampire sends against us."

"I have to go with you." She clutched his arm. "It's me the vampire wants. How do I find him? Tell me what to do, Aidan. I'll do anything to get Joshua back, anything at all." There were tears shining in her eyes, but her chin was up courageously. The nightmare had caught up with her all over again. Little Joshua in the hands of a cold-blooded vampire.

"I will get him back," Aidan quietly assured her.

"No, I won't take chances with either of you. He wants me. I'll go myself. See if he'll exchange Joshua for me," she said desperately. "This isn't your fault any more than it is Stefan's. This isn't your responsibility. I will go to him."

Aidan looked down at her then, his face cold. "I will not allow you to take such a risk. This is my fight," he vowed.

"How can you say that? Joshua is all I have. He's my brother, my only family. I have every right to defend him."

He brushed back her hair, his hand gentle. "Joshua is also my brother, my family. You are my lifemate. There is no question, *cara mia*, who will take care of this problem. You will stay here in this house and do as I say. I will not argue with you about this."

His voice, black velvet and tender, could turn her heart over, but she would not be seduced this time. Alexandria tilted her chin. "No, Aidan, I'm going with you. If you can save only one of us, it will be Joshua."

His eyes caressed her even as he shook his head. "You will give me your word that you will do as I say, or I will send you to sleep until I return. And if you are sleeping the sleep of the immortal, you will be unable to aid me should I have need of it. I must go now. I am wasting valuable time, time Gregori earned for me at great cost to his own strength, I am certain." His mouth brushed hers. "What shall it be? Do you sleep while I go? Or will you remain here awake to aid me should it become necessary?"

Alexandria shifted away from him but nodded her compliance. "It isn't as if you're leaving me a lot of choice, Aidan," she said softly. "Go then. But nothing had better happen to you, or you'll see what a human woman can do when she's good and mad."

"Former human woman," he corrected.

And he was gone. Just like that. One moment he was solid and real, the next he was a rainbow of light streaking through the narrow tunnel of rock upward toward the fog-shrouded sky.

Alexandria sat for a long time, her hands folded in her lap. Aidan would be all right. He would have to be. And he would bring Joshua home to her. She believed it because she had to believe it. When she tried to get to her feet, she found herself shaky, her legs weak. It took determination to find and pull on her jeans. It was difficult to believe that just last night Aidan was making love to her, and now he was out fighting a monster.

She made her way slowly along the tunnel, holding on to the wall, her hand trembling as she opened the entrance leading to the kitchen. She could hear Marie's quiet weeping, the low murmur of Stefan's voice as he attempted to comfort her.

The couple was on the sofa in the sitting room, Marie's head on Stefan's shoulder, his arm around her. They both looked older somehow. Alexandria knelt in front of them and put a hand over their linked ones. "Aidan will bring Joshua back. He knows where he is and managed to weave some kind of protective spell for him. We both think another hunter is in the area and will come to Aidan's aid if need be." Her voice was pitched low and was compelling. "I believe in Aidan, and you must, too. We won't lose either of them tonight."

She could feel the power of what she had become rushing through her. Despite the fact that she was weak and pale and needed to feed, she still felt the power. Her mind was strong, and she had assets she had never dreamed of before. They could be used for good, as now, to ease the suffering of the loyal older couple. Stefan and Marie had grown to love Joshua, and both believed themselves to be in some way responsible for his abduction.

Stefan's large frame shuddered. "I'm sorry, Alexandria, we let you down. The attack was so unexpected, but I should have been with Joshua, kept him by my side."

"I thought he was safe while he was in the house," Marie moaned softly, lifting her apron to cover her face.

Alexandria pushed the apron down and circled both of them with her slender arms. She could hear the blood pumping through their veins, the ebb and flow of life. The scent of nourishment beckoned, but she knew now that she could control herself, trust herself. "No one is to blame for this,

286

Marie. Not you and not Stefan. We'll get through this thing together, as a family. You two and Aidan and Joshua and me. There can be no blame."

Stefan's hand came up to touch her hair. "Do you mean that, Alexandria? It's what you really feel inside?"

She nodded. "Joshua belongs to all of us. It was wrong of me to try to hold him to myself. Now, when he is in danger, we all blame ourselves. Aidan does, because he thinks he failed me. I do, because somehow I let all this happen. You do, because Joshua is a little boy and didn't do as you instructed. The truth is, what happened just happened. And Aidan will bring our boy home to us." She said it with absolute conviction.

Stefan's faded eyes held hers steadily. "And if . . . if something goes wrong?"

She felt the blow in the pit of her stomach but didn't visibly react. She kept her sapphire gaze locked with his. "Then we will all deal with it together, won't we?"

I will not fail you, cara.

Aidan's voice in her mind, the reassurance, brought her a measure of comfort. *Don't think about me right now, Aidan. Be careful. I will be here, merged with you, if you need to draw on my strength.* And she meant to monitor the skies for him. To ferret out any trap the vampire had laid. Aidan would not be alone in this. If something went wrong, he would not carry the load on his own shoulders as he had done for so many centuries. She was determined to share it with him.

"You're very weak, Alexandria," Stefan said softly. "If you're to help Aidan, you must have something to . . ." He trailed off.

For the first time, Alexandria smiled. "It's all right, Stefan. I'm not going to be so silly as to fling myself out the door again."

"I would willingly volunteer," he offered.

She was already shaking her head when a black fury swirled in her mind. Aidan's resistance to the idea had more to do with jealousy than with his vow never to use those who served him, she realized. Alexandria tucked that knowledge away for examination at a better time. "I could never, Stefan, but thank you."

"Aidan keeps emergency supplies. He gave you some once. It is not as good, but it would help."

She shook her head. "Not that yet, either. If there is great need, I will take it. For now, tell me of the others, the guards. Aidan is quite worried about their well-being." She had picked it out of his head, his anxiety for Vinnie and Rusty.

"Vinnie was hurt badly and lost a lot of blood. He had well over a hundred stitches in his neck alone. Rusty fared a little better, but both will be out of commission for a long while," Stefan answered. "I saw to it that they obtained the best doctors available, including a plastic surgeon for Vinnie. I assured both men we would pay the medical bills and compensate them handsomely for their lost time."

Alexandria squeezed Marie's hand gently. "Thank you both. You make things so much easier for us." She slowly got to her feet and made her way to the recliner, where she curled up, drawing her knees up to rest her chin on them. She closed her eyes and allowed the room to fall away so that she could merge herself completely with Aidan. It was where she wanted to be. Where she belonged.

Aidan was well cloaked in the fog Gregori had produced. The dark healer had such an impressive command over nature. The heavy mantle of fog blocked the sun's rays, enabling Aidan to travel without discomfort and to gain an advantage over the vampire still underground until sunset. Most of all, a terrible weight had been lifted from his heart.

Alexandria was with him, accepting of him, of all of him. She could clearly see the beast roaring for freedom, struggling for control, and she didn't back away from him in horror. She didn't blame him for the vampire's desperate challenge or the way Joshua had been abducted. She was afraid for Joshua and for him, but she was not falling apart. She had done as he had asked and tried to reassure and comfort Stefan and Marie. Alexandria was becoming his partner, truly his partner.

As he sped through the fog, he realized he loved her

unconditionally, too. He had never known such a deep, passionate emotion. She had crawled so deeply into him, he was totally lost. He was hopelessly, completely, shamelessly in love. In his wildest fantasies, he had never imagined it would feel this good. He sent up a quick prayer that everything would go as he planned, that the safeguards he had woven around the boy would hold until he could destroy the vampire.

Aidan was moving swiftly, attempting to race the setting sun. The fog had given him a fighting chance, a head start, and he was determined to make full use of it. He streaked through the sky, streaming through the clouds, disturbing a flock of birds and sending them wheeling sharply away from the iridescent light. Gray shaded the trees below, indicating he had only minutes before the sunset. The old hunting lodge was in sight now, deep in the shadows of the tall pines.

Chapter Eighteen

Aidan knew the instant the vampire rose. Earth and rock and moldy wood spewed upward in a geyser through the thick, soupy fog. Rats squealed, racing to abandon the rotted timbers. Cockroaches boiled from the decaying wood, a moving carpet swarming over broken planks. The dilapidated building shuddered. Evil incarnate burst into the air, screaming hatred and defiance, laughing horribly as it sped to the car and its waiting prize.

The shimmering rainbow glittering in the white fog slowly took the shape of Aidan's tall, powerful frame striding through the mist.

The vampire leaned over the trunk of the car, prepared to grab the sleeping child. He stopped abruptly, suddenly wary, his thin lips drawn back in a snarl, exposing long, yellowed fangs. His head undulated back and forth on a skinny, wrinkled neck like that of a reptile. His cold eyes suspiciously examined the trunk, then the blackened ground. He followed the trail of charred bits of flesh. A long, slow hiss of foul breath escaped his mouth, and his red-rimmed eyes swung to take in Aidan's approach.

The vampire stepped back from the open trunk and the sleeping child. "You think to trap me with so cheap a trick, hunter?" he growled accusingly, a clicking sound accompanying his once beautiful voice, now putrefied by his decaying soul.

Aidan halted a short distance away. "We both know I have no need of tricks, dead one," he said softly, his tone so pure it physically hurt the vampire's ears. "That is more your style, using small children as pawns. You have fallen far, Diego. You were once a great man." The voice had dropped an octave lower, and, despite his hatred of its purity, the vampire strained to hear the rippling notes.

"Man," the vampire sneered. "Do not insult me by naming me such a weakling. You have been brainwashed by Mikhail. For centuries he has lied to us, made us sheep. He has driven our people into the ground, attempted to take our rightful power from us. Open your eyes, hunter. See what you do. You kill your own kind."

"You are not my kind, Diego. You have chosen to debase and murder those less strong than you. Women. Children. Innocent humans. I am not like you."

The vampire sucked in his breath, an audible sound of hatred. "It is easy for you to say so, when the scent of your woman clings to your every pore."

"I am two centuries older than you. Even before my lifemate came and brought me light, I did not turn as you did to make my life easier," Aidan said quietly. "Do not abdicate responsibility for your actions. It is not Mikhail or your lack of a lifemate that brought you so low. It was your choice to become what you are."

The thin lips drew back, exposing receding gums stained with red. The white skin of Diego's face was drawn tightly over his bones, giving him a skeletal appearance. He lifted a bony hand tipped with razor-sharp nails and pointed toward the open trunk. "You think you are too powerful for me to defeat, but I am not without my own powers."

Aidan kept his fear for Joshua locked away in some deep, secret part of his soul. His face remained impassive, even serene. In his mind he felt Alexandria gasp as snakes began to swarm up over the car. Aidan didn't move or speak, not even to reassure his lifemate. He was proud of her silence, of the fact that she remained as still and as trusting as ever.

If the vampire was creating an illusion, it was a perfect one. Aidan could actually detect life in the wriggling reptiles. They seemed real enough, although how the vampire could have called so many of them to him so quickly, Aidan didn't know. He attempted to call to the snakes, to draw them away, but they were creatures of the vampire, completely enslaved. The first viper made its way into the trunk. Almost immediately several others fell in after it. Their hollow thunks were followed instantly by a hot sizzling, and the smell of cooking meat filled the air as snake after snake went to its death. Finally the vampire raised his hand, and the remaining snakes slithered back to the ground, curling around his ankles.

"What do you say we dispense with these childish games?" Aidan said. "Come to me, Diego, and remember the man you once were." His voice was so compelling, so enthralling, so hypnotic, that the vampire nearly stepped forward.

Then Diego snarled, the sound harsh and ugly in contrast to Aidan's voice. "I will kill you, then the boy, and take your woman." His smile was grotesque. "She will suffer long and much for your sins."

Aidan shrugged carelessly. "Should you do the impossible and defeat me, my lifemate will choose to follow me, and you will have no chance to get her in your hands. The child will be safe, because there is another hunter in this area, one far greater than myself. You cannot defeat me. No one can defeat him." He said it complacently, with complete confidence.

The vampire screamed again, a hysterical fury that threatened to consume them both. "Gregori! How dare he come to this land? What gives him the right? That is a perfect example of Mikhail's hypocrisy." Then the voice turned appeasing, cunning. "Gregori is not like you, Aidan. You are a fair man. Morality rules your actions. Misguided your hunting may be, but nevertheless you do as you do because you think you must." The vampire looked around and lowered his voice. "Gregori is a cold-blooded killer. He feels no remorse. I have heard tales, rumors, that others swear are true. The healer has killed illegally. Pretending to be the best of our people, he is the worst, and Mikhail sanctions this abomination."

To an untrained ear, that insidious voice would have been beguiling, persuasive. But Aidan could see the gray skin shrunken over the skull. The dried blood beneath the long, yellowed fingernails. The receding gums and exaggerated fangs. Most of all he was very aware of the small, vulnerable boy in the trunk of a car, placed there as the instrument of the vampire's revenge.

"You seek to buy yourself time, dead one. Why? What plan do you have that you would pretend to be my friend?" Even as Aidan spoke, the vipers hissed hideously and swarmed toward him, a slithering mass of writhing bodies.

As the snakes neared his feet, they changed shape, became women crawling toward him, obscenely sexual, hissing, their long, forked tongues flicking at him. Using the fog to cover his movements, Aidan reappeared behind the vampire. As Diego turned this way and that, Aidan struck, a swift, killing blow designed to end the conflict quickly. But at the last moment the vampire leapt away, and his creatures, half female, half snake, growled and spat venom at Aidan, scrambling toward him on their bellies and hands and knees.

Do not pay attention to his illusions. Never take your eyes off the vampire. He waits for your inattention. Alexandria's voice was soft and sweet in his mind, clearing away any cobwebs the illusionist was weaving to confuse him.

He is skilled, this one, cara, he acknowledged.

Not skilled enough, she responded with complete faith in him.

The women on the ground set up a wail, a low, keening, mournful whine that rose on the wind. Aidan smiled at the vampire with a lazy, self-confident smile. "You are trying to call Gregori to our little battle? You are much more foolish than I thought. Even I, who have nothing to fear, would not want to disturb Gregori's solitude. With this racket, he is certain to join us." His golden eyes slashed at the vampire, found the dull, dead gaze, and locked onto it, holding the other man in their molten depths. "I worked closely with Gregori for several years. Did you know that, Diego? What he does, he does coolly and efficiently. There is no other like him. Perhaps in your final moment you wish to test your meager skills against his greatness."

The vampire's bullet-shaped head was undulating again, the skull swinging back and forth rhythmically. He hissed a command, and the obscene creatures of his invention moaned and slunk away. Chanting, he waved a hand at them, and the wailing women slowly shape-shifted back to snakes. Ordinary, harmless garden snakes.

The vampire began to move in a slow, careful, sinister dance. He circled Aidan, the hard shells of the cockroaches crunching beneath his shoes. His head continued to move slowly back and forth, his fangs gleaming and dripping saliva. Aidan faced the vampire stoically, refusing to look at his dancing feet noisily crushing the insects or at the garden snake approaching from his left.

The snake isn't harmless, Aidan. Alexandria's warning was calm. *That's another one of his illusions. It is no garden snake. I can sense the vampire's triumph.*

Aidan held his ground calmly, his golden gaze never once shifting from the vampire's swaying figure. He didn't so much as glance at the snake gliding toward him or betray in any way that he was aware of the danger it presented to him. The vampire's actions were hypnotic, a strange series of steps and motions designed to dull the senses and capture the mind.

As the snake coiled itself to strike only a few inches from the hunter, the vampire stopped, his eyes boring into Aidan's, seeking to mesmerize him. Then, with unbelievable speed, the vampire launched himself forward in an all-out attack. The snake, too, flung itself forward, seeking to bury its fangs in Aidan's leg. But Aidan was no longer where he had been. Even faster, he had leapt to meet the vampire. His hands caught at the bullet-shaped head and wrenched. There was a sickening crack, and the vampire howled, the razor-sharp claws raking Aidan's broad chest.

The talons bit deep, leaving four red furrows. Aidan melted away from the illusionist and reappeared beside the trunk of the car. He risked one quick glance at the sleeping child. The sight of the little boy covered with, charred snake carcasses was unnerving. He wanted to fling the repulsive, evil creations as far from Joshua as possible.

Aidan, do not take your attention from the vampire, Alexandria cautioned. *He is still dangerous. He gathers himself for the kill. Are you all right? I feel your pain.*

I do not feel anything. Aidan's reply was abrupt, clipped, his attention back on the vampire.

Diego's head listed to one side, his grimace a twisted parody of an ingratiating smile at the hunter. Red flames flickered in his eyes. He was gasping for breath, but Aidan was not deceived. The vampire was more dangerous than ever. Aidan would see that danger in the red haze of his eyes and the nails digging blood from their own palms.

"Let me die in peace, Aidan. You have finished me," the vampire said softly, persuasively. "Take the child and go. Leave me my dignity. I will meet the dawn and die as our kind should."

Aidan remained very still, his body appearing relaxed, almost indolent, his shoulders loose, his arms at his sides, his knees slightly bent. The picture of serenity. The golden eyes did not so much as blink. He watched the vampire's movements like the predator he was.

The vampire erupted into cursing, an obscene, guttural

expression of his frustration. "Come and get me then," he challenged.

Aidan merely stared at him, unmoving. He did not allow pity for the misguided creature into his heart or mind. That way lay disaster. The undead felt no remorse for their actions. Diego would drain Joshua dry, torture him to get to Aidan, to Alexandria, then cast the child aside like so much garbage. There was no bargaining with a vampire, no reasoning. The hunter merely waited patiently.

He didn't have long to wait. The undead had no such patience. He leapt at Aidan, shape-shifting as he did so, his head, grotesquely askew on his skinny neck, lengthening into a thick, compact muzzle with long, protruding, razorsharp eyeteeth. In mid-air, the saber-toothed tiger roared as it sprang.

Aidan waited until the last possible moment. Avoiding the long fangs and the massive weight of the animal was easy enough, but it was impossible to get close without those lethal claws tearing at him, trying to gut him. He closed his mind to all pain and cut himself off from Alexandria so that she could not possibly share his suffering. Then his arm was around the creature's broken neck, and he was astride the animal, where the vicious claws could not reach him. Even with his enormous strength, it was difficult to control the howling, writhing beast tearing to get at him.

Slowly, with great care, Aidan was able to apply enough pressure around the tiger's neck to cut off the air supply. The animal went crazy, thrashing and bucking, trying to unseat him. Ferociously it bit and screamed, a high-pitched, unearthly yowl. Tenaciously Aidan hung on. His hand slipped lower, seeking the heartbeat.

Even as Aidan nearly reached his goal, the vampire twisted enough to sink one venom-tipped claw deeply into his neck, just missing his jugular. Blood spurted, and he could feel it running down his skin. The beast was so strong and agile that for a moment Aidan was unsure he could defeat the creature. Then something moved in his mind. A quiet certainty filled him with confidence and strength.

Although he had attempted to shut her out, to keep her from the brutality, Alexandria had never left him. She was there, feeding his strength with her own. Aidan's searching hand found what he was looking for. He plunged his entire fist deep into the maddened tiger, past muscle and into the soft, vulnerable organs.

The vampire raged and screamed, raking at Aidan with his last dying strength, determined to take the hunter with him. As Aidan extracted the pulsating heart, the saber-toothed tiger contorted, shaped-shifting until the withered, gray-skinned vampire lay beneath him, still and silent.

Aidan tossed the decaying matter away from him and hastily put distance between himself and the abomination that had once been a decent Carpathian male. He allowed himself a deep, cleansing breath and sagged against a tree trunk. The wind rustled, picking up strength to carry the putrid scent of the vampire away from him. The night was full upon him, dark and mysterious and beautiful.

Should we come? Do you have need of blood, Aidan?

He could hear the weariness in her, matching his own. It was a difficult task to maintain mental contact when she had just recently learned to do so, especially through so violent a struggle. And she was weak from lack of nourishment. She had allowed him to feed greedily, and she had lent her waning strength to him without hesitation. Even now, her concern was for him.

Stay, piccola, *I will be home soon, and I will bring Joshua with me. Tell Marie and Stefan all is well.* He struggled to keep his voice even so that she would not be afraid for him.

Her soft laughter warmed his heart. *I'm in your mind, my love. You can't hide your wounds from me.*

There was the merest disturbance in the air, just a flutter, no other warning. A large raptor landed on the branch above Aidan's head and slowly folded its wings. Aidan should have known another of his kind was close by, yet he hadn't. As it hopped easily from the perch, the bird's form changed, and it was Gregori who landed lightly on his feet.

He glided past Aidan to survey the grotesque sight on the ground. "He was good, was he not?" he asked softly. His voice was beautiful, a soothing sound that seemed to seep into Aidan's tired body and renew his strength. Despite his darkness, Gregori brought purity and light with him; it clung to him like the aura of power. "Diego studied with the most evil of the vampires. They began banding together in our homeland, thinking to defeat Mikhail with their numbers. When that did not work, they enlisted the aid of human butchers. Now they are turning to travel and trickery. They use many methods to try to defeat us, Aidan. You have done well this day."

"With your aid." Aidan straightened, one hand pressed hard to the flowing wound at his neck.

Gregori glided over the cockroaches and blackened snakes, his feet never touching the carnage as he approached the open trunk of the car.

Aidan could not prevent himself from giving the healer a warning, just in case. "I used your safeguards to keep the boy free from harm." He couldn't believe the healer would ever turn, but he was watchful all the same.

Gregori nodded. "You added a touch of your own. You have grown these years, Aidan. Come here to me." He turned his head then, his strange, pale eyes a compelling silver, his voice low and mesmerizing.

Aidan moved forward despite Alexandria's low cry of alarm. She didn't believe the other Carpathian was evil, but the healer believed his soul was already lost. That made him unpredictable. *Don't go near him! He's so dangerous, Aidan, and I can feel your weakness. It's his voice. Can't you tell that his voice is calling to you?*

He is a great man, cara. *Trust my judgment*, her lifemate reassured her.

Gregori touched Aidan ever so lightly, but the hunter felt heat spreading throughout his body. The healer closed his eyes and sent himself seeking outside his own body and into Aidan's. At once the ancient tongue of their people echoed in the air, through their bodies, a healing ritual as old as time. Aidan felt the pain moving from his body, pushed aside by the greatest healer of them all. The chant went on for some time, but Alexandria continued to share his mind, firmly refusing to relinquish her rightful place. She knew Gregori could feel her presence, was aware that he could read her distrust of him, but she was more concerned with Aidan's safety than with Gregori's feelings.

Gregori slowly returned to his own body, the strain of the healing process revealed by the lines etched into his face. But he casually tore his wrist with his teeth and held out the offering to Aidan.

Aidan hesitated, knowing Gregori was offering far more than nourishment. He would now be linked to Gregori, able to track him at will, should there be the need. The thick wrist dripping precious ruby droplets pressed closer to his mouth. With a sigh, Aidan gave in to the inevitable. He needed sustenance, and Alexandria waited at home, needing it also.

"It is beautiful, this land, in its own way, is it not?" Gregori did not wait for Aidan's reply or indicate in any way that the blood loss was affecting him. "It is not wild and untamed like our mountains, but there is promise here." He did not wince as Aidan's teeth sank deeper into his skin.

Strength such he had not known in years poured into Aidan's body. Gregori was an ancient, his blood far more powerful than that of men of lesser years. The nourishment revived Aidan instantly, took away pain and weariness, and brought a vitality he had not previously experienced. He closed the wound carefully, meticulously, with great respect.

"I am in your debt, Gregori, that you have aided me this day," he said formally.

"You did not need my aid. I only made things easier. Your safeguards for the child would have bought you the necessary time even without the fog. And you had enough strength to survive the sunlight in your disembodied state even without me. You owe me nothing, Aidan. I have been lucky in my life to have a few men I could call friend. You are one." Gregori sounded as if he were already far away.

"Come to my home, Gregori," Aidan insisted. "Stay for a while. It might help to ease you."

Gregori shook his head. "I cannot. You know I cannot. I need the wild places, the high reaches, where I can feel freedom. It is my way. I have found a place many miles from here. I will build there to await my lifemate. Remember your promise to me."

Aidan nodded. He felt Alexandria moving in his mind, offering closeness, comfort.

"See to the child, Aidan, and your woman. Even from this distance, I sense her anxiety for you, for the boy. And she needs to feed. Her hunger beats at me. Do not waste your time worrying about me. I have taken care of myself for centuries." Already his solid form was wavering, shimmering, dissolving into droplets of mist. His voice came back, disembodied, strangely hollow, yet still beautiful. "That was quite a feat you performed today, and in broad daylight. Few can do what you did. You have learned much."

Aidan watched him disappear, the mist streaming into the surrounding forest until it, too, was gone. Gregori's acknowledgment of his achievement made him proud. He felt like a child receiving praise from a revered parent. And since it was from masterful Gregori, who chose to live alone and befriend but few, he felt especially honored.

Very carefully, with infinite patience, Aidan unraveled the safeguards around Joshua, then gently lifted the boy from the trunk. Blackened snakes fell onto the ground, scattering around Aidan's feet. He had much work to do, but he could no longer bear leaving the boy in that awful trunk with the creatures of the vampire's making.

Aidan carried Joshua to a grassy knoll beneath a pine tree and laid him on the ground, tenderly brushing back his blond curls. *He is fine, Alexandria, just sleeping soundly as I commanded. I will wake him when I return him home. Then we can deal with what he saw.*

Just hurry. I want to see him, hold him in my arms. And Marie can scarcely believe me when I tell her Joshua is out of danger. There was eagerness in her voice, but also fatigue, indicating her waning strength.

Worried, Aidan left the boy sleeping peacefully while he returned to the revolting battleground to complete the distasteful task of destroying the vampire for all time. The separated heart and the body, along with all the tainted blood, had to be burned to ashes.

Looking skyward, he built the electricity, weaving the veins of lightning and increasing the friction until it arced and crackled. He directed a bolt to the vampire's body, spinning a ball of fire from the resulting sparks. The vampire's body writhed repugnantly, the stench rising to fill the night air. A few feet away, the heart seemed to move, a subtle, deadly pulsating that gave Aidan pause.

Uneasy with the unknown phenomenon, Aidan directed the flames at the heart and incinerated it quickly, reducing it to a handful of ashes. The body contorted grotesquely, nearly sat up, and a long, mournful wail rose on the wind. The sound was hideous, and as it faded into the night, the notes changed to ugly, taunting laughter.

Immediately, Aidan swung around, his golden eyes restless, searching the land, the trees, the sky for a hidden trap. His body was still, listening intently for any betraying sound. In his mind, Alexandria was holding her breath. And then he heard it. A soft, insidious rustling. Stealthy. Furtive. A brush of scales sliding through pine needles.

Joshua! Alexandria's burst of revelation, of horror, came on the heels of his own.

He moved with supernatural speed, faster than he had ever moved in the centuries of his existence, crossing the distance to the grassy knoll where he had left the child. His hand found the snake, grasped it, and jerked it away from its goal. The thing hissed and coiled around his arm, desperately squeezing his muscles, sinking fangs into the fleshy part of his thumb. It bit again and again, injecting poison into his body, its every instinct commanding it to carry out the vampire's revenge. Aidan tore the snake apart, flinging it into the flames consuming the body of the undead. Noxious fumes rose into the air, green gases that spun and whirled, then disappeared into the black smoke.

Aidan sank down beside Joshua and pulled the child into his arms. He made a slow, careful inspection of every inch of skin to assure himself the boy was unharmed. He waited for a reaction from the snake's venom. Within minutes, his lungs began to fight for air, and he felt nauseated, but it was not nearly as bad as he expected, considering the venom was aided by the vampire's hatred. It took him a moment to realize it was Gregori's blood that was neutralizing the poison's effects. He could feel the struggle taking place in his body, but Gregori's blood was far stronger than anything the vampire could produce. Within minutes, Aidan was fine, his heart and lungs as strong as ever, the venom oozing out of his pores.

He lifted the boy into his arms and launched himself into the air, wings spreading as he made his way across the sky toward his home and his waiting lifemate. He had hardly landed on the third-floor balcony before Alexandria was attempting to pull the child into her arms, laughing and crying at the same time.

"You did it, Aidan! I can't believe you did it!" She was deathly pale, her arms trembling with weakness.

Aidan could hear her heart laboring, her lungs wheezing, struggling to function though her blood supply was low. Despite his desire to sweep her up and care for her needs, he placed Joshua in her waiting arms.

"Look at his poor little face." She was crying, the tears falling on Joshua's bruises and swollen eye. "Oh, Aidan, look at him."

"He looks wonderful to me," he said softly as his arm circled her waist. He took most of the boy's weight himself. "Let's get him into bed and wake him up." He could hear Marie and Stefan clambering up the stairs to join them. Alexandria's hunger was beating at him. Everything male, everything protective and Carpathian in him, rose up to demand he care for her. Joshua was safe. It was time to see that his lifemate's strength was restored.

"Oh, Marie, look at his little face," Alexandria cried to the older woman. "That horrible creature hit him."

Marie was openly sobbing, taking the child from Alexandria. Stefan, too, had to hold the little boy.

"He is fine, just asleep," Aidan reassured them all. His concern was for Alexandria now. "We will put him in his bed and awaken him. He will be told this was a kidnapping attempt, to extort money. He will accept that explanation and understand having guards anytime it becomes necessary."

Stefan carried Joshua to the small room off theirs. Marie dressed him in pajamas and produced a cold cloth to bathe his black eye. Alexandria sat on the edge of the bed, Joshua's small hand in hers. Aidan knelt beside her, an arm around her waist. "Joshua, you will awaken now. Alexandria needs to see your blue eyes." He whispered the words softly, his voice compelling, seeping into the boy's mind and beckoning him back into their world.

Joshua erupted into violence, fighting hard to free himself. It was Aidan who subdued him, protecting Alexandria with his own body despite her efforts to get to the boy. "Listen to me, Joshua. You are home with us. You are safe. The kidnappers no longer have you. I want you to be calm so that you do not hurt Marie or your sister." His voice, as always, was serene and beautiful, so compelling that the boy ceased his struggles and peeked up at them cautiously. When he saw Alexandria, he burst into tears.

She burrowed past Aidan's large frame and caught Joshua to her, dragging him into the protection of her arms. "You're safe now, little buddy. No one is going to hurt you."

"There were dogs, big dogs. There was blood everywhere. Vinnie was being eaten. I saw him."

"Vinnie was very brave and tried to save you from the kidnappers," Alexandria soothed him, stroking the blond curls from his forehead. "He's in the hospital, but he's alive and is going to be fine. So is Rusty. We'll take you to see them in a few days. We should have told you about the possibility of someone trying to take you away from us." She touched his eye with a gentle fingertip. "I'm sorry that I didn't confide in you. You're old enough to know these things."

"Is that why you were afraid to live here?"

"Partly. Aidan is a very wealthy man. Because he loves you, loves both of us, we will always be at risk. Sometimes we will have to have guards. Do you understand what I'm trying to tell you, Joshua? This is my fault, that I didn't make you understand the danger we could be in."

"Don't cry, Alex." All at once Joshua was using a grown-up voice. "Aidan came and got me, didn't he?"

She nodded. "He sure did. No one is going to ever take you away from us. Not ever."

"Next time, when Marie and Stefan tell me to stay in the house, no matter what, I'm going to do it," Joshua decreed. He examined Alexandria with anxious eyes. "What's wrong with you? You're so white."

"This has been very scary for all of us, Joshua," Aidan said. "Marie and Stefan will look after you while I put Alexandria to bed. She needs to rest. And do not worry about Baron. Stefan kept him safe for you. Your puppy can stay with you while I take Alexandria to bed."

Alexandria shook her head. "I'm not going to leave him, not for a minute. I'll stay here until he falls asleep."

"No, you will not, *cara mia*," Aidan said firmly. He stood, a graceful, fluid movement that set her teeth on edge. His hands caught her easily, lifting her and cradling her against his chest. "She needs to rest, Joshua. I will bring her to you later."

"That's all right, Aidan," Joshua said, man to man. "She needs to be in bed more than I do."

Aidan grinned at him and took her out of the room, heedless of her squirming. "He is right, you know," he murmured against her neck. "You do need to be in bed. My bed." His breath was warm and teasing, an invitation she found nearly impossible to resist.

"I think you're insatiable," she accused him, but her arms crept around his neck, and her body relaxed against his.

"Where you are concerned, it is true," Aidan agreed. He was moving quickly through the house, into the tunnel, his body already tightening in anticipation.

Her hands slid inside his shirt, caressing his chest. Her mouth moved over his neck, found the streaks on his chest, and her tongue wandered, caressed, a loving tribute to his courage.

Once in their chamber, Aidan lowered her to the bed. With his gaze holding hers, he began to unbutton his shirt.

Alexandria slipped her sweater over her head and tossed it aside.

He reached out, his hands spanning her ribs, dragging her close, nearly bending her backward so his mouth could take advantage of the invitation her body was offering. She smelled good, fresh, her skin like satin. At once his body raged for release, an urgency he was becoming familiar with. Her hands were at his slacks, sliding aside the button, the zipper, pushing the fabric from his hips.

He groaned when she cupped him in her hands, caressing him. His own hands were rougher as they tore aside her clothing so that her skin was hot against his. "You make me crazy, *piccola*, absolutely crazy," he whispered, and he lifted her into his arms. "Put your legs around my waist."

Her head was bent, her mouth wandering across his chest, her tongue lapping at his pulse. "Feed me," she whispered back, her tone so sensuous, his legs nearly gave out.

His hands were on her hips, holding her still so that he could push into her velvet sheath. He cried out when her muscles slowly allowed him entrance, when she clenched around him, hot and tight and velvet-soft. "Take what you want from me, what is rightfully yours," he murmured, buried deep, welding them together in fire and passion. "Do it, Alexandria. I want you to do it."

His entire body blazed into light, into pure feeling, as her teeth pierced his skin. He surged into her, hard and urgent, reaching, straining, wanting to fly high. Her hair draped around them, brushing at his sensitized skin like a thousand strands of silk. Her hands slid over his back, tracing each muscle. Her mouth on him aroused him further.

Aidan slowed his pace, his thrusting hips strong, his hands tight, binding her to him. She was his. The lifemate he had endured centuries of emptiness waiting for. She was his world. The light. The colors he thought he had lost forever. She was the ecstasy he never knew existed. And she was with him for eternity.

DARK PRINCE

Raven Whitney is a psychic who has used her gift to help the police track down a serial killer. Now she is determined to escape the glare of recent publicity for the peace and quiet of the Carpathian Mountains. Despite her own emotional fatigue, Raven finds herself connecting psychically to another wounded individual somewhere close by.

Prince Mikhail Dubrinsky is the leader of his people but, as his ancient Carpathian race grows ever closer to extinction, he is close to giving in to the heavy weight of loneliness and despair.

Then a female voice enters his mind and tries to console him. Intrigued, Mikhail becomes obsessed with finding this unusual human female. From the moment their minds touch, Raven and Mikhail form a connection. But there are those who incorrectly view all Carpathians as vampires, and are determined to give their extinction a helping hand . . .

978-0-7499-3747-8

DARK DESIRE

Seven years ago, Dr Shea O'Halloran experienced an unexpected and horrendous pain unlike anything she had ever known. It felt as if she were being tortured. Eventually the pain disappeared, but Shea never forgot. She has since devoted her life to trying to understand the cause of the rare genetic blood disorder that is slowly killing her.

The answers to some of Shea's questions start to reveal themselves when she is approached by two men, who accuse her of being a vampire. Shea runs for her life and – following a feeling she can't explain – her desperate wanderings lead her to Romania.

The ancient one known as Jacques Dubrinsky can explain. Seven years ago, Jacques was captured, tortured and buried alive by several humans and a Carpathian betrayer. The years of extreme pain and lack of sustenance that followed have nearly driven Jacques insane. He has been using what is left of his powers to psychically draw Shea to the region. But is Shea to be his healer . . . or his prey?

978-0-7499-3748-5

DARK FIRE

When Darius, the leader of a group of Carpathian musicians, first sees the new mechanic hired to work on the band's touring vehicles, he is astonished to see the red colour of her hair. It has been centuries since he last saw colours or even felt emotions.

Although mechanic Tempest Trine needs the job, she quickly realises that in touring with Darius, she's bitten off more than she can chew. Tempest has always felt different, apart from others. But from the moment his arms close around her, enveloping her in a sorcerer's spell, Darius seems to understand her unique gifts. But does his kiss offer the love and belonging she seeks, or a danger more potent than anything she has ever known?

978-0-7499-3784-3

DARK LEGEND

For two thousand years Carpathian twins Gabriel and Lucian were vampire hunters. But then, Lucian turned vampire, forcing Gabriel to hunt him. Lucian and Gabriel battled each other for centuries until two hundred years ago, when Gabriel sacrificed his freedom, trapping Lucian and himself in the earth of a Parisian cemetery. Now, modern construction work within the cemetery has disturbed their resting place and Gabriel and his dark brother Lucian are raised from the rubble.

Weakened and in desperate need of blood, Gabriel fears he will lose his own soul before he can restore his strength. Fate is on his side when Francesca, a uniquely gifted healer, comes to his aid. Gabriel instantly recognises that she is his lifemate, and must convince Francesca before it is too late: Lucian is on their trail, and will let nothing stand in the way of his eternal conflict with his brother . . .

978-0-7499-3767-6

DARK GUARDIAN

He is the dark guardian of his people. So how, after centuries of a bleak, soulless existence has he, Lucian Daratrazanoff, suddenly come to crave petite, curvy, colourful policewoman Jaxon Montgomery, who foolishly makes it her life's work to protect others from harm?

Fiercely daring, Jaxx will sacrifice anything to shield others. And piercingly erotic Lucian is powerfully, perilously mesmerising – oddly gentle yet clearly a born predator. He has vowed to possess her, to guard her for all time. Yet with his every thirsty kiss, is he drawing Jaxon more deeply into danger . . . and his dark, mysterious desires?

978-0-7499-3811-6

DARK MELODY

Dayan has been searching for centuries to find the one woman who can complete him, a true lifemate, who can save him from the darkness in his soul. Despairing of ever finding her, and on the run from his enemies, something drives Dayan to stop at a bar and perform some of his music. Then Corrine Wentworth walks in, and Dayan knows instantly that she is *the one*.

Corrine wants nothing more than to surrender her life and soul to Dayan, but she is suffering from a degenerative heart disease, and pregnant with her late husband's child. She is also running from the men who killed her husband, the same group of fanatics who are hunting Dayan and his kind.

Dayan must call on his family, and the greatest healers of the Carpathians to aid him in a race against time to save Corrine, whose fate is now inextricably linked to his own . . .

978-0-7499-3851-2

DARK DEMON

Natalya Shonski is a vampire hunter. She hates and fears both vampires and Carpathians alike and has spent her life fighting them.

Carpathian Vikirnoff van Schreider is dangerously close to turning vampire when he discovers Natalya and realises that she is his lifemate. But Natalya is unlike any other Carpathian he has ever known – dangerous in her own right, she refuses to let him fight her battles. But a sinister, mysterious power is after Natalya, and Virkirnoff has to convince her not only to trust him with her heart, but with her life as well.

978-0-7499-3668-6